❧ The Living Planet

The first time I drove on the grass, it screamed like a tormented woman. When I stopped, I found that the grass I had crushed was bleeding—bleeding on my shoes and the tires of the car. It was the red of real blood and I was deeply shocked.

I got the jeep off it as gently as possible.

The Steps of the Sun

WALTER TEVIS

BERKLEY BOOKS, NEW YORK

This Berkley book contains the complete text of the original hardcover
edition. It has been completely reset in a typeface designed for easy
reading, and was printed from new film.

THE STEPS OF THE SUN

A Berkley Book / published by arrangement with Doubleday
& Company, Inc.

PRINTING HISTORY
Doubleday edition / November 1983
Berkley edition / April 1985

ISBN: 0–425–07645–8

A BERKLEY BOOK® TM 757,375
Berkley Books are published by The Berkley Publishing Group,
200 Madison Avenue, New York, New York 10016.
The name "BERKLEY" and the stylized "B" with design are
trademarks belonging to Berkley Publishing Corporation.
PRINTED IN THE UNITED STATES OF AMERICA

For Eleanora Walker,
Dr. Herry Teltscher, and Pat LoBrutto

Ah, sunflower, weary of time,
Who countest the steps of the sun,
Seeking after that sweet golden clime
Where the traveler's journey is done. . . .

William Blake
Songs of Experience

The Steps
of the Sun

⌁ Chapter 1

When they knocked me out I regressed like a shot to my childhood on Earth and stayed there in a kind of wakeful dream for
two months. At times I would become aware of the throbbing
of the ship's engine, of the sleek tubes that fed me, of the
machines that exercised my body and of the soft voice of my
trainer, but for most of the voyage I was back in my father's
house in Ohio with the smells of his cigar smoke and of his
books and the awe I had felt as a child toward the certificates
and diplomas on the wallpapered wall over his desk. There
were faded blue flowers on that paper; it seemed I could see
them more clearly from captain's quarters on my interstellar
ship than I had as a child. Forget-me-nots. There was a
brownish stain near the ceiling over a framed diploma that
read DOCTEUR DE L'UNIVERSITÉ HONORAIRE. I sat on the
green-carpeted floor and stared silently at the stain. My
father, silent also, read from an old book in German or
French or Japanese, stopping every now and then to make a
note on a three-by-five card or light a cigar. He never looked
at me or acknowledged my presence. Mother was out; Father

1

was stuck with keeping me. I felt guilty: Father was busy, his work was important, I was a trouble to him. I must have loved him terribly—his rare, shy smile, his quietness. I did not even hope that he would someday explain his work to me. When he died I still knew nothing about that ancient history he spent his life brooding over. I have never read his books. I had him buried in a fine cemetery, glad to be old enough and with money enough to do it right and well. I was twenty-three when he died and already rich. My father was a scholar—world-famous I was told by Mother—and his style was genteel poverty. I loved him ardently, in silence.

I nearly awoke once here on the ship, when my trainer had allowed his attention to lapse and one of the exercise machines was straining the muscles of my abdomen. I found myself for a moment lying on my back on a red leather bench, groaning upward against steel springs in the ship's gym and with hot tears flooding my face. I had just come from my dream trip to Father's study, awakened fleetingly by pain. The trainer's face was tight with anxiety. As if through a partition I heard his alarmed voice saying, "Sorry, Captain Belson," and I muttered something about love and fell back into my chemical sleep. The astonishing thing was the tears. I had not cried at my father's funeral. I had never mourned him. I had hardly thought of him for thirty years. And here I was at the age of fifty-two, somewhere out in the black reaches of the Milky Way, weeping copiously for him. In sleep I returned to his study and sat cross-legged on his floor, silent. I watched his concentration at his desk. Somewhere outside of me I heard the hum of the ship and exulted, propelled beyond the speed of light toward constellations totally outside my father's understanding.

They woke me two weeks before planetfall. There was a crew of seventeen. I owned the ship; I had bought it a year before. We were heading toward an unexplored planet of the star Fomalhaut, known as FBR 793. It was my first voyage away from Earth.

I have always come awake quickly. There is something feral in me and I welcome it when I awaken. I was on my back in my stateroom and the ship's doctor and navigator were standing by my bed. The doctor was holding a cup of coffee out to me. I ignored it for a moment while I looked around. The room had been painted a pale blue as I had instructed; I could dimly remember the smell of fresh paint in my sleeping nostrils. There was a porthole to my right and one crystalline star, blindingly bright against velvet black, was almost centered in it. I stretched my arms, my legs, twisted my head on my neck. There was strength in my body; I could feel it in my pectorals, my biceps, the muscles of my thighs; the sense of power went through me like a quiet euphoria. I felt my belly; the paunch was gone.

I looked back toward the doctor, reached out steadily and took the cup. There was a white porcelain vase with red roses in it on the desk by my bed.

"Thank you for the flowers," I said.

"Glad we could grow them," the doctor said. "How's your head? Any hangover?"

"Not a bit, Charlie," I said. It was true. I felt wonderful. I sipped the coffee and felt it penetrate the raw emptiness of my stomach.

"For god's sake don't drink it fast," Charlie said. "Bad enough to drink it at all."

I had told them to have coffee ready. "I know myself well enough," I said, and continued sipping.

"It's a new self," the doctor said.

I looked at him over the edge of the cup, over the little red stripe that went around its porcelain edge. "Charlie," I said, "it's a new self but it still likes coffee." I finished half of it and set the cup down. Then I got out of bed, a bit slowly. I was naked and tanned. I looked good. The blond hair on my arms and legs had been bleached a pale yellow by the ultraviolet lamps. "Let's go to the bridge," I said.

"Okay," the navigator said, startled.

"And while I'm dressing, see if you can find me a sandwich."

We were still too far to see the planet. I could have slept another week, since there was very little for me to do when awake. There was little for anyone to do on the ship. But two months' sleep had been enough to get me into shape and to avoid serious boredom. I wanted to do some reading. I wanted the feel of being the owner-captain of a spaceship. I was the first man in history ever to own one and I wanted to savor the experience.

The bridge was a semicircle twenty feet across, at right angles to the ship's acceleration. The acceleration was continuous at one-fifth G even in spacewarp, and it gave us enough weight to walk. For exercise I used springs over cams—zero-gravity Nautilus equipment. There was no such thing as an intergalactic Olympics; had there been, these machines would have prepared the athletes. I felt ready to go for a gold medal.

The sandwich turned out to be Virginia ham and gruyère. With all the cold and the vacuum around us, food-keeping was easy and we had plenty. It was a good sandwich, but half of it filled my shrunken stomach. I gave the other half to the navigator. "How's the uranium?" I said.

"Fine," he said. "Exactly as computed. We could repeat the voyage without refueling."

The bridge was mostly empty deck, carpeted in beige. Its heart was a pair of red computer consoles and a panel of switches. Nothing more complicated than a locomotive. There were six rectangular portholes, and the stars seen through them were splendid, but after a while boring. I had seen them before my sleep and was impressed, but only briefly. The first sight is spectacular; there is no cold mountain sky on Earth that reveals the stars so brilliantly. But I find the sea on an ocean voyage more continuously interesting. It has life in it, while this interstellar panorama, however dazzling, has none. If it should really be, after all, the visible manifestation of a god, I refuse to be awed. I have no need for an inscrutable deity; my father's inscrutability was sufficient. I have enough to do with my life. I need no gods too distant to reveal themselves to me, no presence behind the stars' glitter.

I am no mad Ahab. I am a businessman, looking for uranium. The Earth had wasted almost all she had. I gathered together what I could to power this old Chinese ship and was staking half my fortune on a Schliemann-like hunch that a planet of Fomalhaut would have uranium. "Belson's Bubble" was what the Chicago *Tribune* had called it. Well, to hell with the Chicago *Tribune*.

"Captain," the navigator said, "a message arrived when you were asleep."

I nodded. "Later. How's the garden?"

"Even better than we planned. You saw the roses. It came during the third week out . . ."

I stared at his chubby body, his balding head. "Bill. I said *later*."

"I'm sorry."

"Let's look at the garden."

We went across a catwalk and down a silky ladder with skid-resistant rungs. In the low gravity and with my splendid new muscles I felt like a youthful spider descending a spoke in her new web. I was wearing faded blue jeans and a gray tee-shirt, with gum-soled gym shoes. In low gravity it is easy to slip, and though your weight is slight your mass can bruise you.

It was breathtaking to see. There were tiers upon tiers of lush greens and yellow and red roses spotted among the food-bearing plants, far more dazzling to me than the stars outside. "The hanging gardens of Babylon" my mind said, almost aloud. There were heavy avocados and oranges and grapevines and potatoes in bloom and peas with blue flowers and great trailing vines of Kentucky Wonder Beans. The air was moist and pungent, hot on my cheeks. As we walked, in floating strides, through an airsealed doorway, warm air caressed our bodies. It was like a damp twilight in the tropics. Greenery and flowers and warm, moist air; my heart leaped up at it all. All of it mine.

I picked a tangerine from a heavy-laden tree in a copper pot, and peeled it. It was delicious.

"Okay, Bill," I said. "I'm ready now to read that message."

YOU ARE ORDERED HEREWITH TO PLACE YOURSELF UNDER HOUSE ARREST AND RETURN TO THE EARTH IMMEDIATELY. YOUR URANIUM FUEL IS CONFISCATED BY ORDER OF THIS COURT. YOU ARE CHARGED WITH VIOLATION OF THE ENERGY CODE OF THE UNITED STATES. YOU ARE HEREBY APPRISED THAT SPACE TRAVEL IS A HIGH CRIME AND MIS-DEMEANOR, PUNISHABLE BY A PRISON SENTENCE NOT TO

EXCEED TWENTY YEARS, AND THAT WASTEFUL USE OF FUEL
IS ALSO A HIGH CRIME AND MISDEMEANOR. YOU ARE SAID
TO BE TRAVELING WITHOUT A VALID PASSPORT AND CON-
SPIRING WITH OTHERS TO VIOLATE THE LAWS OF THE
UNITED STATES.

IF YOU FAIL TO APPEAR BEFORE THIS COURT BY 30
SEPTEMBER 2063, YOUR CITIZENSHIP WILL BE REVOKED AND
YOUR PROPERTY CONFISCATED.

U.S. DISTRICT COURT, MIAMI

"What's the date?" I asked Bill.

"October ninth, two thousand sixty-three."

I was seated in the Eames chair in my stateroom. Bill stood
silently by, waiting to see if there would be an answer.

I tossed the paper on my desk. "Tell them we're sorry but
we can't turn around. Say the retros are malfunctioning."
There was a lacquered Chinese table by my chair. I set my coffee cup on it. "Nothing from Isabel?"

"Isabel?"

"Isabel Crawford. In New York."

Bill shook his head. "No, Captain."

"Thanks, Bill. I'd like to be alone for a while."

"Sure, Captain," he said, and left.

On my right was a deck-to-overhead bookshelf, curved with
the slight curve of the ship's hull. It was filled with books:
novels, histories, biographies, psychology, poems. Way up on
the top shelf, bound in leather, sat the seven volumes of
American history written by my father, William T. Belson,
Professor of History (ret.), Ohio University. I had owned
them thirty years and had opened each of them once, for
about a minute. I stared at them then, from my captain's
stateroom on this preposterous voyage of discovery, for a long
time. But when I rose to pick a book it was *The Ambassadors*
by Henry James.

FBR 793 became visible the day before planetfall. I first saw it
as a small half-moon a hundred million miles from Fomalhaut. There was no real thrill; it was just there, another
uninhabited celestial body, a planet called "near-dead" on the

charts. No one had ever set foot on it; it had been studied from a ship in orbit around forty years ago. The ship that photographed it lacked fuel for landing and takeoff, even back in those uranium-rich days.

FBR 793 was the twenty-third extrasolar planet discovered, and, like all the rest, it was without advanced life forms. Whatever the official reasons for the explorations conducted by the United States, the People's Republic of China and the Japanese, there had been only two real ones for sending ships out to interweave the Milky Way. One was the insane desire to find intelligent life somewhere other than on Earth—as if there wasn't enough of it on Earth, and mostly in trouble! The other was the hope of cheap fuel.

Well. Nobody found life, intelligent or otherwise. And there weren't many planets. Most stars didn't have any. And nobody found uranium, or anything other than granite, limestone, chert, and desolation. The whole thing was a failure and it had been abandoned. I picked it up again in my middle age—in what they called a midlife crisis in the times my father wrote of. A geologist told me at a beach picnic once, while spitting watermelon seeds onto coral sand and stroking the brown arm of a languid woman, that he had seen photos of FBR 793 somewhere and they looked like safe uranium to him.

"What's this 'safe uranium'?" I said.

"Somebody at M.I.T. worked it out," he said. "If uranium is formed under a gravity lower than Earth's it would have different characteristics. It wouldn't be radioactive except in a magnetic field." He looked at me. "No meltdowns."

"Jesus!" I said, "there'd be money in that."

"You'd never be able to count it."

I lay there and thought about that for a while. The tide was going out into the tranquil bay on which we lolled. It was about three in the afternoon and sunlight blazed on us. It was Jamaica, I think. I had worked at my desk in a hotel apartment that morning, had been unsuccessfully fellated at lunchtime, was bored with working out mergers, with pineapples and papayas, with Caribbean music, blow jobs that didn't work, Blue Mountain coffee, counting my wealth. I was fifty and worth three billion. *What the hell*, I thought, *space*

travel might be more fun than this. It beats suicide too. I
started phoning geologists and the people who knew about the
few mothballed spaceships that hadn't been scrapped by the
governments that owned them. That was how it started—Belson's Bubble. Had that girl been more effective at lunchtime,
it might not have happened.

In some ways I suppose my ambitions are stupid. I have
more money than I can spend—have had that much since I
was thirty-five. I own country homes, villas, a yacht, a mansion in New York; yet I want to call no place "home"; the last
thing I want is a home. Often I stay in hotels or sleep in my
car. I do not want a study like my father's, some mute terrain
of intellectual combat, some preserve of self-justification. I
will flee from life in my own fashion, will slip around reality in
whatever ways suit my temperament. I can afford it. I make
my money in coal, the stock market and real estate, and I
know the realities. Money does not follow fantasies, except in
show business; and I am not in show business.

I looked at the planet—my planet—half-outlined by its sun,
half dark, and I said, "We'll call it Belson." Why not? I'm
getting on in years.

Belson it is, that big, smart, spherical marvel. When we got
closer I saw it had rings. That hadn't been in the reports, and
was quite a surprise. My heart leaped up to see them through
the windows of the bridge, red and lavender: the rings of
Belson. I was really getting interested. We were a few light-
hours away now, and Belson was huge on the screen, its surface a greenish-gray. I loved the rings.

The ship had begun decelerating the day before and our
gravity had ceased, then reversed and increased to a little more
than Earth-normal; we were slowing down fast. What had
been up before was now down, since we had shifted polarities.
The ship was rotated 180 degrees, while we were all strapped
to cots. It was hectic for a while and a few small, unnoticed
things like paperclips and the ship's cat floated around crazily
while we spun in the changing gravity. That yellow cat drifted,
back arched in alarm, by my face. We stared at each other. Its
eyes seemed to blame me for its condition. "Sorry," I told it.

The other people in the crew were supposed to have been
using the gym but probably hadn't. They were clearly

bothered by the sudden increase in weight. But my muscles were ready for it and it felt good to have heft for a while again. I did a lot of walking that last day in transit, through the engine room, the garden, across the bridge, through the storage and equipment and research rooms. Whenever I passed a port I looked out to see my enlarging planet, Belson. I spoke to no one. The landing would be done by automatic equipment, with the pilot at ready to override if necessary. The pilot was a middle-aged woman with red hair; I had hired her with the possibility of sex in mind—there was something motherly about her and I am drawn to that.

I had no real ambitions for Belson, and I had come to see that. If I found uranium it would be a pleasure, but what the hell. Maybe I had really come all this way to give the place a name, to stake out an unworldly home for myself. Belson had a breathable atmosphere and mild temperatures; a man could live there if he had food and water enough. But the image of myself as the first extraterrestrial hermit had no appeal then and I shook it off.

It was my accountant, a gentle and paunchy Jew named Aaron, whom I first told of my plan to hunt uranium in space. "What for?" he said. He was drinking a Perrier. We were at P. J. Clark's and it was November and already snowing heavily outside the windows.

I looked at him and finished my rum and Coke. "Money."

"You need more money?" Aaron said.

I laughed wryly. "Adventure."

"I don't believe it," he said. "A man can have adventure easier."

"The world needs energy," I said. "Nobody's going to solve the nuclear-fusion problem. The oil's gone—except for what the military has stashed away. They've shut down the fission plants because the uranium's dangerous. And we may be headed into an ice age. Somebody's got to find power somewhere, Aaron, or we'll all freeze."

"Four bad winters don't make an ice age," Aaron said. "There's wood enough to keep us warm. The population's going down, Ben. It'll work out." He fished the lime from his Perrier and licked at it speculatively. "They tried going out in ships when we were kids and they gave it up. Experts. Now they've made it against the law. There's nothing in space but grief."

I liked Aaron. He was solid, and serious, and smart. He liked playing devil's advocate with me. And he had made me think. "Okay," I said, "it isn't adventure."

"What is it then?"

I smiled at him. "Mischief."

He looked at me and frowned. "I'm having a hamburger," he said, and waved for a waiter. "Mischief I can believe. We'll call it exploration for mineral resources and I'll try for tax credits. Let's eat our lunch and talk about something cheerful."

I ordered a rare steak and a chocolate mousse and a mug of beer. That night I called Isabel and took her to see *Così fan tutte* at Lincoln Center. At intermission I told her I was planning to try space travel. She took it in, but with astonishment. We were in my box on red velvet seats, and I was half drunk. The music was grand. During the second act I turned toward her, planning to reach my hand gently up her gorgeous dress, and saw that she was furious.

"What's wrong, honey?" I said.

She looked at me as though she were looking at a disorderly child. "I think you're running away."

I left New York the next day, to begin my search for a ship. Sometimes the city depresses me, now that there are so few taxis and cars and no trees in Central Park and half the restaurants I knew in my twenties have gone out of business. Lutèce and The Four Seasons are gone, but there's a midtown woodstand where Le Madrigal used to be. And the stores! Bergdorf-Goodman is gone, and Saks and Cartier; Bloomingdale's is a Greyhound bus depot. Everybody travels on bus or train because you can't run an airplane on coal. I've never felt that anyplace in this world was really my home. Why not try another world?

The landing was perfect, with only slight help needed from the pilot. We came down at a spot where it was morning, as light as a feather. Outside the portholes Belson's surface gleamed a shiny grayish-black. Obsidian. At a distance was a field of something resembling grass. The sky was a musty green and had clouds like Earth clouds. Cirrostratus and cumulonimbus, high and white. It looked good to me.

The pilot shut off the engine. The silence was overwhelming. No one spoke.

I looked across the bridge at Bill, the navigator. He was recording the landing in the ship's log. That seemed only proper; I felt traditional, and wished for a ship's orchestra to play "The Star-Spangled Banner."

After a few moments Bill said, "I'll put on a helmet and step outside."

"Hold it," I said. "*I'm* going to be the first man to step out there. The readings on the gauges are all right by me; I'm not wearing a helmet." I was shocked by the energy in my voice after the calm I had felt while landing.

Isabel told me that night after the opera, "Ben, I wish you knew how to take it easy. I wish you didn't rush around so much," and I said, "If I didn't rush around I wouldn't have so much money and I wouldn't have you here by this marble fireplace taking off your clothes." Isabel was wearing a blue half-slip and blue stockings. Her naked breasts were like a little girl's and my heart went out to them while the big logs flickered and I still heard Mozart tingling in my ears. We didn't live together anymore, but we were still close at times.

What I'd said made her angry. "I'm not with you because of your money, Ben."

"I'm sorry, honey," I said. "I know you're not. It's just that I'm in some kind of hurry all the time, and I don't know how to stop. Maybe this trip is what I need."

She looked at me hard for a moment. Her face was beautiful in its concentration and her skin glowed in firelight. Isabel is a Scot and it was that Scottish skin of hers—and her lovely voice—that had drawn me to her years before. "I hate you for wanting to risk your life," she said. "You don't need to risk it, Ben. There's nothing to prove."

Oh Jesus, she was right. There was nothing to prove then and there's nothing to prove now. And I knew it. I think I'm addicted.

So I rushed out the hatch of that spaceship onto the dark obsidian surface of Belson in the morning and slipped and broke my right arm. While my seventeen subordinates watched from the big portholes on the bridge, I did a slip and a slide and a cartwheel and was flat on my ass with my right arm under me bent like a paperclip and me screaming. It hurt like hell. The air of Belson was clear and it smelled pleasantly musty; I savored the smell even over the horrible goddamned pain. "Son of a bitch," I said.

Charlie got to me with a hypodermic of morphine. He helped me back to the ship and into my stateroom before X-raying and then setting the arm. It was compound and broken in two places. What a fucking mess! But the morphine felt wonderful.

I hadn't thought of obsidian being slippery. The reports hadn't said anything about it. But it sure was. Belson was a glass planet. And who needed that?

I had a fever the next day while my six geologists and four engineers started seismic testing for uranium ore. Toward evening, huge booming explosions began to rock the ship while I lay dazed with morphine, and spooned myself full of vichyssoise and lemon mousse. Boom! My small Corot fell from the wall. After dark I invited Ruth, the pilot, to watch the movie with me. She accepted graciously enough and I kept my hands to myself. Chemical euphoria was my real companion.

I'd never had morphine before and something in me knew, the minute it began to diddle my nervous system, that this was heavy magic indeed. I felt the thrill of danger in it. There was a *sufficiency* to it, a filling of empty spaces in the soul, that had snagged my bewildered spirit instantly, right out there on the dark slippery surface of a brand-new planet. It was splendid chemistry; when I awoke the next morning not giving a damn for the world I had come to explore but only wanting my fix, I was suddenly frightened. When Charlie came into my stateroom with his syringe I was even more frightened. I told him to forget it, to find me some aspirin. It took him half an hour to find some. That's the modern world for you. Here we were on a spaceship with the most advanced geologic and exploratory equipment and with a sick bay to rival Johns Hopkins. We had a drug synthesizer; we had a computer that could take out your appendix; and the doctor had to borrow

aspirin from the man in charge of the engine room. I felt my
destiny was trying to force me into becoming a morphine addict.

The aspirin helped the pain a bit, but I was edgy. *What the
hell*, I thought, and told Charlie to give me a half dose of morphine. Oh yes.

There are few things in this world that do what they promise, and fewer still that deliver more than you expected. Morphine is one of those; it promised only relief and it carried
heart's ease in its wake. It was chemical bliss for my cluttered
soul. I felt the hook. What the hell. You could go the route of
De Quincey and Coleridge and all those other sad losers. But I
had controlled a lot of things in my life before, and I figured,
Few things are as good as this chemical. I'll ride it for a while.
I knew enough to suspect it might be riding me, but I felt I
could handle that too. There would be a piper to pay. But that
would be in due time.

I found soon enough I could lower the dose and still get
what I wanted. The mornings of the next three weeks I rode a
low morphine euphoria and roamed Belson in a nuclear jeep,
my arm in a sling and Ruth at my side, playing music on the
little ball recorder. It was *Così fan tutte* mostly. I think people
who record live performances are jerks; still, I do it myself
sometimes for the hell of it. It gives me something to think
about during the dull passages, with the little meters and the
tone controls to check. I had recorded *Così fan tutte* that night
with Isabel at the Met. I kept to one shot of morphine a day; in
the afternoons, when it wore off, my price was a headache, for
which the remaining aspirin served until it ran out. I would
visit the seismic sites, driving across the slick obsidian, listening to arias composed light-years away in Austria, and even
when my soul was not singing along from the alkaloid chemistry at work on my brain, it still greeted the strangeness of a
new planet with thrilling of the nerves. There wasn't much to
see on Belson, but I had come to love the place.

The first time I found the grass and drove on it, it screamed
like a tormented woman under the jeep's tires. And when I
stopped and got out I found the grass I had crushed was
bleeding, bleeding on my shoes and on the tires of the car. It

was the red of real blood and enough to disconcert the most euphoric of men. I was shocked deeply. I got the jeep off it as gently as possible.

That night after dinner I found out from the chief engineer, who was also a biophysicist, that the grass was nothing like Earth grass and was incomprehensible to him. It was brown, about a foot high, and did not grow on the surface at all. It was the upper ends of some long, tenuous filaments that went down through the obsidian miles beneath the surface, far below our powers of investigation. No man on board and no equipment either was strong enough to uproot a blade of it. Nor could it be severed. It screamed and bled when crushed, but no one had the foggiest idea why or how. And crushing it did not kill or break it. If it was alive, that is. The biophysicist's name was Howard. He said the grass was some kind of a polymer. Big deal. So is nylon.

And then one twilight, when we were all on board ship eating leg of lamb together, we began to hear something faint and musical coming from outside. For a moment we all froze. I got up and opened the hatchway. It was the sound of singing, coming from a field of grass that began a few hundred yards west of the ship. I went out with the doctor and we walked carefully on the slippery surface, under the light of Belson's setting sun, toward the grass. The grass was singing. It came from all around us.

And the weirdest thing, the thing that raised the small hairs on the back of my neck, was that the voice and the melody were *human*—as human as any of us. You could not distinguish words, yet what it sang sounded like words. It sang loudly and it sang softly and the melody kept changing. For a moment, startled, I thought I heard strains from *Così fan tutte*. Sometimes the grass undulated as it sang, and sometimes it was still. When it moved, the long shadows on it from the low sun rippled with the music. I had never seen anything more beautiful, had never heard anything so moving. For a moment I feared it was the effect of that morning's morphine, but I looked around me at the crew members—at the other six men and the eleven women—and I saw they were transfixed by it too. They were astonished and as moved as I.

Howard fell on his knees by the grass, holding his head close to the sound. I could see that he was crying. Ruth stood by me, staring ahead of herself. Nobody spoke. I was weeping too.

Then the sun set and a moment later the music stopped. Someone turned on a flashlight. We walked silently back to the ship, and when we got there some of us got drunk. There was little to say. It had been the most powerful esthetic experience I had ever felt and was in itself worth the voyage, if anything could be. I had my recorder with me and had had the presence of mind to record part of it, erasing most of the precious *Così fan tutte* in the process. But the grass was better than Mozart, and besides, I was tired of Italian arias. I told no one that night of my recording, since no one was talking much.

The next morning one of the engineers found a scraggly plant growing in a fissure in the obsidian near the ship. That area had been studied closely before and nothing had been found growing. The plant was not like the grass. It did not bleed and you could pick it. Howard took it to his lab for analysis. I was curious; had the singing made it grow?

I played the recording in my stateroom while eating my breakfast croissant, but the music wasn't the same. It was good, but the resonance was gone. It sounded like a big choir and that was all.

By afternoon Howard had analyzed the sample as far as he could. Howard is a thin, stoop-shouldered man, with nicotine stains on his fingers. I found him in his lab, reading a printout. He was smoking a cigarette and looked tired. I asked him what he had found out.

"Well," he said, "it's a salicylate, like one of the organics you find in willow bark and that we've been synthesizing on Earth for centuries. But there's something I don't understand about the molecule."

"What's a salicylate?"

"Aspirin's one," he said. "That's the one in willow bark. Different from this . . ." He held out a fragment of the plant. "But close to it."

"*Aspirin?*" I said. I was shocked. I had carried music with me, and aspirin. Last night the planet had made both.

"It would probably cure a headache."

"Is it safe?"

"I suppose so," he said. "Safe as willow bark."

"I'll take some," I said. My head was aching anyway, since that morning's fix had worn off.

He figured out a rough dose and I took it. It was bitter, like aspirin. Howard protested that we should try it on some lab mice first, but I went on ahead.

My headache vanished in three minutes. Vanished completely and stayed vanished. It was then that I began to believe the planet was intelligent and that it had goodwill. Belson spoke my language. The music had spoken to my heart as directly as that plant had spoken to my nervous system. That kind of a fit cannot be accidental; the odds against it are too strong.

I developed my theory of an intelligent planet and tried it on Ruth. She was polite but clearly didn't buy it. I dropped the subject. Ruth had been having dinner with me since the first week on Belson, but we didn't sleep together and we didn't talk much. She was busy with her scientific thoughts and I with my mystical ones. And my morphine. And I had sex problems.

I named the little shrub endolin. It turned out there was a lot of it around, growing out of cracks in the obsidian. I had come to Belson looking for power; instead I'd found music, euphoria and relief from pain. I was beginning to love this place.

ᖾ Chapter 2

Why did I buy this ship in the first place, this small portable universe? Well, for one thing I had gone impotent. My once enthusiastic and catholic member had become shy, sullen, and would not serve me. Would not serve my lady friends either. There were quarrels, recriminations; I tried resorting to masturbation and, to my dismay, found that was out of the question too. My joint had taken leave of its senses and my senses had taken leave of my joint. It went on like that. I began to feel disgraced. I wanted to kill someone. My therapist said Mother; he was probably right, but Mother was already dead.

Isabel was my eventual port in this storm and kept me from going completely bonkers. She worked with me physically for a few days—and it was indeed work—and then abandoned that, sensibly saying, "It's best to wait awhile, Ben." I moved in with her, into her little studio apartment on East Fifty-first Street, and slept with her and her two big chunky cats in the little loft bed that she had built with her own pale, esthetic hands. Isabel was a good carpenter; she had worked on theater

17

sets for years before developing the courage to try acting.
God, what a tiny place that was! And you could never escape
the street sounds from the windows: the shoutings of drunks
and mad bombers and all-purpose crazies at two in the morning; the steam-powered garbage wagons at four, and the
screeching wood vendors at seven-thirty. Wood was seven
dollars a stick in midtown, and Isabel had a fireplace. It was
the worst winter in forty years; on most mornings the water in
the toilet would be frozen solid. I tried enormous bribes on the
super for heat; he would give me his shy Yugoslav smile and
pocket my hundreds, but the heating pipes remained silent. I
tried, one frostbitten morning when the weight of three
blankets was suffocating me, to bring Isabel to her senses and
get her to sail to Yucatan with me for the winter. But she was
adamant. She held the covers up to her chin and said, "You
know I'm in a show, Ben."

I could feel the little hairs in my nose as stiff as icicles.
"Honey," I said, "you've got six fucking lines in that show,
and one of them is, 'Hello.' " I couldn't see outside because
ice had formed on the windowpanes. And we had a fire in the
grate; I had thrown some sticks on it at four in the morning,
shaking so much from the cold that I'd almost missed. What
would all the poor people downtown be doing, the ones who
couldn't afford wood and insulation and storm windows? The
Red Cross gave out blankets, but there were never enough. I
made a mental note to give a quarter million to the Red Cross.
Or maybe a sheep ranch, so they could grow their own. It was
seven in the morning and I could hear the wind howling
around the corner from Third Avenue.

"Sweetheart," Isabel said, "I'm not going to be your de-
pendent. And I'm warm enough." Isabel slept in long woolen
underwear, hiding all that radiant skin of hers and those
girlish breasts under scratchy BVDs. I slept wrapped around
her warm body, dressed in a flannel nightgown and gym
shorts.

We'd had that argument enough times before, so I gave it
up. Isabel wasn't about to take advantage of my wealth. That
afternoon I hunted around and found a big old coal stove at a
blackmarket shop on Seventh Avenue and got the name of a
dealer. Burning anthracite for private heat was illegal, under

the Nonrenewable Resources Act; it took hard-coal trains to move the food and other essentials around the country, and the enforcement was pretty tough. But I had connections and was willing to take the chance. After all, I was in the business: Belson Mines. I managed after three phone calls to get two dozen cabbage-sized lumps of anthracite and promise of another delivery in five days. Isabel and I were warm enough after that. My dealer, a skinny little fellow in a pea coat, tried to sell me some cocaine along with those black lumps, but in those days I had no interest in drugs. It took a voyage to the stars to get me hooked.

With coal in the grate, Isabel went back to sleeping naked, but it didn't help my impotence. I remember waking up at 5 A.M. sometimes with a yearning in my groin, but if I woke Isabel—no easy task, since she slept and snored like a hibernating bear—it was no good. My scared member would retreat and I would be frustrated and feel like a fool to boot. And have Isabel furious with me for wakening her to another strikeout. "Ben," she'd say, "if you want me take me. But quit waking me up for these *experiments*." I blushed like a child and couldn't get back to sleep. It was horrible. This was after that conversation in Jamaica with the geologist; I began to have daydreams of space travel. I will say this about myself: when I sublimate I sublimate grandly.

So I bought this ship and furnished it, made sure there were a few attractive women in the crew, and set forth to the stars with a limp penis.

"Doctor," I said to Orbach, lying on the leather couch in his office, my big lumberjack shoes resting on the arm, my head against a fat leather pillow, "If I don't get some orgasms soon . . ."

"I wish you wouldn't pressure yourself so much," he said. "There are other ways to use your energies."

"I could lie, pillage and kill. I could run for President. I could travel through space."

His voice was wry. "The last sounds the least destructive." And that clinched it. The next day I told my lawyers to find a spaceship. The one I eventually got was Chinese; it was called *Flower of Heavenly Repose*. I had most of its old scientific gear junked, built a launching pad in the Keys, furnished the captain's quarters with antiques, hired a crew, and took off for Fomalhaut. This took a year. It would have taken five if I hadn't been wound up like a steel spring with celibacy. If I couldn't push myself into a woman's body by an act of will, will would push my body across the galaxy. I hated the spiritual algebra of it, but I understood the equation well enough; I had been robbing Peter to pay Paul for most of my life. That's how you get rich in a world of dwindling resources, a world with its springs running down.

Somebody years before had told me about sleep body-building; you could avoid the boredom of getting into shape by doing it in a long chemical sleep. I hated exercise and the idea had charm, but I didn't feel then that I could disappear from the world of the awake for two months without financial risks of the worst kind. When I learned that, despite the spacewarp tricks my ship was capable of, it would still take three dull months to get across the Milky Way, I decided to grab the opportunity and I had the Nautilus machines installed. I had been developing flabby pectorals and a pot. Firming up my body might firm up its sweetest part too. Hell, maybe in a two-month nap I might have a cascade of wet dreams and get some relief that way. But as it turned out, I didn't; I spent most of my dream time with Father.

I have kept myself in transit ever since I left home at eighteen. I studied metallurgy at one college and Chinese at another, moving from hotel to hotel while I studied. My Aunt Myra in New York left me eighty thousand dollars when I was fourteen. I put it into forests at a good time, and by college I could afford a suite at any hotel I fancied and a secretary to type my term papers. I've never stayed in a plain hotel room; I always take suites. I think I fear being stuck in a single room like my father.

I realize as I write this—as I dictate it—that I am living now in a single room, as I did at Isabel's. I am the sole resident of this moonwood shack, or cabin, the only piece of architecture on the planet Belson. There are no forget-me-nots on the walls, which are the matte silver of moonwood itself, that charming mineral. Still, the thought that I have become the inhabitant of one room and that my condition therefore resembles my father's makes me uneasy. Like him, I spend hours at my desk, reading. Like him, I smoke cigars endlessly. Like him, I speak to no one.

I need to mine more moonwood and build on another room. I need a companion. I need Isabel.

I've lived here four months now, with my little morphine factory and my red computer and with the garden outside. There could hardly be a way of being more alone, except that the planet itself is my friend and lover. When I get morose I can water my garden or shoot up or do as I am doing this very moment: dictate these reflections into the red box that types them up and never makes a spelling error. My fractured life comes rising from a slot, in crisp Bodoni Bold on an endless sheet of Hammermill Bond; there's enough of it now to paper this moonwood cabin, to give me a celestial womb lined with the print reflections of my life.

Since the ship left, there has been no sound but my own voice and the rare singing of the grass. Sometimes the planet shows me its rings. Her rings. His rings. They are seldom visible from here below, although I don't know why. One night last month I was awakened by the grass singing and, *mirabile dictu*, had my first orgasm in years, lying there alone hearing that powerful wordless song and picturing Isabel and the warmth in her Scottish face. That one ejaculation undid a coil deep in my spirit and blew fresh air into my musty soul; I went for three days afterward without morphine. Isabel, I send you my love. I want to marry you if I ever come back to the Earth.

I've known Isabel for ten years and lived with her for five agonizing months, and only now am I coming to realize how much she means to me. Wouldn't you know I'd put twenty-three light-years between us before I would see that? Maybe the distance is necessary to see beyond the fights we had. During our last month together my impotence turned me into a godawful nag; I worked on her case endlessly, nagging her about whatever came to mind, inwardly tearing myself apart with thoughts about all the potent lovers she must have had in her life. I would imagine stupid-looking young men who mounted Isabel's slight body with the aplomb of jockeys. My stomach ached at such thoughts. Yet Isabel gave no justification for them. She was faithful to my forced celibacy while I lived with her, and there were no mementoes of other men around her place. I know because I looked.

I nagged her about her career. I told her she should try for bigger parts in plays, or quit the theater. I would complain about the time she spent shopping for clothes and about the way she seemed to fill that small apartment with shoes and dresses so there was no place for my corduroys and jeans and lumberjack shirts. And yet I knew during all this that I secretly approved, because Isabel looked splendid in her clothes.

I wasn't always that way with her. I could be pleasant enough at times, and Isabel liked my sense of humor and my general disdain for the pretense of the business world. We were also both serious lovers of New York and of New York food. And Isabel knew, as women do, that I genuinely appreciated her good looks. There must have been something about me that she liked or I'd have been kicked out, if only for the messes I made on the floor with my cigar ashes. Isabel's floor was painted white; she had done the job herself not long before I moved in. Six layers, and each one rubbed down with steel wool. I managed to spill a lot of ashes from my Gueveras on that floor and then grind them in later by pacing. Hostility, I suppose. One cold Monday after her play had closed, Isabel spent the day on her knees scrubbing the floor and then giving it another coat of paint. She did this in black panties and socks, bare-breasted, with a coal fire blazing in the grate. I tried to ignore her from behind my *Wall Street Journal*s and my stock reports and prospectuses, but I couldn't keep my eyes off that undulant ass and those lovely breasts that hung down and gently swung from side to side as she scrubbed with a Kiwi brush and then rubbed and then painted. But I kept my hands off her, knowing all too well I had no follow-through available. It was agonizing, and I felt guilty about having made the floor a mess in the first place. There was a big scratch in it where I had thrown and broken a coffee cup in one of my rages over not getting it up. She filled the scratch with plastic wood, sanded it and then painted over it. Bless her heart. And then that evening she bundled herself up and went off to the Morosco Theatre to try for a part in a revival of *Hamlet*. She came home to our paint-fumed apartment and announced she was going to be Gertrude, Hamlet's mother, that it was a terrific chance. Here was Isabel, forty-three years old, as happy as an ingenue with her first part. I should have married her on the spot and started having children. God what a healthy brood we could be making! But instead, I was dismayed by it all and began to think of leaving. We had lived together five months, without sexual intercourse. And I didn't want to get that beautiful floor dirty again. I didn't want to watch Isabel struggle to learn all that blank verse. I remembered *Hamlet* from college; it was a big part.

Eventually I got a suite at the Pierre. It was four rooms and a kitchen on the fourth floor for three thousand a day, plus tax and service. It was warm, since the management had good connections. I took up cooking in earnest.

My best success was pot roast. I got a real pleasure—maybe my only pleasure in those sexually bleak days—from peeling carrots and potatoes and onions, weeping through a dozen onions at a time, standing over my stainless-steel sink and blinking tearily out the window at the empty shell of the General Motors building. I browned the meat in safflower oil, the only oil Isabel would touch, after coating it with durum flour and drenching it in Java pepper. Java pepper was another of Isabel's fetishes. I had to admit she was right too. And I wasn't cooking all those roasts for her either. She never came up to that suite, with its big beige sofas and its oriental rugs; I never invited her.

Oh Isabel! What a pervert I turned out to be, when push came to shove! It's all too clear now as I speak this on Belson: I didn't move out of your place because of the cold or because you were memorizing blank verse. I moved out because I had fallen in love with you. There I would stand in that high-ceilinged old kitchen with its white walls and its wooden countertops, and all the sexual energy that your body had inspired in me—that waist, those hips, those sweet breasts—went into my doleful midafternoon peeling of carrots, my weeping over stacks of shiny brown onions! My analyst, the Great Orbach, would call it sublimation; I call it a fraud and a cheat. I should have been arrested for gross and illicit orality. (Officer, do you see that big man over there, with the glasses and the lumberjack shirt, the one with the stack of vegetables at his elbow? I want him taken into custody and charged with criminal avoidance of manhood.)

I'd had Henri Bendel's send over a set of steel cookware, but all I ever used of it was one big pot. Sometimes the small saucepan for thickening gravy. Twelve hundred dollars, plus the 12 percent New York City tax and eighty dollars for delivery, and all I used was two pans. The damned roasting pan didn't even have a rack in it; I had to balance the meat on top of the carrots and onions to keep it from boiling. But my pot roasts were terrific. I served them with strawberry jam on the side, and a Bibb and arugula salad. Chocolate mousse for dessert. If my alienated member had been less shy, I could have gotten into the pants of every actress on Broadway that season, from the quality of my pot roast and the big wood fires I had in my living room to eat them by. Not to mention my charm, good looks and money. Ah well! What really happened was that I made a lot of women furious with me for not even *trying*. What I wanted was to eat with them and look at them and talk. Sometimes I did try rolling around in the bed, but I knew before I started that it would come to grief and anger. And it always did. I got some heady oral satisfactions with women whom schoolboys would have given their souls to fondle: a Belgian movie star, two leading ladies, a diva, a ballet dancer, the estranged doxy of a uranium man even richer than I, a handful of courtesans who did sex more dexterously than Chinese women assembled radios. The oral satisfactions were nice, but I'd have been better nourished eating fruit. Some very huffy women left that apartment in the mornings.

I had sense enough to realize it was a midlife crisis. I'd been studying the history of the uranium explorations and had come to feel—as a lot of well-informed people felt—that the government had stopped looking for uranium at just the wrong time. It had been the repercussions of all those wasted voyages and all the spent nuclear fuel that finally brought about the CEASE agreement, banning space travel. "Use the fuel at home!" President Garvey had shouted in her schoolteacherly way, and a lot of politicians had breathed sighs of relief.

But the fact was that safe uranium was just around the corner. A lot of experts felt that way; but no government was willing to take the risks anymore. Just one space voyage would use about 6 percent of the Earth's entire supply of uranium. Enough to heat Shanghai for ten years. You couldn't go out into the Milky Way without putting the ship into a spacewarp, and you couldn't do that without a few trillion megawatts at your disposal.

I had been toying with the idea for two or three years, ever since that conversation in Jamaica with the geologist. I did some talking around and found the thing was like ESP, a lot of knowledgeable people were believers; it was just that governments were uptight about it. And private industry was afraid to touch it—especially in those unprofitable times. Hell, the prime rate was 4 percent.

The SALT talks were still going on—SALT 17, in fact— after a hundred years. But it took exactly six months of martinis and tea in Geneva for the whole goddamned world to decide to quit looking for uranium in space. We could still bomb one another into radioactive dust at the touch of a few well-placed fingertips; but we would now sit and freeze because the gamble for energy scared the politicians more than the gamble with Armageddon did. Well. *Plus cq change, plus c'est la même chose.*

I figured it would cost me about eight hundred million to outfit a ship, hire a crew, and go to Fomalhaut. If I could find uranium and bring it back in quantity my profits would be almost beyond measure. Eight hundred million was half of what I was worth. If I lost it all I would still be rich, would still have more money than I could spend in a long lifetime. What the hell. I was getting tired of pot roasts and of angry women. I was unmarried. I hadn't used my stock exchange seats for a half-dozen years, and interest rates were abysmally low. And I am a restless man. I had been looking, unconsciously, for something big to put money into. What the hell, I might captain a spaceship off to the stars. Captain Belson. Why not?

It was insane for me to spend that cold winter in New York with temperatures at twenty below zero when I could have gone to the Yucatan in my boat. Getting coal for a boat was easy enough; transportation came under a special heading in the Energy Act. But the *Wit's End* stayed tied up in the East River that winter and got its hull cracked when the river froze solid in January. It didn't bother me much when that happened, though; I had my mind by then on other modes of transport; I had begun buying the *Flower of Heavenly Repose* and the uranium the trip would take. It was as complicated as preparing a small nation for war and I was thankful to throw my energies into it. I had six telephone lines put into my apartment in the Pierre and eventually installed a staff of five men and seven women on the two floors above mine. When the first warm day finally came, in June, we all toasted the spring together in my living room and got pleasantly drunk on Moët et Chandon. One of my purchasing agents was an amiable fat lady named Alice. She wore pink coral jewelry and sipped her champagne like a bird. Alice asked me what we would call the ship. Peking had just agreed to sell. I tossed off a fizzy mouthful before I spoke. "*Isabel*," I said. "The ship is the *Isabel*."

❧ Chapter 3

Belson has a diameter half that of Earth's—about four thousand miles. It is a great deal denser, though; the gravity is over half of Earth's. I weigh a hundred thirty pounds here; I'm two twenty in New York. Six feet four. Since Belson has no oceans, there is actually a lot more land area than on Earth.

There was no way we could explore it all. My experts back home had picked three sites from the old photographs and we tried each of the three. They were all in the same general vicinity on the planet, each a few hundred miles from the other. We had two jeeps for getting around. You could drive on the obsidian easily enough, although it was rough on the lower back and you had to watch out for skids. I wished I had been able to bring an airplane and the fuel to operate it; I would like to have explored more. But my geologists had assured me, after studying the pictures, that it wouldn't be worth it. If there was uranium it would be within three hundred miles of where we landed, and the rest of the planet's surface would be the same as where we were. Belson had almost no geological features—at least few were detectable. There was no food and little water.

Negative reports kept coming in from the tests. It was beginning to look bad. We had discovered moonwood—a lovely mineral material that could be sawed and hammered and had a silvery surface; but it would hardly be profitable to export it. At that distance even gold wouldn't pay its own freight. Only uranium could really justify the trip. And it was beginning to look like there wasn't any.

When I was fourteen I worked up the temerity to ask my father's advice on choosing a profession. I was a tall and gangly kid then with platinum-blond hair and muscles too weak to hold my body up properly—or so it felt anyway. I was awed by my father and by his silences. I stood in the doorway to his study for about ten minutes staring at those forget-me-nots on the wall and at the array of diplomas below them before he looked up and nodded toward me.

"Father," I said, feeling awkward and callow, "I need your advice."

He nodded again, hardly seeming to see me. There was a mild scowl on his perfectly shaven face. He was wearing a brown sweater and brown flannel trousers; there was gray hair at his temples but the rest of his hair was black. I was the only blond in the family.

"I've been thinking . . . ," I said, groping. "About what kind of work I'll do."

He nodded again, still silent. I felt cosmic pressures in my skull.

"I mean I should study something in college . . . ," I said with a lameness that bordered paralysis, suddenly aware that college was two years away. Why was I asking such dumb questions of a man so clearly occupied with universals?

He spoke, and his voice came as if from the bottom of a well. "What talents do you have?" he said.

I could think of nothing. I felt as ungifted as a tree stump. Actually, I could play the piano very well, was a whiz at mathematics and physics, had a passable singing voice, had written a two-act musical comedy for my high-school drama class, and could read poems in Chinese. I managed to forget all this in the presence of my father's clear unawareness of any of it. "I don't know," I said. Thinking of those words now, I still wince with embarrassment.

"Well," he said, with a distance as great as that of the broad gray Atlantic, "what can I say?" And he turned back to his book.

My mother was equally helpful. I popped the same question to her after she had just come back from a bridge party and was pouring herself a screwdriver in the kitchen. The sink was full of chipped dirty dishes; a Picasso clown hung askew over the stove, with grease on the frame. "Benny," she said, "I am not a vocational counselor. And your hair needs combing."

With that kind of help I decided to take my instructions in life from the outer world. And the outer world, shrinking into itself as it was in those sad, cold days, had this advice for me: make money. It seemed like a good idea. And it was; in the stock market I found my authentic talent.

And yet somehow here on Belson, when the *Isabel* was still my home, I didn't stop to think of what a money-maker endolin could be. It is remarkable stuff—the genuine anodyne. But I was wrapped up in my morphine highs then and in my theory of the planet's intelligence and in brooding about Isabel and in the strange soothing my spirit was given just in riding a jeep across vast plains of obsidian in the afternoons, skirting fields of Belson grass and drinking in the musty smell of the warm Belson air.

The grass never sang again for us. The seismic studies revealed no uranium but a lot of lead. I was getting out of shape again, even though I worked out on the machines every now and then. It was time to head back to Earth, to have myself put to sleep again. So I thought. We gathered a couple of crates full of endolin and about eighty large slabs of moon-wood. The navigator and I worked out a route home, planning to pop out of our self-generated spacewarp at a different set of stars from the ones we had drawn energy from on the way out; I gave instructions to be awakened a day before we arrived at one called Aminidab, a never-visited star that had looked right to some people at M.I.T. I told the doctor to jettison the rest of his morphine. I would go cold turkey the easy way: unconscious. I could have wept. Not for the morphine, which I knew I would have to give up soon anyway if I didn't want to

addle my life forever, but for Belson. I loved Belson and
didn't want to leave.

The night before we left was a bright one, with both moons
up and full. I gave myself a double injection of morphine and
went out for a final barefoot stroll. I walked along the edge of
the grass in a fine euphoric high for miles. The grass was silver
in the moonlight, and the vast, dry, serene emptiness was like
the desert in an Henri Rousseau painting. The obsidian felt
warm beneath my feet. Sometimes the grass sighed gently and
I sighed back at it. I felt as I had never felt before the warm
spiritual presence of that lonely planet, the only one of its sun.
I had become ecstatic with morphine and with my sensitivity
to impending loss. My neck tingled. I began to talk to the
grass. I told it how I felt. It seemed to sigh in response. I told it
about Isabel and about my impotence with her and it sighed
with me. I told it about my daughter Myra and her arthritis,
about her poor, painful life. I talked about how my world was
growing cold and empty after millennia of vigor and bounce. I
became higher, more mystical, moved by what I was saying
and by the splendid isolation I had here in my far corner of the
Milky Way. I forgot the people back on the ship and felt alone
with Belson, *my* Belson. It seemed to me then that Belson was
the finest and biggest thing I had ever known. The rings came
out in the night sky and glowed on my body.

After a while I lay drunkenly in ring light on the grass,
gently so as not to bruise it or make it bleed. It seemed to embrace me with a million small fingers. In my head I began to
hear something like words. At first they made no sense, but
after a while they became clearer. It was the grass speaking to
me: I could tell by the cadence, which was the same as the
singing. The words were both in my head and outside, murmured by the grass. What they said was, "I love you."

They had to come and find me in the morning and they carried
me back to the ship. The doctor said I must have overdosed. I
told them nothing but asked if anyone had heard the grass
speak the night before. No one had.

We delayed leaving for a day while Charlie gave me some
psychological and motor tests. I did fine on them. I knew I
had had no overdose and I knew that Belson had said it loved

me, but I also knew to keep my mouth shut about it. The next day we brought the coils around the ship to within a half degree of zero Kelvin, and when superconduction was in effect we generated the field and slipped into our warp. We popped out fifty hours later, two light-years away, and soaked up energy from a nearby sun. You cut the uranium bill in half that way. It was a reddish sun with no planets and had none of the zip of Fomalhaut. I was already homesick for Belson. I could have cried again. I had the doctor put me to sleep. All the way to Aminidab I dreamed of New York and Isabel and of the voice of the grass saying, "I love you."

The way I felt about Belson's intelligence was something like the way I feel about the stock market. The market is a dumber entity; it is blown around by half-baked gusts of emotion. The way to handle it is to learn everything you can about it and then depend on intuition. The intuition may *feel* mystical; but, in my case anyway, it isn't. I know what I'm doing with the market and I have the bank accounts to testify to that. I never developed a profession for myself after those consultations with my parents, but I'm not a fool. I trust my mystical feelings. I believe that Belson loves me.

When I was about twelve I played an old game called Monopoly with a kid I knew. My father had given me the game for Christmas; it was something from his collection of memorabilia from the twentieth century. And maybe it was a subliminal nudge toward the robber-baron capitalism I was eventually to espouse for myself, to fill in the time. The kid's name was Toby. We played in the living room of his house for a dollar a game. Toby was a rich kid by my standards of the time. My family lived in a permoplastic bungalow near the campus; his had a fourteen-room stone mansion. Toby's father was a judge and owned an alcohol-powered car. Toby himself was a ferocious competitor, more so than I; but I always won. I picked up all the necessary principles of the game the first time around. The basic philosophy was to go for broke, take every sensible risk you could. It was a solemn lesson for me. It was that philosophy that helped send me to Belson, and it was that philosophy that made me overrule my navigator and choose a potentially wasteful stopover at Aminidab. All I knew about Aminidab was that it was a sun of

the same spectral type as Sol. No one had ever gone near
enough to see if it had planets, but the astronomy people at
M.I.T. had picked it as a good risk. After all, for all the exploring that had been done in the twenty-first century, not one
star in a million, in the Milky Way alone, had been observed
closely enough to see planets. Computers had decided on the
ones to look at. There are a whole lot of stars out there. They
haven't been counted yet. It is gratifying to think they never
will be.

Well. When they woke me up they were clearly excited.
Nineteen planets had been spotted and we were still quite a
distance away. You can't pop out of a warp near a star; you
pull out a few thousand million miles away and then creep up
on it. We were still creeping.

I felt fine and saw I was back in shape again. I drank my
coffee and headed for the bridge. There was Aminidab, and
there, like specks of light, were its planets. They looked like
dust motes by a light bulb.

Aminidab turned out to have, all told, thirty-four. I was
exultant and gave orders to work out a path for a quick
photographic circuit of each..

"That'll take a lot of time," Ruth said. "And fuel."

"I know it," I said. "But, Ruth, there's going to be uranium on one of them or more. Come on. Let's go for it." For
the time I had forgotten Earth and Isabel. I could smell success and it was turning me on. I wanted uranium. Of course I
wanted uranium for the money it could make me and for the
simple success of my voyage and to confound my enemies
back on Earth. But I wanted, more importantly, to provide
the world with safe and easy power again; in the days before
leaving I had daydreamed of finding trillions of tons of it on
some far-off planet. It was possible. It didn't have to be as
scarce, even with its half-life, as it was on Earth. There were
younger planets. There might be vast mountains of it somewhere—mountain ranges even. Yet it was, I knew, a daydream
of an impotent man: endless potency.

The third planet we photographed looked so good to me
and to the geologists that I ordered a landing right there. It
was a dense little world, half under water and with a lavender
sky. We skimmed over part of its surface, in low orbit, gawk-

ing. There was plant life all over. The oceans were pink. I liked
it. Not with the deep affection I felt for Belson, but I felt
sanguine about this planet. It looked young. It had energy.

We found a kind of mossy plain and landed. This time Ruth
did the landing herself and made a good, simple job of it. My
respect for her doubled. Ruth was a good woman; she just
didn't have much to say. Her red hair had gotten very long on
the trip and I liked the way it fell over her competent
shoulders. But when I praised her for the landing she seemed
cool when she thanked me. Something was going on there, and
it must have gotten worse during my long sleep.

Before opening up we checked the atmosphere. There was a
lot of oxygen—twice that of Earth. The rest was nitrogen and
traces of inert gases like argon and xenon. We had better be
careful about fires, the doctor said, and not breathe too
deeply. You could addle your brains with too much oxygen.

The plain we were on was about ten miles from a place that
had photographed out as mildly radioactive. There was a lot
of water on this world, and if the uranium turned out to be
there we could stay indefinitely. I liked the idea of exploring.
What the hell, it looked a little like Jamaica, except the colors
were all wrong. Orange tree trunks, for instance. The gravity
was eight-tenths Earth-normal and there were heavy pink
clouds in the sky. We touched down in a storm of warm,
tropical rain. It kept up for two days. How it all drained off I
don't know. It was a furious, drenching downpour and it
pounded on the ship's hull like hail on a plastic roof; the noise
was almost deafening. It was frustrating. We didn't dare go
out for fear of being drowned. Here we were on this lively
planet, ready to get our jeeps out and throw ourselves into the
explorer's dream of a lifetime, an adventure beyond the
childhood imaginings of any of us, and we had to stay inside
because of rain.

I finished *The Ambassadors*, had a morose and silent dinner
in my stateroom with Ruth, who excused herself right after the
mousse, and lay on my bunk, listened to the rain and thought
about my early days in Athens, Ohio.

When I was a kid in Athens there were horses everywhere.
The Energy Acts of those days classified burros and horses
as solar—since they ate vegetation—and a person could have

as many as he could afford. Athens was a hilly place, with
its small university built two hundred years ago in the Ap-
palachian foothills; and although people had bicycles, horses
were the best way to get around. It's a lovely little town still, I
suppose, although I haven't been there for twenty years. We
had a sweet-tempered chestnut mare named Juno, and some
nights when Father was reading in his study and Mother was
asleep on the living-room couch I would go out to the garage
and sleep with Juno, lying on her moist and tickly straw, soaking in her body warmth and her body smells, listening sometimes to the fluttering and groaning noises she made in her
sleep. Juno died when I was fifteen, and I mourned her more
than I would mourn either of my parents.

My father supplemented his professor's income by having
Juno serviced and selling the foals. She never failed to produce, bless her heart. She gave birth to a succession of colts in
deep, rich, glossy browns and blacks, and she nursed them
with love and patience, watching them grow and urging them
on. Her grief when Father sold them was, to me, palpable. I
could feel her mourning. I made a special point of sleeping
with her on the nights after a colt of hers had been taken away,
regardless of how cold it might be in the garage, and she would
nuzzle me in her sleep sometimes and the garage would fill for
a moment with the resonance of her doleful, motherly voice in
its sad whinnying. I knew how she felt. I would have whinnied
along with her had I known how.

When Juno died she wasn't replaced. My father had taken
an early retirement to do research, and the three of us were on
a reduced income and couldn't afford a horse. Father hardly
went anywhere anyway, and Mother had undergone two bad
falls from Juno. Juno's body was sold to the recycling plant
on the edge of town and I retreated farther into myself and my
dreams of wealth. There was no one left in that grim household to love.

I remember my mother coming out to the garage one night
when Juno was still alive and I was lying against her flank
half-asleep, dreaming already of stock-market quotations and
of the killings I would make. Mother was wearing a pink
chenille bathrobe. She had a candle in her hand and her face
was as puffy as bread dough and her hair wild. "My God!"

she said, seeing me. "You fool. That horse could roll on you and kill you. Or kick you to death."

I opened my eyes and stared at Mother. I could have stood up, easily, and beaten her senseless. Juno wouldn't hurt me. I stared at Mother and said nothing.

Mother suddenly seemed to weaken and become confused. She put a hand to her forehead, and even in candlelight I could see the blue veins in it and the trembling. She looked at Juno and spoke as if to her. "What's going to become of me?" she said. Juno was silent. So was I. Mother turned and went back to the house. About a half hour later I got up from the straw and went through our vegetable garden to the living-room window and looked in. There sat Mother on the sofa with her robe open and a drink in her hand, staring at the gray floor of our living room. The study candles were out; my father was in bed. It was about three o'clock in the morning; I could tell that by the stars. In those days we still were allowed electric light until 10 P.M., but it was far later than that. Mother had lit six candles and was sitting there as though hypnotized, the flesh on her cheeks sagging, her breasts exposed, sagging, her arms sagging at her sides. Whenever I hear the phrase "spiritual bankruptcy" I think of Mother sitting there, an empty woman.

Mother was dead within a few years, and shortly afterward my father died. I was thirty before I found out that my father was not a famous scholar at all but just another university hack, his whole lifetime worth at most a couple of footnotes in the work of a real historian. What fools they were, with their unlived lives! What cowards! I have tried to erase them from memory but I cannot completely; something in me can still, in the dark of night, ache for a parental touch that I cannot even remember, ache to be held by them. At such times I force my memory back to Juno, and Juno, as always, comforts my hungry spirit.

It was Ruth who asked me, in a kind of shy, distant way, if we shouldn't give our rainy planet a name. I didn't hesitate. "We'll call it Juno," I said. My heart was gratified at the thought. I looked out the window at the heavy rain and the shadows of strange trees burgeoning up from the wet soil. What a fecund place, what life!

• • •

When the rain stopped I was the first one out the hatchway, walking more soberly this time but my heart exultant. The air smelled of wet grape leaves and was as moist as in a greenhouse. There was a breeze; I could hear rustling, paperlike, from the distant forest. The grass had a rich green hue and was spongy underfoot. What a place, what a splendid place! I was high with the thought that this could go on forever, with thirty-three more planets around this sun alone! Actually it was a pair of suns; Aminidab had a small red twin called Casca and I could see it just above the distant horizon.

I turned back toward the ship. Ruth was standing in the doorway looking out, her face morose.

"Come on out, Ruth!" I shouted, and she smiled faintly and walked out and stood for a minute. I jogged over, put my arms around her and gave her a hug. Then I pulled back a bit and waved at the others inside. "Come on out!" I shouted. "Bring some wine and we'll have a picnic!" I looked back at Ruth. She was shaking her head at me, in a kind of motherly mock-alarm. Her face had brightened considerably. It suddenly occurred to me that I had never told Ruth I was impotent, and I immediately realized she must be miffed at me for not even trying to get in her pants. Jesus, I can forget the simplest social obligations sometimes when I get wrapped up in myself, as I was on Belson.

Well, we had the picnic there in our first few hours outdoors on Juno and we had a great time—all eighteen of us. When I had awakened a few days before from my long nap, I noticed a certain coolness in the crew and interpreted it as pique at the way I could sleep away most of the trip, while they had to contend with the tedium. Probably bitching at one another too, and getting into sexual complications the way people will. The idea of a picnic was an inspired way of getting past hard feelings and inaugurating a new camaraderie in this new world of ours. It worked splendidly. One of the seismic engineers, a normally quiet woman named Mimi, produced a guitar and began singing old twentieth-century songs. "Downtown" and "Let It Be." Howard and another engineer brought out bottles of red wine, a wheel of cheese, some cans of tuna fish and six loaves of rye bread; we found a dry place on the spongy ground and sat around together and sang along, with our mouths full of food. We kept passing wine bottles. It was delightful. Nobody was worried about dangerous life forms, and there really wasn't any need to worry. If there were any animals—which was very unlikely—they could hardly have *homo sapiens* on their diets. We drank the wine and watched the suns move across the sky at a merry clip—since Juno's rotation took a little less than eight Earth hours—and then were entertained by a night with five moons and the twinkling of about a dozen of our nearby fellow planets. Despite the brightness of the sky, I could spot Sol as it rose, looking nondescript, just another Spectral Type G, Main Sequence, star. That little pinpoint flicker in Juno's purple sky was the sun of my old Earth, the blazing god of its ancient religions; from here I saw it as just another distant rhinestone among handfuls of them thrown across the night sky. Ninety million miles from Sol would be Earth, too small to see, where Isabel lived. I waved toward Isabel, a bit sadly, and fell asleep for a while on the grass.

Later that night I found myself briefly alone with Ruth and almost told her about my sexual problem. I wasn't sure that I was still impotent; I just had, then, a lack of interest that might have merely been desuetude—a kind of "solitary confinement blues," as some of my friends in prison used to call it. I spent two years in a prison in New Jersey, back when I was young and in too much of a hurry to assemble my first ten million. It had to do with price-fixing. Alleged. I managed to get market reports in my cell and found ways of sending out buy-and-sell orders. I was worth about twelve million when I got out, so the experience paid off well enough, although I did get restless in jail. When I left I had managed to corner the marijuana market in the prison; it had been done largely in a spirit of play. *That* was the only real price-fixing I ever did: I got it up to three hundred an ounce for mediocre Jamaican and passed my holdings on to a friend—a murderer and there for life—who was grateful to take over. He sends me Christmas cards and an occasional moody letter. Eduardo had murdered two wives; I knew how he felt.

Most of us didn't sleep that short night, our first in the open for some time. The first sun, the little one, was back up three hours after the big one had set, and it made a pleasantly soft light to explore by.

The forest was made up of those trees with slim orange trunks. The trunks were warm and leathery to the touch; the leaves were membranous and translucent, with a kind of ivory-colored Spanish moss hanging from some like old lace; they rustled pleasantly in the grapey wind. We looked for fruit but there was none. The forest was large and the trees were all alike. We kept on walking through it. There was little chance of getting lost, but just to be sure I marked our path occasionally with a page from *The Ambassadors*, which had somehow wound up in my jacket pocket. After a while the second sun came up, the light changed from red to yellow, and it began to get warm. The spongy grass became harder underfoot as its moisture evaporated. I was getting hot and sticky and was thinking about going back to the ship for the nuclear jeep when we came up over a slight rise and Ruth, who was the first up there, shouted, "Wow!" and we all came up alongside her and gaped. Below us stretched a broad valley all the way to the horizon, with trees and bushes and plants: brown and crimson and mauve and yellow. The small hairs on the back of my neck prickled.

We were all still a bit high from the picnic and from being up all the brief night; we rushed down the hill and started looking at the different plants, first in childish delight and then trying to find things that seemed edible. I found some long pods growing from a yellow bush and picked them; they were slippery and smelled grassy in my hand. Ruth found something that looked like an avocado, and Howard found stalks like celery. We began gathering in earnest, shouting at one another when we found something that looked good. You could move fast and easily in that gravity and we were all over the place. Nobody dared bite into anything yet; it all had to be tested first for poisons and digestibility. We loaded ourselves with this astonishing harvest, laughing and joking. It was a profound release after the long trip from Belson and the days of waiting in the rain.

We found a lot of things that looked like food. Howard and Sato, our biophysicist and our physiologist, checked them out with beakers and computers and lab mice and found that half

of them were indeed edible. Protein, carbohydrates, fats. Just
like Earth. My yellow pods had little orange peas in them that
tasted like almonds. Howard's stalk was as crisp as celery but
tasted like fish. And someone had picked mushrooms that
looked suspiciously like Earth mushrooms and in fact *tasted*
like mushrooms. Sato muttered something about "interstellar
spores" and I shrugged. I didn't really care if they were fun-
goid cousins of what grew on Earth, carried here by astral
winds or by the hand of God; they were nearly as good as
morels and they would be splendid on steaks or in an omelet.
The big orbiculate leaves of the orange-trunked trees were
edible but tasted like kerosene. There was a plant that was like
wheat, and I later got some kernels from it and ground them
up and made a few passable loaves of bread. I had learned to
bake during those morose days at the Pierre. The flavor was
slightly acid but it worked out fine with the mushrooms when
you fried them and made a mushroom sandwich.

I was really beginning to feel good with the crew. The picnic
had begun it, and finding new foods and sharing them ce-
mented it; we had become a family. When I saw Sato walking
hand in hand with Mimi, I felt a warmth in me that I had never
felt, even for my daughter Myra with her unlucky body and
her doleful eyes.

I went to bed early that night and dreamed for a while of
Myra.

The next morning everyone was a bit tired at breakfast. But by
the second cup of coffee we were all charged up again. Within
a half hour our chief engineer, Annie, was outside in her
overalls supervising the unloading of the two nuclear jeeps and
then having a plant wipe installed on the front of the bigger
one. Mimi and Sato left their breakfasts half finished and
went off to the equipment lockers to break out the uranium
detection and sampling gear. The geologists started a discus-
sion of three possible mining sites that our computers had
picked from the infrared photos, taken while the ship was in
orbit. The nearest site was seventeen miles away, but the
likeliest was six miles farther. The basic problem was ground
transportation. You could hardly use the *Isabel* for short
hops.

I finished off my pancakes and bacon and stayed out of it
for a bit. But when I'd had my second cup of coffee I spoke
up. "Let's go for the big one first," I said. "Annie can go in
front with the wipe and we'll follow with the gear."

Arturo looked up from his charts. "What about the
seismics?" Arturo was chief geologist and looked testy.

"We won't do seismics. I have a hunch we won't need them
here. This first time out I'm going to put my faith in a
shovel."

Arturo looked at me with dismay for a moment. Then he
said, "Captain, with all respect, we have to zero in on a thing
like this. You can't just start digging . . ."

He was sitting across the table from me. I stood up with a
cigar in one hand, reached the other hand out to his chart, and
pointed to a spot where a group of computer-drawn lines con-
verged. "We're looking for a mineral with an atomic weight
of two thirty-five," I said. "And there is something very
heavy right there—twenty-three miles from here."

"Captain, the photo equipment isn't capable of that kind of
discrimination. It could be thorium or actinium. It could be
lead."

"We'll see what it is," I said.

In an hour we had our two-jeep caravan set up. I sat with my
Sears, Roebuck shovel in the driver's seat of Annie's jeep, and
the other one followed with three geologists and their equipment. Annie had a wipe cylinder installed on each of the front
fenders and she blasted while I drove at a steady five miles an
hour. At first she was very careful and businesslike with the
big silver tubes, but after a bit she started getting into it and
operated the controls as though she were firing six-guns: *Zip!*
Trees and bushes puffed away in pink bursts of cloud. *Zap!*
Great lavender flowers vanished as we humped and rocked our
way along the denuded ground, and stands of leaves the size of
rowboats fell into dust.

I had fed Arturo's chart into the jeep's readout machine;
my navigating behind all this molecular devastation consisted
of keeping two little green lights on the dash superimposed.
More accurately, bringing them back together every time I hit
a big hump and they veered apart.

It took four and a half hours to get there and I suspected the three behind us wanted a break. But I didn't want to stop and we pushed on until the beeps of the homing device on the dash got loud enough to let me know we were very near our destination. I pulled up, turned off the ignition and got out. I was shaky from the ride but excited. I could smell uranium. Or, more precisely, money.

The other three came dragging up in a minute, looking dusty and weary, and I handed out beers from the back seat. Then I took my shovel and pointed toward a rise just ahead. It was a kind of grassy hillock about the height of my mansion in New York. We all took long swigs of beer and then I said, "I think that's an outcropping and I think it's what we're looking for." I looked at Arturo, who had been in the second jeep. "What do you think?"

He nodded a bit coldly. "That's where the lines on the chart converge," he said. "But there's nothing radioactive around here. It's probably lead." He was holding a Geiger counter.

"If it's safe uranium it won't affect a counter," I said.

"Don't be sure," Arturo said. "Nobody's ever seen safe uranium. It's only an educated guess." He looked skeptically toward my hill. "Maybe a hopeful guess."

"This is one hell of a time for that kind of talk," I said. "I'm going up."

Before anyone could say anything, I had started up the hill. It was overgrown with some kind of matted, pinkish vegetation, with no handholds; but in the light gravity and the good shape I was in I managed to scramble my way up. I looked back and saw the rest of them beginning to climb. I turned back to the summit I stood on. It was a flat place, a bit larger than a pool table. I took a firm grip on my shovel and started digging.

By the time the others were on top and were standing, sweating and a bit annoyed, looking at me, I had dug through the topsoil. I raised a shovel load now of a mustard-colored mass and held it out toward them. It was very heavy stuff, whatever it was. "I'm no geologist," I said. "Can somebody tell me what this is?"

Annie was the first to reach for it. She took a pinch between her fingers and sniffed it. Then she took the equipment case from her shoulder and got some little electronic machines out. Arturo did the same. When he felt the stuff and its heaviness and then rubbed some in the palm of one hand, he showed surprise but said nothing. The four of them worked on the samples for several minutes in increasing but silent agitation. I felt excitement growing in me. It was like the feeling you get when a stock begins to move up and you sense that it's going to go through the roof.

Annie spoke first. "My God!" she said, "I read uranyl nitrate at eight-six percent."

"Unstable but not radioactive," Arturo said in a hushed voice.

"I cannot believe this," Mimi said, with a thrill in her voice. Suddenly she stood up. My heart had begun pounding like a triphammer. She threw her thin arms around me and hugged me with astonishing strength.

I hugged her back, and then the others piled around us in a big huddle of arms and bodies. "I believe it," I said. It turned out the whole hill and the ground for acres around it were 86 percent uranyl nitrate—a U236 compound and yet as safe as buttercups. The other 14 percent would be no trouble for the *Isabel's* refining equipment. The only problem was getting it to the ship; we had a hold capacity of sixty tons. Hauling that much ore twenty-three miles in jeeps would be a pisser. The best idea was to take the *Isabel* up into orbit and bring her back down again as close to the hill as possible.

But when I told Ruth that was what I wanted, she said, "Look, Ben. Maybe I can jockey the ship over without all that fuss."

And she did. We got everything back on board, strapped ourselves into our bunks, and Ruth brought the *Isabel* shuddering up to a few hundred feet of altitude, tilted her forward for a moment, and then brought her shuddering back down on her own white tail flame. It was a gorgeous maneuver; I was astonished that it could be done at all.

When we stepped out a half hour later over smoking ground, we stood twenty yards from my hill of uranium. Ruth stood beside me looking modest but clearly pleased with herself. I turned and shook her hand warmly.

• • •

The next morning we opened the big hatchways and lowered the processing machinery to the surface. The two enjays—the nuclear jeeps—were fitted with backhoes, and Mimi and Sato each drove one while Annie had the metallurgical plowing equipment taken out and got it in place. By afternoon, fourteen people were working together and a steady stream of uranyl nitrate was moving along conveyor belts.

The *Isabel*, seated on her retros as she was, is nearly as tall as the Washington Monument, and a great deal thicker. I walked around her several times while the preparation of this cargo was getting underway, the piling-up of our bonanza, and then I stopped for a long silent look at the heavy boxes now escalating their way up to the empty holds. The thrill of discovery was gone. I watched this accumulation of potential wealth with something like weariness. It was beyond doubt the apex of my financial career and a mineral find almost beyond the dreams of Cortez in Mexico, yet I found myself without enthusiasm. *Maybe I'm just tired*, I thought. I went back on board and into my stateroom, took a bottle from the cabinet and poured myself a stiff drink. The *Isabel* was shuddering as her holds began to fill. I took a long swallow of Bourbon and sat wearily in my Eames chair. What it all meant for me then was merely more money. I had won my original gamble and was bringing off a coup that would stagger the financial communities of the world. Juno uranium could reverse the decline of New York, of the whole United States. If an ice age really was on its way, this uranium would keep the people of the world from freezing, would open up new possibilities even for the poorest. Especially for the poorest. And I could be, in a few years, the richest man alive.

I finished my whiskey and poured another. I felt weary. I felt as though I had done nothing and solved nothing.

❧ Chapter 4

I believe that in the twentieth century a person could become a
billionaire on four or five correct guesses and on being in the
right place at the right time three times. The United States
economy underwent a steady expansion during that century. A
tenacious but lucky fool could quadruple his inheritance with
less skill than it took to win at Monopoly. Quite a few
tenacious and lucky fools did just that, and then went on to
work widespread mischief with their radio stations and their
crusades for Christ—that Gentile, middle-class Christ of the
Texas billionaire!—and their John Birch societies and their
general loutish arrogance.

There are still men and women of that kind around and I
know some of them pretty well. I don't socialize with them at
their prayer breakfasts and their Permastone country-squire
mansions, but I sell real estate to them from time to time.
They are a rarer breed in the twenty-first century than in the
last two. Ours is a dwindling economy. Energy sources and
population have been shrinking for seventy years. If a person
in 1940 had bought almost *anything*, from canned-soup fac-

tories to Australian ranchland, and hung on to it for twenty years, he would have enriched himself enormously and along the way gained a reputation for perspicacity. His sons and daughters would have been written about in the papers as though their lovers and their art purchases and their drug addictions were of national importance.

Well, it doesn't work that way anymore. If you hang on to what you own, it loses value. Markets keep getting smaller; there are fewer people to buy canned soup. Even with the Chinese now using armpit sprays and mascara and perfumed toilet paper, the world market keeps getting smaller.

I have several ways I rely on for making money; the chief one is knowing when to sell and what to sell for. There are lots of things for sale out there and, as always, some are bargains but most are not. I buy the bargains and I know how and when to sell them. I am not a producer of wealth or of much that society needs or wants; most people like me are the same and always have been; we are really people who are either smart enough or powerful enough or rich enough to begin with, to be able to take advantage. Marx called us jackals, and, as usual, Marx was right. I'm worth about two billion and I sometimes hate myself for it.

When I was in my late thirites and making a lot of money in the declining real estate market, I went through a period of a few years collecting impressive-looking buildings on bankruptcies and by finding weaknesses in the networks of mortgages that were common in those days. It was easy, once you grasped that things were going bad faster than anybody else thought they were. It was the 2040s, the time of the uranium bust. Nobody was having any babies; the military had its crude hands on all the crude oil; whole industries were reeling; just taking the Mercedes limousines away from all those gray-templed hustlers who sat on their boards had thrown most U.S. corporations into tailspins. I was selling short like a mad Arab at a bazaar; I rescued real estate from the courts, spiffed up its paperwork, found ways of unloading it and then found ways of writing it off. Jolly times, if you had the nerve. During all this a lot of buildings passed through my hands and I hung on to a few that suited my fancy. I wound up owning what had once been a fine arts museum in San Francisco, which I lived in for six months because of some tax advantages. I also owned a house in Georgia, four banks in Dallas, the Japan Camera Center in Chicago, two solid blocks of Park Avenue in New York, and a baroque, five-story mansion at Sixty-third and Madison. I decided one rainy Thursday to make it my family home; I spent three months knocking out walls and redecorating—over fifty workmen would be there sweating away at any given time.

I think that place reflected my time in prison more than anything else. I had learned to shoot passable nineball in jail and I had a billiard room put in my mansion, with a fine nineteenth-century mahogany table. I almost never played anymore, but I loved looking at the way the green baize surface glowed under the Tiffany lamps. I had been claustrophobic sometimes in my cell and couldn't sleep; I had a whole floor of that place as my master bedroom, with a huge bathroom each for me and Anna and an unfinished pine floor big enough for basketball. I furnished the main living room in eighteenth century; I had fallen in love with that from a picture book at the prison library: *English Eighteenth-century Houses*. There were gold armchairs with white brocade seats and cloisonné snuffboxes and clocks with cherubs on their faces. I bought two Fragonards, and a chandelier from a French palace. But all I remember using that room for was playing three-card stud with my accountants. We didn't entertain. Anna spent most of her time in the bedroom, reading or making hooked rugs.

During the redecorating Anna was living with her parents upstate, in their parsonage in Watertown, and on the night before she and our daughter Myra were to come and make a grand attempt at living with me, I went to the place and poured myself a tumbler of Japanese Campari in the cathedral-ceilinged kitchen and walked around in a kind of euphoric daze for hours. I allowed myself to imagine being a paterfamilias on the grand scale. Since Anna and I had only one child, it would be necessary for us to start breeding fast, but that seemed okay at the time. There was a big nursery on the top floor. What the hell; we could have six or seven kids and reverse the trend. I didn't know anybody else who had children. There alone in that big spooky expensive place I visualized the bustle and warmed to it. Moonlight came through high casement windows onto the floor of my cavernous living room and glistened on the cherrywood grand piano. I sat on the bench and played "Stardust" and "Bridge over Troubled Waters" soulfully and drank more Campari. I got up and went to the billiard room and played myself a game of nineball. I still remember: I ran the first seven and then miscued on the eight. I walked down to the wine cellar and counted the whites, took the walnut and brass elevator up to the fourth floor and surveyed the guest suite, done in early twenty-first century, with everything pastel and puffy, even the kitchen and butler's pantry. I smoked a Japanese cigar, drank a glass of Japanese whisky, turned on my Japanese music system for a while, glanced through the Japanese section of the *Wall Street Journal* and thought briefly of buying a resort hotel near Osaka. But I wasn't really interested, and Japanese investments troubled me; I knew her depression would worsen from buying American coal, as indeed has happened. My spirit was troubled there in my mansion and I didn't know why. Yes, I did. It wasn't going to work out, and I knew it then.

I still had my methane-powered Bentley in those days, and I used it to pick up Anna at Grand Central the following morning. She had traveled second-class on a wood-burner, sitting erect on one of those plastic seats by dirty windows, and had brought exactly one small suitcase with her. Samsonite. That was Anna. It wasn't exactly religion with her and she had taken no vows of poverty. But my God, did she gall me. Yet she wasn't really stingy in the soul—just closed off somewhere. Often I would wind up spiritually on her side and cursing myself for being oafish and rich. Her suitcase was half full of books.

Anna and Myra and I lived in that mansion for eight months. Toward the end of it the student riots began. Things were bad all over and the students had decided capitalism was to blame. I had no real quarrel with that, although I felt the scarcity of fuels deserved at least equal billing. For a few days of it a lot of the sons and daughters of the upper-middle class decided *I* was the enemy, and I got edgy when they started chanting things like, "Belson go home." Hell, I *was* home.

They hanged me in effigy, and it was a damned good effigy too. Art students. I'll never forget that stuffed manikin with my steel-rimmed eyeglasses and my characteristic lumberjack shirt and the cigar. It looked so mournful being hanged under the gaslight there at Sixty-third and Madison, my replica head at one side as if in a daydream and my feet jumping around as drunken students jerked the rope. I stared at it a long time from my billiard-room window. Then they burned it and I gasped as it blackened. What a sensation! What a deadly preview! Still, I liked being the star of the show.

Anna saw that effigy too, I'm certain, from her bedroom window. She was a lot more cheerful the next morning. At breakfast she joined me for her Rice Krispies, and for a moment she even hummed a tune. But when I suggested we bounce around in our Louis Quinze bed for a while it was nothing doing. She wanted to finish Proust. I should have divorced her on the spot, citing cheerfulness toward effigy burning as grounds. Denial of conjugal rights. Overweening literacy.

I had never paid much attention to television, but when I moved into that mansion I decided to install the best. People told me the technology had been improved a lot and it was patriotic to patronize it. Since the death of Hollywood in the first part of the century and the demise of General Motors at about the same time, the United States had led the world in only two technologies: fast food and television. During the Depression of the 2050s holographic TV had improved enormously. So I had an RCA set installed in what had once been a third-floor sitting room. It consisted of six projection posts against the room's longest wall, and I'll never forget how I jumped when I first turned it on after the installers had left. A group of real people—dancing and singing frenetically—suddenly appeared in the room, life-sized and skimpily dressed, all of them grinning at me like idiots. The sound was real too, loud and sexy and terrible; it was Broadway synthetic music of the worst kind. It turned out they were doing a commercial for life insurance. I'd had no idea. And the whole thing only used a hundred and fifty watts. I left the set on, went to the bar in the next room, got myself some whiskey, and came back and joined my illusory guests, now a middle-class family in turmoil. A soap opera. It was quite a sensation to move among them, a drink in my hand, and hear talk of their electronic hysterectomies and multiple infidelities. They were very earnest. Things were pretty low in my life at the time. I seldom saw Anna, and Myra spent all her time with doctors and lovers. I ran my businesses pretty much from my head, and a dozen phone calls a day made up my labors. I was on hold— both financially and emotionally; I got hooked for a while on television. It was a sign that things were falling apart, that my plan of settling down in New York was unreal. Something in me welcomed the riots when they came. I haven't watched TV since. I do believe that shooting morphine is better for the soul.

Anna was the child of an improbable marriage between a little dandy of a Presbyterian minister and a big-boned grand-lady Episcopalian. Her mother, who had never attended her father's church, was far too grand to get out of bed before noon; she had lain on satin with her quilted robe and quilted eyepads while Anna took charge of two younger brothers.

I visited them one summer vacation, when Anna was home from Elmira College, where she studied French Literature. Her family kept her so busy, fixing this and taking care of that, that we hardly had any time together. She spent one morning preparing a Fourth of July picnic for all of us, and when the Fourth came her mother decided that Anna should put away the chickens she had roasted the day before and cook a ham instead.

"Mother," Anna said, in despair, "I have to hang up the wash. And where will I get a ham on the Fourth of July?" She stood there looking at her mother, trembling.

"You'll work it out, dear," her mother said. She turned and walked back up the stairs to her bedroom.

And Anna did in fact work it out. She got the clothes dry and bought a ham and cooked it and had a picnic dinner for six people. That evening she cleaned up the kitchen, fixed the damper on the wood stove and rearranged the books in her father's library.

"That girl sure is a wonder," her father said sweetly, puffing his pipe. At the time, I thought so too.

• • •

I spent two days after they hanged and burned me in effigy getting police protection and having steel shutters put on the windows of the bottom two floors. It was a private police firm, a subsidiary of Cosa Nostra. There already was a high wall around the building with a stand of barbed wire on top. During this activity I hadn't seen Anna or Myra, but when it was all over and I was in the billiard room one evening idly shooting the three ball around on the table, thinking things over, who should walk in but Anna. She was wearing a faded green housedress and she looked tired.

"Hi," I said. "Where've you been lately?"

She frowned a little. "Around the house," she said. "Staying out of your way."

"You wouldn't have been in the way. I've just been telling men where to put things."

"You should have asked me to help." Her voice was weary. "Ben, pour me a beer, will you?"

She seemed so relaxed and tired and familiar that my tension dissolved. "Sure, honey," I said. I went to the little bar at the end of the room and got two bottles of Peruvian beer and two glasses. Anna seated herself in a big velvet easy chair. I set the glasses on the table beside her and poured them both full, with big foamy heads. I pulled a smaller chair over to face hers, took one of the glasses, and sat down. Anna seldom drank, and I took this present willingness as a good sign. I sipped my beer slowly and waited for her to start a conversation. She clearly had something on her mind.

Finally she spoke up. "Ben," she said, "I think I could go crazy in this house. There's nothing here for me to do."

I stared at her, crestfallen I guess. I had been hoping for something positive. "You should get out more," I said. "Meet people. We could go to the theater or the ballet." I felt stupid immediately, saying it. There were riots and demonstrations out in the streets of New York and I was one of the prime targets of them. My wife should hardly be out at soirees or politely applauding the ballet. I always seemed to be saying stupid things to Anna.

She just looked at me wearily. "It's like it was when we lived at the Pierre, Ben," she said.

"I don't drink as much as I did then. And I'm home a lot more."

She looked at me fiercely for a moment. "You were drunk all the time," she said. "Or at least whenever I saw you, which wasn't often. Now you're drunk only part of the time."

That was her first acknowledgment that I had cut down, and I was glad to hear it. "Look," I said, "we could read books together, the way we did when we were first married. We should take a trip to Europe and go back to some of those places in Florence. Or that house in Brussels."

She just looked at me and sipped her beer thoughtfully.

"Hell," I said. "In a week I can be finished with these damned mergers and with a coal deal I'm trying to make. I'll have time on my hands. We can get . . . can get reacquainted." I looked toward the big casement windows that faced Madison Avenue, where my new floodlights made the tops of the two big maples glow theatrically, as though for a stage setting. Then I looked back at Anna and saw that she was crying. "What's wrong, honey?" I said.

She went on snuffling for a minute and then took a substantial-looking handkerchief from the pocket of her dress and blew her nose powerfully. "Ben," she said, "I had a miserable time when we went to Europe. I hated that house in Brussels. I spent the time hooking rugs and trying to get some heat in that *kitschy* place while you paced around and fretted and made three-hour phone calls. It was horrible." She blew her nose again, more softly this time, and then looked at me balefully. "What makes you think it'll be any different if we do it again?"

"I didn't know . . . ," I said. "I thought you liked Europe that time."

There was hatred in her eyes now and in her voice. "I told you a half-dozen times when we were there I wanted to go home. I told you I hated Belgium. I felt uncomfortable in the restaurants, and the movies were insipid."

"Honey!" I said. "I remember." Actually I hadn't, until she spoke of it. I felt immediately guilty. But, damn it, it had been ten years before. "And didn't I have French movies brought over and we showed them in the living room? And I got a good cook and we ate in."

She stood up all of a sudden, with her half-finished glass of beer in her hand, and stared at me and said, levelly, "You son of a bitch, Ben. It was just like that. *You* did this for me and *you* did that. You were telling me then how *you* were going to straighten things out and how *you* were going to change. Well, you didn't change and you're not going to and I'm ill with it. I have a sickness unto *death* of hearing about you and what you are going to do and how things are going to be different. There are only two things you do, Ben; you make money and you talk about yourself. And I'm sick of both of them." She stopped and finished her beer.

Something in me was cringing. I knew what she said was true. I was obsessed with myself and with making money. But, damn it, I did pay attention to her when she spoke up loudly enough to compete with the three-alarm fire that was sometimes going on in my head. I felt wretched. "Anna," I said, in all sincerity, "what do you want?"

And then she did something I had never seen her do. She gripped her beer glass, swung her arm, and threw the glass like a hardball against the far wall. Straight as a rocket. It crashed, fell, tinkled on the floor.

"Jesus!" I said, impressed.

"What I want," Anna said, "is for those rioters out there to come and get you personally and hang you. And then burn you. I hate your insides, you self-centered son of a bitch."

I just stared at her. I had sensed that she was furious for a long time—years, I think. And there it was. It seemed to clear the air in the room.

"Damn your egomaniacal *soul*," she said, and then turned and left the room.

I sat there for about twenty minutes. Then I got up, went to the pool table, racked the balls into their triangle, broke the rack, and started shooting straight pool. I ran all fifteen of them. But my stomach was in a knot. I *was* a son of a bitch. Self-centered and money crazy.

When the Mafia first came out of the closet, merged with the Teamsters and listed itself on the New York Exchange, I stayed away from the stock. Cosa Nostra Industries. I was

suspicious, despite the predictions of better shipping of goods
across the country. Well, as usual, I was right; shortages got
worse in New York, and the arrival of food and goods became
even more whimsical. During that time in my mansion there
were never any potatoes available except on the black market,
but there was an abundance of pears. Damned good ones too.
After I finished running that rack of balls on the pool table, I
went down the elevator to the living room, where there was a
big Sèvres bowl of yellow and red Bartletts. I began eating
them and pacing around, dripping juice on the floor for a
while until I got a plate and held it under the current pear.
They were remarkable—as succulent as fruit could be—and I
must have eaten a dozen of them. "Orally deprived," the
Great Orbach had said of me, "lacking in deep and vital
nourishment inside." It was sure true. My mother's breasts
had looked like rotten turnips to me. When I drank I drank
seriously. Planning a real estate sale or a merger I could chew
my thumbs until they blistered. If I didn't have the metabol-
ism of a Brazilian fire ant I'd be fat. But I only sleep three or
four hours a night and I'm normally pretty lean.

So I gobbled down those pears in my guilt and anger and
helplessness and remorse over Anna. We had been married fifteen years and it seemed to be only grief. I ate another pear,
dribbling juice down my chin, striding across the living room
in my lumberjack boots. *Jesus!* I thought, *what does she
want?*

I said that aloud, *What does she want?*, several times, and
then realized I was fighting back the answer. It was obvious:
she wanted me to care about her. And the truth of it was that I
didn't. Not anymore. Anna bored me. There was a sweetness
in her somewhere—a kind of lost child—that appealed to me
strongly. There was that intelligence that had drawn me to her
in the first place. But right now it was all dust and ashes. It
wasn't enough. I ate another pear, more slowly this time. It
would have tasted better with a little hard cheese, but that was
two floors below, in the kitchen. I pictured Anna's face as it
had looked in that parsonage with her cultivated, genteel family. She had seemed so smart, straightforward and fresh. So
unlike anybody else I knew. She'd had a nice round bottom

then too, and big, amused eyes. Talking to her was like talking to an old friend. She didn't flirt. She wasn't devious. I felt I should grab her right then and marry her.

I proposed after we had known each other three months and she accepted. She told me the truth: she wanted to get out of that place near Canada, see the larger world. She didn't want to finish college and be a schoolteacher. She wanted something "different" she said. Well, I never found out what that "different" thing was—although God knows I tried to. And she never did either. She didn't know what she wanted; how in the hell was *I* supposed to?

I took her to an inn in Jamaica for our honeymoon; we stayed in a suite with a private swimming pool and private dock and our own croquet course. The bedroom was enormous, with white furniture and beds and white walls. There were nineteenth-century British paintings of flowers and horses and landscapes on the walls and three vases of flowers in the room. We had two bathrooms, tiled and huge, with a giant bowl of hibiscus in each—pink for her and blue for me. There was a stone balcony forty feet long over the rocks where the Caribbean splashed in clear blue and foam.

It was our wedding night. I had undressed quickly in my bathroom and was lying, wearing only a pair of black briefs, on one of the two king-sized beds, my hands behind my head. I was pretty inexperienced sexually myself, and Anna was a virgin.

So much for the Fergusson pill and the "liberation of the body"—I was as scared of sex as they had been in the Middle Ages. So was Anna. We had talked about it.

But she had not said anything to prepare me for what happened next. We had gotten off the plane still wearing the dressup clothes from the wedding. She came abruptly out of her bathroom now, with her white blouse still on and with some kind of godawful sexless rubber girdle on her bottom. She walked over to the bed in her matter-of-fact way, planted her feet like a shortstop, turned her back to me and said, "I can't get this thing off." I was sort of spellbound by all this. It was Anna's way of behaving all right, but I had expected something different for a wedding night. I sat up in bed, reached over and unhooked a little steel hook at the top of the thing. It felt to my fingertips like Rubbermaid.

"That's better," she said and then proceeded to loop her thumbs under the waistband of that damned rubbery white garment, pull it down an inch and then, abruptly, let it go with a loud *pop*. She breathed an audible sigh of relief. She took it off an inch at a time that way. Pop, pop, *pop*, I can still hear it.

I had not expected Anna to act like a courtesan. But, Jesus, she seemed to be trying to tell me something awful with this.

"Jesus Christ," I said, "what's going on?"

Her voice was taut. "I just couldn't get the thing *off*," she said.

"Why did you wear it in the first place?" She didn't need a girdle. Her ass was fine.

Then she began to cry.

"I'm sorry, honey," I said. That must have been the first of a million times I was to say that. *I'm sorry, honey.* Christ! I should have read the handwriting on the wall right then and bolted back to New York. Let my lawyers handle the annulment. But, as usual, I thought it over and figured I was in the wrong. If only I could trust my feelings with women the way I do with money! I'd be as fulfilled as a fat Japanese Buddha floating on a lotus leaf.

"The lady at the store told me I needed something to wear under the suit, and I bought it. I wanted to look right for you."

I shook my head. She turned to look at me, standing there with a white Synlon blouse on and that big dumb rubber thing lying on the floor like a discarded chastity belt. Chastity belt is right. I've learned since that there are nuns everywhere.

"Well, she should have sold you a pair of scissors to get it off with." I was trying to be amusing. But it wasn't funny. Goddamn it, it was *terrible*. I felt like a son of a bitch for being angry. I had loved her for her plainness, hadn't I? What did I expect? Poor girl—how could she know how to be graceful on her bridal night?

Anna looked devastated. "I'm sorry, Ben," she said. "I guess I don't know how to be a bride."

"Honey," I said, "it's okay. Just throw that thing away

and get yourself naked and come back. If you feel self-conscious naked, wear something. Just something that isn't made of rubber.''

She smiled. "Okay," she said, and went back into her bathroom.

She came back after a while wearing a white gown. She had put on perfume. She lay in bed by me and we talked and both of us got to feeling better, but something in me was apprehensive. We didn't make love until the morning, after breakfast. She bled a little on the sheets. When I walked out of the shower afterward I saw that she had the sheets off the bed and was in her bathroom grimly rinsing the blood out. My stomach sank. But I said nothing to her. *What the hell*, I thought. *She'll change*. But she didn't.

After two hours or so of eating pears in the living room, I went into a bathroom and threw up. Then I went to the phone and called Arthur Freed, one of my lawyers, got him out of bed, and told him I wanted to get a divorce and I was willing to pay substantial alimony.

I still felt sick and my mouth was full of a sour-sweetish taste from all the pears. But something in my heart felt lighter. I had been putting off that divorce for fifteen years.

I'd been seeing Isabel from time to time, ever since I'd backed a revival of a play she had a small part in. I waited until sunup and called her and asked her to have breakfast with me. She agreed, sleepily. By nine that morning I was in her apartment and we got into her loft bed together, while her two big, loutish pussycats watched me fumble, moan and fail. I had become impotent. Son of a bitch!

In a cover article a few years ago, *Newsweek* called me "a scrappy child of the times" and went on to speak of those "times" as being "the orphan offspring of the twentieth century." In its half-assed way *Newsweek* was right. My father buried his life in the past; I live very much in my own century. I was born in 2012, when population in the industrial societies was plummeting. It's a wonder I was born at all. The last gas station in America closed when I was four. Faster-than-light travel was perfected when I was seven, and when I was in high school the frenetic search through the stars for uranium was

on, with hundreds of ships like the *Isabel* scanning the Milky
Way for what the *Tribune* called "the galactic Klondike."
Fuel for that venture reduced the world's supply of enriched
uranium by half. God knows how much was thrown into the
stratosphere during the Arab Wars, blowing up those half-
empty oil wells and the spanking new concrete universities that
dotted the sands of the Persian Gulf.

If my century is the "orphan" of the twentieth, it is the
1990s that conceived my times. More precisely, the year of
conception was 1997, when Fergusson invented his pill.

Fergusson was a cranky old celibate whose contraceptive
had all the necessary characteristics: it was cheap, easy and
safe, and you didn't have to remember to take it more than
once. It was also nonsexist; a man or a woman could get sterile
with the same pill. The first Fergusson kits came out several
years before my birth, and it is to my everlasting astonishment
that neither my mother nor my father took one of the reds and
prevented me and this account of them from coming into
being. A kit was a small plastic bottle with two pills—one red
and one green. If you swallowed the red you were sterile and
you remained that way until you took the antidote—the green
pill. You were sterile for a weekend in Mexico City or for your
lifetime, as you chose. A Fergusson kit cost almost nothing to
manufacture; they sold for the price of a Pepsi-Cola—two
dollars. The World Health Organization gave them out free in
Latin America and India. The Roman Catholic Church nearly
strangled on its apoplexy; the Pope crinkled his wise old
Japanese eyes in pain. The press and pulpit were full of talk
about God-given procreation and the warmth of families.
People nodded agreement sagely and took the pill. Minority
groups shouted "chemical genocide" and maternity wards
closed down. Bantu tribesmen gave their young reds as part of
traditional puberty rites. No igloo in the Arctic was without
them. And everywhere the greens were left over. They seldom
got taken. "Collective suicide" *Osservatore Romano* called it.
A few dutiful Irish had broods of sulking babies; the rest of
mankind breathed a sigh of relief. The price tag had finally
been removed from copulation. The next generation was half
the size of the previous one.

Myra was born from my deliberate taking of a green on a

Friday night. At the first sign of Anna's pregnancy, I popped
a red.

During the nine months I lived in that mansion and tried to
be a family man I would, from time to time, feel guilty about
my style of life and about all the money I had. I have always
been a Communist manqué, perhaps even more so than Isabel.
And Isabel was born in a Communist country and went to
Maoist schools. My parents seldom spoke at the dinner table
in more than grunts; when they did speak it was usually to remind me that a family of six in India could have been fed on
the vegetables I didn't want to eat. I silently wished in those
days that I had a postpaid jiffy bag by my plate, into which I
could dump my uneaten Spam and mail it off immediately to
some address in New Delhi. I still pay a dole in guilt for my af-
fluence.

Sometimes I would roam through the long hallways and
parlors of my big house and find myself thinking, "What a
waste!" I would decide glumly to turn the place into a shelter
for homeless drunks or a hospital, that I myself really needed
no more than a single room. But then I would console myself,
as one does at such times, by thinking of worse cases. If I
looked across the street from my big dining-room window I
could see the facade of a mansion bigger than mine, with a
brass plaque that read THE PENNY NEWTON MEMORIAL
SHELTER. Penny, dead a dozen years, was the last of that family of oil barons and electronics wizards; she had put her hundreds of millions into endowing a five-story mansion to be
used as a home for stray cats. There were about six thousand
pussycats living across the street from me, and brigades of
uniformed men searched the city for more, while a staff of
veterinarians and nutritionists kept the residents glossy-coated
and bright-eyed. There were still plenty of families in Harlem
with rickets and frostbite. Ratbite too. What the hell, at least I
had earned my money. Penny had done nothing in her entire
life but attend the ballet, play whist and accumulate dividends
from the fortune her father had cheated other people out of.
My general feeling was that the wealth of most of my neigh-
bors was as unearned and as trivially spent; Penny's cat home
was merely more blatant. Property is theft.

●   ●   ●

After several days of it, the loading got to be routine, although some crew members continued to go around in a kind of protracted excitement. I was neither thrilled nor glum, but I realized my emotional distance from the ore that continued to pile up had separated me from the crew too, canceling the picnic as it were. I made the motions of supervising the work, but I gave no orders or instructions. It was Annie with her tanned, serious face and her quickness who ran the show. Under her supervision the raw Juno subsoil was fed into machinery that refined and compacted it and processed the pure uranium into heavy yellowish pellets about the size of a twenty-dollar coin but an inch thick. The *Isabel* had brought a supply of boron moderators just in case radioactivity had to be contended with, and these were, on Annie's orders, placed between the pellets. Stacks of twenty pellets alternating with twenty moderators were then covered with transparent, high-density sheaths. The result looked like some kind of gargantuan candy roll or parfait; it would be placed carefully in a plastic case along with nineteen others of its kind. The cases were numbered and loaded into the *Isabel's* storage by a crane.

This was not a neat and smooth operation, as in a Japanese holovision factory. Nobody wore a white lab coat, and there was a lot of dust, noise, confusion and sweating. But the boxes, looking sturdy and potent, were stacking up in the holds at an exhilarating pace—exhilarating to the others, if not to me.

I worked out in the gym every morning during these days. I took Artaud, my trainer, off the work crew for enough time to help me get the zero-gravity springs off the machines and replace them with weights, but I didn't need his help in working out. The crew was invited to use the gym too; but I was usually in there alone, shortly after a light breakfast, putting myself through a pretty grueling sequence. It would be painful sometimes, doing repeated movements against those weights, but it accomplished something very necessary for my spirit.

After working out I showered heavily, dried off with one of the *Isabel's* heavy towels, dressed in jeans and lumberjack shirt, and went outside to make a show of being the captain of this busy and cheerful crew. Every now and then I lent a hand if one of the conveyor belts jammed or a slowdown cropped up along the line. In the afternoons I would go to my state-room and spend some time trying to plan out my course of action when I returned to Earth with the *Isabel's* cargo. I would try to concentrate on some of the basic decisions: should I set up my own power plants or try merging with businesses like Con Ed? Should I merely sell uranium, confining myself to the fuel market in the way I had started out, hauling coal in a wagon? Should I buy more ships and have a fleet of them ferrying fuel to Earth? Should I go into the electric-car business or even the lighting and small-appliance business, which would be booming as electricity became abundant again? I somehow could not really focus on these questions. It lacked substance. It all seemed foregone.

At night I had supper at my desk and then played solo chess or read. I usually drank, alone.

One morning in the gym, during the second week of loading, another person came in just after I had started working out. It was Howard, dressed in yellow shorts, looking skinny and embarrassed. Howard is an intellectual, he'd been a professor of biochemistry somewhere for years, and he looked comical standing in the hatchway.

"Come on in," I said, heaving my legs up against a hundred and fifty pounds.

He seemed heartened by that. He came over and strapped himself into the hip-and-back machine, next to mine.

"Did you warm up first?" I said.

He nodded. "Stationary running, in the mess hall."

I grunted and continued. For a while we both worked silently. We unstrapped and changed machines; Howard moved to the leg raise I'd just left and I moved to the leg curl. He set the weights down to sixty and we began working our machines in unison. "Captain," Howard suddenly said, panting, "do you have trouble sleeping here? With the short days and the two suns?"

"No," I said. I didn't say that I was usually drunk by the time I turned in.

He nodded. "One of those suns is always coming up just when I'm going to sleep."

"Close down the hatch by your bunk," I said. "Put a pillow over your head."

"Yeah," he said, unconvinced. "I could do that."

For a while there was silence except for the squeaking of the cams and the clunking of the weights in their tracks. When we got up to switch to the next machines he spoke again. "I keep thinking about my wives when I go to bed."

"Wives?" I said.

"Six."

That was a serious number. But I didn't want to talk about women just then. "Where are you from, Howard?"

He lay down on the leg-curl bench and awkwardly got his heels under the lifter. "Columbus, Ohio."

"Isn't that where Ruth's from?"

"Yes. Ruth's my sister." He strained to lift the weights but nothing happened.

"I'll get it," I said. He was trying to do the hundred pounds I'd been using. I set it back to forty. I was a bit shocked to think of this skinny guy as the brother of Ruth, with her hefty build. "I didn't know that," I said. "You sure don't look alike."

"I favor our mother."

I seated myself in the overhead press and began working.

"Ruth's a smart one," he said.

I didn't reply. Howard annoyed me, as much in his tone of voice as anything. I knew that if some part of me had given up back when I was a dirty-kneed kid I could have grown up to be like him. I pushed hard at the weights, repeating fast until I could feel the sweat pop out and hear myself groaning with the effort. If my father had seduced me into imitating his aloofness and if my mother had hidden her chaos and self-hate better, instead of letting it all hang out there in the kitchen where gin bottles outnumbered spice jars . . .

I finished, unstrapped and wiped the sweat off with a towel. The hatch was open and from outside came the muted shouts and grinding sounds of the loading operation. I waited for Howard to finish and then said, "I've had women troubles lately myself. How do you feel about marriage, after six tries?"

He puffed heavily for a while. Then he said, "I'm not sure. Every time I do it I have high hopes. But then the fighting starts."

I took a towel from a hook on the bulkhead and handed it to him, for the sweat. "Over what?"

"Money. Sex. The way she dresses. What we eat." He dabbed at his chest and armpits. "You know."

"I know." I wrapped my towel around my neck and did a few knee bends. Outside the porthole I heard Annie shouting orders to someone.

"Are you married now?" I said.

"No. But I think about trying again."

"Maybe that's why you can't sleep."

"Could be."

I finished my workout in silence and showered before Howard was through his. During my shower it occurred to me that I might not go back to Earth with the *Isabel*.

The next morning I decided to go back to the valley by our original landing site and pick some food. I wanted to get away from all the activity around the ship. Annie had worked out an improved system by then that didn't require the smaller jeep. I had the earth-moving rig taken off it and invited Ruth to go along with me. She accepted, and we took off on the long drive. We didn't talk much during the trip. I drove it at fifteen miles an hour and had to pay attention to the road.

I parked at a place where Annie's road came within a few hundred yards of the valley. We got out, carrying buckets for the food we were going to pick, headed into the forest, and began walking along one of the lanes between orange-trunked palms. "Ruth," I said, "how'd you come to be a star pilot? Is it something you dreamed about when you were a kid?"

She looked over at me. "I took it as an elective in college."

"An elective?" I said. "What kind of college gives electives like that?"

"Ohio State. I was studying to be a railroad engineer. *That* was my dream when I was a kid. I wanted to pull the cord that blows the whistle."

I knew what she meant. "Have you ever done it?"

"Nope." There was a hint of melancholy in her voice. "I never have."

I started to say something else when she went on. She seemed looser now and eager to talk. "There was a course in astronavigation on Tuesday and Thursday afternoons, and it fit my schedule. I had thermodynamics and steam-power systems in the mornings, and I wanted something simple after lunch. I thought astronavigation would be easy, because nobody was piloting spaceships anymore."

"Why were they teaching it at all?"

"Well, they still had the equipment. The Sony Trainer and videospheres from the days of the Uranium Bust. Their landing simulator was a dream. I made an 'A' in the course, and took another. It was still a glamour course."

"Really?" I said. "It must have been twenty years since anybody had flown a spaceship . . ."

"You're forgetting the TV shows," she said. "Remember those space adventure stories?" She stopped walking for a moment and looked over at me, with her eyes just a bit wide. She looked very attractive that way. "You know," she said, "we've actually *done* what they were doing in those shows. We've found *uranium!*" I thought Ruth was an unemotional type; this was the first time I had heard a thrill like that in her voice. It was a pleasure to see her like that. "We sure have," I said.

"How much money do you think it's worth?"

"Trillions," I said. "It's a fucking king's ransom."

"Then why aren't you more excited?" she said. "You're supposed to be a . . . a *tycoon.*"

That was a funny word for her and I had to laugh. "Ruth, I really don't know. I think about hauling this cargo back to Chicago and New York and the things I have to buy and sell and all the wheeling and dealing I have to do and it just bores me."

She was still looking at me. She stopped walking and bent down and pulled a blade of grass and began chewing it. We all did that every now and then; the grass on Juno had a pleasant licorice flavor. In fact, I think it's habit-forming. I thought sadly of Belson grass. And then Ruth said something that shocked me. It was as though she were reading my mind. "Something happened to you on Belson, didn't it?" she said.

"Yes."

"Was it morphine?"

I thought for a minute. "No."

She nodded. "But it was something . . . something mystical," she said.

I was surprised at her knowingness about me, but I remained silent.

"Come on, Ben," she said. "It's been written all over you since that morning we had to carry you back to the ship."

"Even during the picnic?" The picnic had been about a month before this.

"Even during the picnic." She smiled. "You were very sweet then and we all loved you. But a part of you was somewhere else."

"I was thinking about Isabel. A woman friend."

She frowned. "It was something else, Ben."

"Yes," I said. "It was." But I didn't want to talk to her about how it felt to hear the Belson grass, holding me in its thousands of gentle fingers, saying, "I love you."

"Come on, Ben," Ruth said. "What's the matter?"

I looked at her closely. She was really very good-looking. "Well," I said, "sex, for one thing." I bent down and pulled a piece of licorice grass myself. "I've been impotent for the last couple of years."

"Oh," she said.

I laughed wryly. "Yeah," I said, suddenly feeling very relieved.

We had come to the rise and we began scrambling silently down the hill. When we were about halfway down I stopped and let Ruth go on ahead. I stood and looked around and then up ahead at the enormous valley that stretched ahead of me to the horizon. It was as splendid a vista as a man could ever want to see. I drew a deep breath of the delicious air and thought with a profound historical thrill, as deep as my genes: if mankind ever leaves a shattered Earth to live elsewhere in the universe, it should be for Juno. This was a second chance as vast and breathtaking as the one spread before the eyes of Columbus and his sailors—those rapt men from the alleys of Barcelona and Seville. The hairs on the back of my neck prickled. Planetfall had confused me; with the heavy rain, the frustration, I had missed this thrill at the time, intent merely on exploration and discovery. It had caught me now, after my conversation with Ruth. I was staggered by this planet, its breadth and diversity—its beauty and life. A part of me had been searching, all my life, for a home; my bags had always been packed. And here it was.

I looked up. Two suns shone pleasantly down on my body. At night there would be a half-dozen moons. Everything about this place was generous, replete, fulfilling. I breathed as deeply as my lungs would allow, exhaled, and walked slowly down the rest of the hill, into the valley.

Ruth was off a bit to my right and I started to walk toward her, but then decided to stay alone for a bit. I walked to my left, toward a small field of mushrooms that grew in Juno's open suns. Ruth waved at me and I waved back and bent to picking, and after a while my exalted feelings began to leave. I began sweating. It was hot. I looked over toward Ruth; she was gathering the little red berries we had discovered a few days before. As I was looking toward her she stood up and arched her back and stretched. She was sweating too and the cloth of her blouse was clinging damply to her full breasts. How pleasant to see that!

I took my shirt off and began working in earnest, pulling up the little gray mushrooms, dusting them off, and filling my bucket.

I stopped for breath after a while and looked up. Ruth was standing near me barefoot, resting herself. Her hair was wet from perspiration. "Remember what Charlie said about UV," she said. "You can get a burn from those suns."

That annoyed me a little. "I won't get sunburned," I said.

"You're the boss," she said. And then, "Ben. I wish you weren't impotent."

I felt relieved that she had said it. "Thank you," I said.

"Would you like to make love anyway?" she said.

I must have just stared at her.

"You know," she said. "There's a lot we could do . . ."

"Yes, I know," I said, coming out of it. She stepped closer and laid a hand lightly on my forearm.

I was embarrassed. "Ruth," I said, "you're a fine woman. But I don't think I'm ready yet . . ."

She looked hurt for a moment. She let go of my arm and blushed. "Sure," she said, "I understand."

I didn't know what to say. I felt like a fool. A part of me

would like to try myself with her on a field of spongy Juno grass under the palms. I could be an effective lover sometimes without the use of the essential. It had certainly been a long time. But I didn't want to. "I'm really sorry, Ruth," I said.

"It's *okay*," her words said, but her voice said it wasn't.

When we got back to the ship at first sunset, I found I was badly sunburned.

I had supper with the crew that night and they were high with excitement over the cargo, but I was miserable. I was painfully red and I felt foolish for letting myself get that way in the first place. I felt awkward about what had happened between Ruth and me.

I was halfway through the meal before I thought of endolin and asked Charlie where he kept it. He got up from his roast beef and went to his sick bay and got some. It was a little plastic cup of dried leaves. I took a pinch, waited several minutes for the annoying pain on my back and shoulders to go away, and nothing happened. Charlie had returned to his roast beef and to a joke he had been telling the navigator. When we had arrived at dessert, he got up and came over to my seat at the head of the table.

"How're you feeling, Captain?" he said.

I looked up at him. "How long since I took it?"

He checked his watch. "A dozen minutes."

"Well, it isn't working," I said.

"Give it a few more minutes," he said.

I looked at him. "It's not going to work, Charlie."

"I'll get you some more," he said.

I looked at him. "Don't bother," I said. "Get some morphine."

He stared at me for a minute. "*Ben*," he said, "you kicked it . . ."

Inside, I was as astonished as he was. As far as I knew, I had hardly missed my chemical euphoria since the trip from Belson to Juno, and yet here I was with my attention suddenly fixed on wiping out the discomfort of a goddamn *sunburn* with, as they say, morphia. I was not only astonished; on some quiet level of perception and feeling, I was terrified. But my voice was unruffled and I felt outwardly as calm as a madonna.

"Get me fifty milligrams, Charlie. I know what I'm doing."

"Ben," he said, "we jettisoned what I had left. Remember?"

"I remember," I said. "But you can make it. Go make me some."

The ship had a drug synthesizer. For some reason you couldn't make aspirin with it, but you could make atropine, propranolol, prednisone, and two hundred milligrams of morphine sulphate a day—enough to keep a heavy spirit permanently afloat.

Charlie shook his head. "Ben," he said, "as your doctor I can't allow it."

I stood up. I'm pretty tall and Charlie isn't; I towered over him. "Charlie," I said, "I am the captain of this ship. You aren't making a house call. Get me that morphine."

He said nothing and went and got it. I took the syringe from him right there in front of everybody at the mess table and shot myself in the throat with it, just like they do in the movies. Doing it I was outwardly calm, slightly theatrical. Inside I was astonished. I sat down again and waited. The fear went away. Euphoria settled over my unquiet spirit like a luminous dust.

So I was hooked after all. Part of me thought, with wonderment: if I was going to do this, why didn't I do it with booze back in my forties in New York City? They have spiffy hospitals there for the well-heeled lush, and a man can ricochet around with a liquor habit for years and hardly suffer from it at all. I had sure come close to going that way—close enough that Anna thought I was an alcoholic. Her position was biased, however; I was drunker than usual around her. Anyway, here I was twenty light-years away from methadone centers and rehabilitation programs and emergency rooms, turning my bloodstream into a chemical bath for my brain. I am at heart a gambler and I am drawn to the edge. I stood now at an edge I had not dreamed of visiting until I broke my arm in my puppydog rush onto the slick black surface of Belson, my namesake planet.

It was then I made the decision to stay on when the *Isabel* went back with its cargo of uranium. I would write out instructions to Aaron and to Met Luk San and to Arnie; they would start buying utilities for me, selling my six million acres of woodlands, putting me in the electric-automobile business and, most of all, into the business of selling safe uranium. The instructions could be sent the minute the ship got into space-warp; they could get the whole thing started and when I got back to New York I would do the necessary tinkering with it. My uranium was in itself a brute fact; any bright student at the Harvard Business School—that training ground for fledgling swindlers—could work out a reasonable plan for making ten billion dollars from the *Isabel's* first cargo. There was a lot of rationalization in that; I knew I should get my ass back on Earth if I wanted things to go right, that you didn't send boys to do men's work. But down deep I didn't care. I wasn't ready to get involved. I might lose a few billion by not being there to decide whether to start buying electric clock factories or get into the highway construction business, but damn it, *everything* was going to start paying off like a gambler's dream when all that power hit the hungry world. There was no way to lose, if I sold my wood, coal, solar plants and shale oil convertors and bought everything else in sight. Anyway, I had enough money already. And the *Isabel* now had enough uranium to buzz around the cosmos forever. Meanwhile I would have my fling with euphoria. I couldn't O.D.; the synthesizer wouldn't produce it that fast. What the hell, I had planned *suicide* once, in Mexico. People do that all the time; they did it over the Dow Jones Average back in the last century, dropping themselves onto Wall Street like garbage, over margin calls. Reason would dictate that if a man is ready to kill himself he should try something outrageous first.

I think the crew would have been less shocked if they found I *had* slit my throat, when I told them I was going to stay. "Look," I said, "it's nothing personal. I'm going to stay on until you people get back and I'm going to stay high on morphine while I do it. I'll kick the habit in sleep on the way back. I know what I'm doing."

But they looked at me as though I had gone berserk.

The night before the ship was to return to Earth I went to my stateroom alone and had a thoughtful supper of veal and Juno mushrooms with a half bottle of claret. It was dark out-

side my porthole; none of the moons was in view. I turned on
the ball recorder and played the song of the Belson grass and
let a pleasant melancholy suffuse my spirit. I had a small
power hypodermic filled with morphine sulphate near my bedside. It was made of glass and chromium, like a fine camera.
The sight of it was a deep comfort. The claret's alcohol felt
good in my veins—a shy, chaste sprinkle of euphoria; but
morhpine was more to the point.

I picked up the syringe speculatively, held it up to the light
on my desk. The addict falls in love with the tools; I found the
syringe a pleasure merely to hold lightly in my hand. Phallic.
Soon I would force the drug into my neck, not far from the
jugular vein, in what I had come to call the "Dracula spot"—
halfway between brain and heart.

I set it down for a moment. There was a knock at my locked
door. I was startled and annoyed. I got up from my chair and
opened the door. It was Ruth. She was wearing her plain khaki
pilot's uniform, but her hair and skin looked fresh and bright.

"What is it?" I said.

"I'm sorry to interrupt, Ben. I want to talk to you."

"Okay," I said and let her come in. She seated herself on
the edge of my bed and I went back to my Eames chair.

"Ben," she said, awkwardly. "We may not see each other
again."

That was a surprise. "You're coming back with the ship,
aren't you?"

"I don't think so," she said. "I only signed up for one
voyage. I don't think I should be away from my eight-year-old
any longer than that."

I was impatient with this. "I'm sorry to lose you as a pilot,"
I said. "Mel should be able to get someone else, though."

"Ben, I want to give you my address and telephone number
in Columbus, Ohio. I'd like to stay in touch."

"Sure," I said. "Sure, Ruth." She handed me a square of
paper with writing on it and I slipped it into my billfold where
I keep papers with such things on them as the names of
Isabel's cats and last September's price of wheat in Chicago.
There's a forest of random information in there waiting for
me to broadcast it into my central computer in Atlanta.

I felt something else was called for from me. "Ruth," I began, "it's a pity we didn't become lovers."

She shook her head. "That's okay now," she said. "But I don't think you should stay on Juno. What if you get sick or break a leg?"

"I won't get sick," I said. "The microorganisms for that aren't around here. And I won't break a leg in this gravity. I'll be okay."

"Ben," she said. "It seems so damned foolish. You need to be on Earth, selling the uranium. Making deals."

I was beginning to get angry. I didn't need this motherly concern. "Damn it, Ruth, I know what I'm doing. I'm sending back enough instructions to keep my people in New York busy for a year. I need time to myself. I need to ride my morphine habit, too . . ." I nodded toward the hypodermic on the table.

Her face opened a bit at this frankness. "Are you really hooked, Ben?"

"I don't know," I said. "I love it a lot."

"What's *wrong?*" she said. "Why should a man so lively and strong and rich . . . ? Hell, Ben, there's so much *to* you. You don't need drugs."

Somehow I became furious at this. I could have slapped her. "How do you know what I need?" I said. "How in hell do you know what goes on inside me?"

She stared at me. "I'm sorry. But I think you're a fool to spend months on Juno alone. You can withdraw from your habit in a long sleep. You did it before."

"I want to do it this way, Ruth. I'm fifty-two years old and I know what I want to do for myself. I'm not ready to go back to New York and start making money. I have a dozen people whom I trust to run my businesses. I'm on vacation." I settled back into my chair.

She sat and looked at me for a long time. "Okay, Ben," she said, and stood up. "I've said what I had to."

I could see that she was really pretty and kindhearted and something inside me reached out to her. But I pulled back from the feeling. I did not want to make love to her and I wanted to be alone with my hypodermic. I held my hand out to her. I was shocked to see that it was trembling.

She shook it and left. There was ice in my stomach. Old, glacial ice.

I locked the cabin door behind her, picked up my syringe and lay back on the bed. I held the head of it to my neck, just below the mastoids, and gently squeezed the handle. Oh yes. Comfort came down.

And as my high settled in for the night a relay somewhere in my head clicked into place and my decision veered toward its real direction. I would not stay on Juno. It was not Juno my heart longed for, with all its abundance of life and power. Not Juno at all.

✤ Chapter 5

I looked at them all sitting around the table, drew in a breath and said, "We'll activate the ship's coils at nine A.M. tomorrow. The *Isabel* should be in orbit by noon and info a warp an hour after." My head ached, but my mind was clear.

"Terrific, Captain!" Charlie said. Ruth smiled toward me. Everyone looked cheerful. They had known we would be leaving tomorrow, but this was the first official announcement of it.

"Before you start planning your homecomings, I have some news for you that you won't like," I said. I paused only a second. "We are taking a detour by Belson. I'm staying there."

They were dismayed and they fussed and fumed about it. I thought for a while they might even mutiny. But evenutally they accepted it. We were, as I had said, in our warp shortly after lunchtime the next day. By suppertime I was in my chemical sleep. Twelve days. That was the time from Amini-dab to Fomalhaut. It was taking them twenty-four days out of their way home, and I didn't blame them for being pissed. But

there was enough fuel for it and I promised them all a bonus
for the extra time.

When I came out of my sleep and went up to the bridge and
looked out the window, there was Belson at about the size the
moon is when seen from Earth. It looked as empty as the
moon. I had awakened with cold in my gut and remembered
no dreams; the sight of that planet of black glass sent a deep
chill into my soul; it was all I could do not to quail at it and tell
Ruth not to land. Where did these spooky feelings come from,
anyway? I had never felt anything but love for Belson—even
when it had broken my arm.

I steeled myself, shook off the bad feelings as well as I
could, and told Ruth to pick a spot on the other side of the
planet from where we were before. She was shocked to hear
my voice. She had been sitting hunched over the controls when
I came in and hadn't looked up. Somehow she had cut her
hair. It looked nice short. She blinked at me and then frowned
slightly. "Good morning, Captain."

"Good morning, Ruth. Find us a big plain of obsidian and
come down on it. I don't want us hurting the grass."

"Okay, Captain," she said. And she did it. Within two
hours she had set us down on the planet's day side without
even a bump. Out the portholes was Belson, looking the same
here as on its other side. And my spooky feelings had evaporated. I couldn't wait to get out there and start making my
homestead.

It took a week. On the first day we explored the new area
just to make sure. There was a higher proportion of obsidian
to grass here, but that was the only difference. On the second
and third days I erected myself this shack of moonwood, with
the help of five crew members.

We outfitted it from the ship. We carried out the little red
computer that I use for writing this journal, four of the
Nautilus machines, eighteen cases of wine and, from the ship's
garden, an array of hydroponics. I have my Eames chair, a
mattress, my books and a very serious voice-activated recorder
for recording the song of the Belson grass. A lot of food, a lot
of whiskey, the drug synthesizer, seeds and hydroponics. I am
relatively happy now.

My stateroom aboard the *Isabel* was not much bigger than

my bathroom at the Pierre; it barely held my narrow bed, my Eames chair and a small desk. Above the desk was a narrow bookshelf, and to the right of it a hatchway that led into my private head. Whatever Chinese had designed the head had placed things so that when I sat on the john I faced a porthole that gave a view of the Milky Way; the clarity of the view was, shortly after I arose in the mornings, breathtaking. Being in spacewarp and at an analogy travel rate of two hundred times the speed of light did not affect it. I sat on the can in the mornings and watched the starry universe.

There was a kind of anteroom to the stateroom, and it was much larger. The Chinese had used it as a captain's mess and boardroom for staff meetings. Since I either ate with the crew or with one guest in my stateroom and since there were no staff meetings, that room was the ship's gym. During my long sleep I had been carried from my bed daily, worked out and returned; I had had the gym installed next door to simplify that maneuver. There were five Nautilus machines in there; after I was wakened I would work out for an hour each morning and then shower back in my head. It was a good routine. It was good to be away from the Earth and without a telephone, to eat breakfast alone and then move my bowels and then build up a sweat on the equipment. I especially liked working my pectorals and quadriceps until they bulged and hardened. I still work out here on Belson and the machines are better; they have regular weights now instead of springs. But sometimes I miss that little gym on the *Isabel*; I'll be working away at leg curls, say, and my mind will go back to those days, to my scrambled eggs eaten at my stateroom desk, to the satisfactions of the journey I am still taking, into myself. Looking back on it, now I feel that my decision to come to Fomalhaut was inspired. The Belson grass and all the things that happened on Juno, even the dreams of my father's study, were important in bringing about change; and yet sometimes it seems that my mornings on the *Isabel* alone, my breakfast, my shit, the stars, the Nautilus machines and the sweat that covered my hardening body and the cold shower afterward were what really changed me and began to thaw the glacier that was crushing my soul.

Many middle-aged men can't seem to change their lives at

all. The more scrubby and dour things get, the less rewarding the compensatory pleasures become, the more we tend to hang on and to fear attempting a new bargain with life. I felt that way before I bought the *Isabel*. The only thing was that I damn well knew my life was getting worse. I wasn't moving anywhere, and the price for staying where I was was going up. Much of this was invisible to me; but the same voice that could tell me to sell a company no matter what the stock was going for was telling me to pull out. Good ratios all around. Good performance record too. But time to unload nonetheless. Time to sell, move, get out.

I saw my father die. He was the age I am now—fifty-two. Somebody had taken out his false teeth and his mouth closed up like a fist; a sound, half gag and half rattle, came from somewhere inside. It was as though whatever soul he owned had shrunk like a handful of dried peas in a never-opened pod and it was rattling around inside him now. *Too late*, I thought, *too late!* He needed a shave. It was the only time I had ever seen him in need of a shave. Somehow for once he looked like a man, in that last grim spasm. The son of a bitch. That was his price for staying where he was. One long soul-shaking shudder and down the tubes. Well. If there's a life after death he's probably avoiding it now.

As, come to face it, I am avoiding my own life.

Well, to hell with my life for now. That mess back on Earth. Isabel and money; money and Isabel. Anna! Some nagging voice in me tells me to feel guilty because I am lying on my ass on a barren planet and shooting dope. Because I am not *engagé*. Because I am shunning relationships. Because I have become asexual and detached. Well to hell with that voice. It's the one I ignore when I want to make money. I am going to lie on my foam mattress and listen to the grass when it chooses to speak to me or sing to me. I have been a sick man lately; I need respite. I need to do what I need to do to get well. My father decided to die when he was my age; I decided to come to Belson. It beats death. And I can go back.

And that's how I got to where I am now, tending the seedlings in my hydroponic garden, twenty-three light-years from New York and as alone as the prisoner of Chillon. The *Isabel* left for Earth three months ago and I fell into my routine here on Belson as though I were born for it. It has been a spare and nearly empty time and one my soul has needed. For some reason during the last week—I count by Earth time on my Chinese watch—each Belson day at twilight the rings have come out for about a half hour and glowed like a giant and perfect rainbow in the green sky. That is the climax of my Belson day; I feel the rings do it because I'm here. Belson's first resident. I take no morphine after ringtime; I lie on the hard foam mattress on my moonwood porch and stare up at the sky. Sometimes I look at my former sun, Sol. From here it is an undistinguished speck of a star, and because of its distance I see it as it was twenty-three years ago, as I saw it when I was thirty and afraid of love.

Sometimes I fall asleep while staring at the sky. Sometimes I read by the light of a little nuclear lamp, or dictate into my red computer as I am doing now, writing this. I am never lonely here. Sometimes the grass sings to me. Often I lie on it, but it has never again said, "I love you."

As the ship left Belson, first trembling, then roaring and howling its way upward to and immediately beyond the clouds, great fissures appeared in the obsidian plain around me; the *Isabel* disappeared upward with an alacrity that was astonishing. I had never watched a spaceship take off before and it was spectacular to see all that power unleashed. The air smelled electric—some mixture of ozone and of the unburned residue of the *Isabel's* solid fuel, used only for takeoff and landing. She had vanished from the sky with Ruth and Howard and Mimi and all the others aboard, and the smell remained. She would go into orbit, then go nuclear and, after a half hour or so, when her capacitors were charged, into spacewarp, somewhere both within and outside the knowable universe, shimmering, taking that nondimensional road back to Sol and Earth and her landing pad in the Florida Keys. And I was here alone, as far from home as a man had ever tried to live. For a few moments my arms and knees trembled. I was scared shitless.

I stood there and then I looked around me at the glass planet where I stood and where I had elected to live for six months completely alone. Alone without even the cockroaches

famed for friendship with Devil's Island prisoners, growing
their cave beards in solitary; alone without the consolation of
a bird, a snake, a distant rustle of tree limbs. *What in the
name of God was I doing?* What was I doing to myself? And
the word jumped into my head as alive as Athena when she
sprouted from the brow of the Cloudmaster himself:
masochist. Ben Belson, masochist.

Oh, yes. The cat is out of the bag, the cards are turned face
up on the dirty green cloth, and the Devil has come out from
behind his disguise as Dolly the Chambermaid. I could have
left Anna in a flash, with her rubber girdle at her feet. Divorce
is awfully easy. I'm rich. I did not leave Anna, not for all
those years of berating myself for being the wrong kind of
husband for her. What a goddamned painful tango we
danced. Well. You marry a woman like Anna when you're
afraid.

Afraid of love. I might as well face it. That's the truth of it.
I was afraid of Isabel and that's why I moved out of her apartment and into that suite at the Pierre. That's why I came chugging halfway across the cosmos in this Chinese spaceship—
Flower of Heavenly Repose. Oh yes. Look here, Officer,
my name is Ben Belson, the celebrated millionaire financier,
friend to famous and beautiful women, theater buff, prowler
of the galaxy and closet Marxist. Big hands, big feet, big prick
and a booming voice. And a big, throbbing, empty hole in my
heart.

The day after Isabel got the part in *Hamlet* we celebrated with
steaks at a neighborhood restaurant. Isabel was radiant. Her
complexion was luminous against her gray sweater and silver
jewelry, her curly gray hair. I was pleasant on the outside but
inside sullen. She had three glasses of wine; I had club soda. I
had nearly given up drinking a few years before, after spotting
some handwriting on the wall about what happened to people
who drank gin with their scrambled eggs. In those days I was
free of bad habits—especially of fucking. I smiled as Isabel
drank her wine and talked about how much the part meant to
her, but inside I sulked like a child.

That evening she sat by the fire with a cat in her lap and a
beat-up paperback of *Hamlet* propped on the cat. She was

underlining Gertrude's speeches in red. I busied myself cleaning up the breakfast dishes, clanging pans from time to time to
let my presence be felt. Fifty years old and often on the cover
of *Time* or *Peking*, a "basic force" in world finance, as
Forbes called me once, the terror of boardrooms and a mover
and a shaker on Wall Street, and there I am in Isabel's little
New York kitchen clanging the frying pan against the steel
sink because I'm pissed and jealous. Because she's more interested in a play than in me. Because I can't get it up with her
and haven't in the months we've lived together. *Clang* goes the
pan as I set it back on the wood-burning stove, scrubbed. And
from here in my self-imposed exile on Belson I can see I was
angry with Isabel because she was a beautiful, smart, erotic
woman who wanted me to fuck her. *The very idea*, I was saying in my heart, as I scrubbed bacon grease off that morning's
breakfast plates. *Who in the hell does she think she is?* said
that scared child in my mossy old rib cage. I dried the silverware with a cloth and could hear the cat purring in Isabel's
lap. I wanted to wring its neck. Inside me an angry virginity
smoldered, grimly loyal to a pair of miserable ghosts. I started
throwing the silverware into its shallow drawer. *Take that,
you goddamn knives and forks! Son of a bitching, goddamned
spoons!* Isabel murmured pleasantly over her text, underlining
speeches, occasionally stroking the big cat, Amagansett, in her
lap. I slammed the silverware drawer shut and stated, with
great control in my voice, "*Hamlet* is an overrated play." Ben
Belson, literary critic.

"Huh?" Isabel said. There was an edge in her voice; she
had picked up the sound of a gauntlet falling. "What's that,
sweetheart?"

"*Hamlet*," I said, "is an overrated fucking play. It's too
long, too wordy, and it has too many corpses on the floor." I
dried my hands off on the towel, walked over and stood by the
fire. The other cat, William, saw me coming and slinked away.
Those fucking beasts pick up vibrations. "Nobody really
knows what *Hamlet*'s about, either. That's a lousy recommen-
dation for a play."

Isabel marked her place with an ivory bookmark and then
looked up at me coolly. "T.S. Eliot said it's about a boy's
disgust with his mother."

That one stopped me for a second, but I shook it off. I was in no mood to explore my own psyche. What I wanted was to work on Isabel's. There she sat, content by the fire, happy in her career and her pussycats, warmhearted and serene. And here I stood with a rage in my otherwise empty heart and my big, calloused hands trembling. I got those callouses from chopping cords of wood, in fury, at my country home in Georgia, every time the Dow went the wrong way. Inside, there in New York, I am a complete mess, a bridge hand without a face card, a barren, angry hulk of impotence, a sick and furious motherfucker, and I say to Isabel, "Is something bothering *you?*" She should have brained me with a lump of coal.

She looked up at me steadily before she spoke. "Ben," she said. "You look ready for homicide, or worse. I don't want to talk about Shakespeare with you right now."

A part of me recognized that she was completely right. So I counterattacked. I tried to relax my features into something more amiable. Plausible anyway. I went back to the kitchen—actually just a space along one wall with a small stove and a dish cabinet in it—and started heating water for tea. I looked at my watch. A little after 11 P.M. "Isabel," I said. "You can get awfully snotty when you talk about the theater. Do you feel Shakespeare's something holy? Too holy for a businessman to discuss?"

The black cat leaped off her lap at that one. "Ben," Isabel said, "for Christ's sake come off it. I'm not a Shakespeare snob and you know it."

Something glowed in me. I had her there. "What about that time we saw *Henry the Fifth?* All that talk you gave me about the audience not being able to feel the cadences." I was standing by the fireplace again, striking a pose of sweet reasonableness. "The fucking *cadences.*" I looked at her face. I could see I had hit home. Something inside me thrilled at it.

"Damn you, Ben," she said. "If you didn't have a bloody tin ear yourself you'd have known what I was talking about. Shakespeare was a poet."

"Bullshit!" The fact was that I didn't know beans about Shakespeare but I did sense that Isabel had mixed feelings about liking him and being in one of his plays. I felt I had something there. "Bullshit!" I said again, getting into it.

"Shakespeare was a middle-class Englishman and he sucked up to aristocrats and the only people he endowed with classy feelings were princes and generals and emperors. The rest of his characters are drunks and clowns."

Isabel didn't even look up. "And women," she said. Then, "Your tea water's boiling."

"Thanks," I said, and walked back to the kitchen wall with what felt like controlled dignity. Actually, my mind and heart were a muddle. One thing about impotence: you miss the clarity that comes after an orgasm. Sometimes it felt as though my unspilled semen was backed up to my brain and had shortcircuited half the connections there. And what was there to do about such a muddle except to shout at Isabel? "I hate snobbery!" I shouted. "Goddamn it, I hate the way you want it both ways, Isabel: you want to be a Communist and bleed for the masses and you cultivate the tastes of an aristocrat. Antique English silverware"—I gestured toward the nail on which hung Isabel's safety-deposit key; she kept her Georgian service for twelve in a vault—"and antique furniture. You wouldn't let a veneer in the door. You wouldn't so much as set your pinky down on a surface that wasn't hand-rubbed by forelock-tuggers in a fucking English sweatshop. You're proud as a pumpkin of being a daughter of the People's Republic of Scotland, but the only barricade you've ever stood near had footlights on it."

I felt a muted brotherhood with Shakespeare. *Way to talk, Bill!* I looked at Isabel and it seemed as if she were far away. Everything seemed far away. Isabel was staring into the fire, where my Mafia coal was burning. Her face was pale and drawn—impassive. Then she raised her eyes to my face silently and I saw something awfully, horribly hurt there, something that twisted me in the stomach and suddenly brought me back into the room with her. "Why are you talking like that, Ben?" she said.

I thought suddenly of Lulu and Philippe, the two California seals at the Central Park Zoo. I would walk up there sometimes around noon to buy one of the four-dollar hot dogs that the vendors sell. I needed to get out of the apartment from time to time and I'd walk up Fifth Avenue, by all those empty stores and then, near the park, by the run-down apart-

ment buildings. The park itself was always a bit depressing, its
trees long gone to wood thieves, and the zoo was full of empty
cages that nobody wanted to have heated anymore. There
hadn't been an elephant in the place for forty years. But there
were still some birds and an aquarium, and the big heated pool
was still there with its two California sea lions. I'd buy my hot
dog with sauerkraut and mustard and then go, huddled
against that awful winter in my mackinaw and scarf and long
underwear, and look at the seals while I ate. When they swam
they rubbed their smooth bodies against one another in a kind
of continuous "Hello." The love in this was perfectly clear
and as easy as sunshine, even in what must have been for those
displaced Californians a frigid environment. To say the least.
Yet they were full of life and of straightforward affection for
one another. Why couldn't Isabel and I, two grown *homo
sapiens*, be like that? Why couldn't *I*? What the hell? What
was wrong?

Isabel appeared to be on the edge of tears, and there was a
grimness in her profile that moved me. There was old Scots'
darkness in her eyes and heaviness in her brow. "My God,
Isabel," I said, "I'm sorry as hell. What am I saying?"

She looked at me quickly and then looked away.

"What do I know about Shakespeare?" I said.

She spoke quickly and her voice was soft and distant.
"That's not it, Ben. It's not Shakespeare."

"I know," I said, becoming explanatory now. "I know it
isn't. I don't know why I . . ."

"Don't explain, for Christ's sake," she said. "Just shut up.
You're not talking to *me*. You haven't talked to me all evening." She stared at me hard. "Don't you know, Ben, that the
things you say *hurt?*"

I stared at her. "I'm sorry, honey," I said. "I'll fix tea."

On her bathroom wall Isabel kept a hologram of herself as a
seven-year-old, taken for her first day at Socialist Primary
School in Paisley. She wears a hand-knitted sweater and a kilt
and her eyes hold a look of anxiety. Isabel's father was at sea
for most of her childhood, and her mother was as cold as
mine. Sometimes toward the end of our stay together I would
see that same anxious look in Isabel's eyes, in her early forties.

In the hologram she holds a striped cat in her lap. Something in Isabel's psyche had always drawn her toward cats, and when I moved in with her she had the two, Amagansett and William. I remember shouting at Isabel once in the middle of the night that I could probably get it up for her if she weren't so damned anxious about it and her saying, levelly, "Don't get it up for *me*, Ben. Get it up for yourself!" and knowing with a knot in my stomach that she was right, I padded for refuge into the bathroom and found the two cats huddled behind the base of the sink. They stared up at me with pained, curious eyes. I looked at them silently a minute and then said softly, "She knows *everything*, boys."

My red Chinese computer also reads. I can set a book in its drawer and it will turn pages and read aloud in a pleasant, avuncular voice with a midwestern accent. Sometimes I do that with my library books when my eyes are blurred from morphine or I just don't want to open them. I set the drug synthesizer to make ethyl alcohol, mix it with grape juice from my garden vines, and drink myself into a near-coma while my computer reads the short novels of James: *The Lesson of the Master, The Beast in the Jungle, The Pupil.* I've never read them sober; I'm not sure which has the ball-less William Marcher as protagonist, but I know I see him looking like my father. Distant, lost in terminal self-regard.

I speak in this journal as though my time on Belson were spent in reading and thought; in fact, much of it is passed in the grip of an uneasy lassitude. For the last five days I have been incapable of action or reading or of amusing myself in any significant way. I merely pass time. Often I feel like a fifteen-year-old hanging around the drugstore waiting for someone to drop in. Yesterday I merely waited all day for Fomalhaut to set.

When dusk comes, the sky has a way of modulating its colors that evokes feelings I have no names for. There is nothing like it in the skies of Earth, no pinks and yellows to match these pinks and yellows, no blue-grays so somber as Belson's. Last night I felt a gentle suffocation as I watched Fomalhaut descending. As it touched the magenta horizon and reflected from the thousand acres of obsidian the suffocation was relieved and my heart expanded with my lungs and I became for a moment dizzied with happiness.

It is a terrible comment on the nature of capitalism that a man as baffled by himself as I can be so successful at it—that I could become so rich and so confused at the same time.

Three days after I moved in with Isabel the temperature dropped to eighteen below zero. It was November 1, 2061. All Saints' Day. Isabel had a matinee and an evening show and she was out of the apartment all day. I managed to get out onto the icy streets and buy enough wood to make a big fire in the fireplace; I spent most of the day huddled by it, wrapped in a blanket, reading a book called *Nuclear Fission in the U.S.: The Loss of Denver.* I don't know why I didn't find myself a warm hotel room. Yet something told me I should stick with Isabel for that winter, and I didn't really question it.

She got home a little before midnight, wrapped up in a heavy coat with artificial furs and looking like a Russian countess. Her cheeks were as red as apples. She blew steam by the doorway, stamped her boots and sang out, "Hello, darling." It thrilled my heart, grumpy as I was, to see her like that.

But a blast of icy air had hit me from the open door and I suddenly found myself furious. "Shut that damned door!" I shouted. And that was the way it often went from then on.

Sometimes, walking through the park that winter, dressed in a parka and muffled like a seal hunter, I would hear Isabel suddenly break out in song:

> *I like New York in June,*
> *How about you?*
> *I like a Gershwin tune,*
> *How about you?*

Her voice was so direct and unaffected that the old child in me wanted to cry at the sound of it. We held hands a lot, squeezing hard to feel one another through mittens.

We walked every day, no matter how cold it was. Isabel is

the only woman I know who shares my love for walking the streets of New York. Her gray hair glowed in winter sunlight and she would face the icy air with zip and aplomb; I think I loved her most while striding briskly up Madison or Fifth Avenue in December, seeing the stares she would get from Chinese tourists muffled in their Korean scarves.

Sometimes she would window-shop. At first this was annoying; it seemed to be the customary female dumbness. But gradually I saw that Isabel was as perceptive about clothing as she was about the paintings in museums. She knew a lot about shoes, for instance—more than some people know about life. She had a sense of the sheen and poise of a shoe and eventually made me see it for the piece of minor sculpture it could be. But when I offered to buy she said there wasn't room in her closets.

Eating at restaurants with her was delightful, and we did it a lot that winter. I think I began to love her a dozen years ago when I first saw her eat *truite fumée*. She would cut it neatly with her knife, slide an ample slice onto her fork, push a dozen capers on top—still using the knife—and then put it into her mouth and chew with serious concentration. There was nothing prissy in this; Isabel was a formidable trencherwoman and her eating was punctuated with little sighs of pleasure. That was when I was married to Anna; I was backing a play that Isabel had a tiny part in. She had also carpentered one of the sets. I was taken by her intelligent face and her figure and asked her to lunch. Nothing developed from that meeting for a long time, but watching her eat made my heart go out to her. I love people who like to eat and don't get fat doing it. This woman ate with gusto and had a waist like a girl's. In the twelve years I've known her her hair has become grayer but her figure hasn't changed. I tingle now to think of that figure, to remember her putting away *truite fumée*.

We laughed a lot on our walks and in restaurants. We hugged each other spontaneously from time to time. I was delighted by her in hundreds of small ways. But whenever we tried to make love during those five months I found myself with a knot in my stomach and some old smoldering fury in my loins. What had been a happy afternoon of walking and chatting could become a nightmare; sometimes I became withdrawn and bitchy for hours. I should have quit trying altogether; Isabel herself told me I should quit, but I found ways to override her objections. I told her my sexual failures needn't upset her, that if she were really turned on it might help my problem, that maybe at depth it was she who was afraid of sex. For about two weeks I had her buffaloed. Everybody has sexual fears; I developed Isabel's like an impresario, trying to cover up my own.

She saw through it eventually. "Goddamn it, Ben," she said in the middle of a cold night in the loft bed. "You're the one with the problem and you're trying to blame me for it."

I fumed and blustered for a few minutes and finally fell back to sleep. In the morning I waked to see her sleepy-eyed and a bit grim-faced, and said, "I think you're right."

Things were better for a while after that. I left her alone and quit trying to act on every sexual tingle I felt—and I felt plenty of them. I slept better. But there was a lot of fury in me, and I felt it building. Much of the time I was good-humored and enjoyed doing what little work I needed to do—which took about three hours a day, mostly on the phone—but inside a pressure was building. I was becoming a time bomb, looking for an excuse to explode. I was scared by this and at the same time exulted in it. Living with Isabel and hating myself for impotence, I had become a sullen, angry, dangerous child.

⚘ Chapter 6

My hydroponics garden stands out now in green against the gray of Belson's surface, alive against that bleak obsidian. It is remarkable what Fomalhaut can do to power a vegetable, more remarkable that plants bred to the light of Sol flourish under this blue star. They do it with chemical fertilizers recycled, and recycled water. Part of the fertilizers are recycled through me; I defecate into a hopper that feeds the system, and then add potash; I eat the same rearranged molecules over and over. Orbach would love it; it fits his thesis that my personality requires self-nourishment.

I find deep pleasure in seeing those lettuces and carrots and beets and asparagus growing in their plastic troughs. They cover a half acre of surface that for billions of years has been lifeless. I walk down the rows, encouraging my plants, rubbing their wet leaves tenderly, muttering to them sometimes, sometimes pulling a leaf of lettuce or spinach and eating it there in the rows, warmed by blue Fomalhaut, alone and happy with my vegetable companions.

Since there are no seasons here, every season is growing season; I am already on my second crop and am improving the breed. Why can't you just let things *alone?* Anna would say at times in anger. Well I can't. I don't want to. So I save the best plants for seed, sensing that the new spectrum of Fomalhaut is an evolutionary spur and that some of my varieties will thrive on the short day-night cycle. Luther Burbank Belson, prodding his bush beans into stardom. It has worked, especially with the carrots; I've never seen such big, firm, orange carrots. I had Annie pull out one of the nuclear cooking coils from the *Isabel's* galley, and I cook my vegetables on that. It requires twenty minutes at Belson air pressure to produce a carrot *al dente*—neither crisp nor mushy. They are superb with Java pepper.

I remember now the pattern of sliced carrots on Isabel's white floor the day I cooked the leg of lamb.

It was the first time I had ever roasted a leg of lamb, but I hadn't told Isabel that. My career as a cook had begun for all practical purposes in her apartment; I knew how to scramble eggs and make a grilled cheddar sandwich when I moved in, but that was it. I started taking over the kitchen at Isabel's when I felt I had to create something for her and me, something elemental and sensual. For one orifice if not the other. Orbach pursed his lips when I told him that, but he didn't look convinced. "Hell," I said, "I've got to do *something*. I can't fuck, and I'm bored with making money."

"Benjamin," Orbach said, "cooking is a fine and creative thing to do. But it wouldn't be wise for you to pretend you are a woman when you're having difficulty being a man."

"Come on!" I said. "I'm not pretending I'm a woman. My mother opened canned spaghetti for supper. And complained about it. She spent more time in the kitchen drinking screwdrivers than she did at the stove."

"Maybe you want to teach her to be domestic," Orbach said.

"Isabel?" I said.

Orbach frowned. "I'm not sure," he said.

"I'm not sure of *anything*," I said, "except that I love to bring her coffee in the mornings and drink it with her."

"Bring her coffee?" Orbach said. "Who?"

"Isabel, goddamn it!" I said. "If it was Mother, I'd bring her a martini."

Orbach smiled wanly at that. "Benjamin," he said, "as a child you had to nourish yourself, because there was little other nourishment around."

I lay on the couch and looked at the water stain on Orbach's ceiling. "I get tired sometimes," I said. "I get damned tired of the whole fucking *weight*."

"Clearly," Orbach said, with sympathy. "I'd like to use chemical recall with you for the rest of our session today. I'd like to give you sorbate and take you back to your infancy and see if we can find out what you were thinking."

I felt myself sweating. I hadn't used chemicals in therapy for several years. They scared me. "Those pills pack a terrible hangover," I said. "I need a clear head for . . ."

"For what?"

"For cooking supper tonight," I said.

Orbach shrugged. "Very well. Perhaps some other time."

The supper of which I'd spoken was the leg of lamb. I'd noticed it on sale that morning at thirty dollars a pound and bought it impulsively. I then wound up carrying it around with me while I spent a couple of hours with my lawyers, who were too polite to ask what in heaven's name I was doing with a leg of lamb in a plastic bag.

It took me awhile that evening to figure out the controls on Isabel's oven, but I managed. The combination of those electronic gadgets and a heat source of hickory wood has always seemed disorderly to me. It was a Wednesday and there would be no evening performance of Isabel's play, so I had plenty of time. I cut slits in the fat and pushed in slivers of garlic, then rubbed the whole phallic thing with rosemary and coarse pepper. I had it in the oven by the time Isabel came home from her matinee; she gave me a quick kiss and a pat and went off to take a bath. I was beginning to feel very professional about this meal. I peeled away at my carrots, happy as a clam. Since the bathroom of that little apartment was only a few yards from the stove, I could hear Isabel splashing away merrily.

After a while the cats started nosing around at my ankles and looking pushy. It was time for their supper and I should have fed them, but I didn't. The black one, as heavy-looking as a bag of cement, began meowing in his choked way. The brown-and-white, shyer, looked at me reproachfully. *Get out of my way, you dumb bastards,* I thought at them, viciously, not wanting to say it aloud in Isabel's hearing. The black one croaked at me louder. I wanted to tell him to go back to cat school and learn to meow properly. I began to think I should open a can of food just to shut them up. I looked at them again, at their pushy, imploring faces, at their *insistence,* and thought, *Fuck you, boys. Your lady friend can feed you when she gets out of the bath.* They looked at me as though they shared an I.Q. of 3 between them. I grabbed a saucepan and threatened them with it. They slinked away.

A minute afterward, Isabel came out of the bathroom stark naked. I wanted to take her right there, but I restrained myself. Isabel could be testy about sexual advances that led nowhere. My balls had begun to tingle at the sight of her and I really wanted to drop to my knees for a while and let the lamb be well done if need be. But I pulled back from the tingle and cut it off somehow. That, I should have known by then, is how you get blue balls. That's how you get into fights over whatever is handy—like carving a leg of lamb. I should have gone ahead with Isabel and let her decide whether she liked it or not; it would have saved a lot of grief.

Instead, I started fussing with the peas and managed to spill a third of them down into the wood fire, where they hissed at me in derision. I could feel the inanimate world gathering itself for one of its attacks on my person. I began to feel like hunting down the black cat and strangling him. I reached for the oven door and burned my hand. Instead of shouting, I gritted my teeth. Stoicism. It gives you blue balls in the soul.

But I did manage to control myself enough to get the peas into a bowl and then to get the lamb out of the stove and onto a big plate for cooling. It looked terrific. Very professional. I felt a lot better. I spooned out the carrots and circled the leg of lamb with them. It was shaping up like a sculpture. I was cheerful again despite the tight feeling in my stomach. I remembered we had fresh parsley in the bin. I got some and put it at one end of the plate. *Voilà.*

Isabel had pulled on a pair of jeans and set the table by the window. I was standing by my masterwork, waiting for praise.

And then my stomach sank. Somebody had to *carve* this fucker, and I'd never carved anything in my life. When I was a kid my mother managed to roast a turkey once a year, on Thanksgiving, with a kind of cold, hungover resentment. She always carved it herself, while my father sat around looking bored. I think that, down deep, I was waiting for Isabel to get up and carve, like Mother. She came into the kitchen, in fact, and I felt a sigh of relief in myself. But what she did was exclaim over how beautiful the lamb was. And then she said, "Hurry up and carve it, Ben. I'm hungry!"

Jesus, did I want to throttle a cat just then! If I could have just done it—or just kicked a cat around the living room for a minute, I could have sliced up that roast the way an orchestra leader slices air with his baton. With a pinky sticking out as the slices fell with gentle plops on the serving platter, arranging themselves prettily between disks of carrot. But what did I do? I gritted my teeth, stuck a fork into the roast, took a big kitchen knife and started slicing as though the lamb were a loaf of bread. Immediately I hit a bone. I tried the other end. Another bone. I slipped the lamb, greasy now and still too fucking hot, over on its side in the plate, which was now filling with juice, soaking about half the carrots and giving them the color of wet orange socks. Burning grease was sticking to my fingers. I shook it off. Some of it landed in the peas. I began slicing at the first end of the roast, but from a different angle. There was another bone. How could a white, furry lamb walk around with so many goddamned *bones* in its legs? How could the bones be coming from so many different *directions?* My cheeks were burning as though rubbed with Brillo; Isabel was watching every move in tactful silence.

And then, as I stood ready to turn my knife against anything that lived, there was an abrupt, loud *plop*, as though someone had dropped a fish on the kitchen counter. It was William, the normally shy cat. He must have jumped down off

an overhead shelf where he'd been hiding since I'd scared him
away with the saucepan. I stood frozen, staring. During my
carving I had managed to get loose a piece of lamb the size of a
poker chip. William took that piece demurely between his
teeth, leaped to the floor and scampered across the room. I
gripped my Sabatier, visualizing the mess in the apartment
from feline decapitation. William huddled with his find in the
corner, under Isabel's bronze urn of pussywillows. The black
cat slinked over to join him. Clearly a coconspirator. I
picked up the roast, plate and carrots and all, held it over my
head the way King Kong would hold a subway car, and threw
it at them with all my strength. It whammed into the bronze
pot with a thud that enriched my soul with relief. The plate—
Isabel's best Delft—flew apart like a comic-strip firecracker.
And the carrots spread themselves over the white floor like
abstract expressionism. Like the perfectly placed rocks in a
Japanese garden.

But *Isabel!* The poor dear woman. She stared at me in terror, and then she began to cry great rolling tears of grief. "My
cats!" she sobbed. "My Delft platter." She ran into the bathroom, slammed the door and locked it. I stood motionless,
staring at the carrots on the floor, at the chips of china. The
cats had disappeared. I shrugged, got a can of cat food from a
shelf and opened it.

We were civil with one another after that one, walking on egg-
shells for about three days. Once, for no apparent reason,
Isabel began to cry while reading her *Hamlet*. The air of the
little apartment was thick with grief; I had no idea how to cut
through it. On the fourth day I told Isabel I was going to move
to the Pierre. She smiled faintly and said, "That might be
best."

It was early May when I moved out, packing up all I had
lived with during the winter into one Synlon bag, paying off a
few of Isabel's major bills—her rent, the telephone bill, the
winter assessment—before I left. She was at a rehearsal at the
time. When I signed the checks my hand shook and I cursed at
it for shaking. Another goddamned unreliable member. I
looked around the place, nodded with controlled civility to the

sleeping cats, bent down to pick up a two-dollar piece I had dropped on the floor probably a week before, sighed melodramatically, and left.

It was a surprisingly warm day and I had my heavy mackinaw unbuttoned as I walked up Park Avenue. There was a nice sense of life and bustle, with a lot of horses and a few methane taxis in the streets and people bicycling happily. My spirits picked up. I began to whistle.

Half the people on the street were Chinese. By midsummer New York always seems to be a Chinese city, a kind of cultural suburb of Peking. The Russians are ahead of everybody else at heavy industry; the art comes from Buenos Aires and Rio de Janeiro; the political life in Aberdeen and Hangchow is far more lively than New York's; and if you want to make a really big business arrangement you go to Peking, the world's richest city. But New York is still New York, even with its elevators not working and a total of one hundred fifty taxis permitted to operate (Peking has thousands, they are electric powered and have leather upholstery). But Peking is still a stodgy businessman's city, with all the old China erased from its neoclassical architecture. The Chinese come to New York for the civilized life. New York is the major city of a second-rank power, of a country whose time is slipping away; but it still has a bounce you don't find anywhere else. There are restaurants with white tablecloths, with waiters in tuxedos that look like they came from the last century, and, however they beer-feed and hand-rub their fat old steers in Japan, the Kansas City steak served in a New York restaurant, with the dim lights and the polished wooden bar and the tuxedoed waiters, is still one of the delights of the world. And New York theater is the only theater to hold anybody's interest for long; American music is the most sophisticated in the world. The Chinese are still, behind those stuffy facades, the greatest gamblers on earth and the trickiest businessmen; they've accommodated their ideology and their asceticism of the last century to their present wealth with the ease of the Renaissance Popes; they are Communists the way Cesare Borgia was a Christian. And they love New York.

The Pierre is a grand place and I know its people well. I

moved in there first when I was twenty-three and working on downhill mergers; the same man still tends bar in the afternoons and he calls me Ben. His name's Dennis. I always ask about his kids. He has a son in the wood business in North Carolina; his daughter runs the office at the Jane Fonda Theatre. The manager says they're going to name my suite the Belson Suite someday and I tell him I'm all for it, that it'll make it easier to get my mail if there's a plaque on the door. They always have fresh flowers for me when I move in. What the hell, something deep in me likes to live in hotels, to be ready to check out at any time. To live by the day and pay by the day.

I had an appointment that afternoon with Orbach, up on Eightieth Street. I looked over the suite, smelled the flowers, called Henri Bendel's to order my cooking pots, and decided to walk to Orbach's and pick up a few cookbooks on the way. Maybe there would be spring vegetables in, from the South, if the Mafia wasn't in disarray from its quarrels. I called a couple of lawyers and gave them my phone number and left.

Walking up Third Avenue, I found myself looking in store windows, not at cookbooks but at clocks. I was doing that a lot these days, developing a fascination with timepieces, with the passing of time. I noticed birthdays as I never had, would remember trivial things that had happened on a given day a year before. This started when I turned fifty. I was becoming aware that my days are numbered, that I am going to die and rot like everybody else and that I'd better get my ass in gear if I want to live my life as Ben Belson and not as some fucked-over replica of my father. I know I've made a lot of money and fame for myself, have traveled everywhere, have bedded a lot of women and eaten a lot of the world's best food, and my father did none of those things. But for twenty years something in my soul has been on HOLD, waiting, going through the motions of having a filled and good life but inside feeling morose and sullen. And there, looking at clocks in yet another Third Avenue window, I was waiting for the time to run out, waiting to join my father in the underground brigade—to terminate, with the smell of wet earth.

And, realizing that, or some of it, I was seized with anger of a kind I hadn't felt in years. I wanted to rush into the store and smash every clock in the place. Instead, I went in and bought a Chinese wristwatch. I'm wearing it now, here on Belson. I am an eccentric in many small ways; this watch is the first I've ever owned. Now that I have time to reckon with.

A voice in me cries desperately, *Hurry, Ben!*

Looking back on it, I can see that picnic on Juno was a turning point for me. I have become even more of a hermit now than ever before; but something happened there on Juno that moved a big chunk of the gray old glacier inside. In college I never sat around and drank with my classmates; if I were with two or more people at a time something became stiff in my soul. I did not hate people; I never have. But there was a coldness in me that would, to my despair at times, cut me off from my fellows. Somehow it dropped from me at that picnic and I felt an easy comfort in the presence of the crew that I had never felt before. Mimi sang "Downtown" and "Michigan Water Blues," and I drank red wine from a passed-around bottle and lay back on that moist grass in the grape-flavored air; I would look at the faces of the crew and silently beam. Sometimes between songs everybody would be silent, listening to the quiet, papery sounds of those extraterrestrial leaves blowing in that fruity breeze, feeling the rich, oxygen-laden air on our cheeks. I thought from time to time of Juno herself, the original Juno who slept on hay and whose massive nostrils exhaled steamed horse breath into the Ohio night air at my side, and some of the deep old fondness I felt for her was transferred to this new and generous planet and to the people, mostly young, who lay about on its spongy and inviting surface with me.

Yet here I am alone on Belson.

Still, I have my vegetables. And my morphine. The rings are out. It's time to shut off the computer that is typing this, collect the morphine from the synthesizer, and shoot up. I wish I could masturbate right now, here alone under the rings of my own namesake planet.

I first came to New York in 2025. I was thirteen. Aunt Myra

had suggested I spend one of my high-school summers with her on the Upper East Side. I'd never met her. My parents sent me off on a Greyhound bus, telling me the city would help in my education. I bought my own ticket, and what Aunt Myra didn't pay for in New York I paid for myself. I had a large coal route in those days in Athens. Burning coal in home stoves was still legal, and I pulled a child's wagon around the poorer parts of town selling it by the lump: two dollars for the small ones and four for the large. My markup was 40 percent. I hauled that damned wagon up and down hills about eleven miles every day after school and my shoulders would ache from it for hours afterward, but I wound up, at fifteen, with a 5 percent interest in the mine it came out of. By the time I was thirty-five I owned most of the coal in America that the Mafia didn't. I can picture myself now on that bus in my white shirt and tie and with a half-dozen hundred-dollar bills folded up and safety-pinned inside my shirt pocket. Half a fried chicken and two hard-boiled eggs in a paper sack beside me on the seat until I had a chance to throw them away. A fresh haircut. That may have been the last time in my life I wore a necktie. Except for my wedding.

The bus was a coal-burner and there was something wrong with the boiler; we kept losing power on hills. The trip took almost three days. I ate soy protein-and-gravy sandwiches at bus stops all along the way, and in men's rooms in Pennsylvania and New Jersey read graffiti of the rankest kind I have ever seen. I knew almost nothing about sex except that it had something to do with social class and that people like my parents were alarmed by it; those graffiti shone in my brain like neon. Many of them were illustrated, with low draftsmanship but high energy. It was for me a connection, however disquieting, with an outside world in which things went on I had thought went on only in my own head. A couple of those drawings are still in my memory; they can still send a wicked thrill into my balls.

For several hours between towns in Pennsylvania an amply built young woman with glasses and dark nylons sat beside me. For a while she made bland comments on the scenery and on her job as a small-town video librarian; then she slept. As her body adjusted itself in sleep her skirt inched up her thighs. Oh Jesus, I remember those thighs! Those cheap dark stockings, the white flesh above them! She snored lightly, with her lips parted. At the first sidelong sight of inner thigh my joint rose with the mindless alacrity of a Marine's salute. The smell of her Woolworth perfume intensified in my nostrils. I had become so sensitive, so alert, that I could even smell her flesh in its genteel sweatiness from my circumspect position sitting erectly beside her. Erectly. I could have driven nails with it. I pretended to be reading a book.

It was midafternoon; there were few others on the bus. If I were on that bus now I would reach my hand out toward her open lap rather than my own closed one. But what did I know then? I looked around and saw that no one was looking. I allowed myself to turn my head slightly, enough to see what was now a dark hiatus between her thighs, parted and inclined toward me. I let my hand fall gently in my lap and in that moment discovered self-abuse. My palm, touching myself, was instantly wet. My blood circulation had become disorderly; I felt faint. The pleasure had been momentary but so intense as to open a door in my spirit that has never closed. I saw in a flash that my parents were fools and that the world had punch.

An hour later I slipped my right hand into my pants pocket and did it again, more slowly. It was ecstasy. To hell with my undershorts. I would throw them away.

I would have given my soul to slip myself inside what that pink margin hid from view, to have felt it grip my adolescent member. It did not occur to me she might have liked it too. She had said she was on vacation for a week. I could have taken her to a Holiday Inn in some Pennsylvania coal town and we could have fucked ourselves silly. Oh Christ!

My Circe aroused herself from sleep, blushingly pulled down her skirt, and got off at New Hope, Penn. I never learned her name, nor what town she lived in.

Aunt Myra was my father's older sister and had always been a shadowy black sheep of the Belsons'. I had not met her before that summer of my thirteenth year. Myra had clearly been around. I knew she'd gone to Duke with President

Garvey, had played bridge with Kronstadt the demon poet, had written the lyrics for an operetta, was rumored to have had a baby by her chauffeur, and had been the mistress of three different millionaires. The last of these had left her a small fortune in cash and an apartment hotel in the East Eighties. She had lost the cash in the depression of 2004. Myra, my mother said in icy reflection over a martini, had taken her financial advice from Arab astrologers and Roman Catholic choirboys. She had lost the apartment hotel but managed to hang on to the twelve rooms of its penthouse for her lifetime. She owned nothing else.

Aunt Myra was about sixty-five that summer. She wore faded bib overalls and walked barefoot around her apartment, smoked Black Russian cigarettes and wore gold-rimmed glasses over which she peered at me in a kind of bemusement. She popped vitamin pills continuously and laughed a lot. She was a bit under five feet tall—I towered over her, even at thirteen—and despite crow's-feet, gray hair and gray tee-shirts under her overall bibs, she looked youthful. I had never seen anyone like her. I arrived at her place about suppertime, having adjusted my tie a half-dozen times in the elevator. I was carrying my cheap suitcase. I felt awkward as hell. When I knocked on the elegant gold-and-white doorway of her penthouse I expected to be greeted by some kind of sagging debauchee with dewlaps and a gown. What met me was this pretty little person in overalls and bare feet.

"For Christ's sake. Come on in," she said, peering up at me over the gold rims of her glasses. She held out a tiny unmanicured hand and I shook it. It felt cool and friendly and as small as a child's.

"How do you do?" I said in the reserved way I had learned from Mother.

"Let's have something to eat," she said, and led me through a big empty hallway to a cluttered living room. But what clutter! One wall was covered with paintings and watercolors; there must have been twenty of them. Bright as an African stamp collection. Oriental rugs all over too. A black corduroy sofa. A half-dozen tables. Cats—six or seven cats. There were four cats on the window ledge, below high windows overlooking Central Park. It was a park filled with trees in those days. We passed through this astonishing room and into the kitchen. It was done in a spare way—Hungarian peasant, a turn-of-the-century style in rich people's kitchens. Crude ceramic tiles, blue and white, on the walls. A grass rug on the wooden floor. Oak countertops. A terra-cotta stove. But she had a refrigerator, the first I'd seen. In Athens we used iceboxes. When Aunt Myra opened the door of her big brown refrigerator I saw shelves with bright jars and bottles, fruits and vegetables, like a picture in an old magazine. What she fixed me for dinner that night was a thick slab of pâté de foie on Bibb lettuce, a dozen tiny cornichons and a glass of Polish lager. I'd never eaten that eccentrically before. Dessert was chocolate mousse. It was delicious. I've been eating it ever since, in extended tribute to Aunt Myra and her liberation of the spirit.

She handed me a cracked Haviland plate with the lettuce and pâté on it and then the beer in a crystal pilsner glass and I stood there stupidly holding it while she fixed herself the same. Then I followed her out of the kitchen, and it took me a minute to realize that we weren't going to sit down; this would be a peripatetic supper. I worked up the nerve eventually to set my beer glass down after one sip of the bitter stuff—it was my first taste of beer—and started eating the pâté with my fingers. Myra led me around the apartment. She had four bedrooms, three of them empty and from which I could pick the one I wanted. I chose the one with the most windows. Its furnishings were all gray and white, and it had a little Corot on one wall—two old men at a table.

While we walked around she talked from time to time in a pleasant voice about the apartment and about her cats. She asked me about my father in a kind of offhand way, and when I said he was doing okay she sniffed and said, "*I* never could figure out that boy. He was always so goddamned *calm*." It was strange to hear that and to realize that Aunt Myra was fifteen years older than my father and, from the tone of her voice, didn't care about him much. She was nothing like my father or mother, nothing like any adult I'd known. She may have been the last person I loved—and it was love at first sight.

That summer with Aunt Myra gave me a sense of the

possibilities of a city that has never substantially diminished. I
have forgotten the plays and ballets we saw, but I remember
the marble floors, the high-ceilinged lobbies, the soft lighting
at the bars between acts, and the expansive feeling to be in
New York City at the theater. We saw holo shows and two
museum openings and sky music concerts in Central Park. I
remember elevators, before the Energy Acts outlawed them. I
remember the lights in the upper floors of skyscrapers at
night. And most of all, I remember walking down quiet streets
on the East Side between rows of old brownstones, looking
into the windows of brightly lit apartments, wanting to live in
one more than I'd ever wanted anything before. I became a
spiritual New Yorker while walking the East Seventies between
Park and Second Avenue at the age of thirteen.

I also learned about eating from Aunt Myra—salads and
desserts, arugula and chocolate mousse. My diet is a tribute to
her memory. Myra taught me another thing—chess. After a
week of shows and concerts, she announced that we were
going to spend a night at home and entertain ourselves. "Do
you play chess?" she asked me, looking up over her glasses. In
her hand was a plastic packet the size of a billfold.

"No," I said. "I play Monopoly."

"Well, you can play that too with this thing. This electronic
marvel," she said. "But a smart young man should know
chess."

I started to say that no one played chess anymore, for the
same reason no one ever did arithmetic: human effort had
long been outclassed at that kind of thing. Luck games were
what my generation played. But Aunt Myra was no dummy;
she might have a point. "Okay," I said, "will you teach me?"

"I'm going to roast a duck," she said, "and then change for
dinner." She had just come home from shopping and was
wearing her striped coveralls. "This will teach you the game.
Learn it and we'll play during supper." She handed me the
thing. "Unfold it on a table somewhere and press the red
spot." Then she went into the kitchen.

It was made of some kind of rough old plastic and it looked
well-worn. I took it into one of the living rooms where a
walnut refectory table sat by a window, pushed a few ginger

jars, paperweights and African violets aside to create a space, and then unfolded it. It turned out to be a big white square about the size of a Monopoly board with a red dot at the lower left-hand corner. I pulled up a chair, seated myself in front of the board, and pressed the dot.

The surface was immediately covered with print, like a menu. Backgammon, Checkers, Chess, Go, Monopoly, Snakes and Ladders, Bridge, Poker, Canasta, Casino and so on, were listed down the left side, with a red dot to the left of each. On the right, in capital letters, were three options: 1. RULES AND INSTRUCTIONS, 2. PLAY, and 3. OPPO-NENT PLAY (CHOOSE LEVEL). This last was followed by the numbers one through twelve. At the bottom right-hand corner, in gold letters, was written MYRA BELSON.

I pressed "Chess" and "Rules and Instructions." The print vanished and was replaced by a large chessboard, with green and ivory squares. A soft voice from the board said, "*Voici le Jeu d'Échecs . . .*"

"English," I said, aloud.

"Yes," the board said. "This is the game of chess, invented in India and modeled on warfare. It is played with thirty-two pieces, or *men*, as follows: Here is a pawn . . ." and the silhouette of a pawn appeared in the middle of the board. "Each player has eight pawns, placed on what is called the sec-ond *rank*." The pawns appeared, black and white, in their starting positions.

I began to get interested. I could hear Aunt Myra banging pans around in the kitchen. I got up and went to get a beer before continuing. She had the duck in a pan and was slicing an orange for the sauce. I'd never eaten duck before. "What do you think of chess?" she said.

"Looks interesting.".

"No sex and laser rays," she said. She was referring to the kinds of pocket games people generally played, with 3-D visuals and all the screams and curses.

"That's all right with me." I took a liter of Nairobi beer from the refrigerator and a glass from a cabinet.

"Enjoy it, then," she said. "But go easy on beer. You're young."

"I'll never be an alcoholic," I said, thinking of Mother.

"That's good," Aunt Myra said, putting her sliced orange around the duck. "Addiction is a pain for everyone concerned. I understand your mother is a lush."

I'd never heard anyone talk that way before. "She drinks a lot of martinis," I said.

"Mmm," Aunt Myra said. She took down a mixing bowl and began making some kind of dressing in it. "I advise you to stay away from home as much as you can. Your father's a cold fish and your mother drinks."

"I work a lot," I said.

"Do you like money?"

"Yes."

"Good. That's a start. You need a love affair."

"Maybe." I didn't say I was terrified of girls. Terrified. I also didn't say I'd discovered sex on the bus coming to New York.

I took my beer back to the table and went on with the lesson. Outside the window late sunlight shone on the facades of old mansions across the street. I thought for a while about sex and money and what Aunt Myra had said about staying away from home. I wished she would invite me to live with her; I was crazy about Aunt Myra and crazy about New York. I drank down a long glass of beer, feeling the spiritual warmth it gave my belly, and went on with chess. You moved the pieces by touching the silhouette with your finger; the piece vanished and reappeared on the square you touched next. The opponent's pieces moved on their own. The voice gave instructions and recommendations, and after a couple of practice games where it showed me what I'd done wrong, I told it to be quiet and played against the board in silence. I was using the first level of the board's flexible computer—built, I suppose, into the molecular structure of the plastic—and on the third game I beat it by queening a pawn. I was playing at level two when Aunt Myra brought in her blue Spode platter with a golden duck à l'orange on it. We ate with our fingers and played chess. Myra beat me thoroughly, and gave me some advice that was a lot more helpful than the machine's. We played fast games until two or three o'clock in the morning; she won them all. It turned out Myra was a rated player and had won tournaments when young. I was hooked on chess.

I stayed with Myra six weeks that summer, and it was the finest time of my life. She was the zippiest person I'd ever met. I adored her. I could have cried when I left, even though she invited me back for the next summer. She gave me the chess set as a going-away gift, and I played against the computer at level four all the way back home. I never showed the set to my parents; they never knew I had taken up the game. As if it would have mattered.

I never saw Aunt Myra again. The following winter was the first New York was to undergo with no oil for heating. In February the temperature dropped to fourteen below zero, and Aunt Myra died of pneumonia, along with thousands of others. The world was getting grimmer.

ᔕ Chapter 7

For what must have been a quarter of an hour, I stared at the empty sky overhead where the ship had disappeared from view. This was months ago. My neck was stiff from craning, gawking at the sky from which humanity had just disappeared. I was the only *homo sapiens* around, yet it wasn't really a new feeling to me at all.

The cabin has a porch on it; I went over to it finally, sat down, and stared for a while at the obsidian plain in front of me with its field of Belson grass at a distance. The obsidian near the cabin is a grayish green, and evening light makes it appear blue. The sky was green, as it sometimes is at twilight. The rings were not visible. Fomalhaut was dropping toward the horizon. Feeling the silence I began to whistle.

One of the strangest things about this planet is the silence at sunset; I've never gotten used to it. Some part of me expects to hear the sounds of crickets and tree frogs in the warm air—or at least the buzzing of gnats. But the only sound I know of that Belson makes is the singing of its grass—those polymeric strands that go below the surface to some obscure molten intelligence at Belson's center, to some hot old chaos like my own.

I got up finally and went inside. The cabin interior had two pieces of furniture: the Eames chair and a big moonwood slab sitting on four posts for a table. On it sat the drug synthesizer, a nuclear lamp, a pile of plastic sheets, a stack of legal notepads, a pair of ball recorders, and the computer.

There were two large windows with shutters on them to protect me if either beasts or weather should appear, although I expected neither. The light from them was weak. I turned the lamp on low. There was a pile of morphine crystals already accumulated in the receptacle of the machine; I ignored it and walked to the back wall where a moonwood shelf was my kitchen and made myself a drink of gin and water, with a little lemon juice in it. It struck me then for the first time that the cabin was familiar. I looked around me. I could have been in Isabel's apartment in New York!

The kitchen was a space along the back wall and windowless, as hers was. The dimensions of the room were about the same. Where Isabel had a sleeping loft I had a sleeping porch. Aunt Myra's little Corot hung on a side wall exactly where Isabel had hung a Malcah Zeldis. For a moment *déjà vu* made the hairs on the back on my neck tingle. What was I trying to do here across the Milky Way from New York? Keep alive the memory of five months of fighting and impotence?

I sighed aloud at that thought and then walked across the bare floor of the room and out the door. I had spent a week building the place, cutting the balsa-light moonwood with a hot molecular wire and then fitting slabs of it together to make a cabin. Yet in all the time of construction it had never occurred to me I was making a simulacrum of Isabel's New York apartment.

I walked outside, going carefully on my gumsoled shoes, past my little cluster of wet springs with their purity meters and along my hydroponics troughs with their accelerated seeds. Those seeds were already coiling under the brown medium in the troughs, ready to spring up green in a few Earth days. I was feeling much better. I took another swallow of gin. It was getting dark now. I walked slowly across the green-gray plain, away from the setting sun and toward the grass.

There was a field of it as broad as a Kansas wheat plain, a few hundred yards from my garden-to-be. I walked slowly toward it. The surface underfoot was now striated with cloudy bands of purple.

After a moment I passed a patch with cracks. In the cracks grew endolin; I could see it there, the color of heather. I bent and pulled a pinch of it. My neck was still sore from staring at the takeoff and after. I chewed and swallowed the endolin and as I continued walking the pain eased. Wonderful stuff, when fresh. If only it could speak to the soul the way morphine does. The way the grass had done.

I stopped at the end of the field. At nighttime there is usually a breeze here; one had just sprung up. The light was weak, and the grass looked gray and silky. The sky was a deep emerald. I stood at the edge of the rippling grass, finished off my drink and said, "Hello. I'm your new neighbor." The grass waved silently in the wind but said nothing.

I stood there alone for a long time while the sky turned black and the stars came out. There was a pink light from the only moon up, off to my left. And then for a minute I was seized with loneliness. I missed Isabel. I wanted her looking at that black sky with me. I did not want to make love to her, not even necessarily to kiss her. I just wanted her with me.

I turned and went back to my cabin, had another drink, and played the part of *Così fan tutte* that was left on my recorder. I'd had the machine on the seat arm between us; at several points on the recording I could hear the rustling of Isabel's dress, there at the Metropolitan Opera.

For the next few days I busied myself making simple pieces of furniture. The moonwood came from an outcropping about a hundred yards to the south of my cabin. I cut boards from it with a hot wire slicer, much like using a cheese knife on gruyère, and then nailed them together into a chair and two small tables and a set of shelves. The nails were pieces of heavy wire cut in the *Isabel*'s machine shop and fed into a forming machine that gave them a point and a head.

Every few hours I would take a break from the carpentry, not because it was difficult but because I wanted to stretch the project out. I would shoot a little morphine and then go out

looking for endolin. There was a lot of it. At least once a day I
would go stand at the end of the grass and speak to it, but it
never spoke back to me.

I discovered something important about endolin. I had ac-
cidentally gotten a few twigs of it wet once while checking the
irrigation flow in my hydroponics. I'd set the twigs on a two-
day-old lettuce plant so I could use both hands to tighten a
plastic fitting. Some water sprayed the endolin. Later, when it
dried out in the sun, I saw it had changed color, from heather
to a dark brown. When I picked it up, a fine grayish dust
sifted down from the twigs onto my hand and onto the
ground.

The drug synthesizer has an electronic analysis device as a
doublecheck precaution. You can read out the formula for the
drug you just made. A person wouldn't want the machine to
slip up and make strychnine by mistake. I used the analyzer to
check out the gray dust from the endolin and found it was the
pure alkaloid, just as Howard had written it down for me. The
rest of the plant turned out to be mostly cellulose. So the gray
dust was concentrated endolin. Very concentrated; its weight
was less than a fiftieth that of the twig.

It occurred to me immediately that the stuff might keep better in this form. I spent a few hours gathering a bushel and a
half of the twigs. Then I wet them down thoroughly and
spread them to dry in the next day's sun. When they had dried
out I picked them up a few at a time and shook them carefully
over a large plastic bowl. Eventually there was a half cup of
gray powder in the bowl. I checked it on the analyzer, saw that
it was indeed the alkaloid, sealed it into a folded-up square of
plastic, and irradiated it just as I was prepared to irradiate lettuce and peas for preservation. In the nearly two months since
I tried that, it has worked perfectly. A three-milligram pinch
of the dust, stirred into water and swallowed, will cure the
worst morphine hangover in about a minute. There are no side
effects. My health here on Belson is perfect. Ben Belson, pharmacological researcher. With a patent on this stuff, back on
Earth, a smart man could get a 15 percent interest in Parke-
Davis, or Lao-tzu. It's a business I've never fooled with, but
what the hell.

So that added another project to my daily rounds: preparing

concentrated endolin. The analyzer's scales have a beam, so that whatever gravitation I'm in will give constant readings. I now have fifty-three pounds, Earth weight. That's almost all the plastic bags I can spare. It's enough to cure all the hangovers in Japan. They can stir it into their tea.

What a narrow, limited life this is! And how it has grown on me, how I take to it so easily! I am not homesick and I am not lonely anymore. Or if I am lonely I don't know it. Sometimes I think I swim in loneliness the way a fish swims in water, unaware that it is wet.

In my third month I began to shoot dope in dead earnest. My veins swelled with morphine and my brain became a hot fog, burning with euphoria. Sometimes there were nightmares. I saw in sharp detail De Quincey's three old women, constructing themselves with gold knitting needles, their bodies self-knitted and self-purled for me. One resembled Aunt Myra, but when I spoke her name she looked away. Eventually all three burst into white flame and I heard myself screaming.

At the start of the fourth month I stayed on my back in bed for over four days, until the Shartz machine's morphine reserve was gone. When I finally got out of bed I fell to one knee and thought for a while of never getting up. I might have stayed there and died if I hadn't been hungry. There was a large pail of water by my bedside, but no food. I hadn't eaten in four days. My stomach felt stuck together and my head was primarily a pulse.

I pulled myself up and slowly walked outside, like a sleepwalker. It was midday and I squinted. At first I thought I was seeing another hallucination: the plants in my garden were black. I blinked and stared and scratched my funky armpits. Hair came out and stuck under my nails. For some reason the soles of my feet were sore. It was no dream. My garden had died. Black as sin. I fell once on my way to the lettuce—my dear lettuce. The leaves were like huge flakes of ash and they became powder in my trembling hand.

I stooped to my carrots and dug three up with my fingernails; what was beneath the ash leaves were brown crumbly shafts with a sour smell to them. I sat in the center of my garden, surrounded by ash and bad smells, and I remembered lying on my bed in chemical bedazzlement and looking out the door to see a black rain falling from the lavender sky and smoke rising from my garden as the rain hit my beloved plants. I had taken it for hallucination, on a par with the three self-knitted maiden aunts—the kind of thing that goes away. It didn't go away.

I lit a cigar and continued sitting. My hands still shook but my head was beginning to clear. What I needed was a dozen raw eggs and a bottle of whiskey, but I let the cigar be my pacifier while I added it up. Clearly there was more to this planet than met the eye. It had pulled a fast one on me, with its death rain. What would have happened to my body had I been outdoors during the rainfall? Would my skin have gone the way of the lettuce? Must I now escalate my imitation of Robinson Crusoe and make myself an umbrella out of what was available? I dropped that for a while and thought of food. The *Isabel* would not be back for months. I had four boxes of irradiated meat behind the cabin and two dozen cartons of dried food by my sink. There was a large supply of vitamin pills and protein tablets.

I had a frightening thought, bit down on my cigar and pushed myself up. I padded back to the cabin and then around it, to where the meat was stored in sealed plastic cartons. My premonition was right; the rain had eaten through the cartons, turning them gray. Inside each, where lamb chops and steaks and pot roasts had lain ready for cooking in molecular suspension, now lay stacks of individually wrapped hockey pucks— dark and shriveled and smelling to high heaven or whatever it was above the inscrutable Belson sky. I stepped back from the smell and stared upward for a long while with an Old Testament feeling, wondering what celestial visitation this perverse planet had prepared for me. In my mind were the words spoken to Job: "I alone am escaped to tell thee." Son of a bitch.

Nothing fell from the sky on me and I did not become covered from sole to crown with sore boils, although I was ready.

I thought of a fissure in the obsidian nearby and walked over to it. I grabbed a handful of endolin and crunched it down raw, without a chaser. The taste was bitter and clean in my dry mouth. Then I went back into the cabin, opened up my one window to let some of the bad air out and then washed my face with the water left in the bucket. That felt better, and by then the endolin had eased my head.

Along the far wall of the cabin was a long moonwood shelf with over a dozen plastic cartons of dried food. I took a deep breath and walked over, a part of me thinking that surely nothing could have happened to my dried beans and potatoes and synthetic protein. But another part of me knew exactly what was going to be the case. I broke the heavy seal on one of the cartons and lifted out a plastic pouch of what should have been dried eggs. Inside was a light-brown mush—a kind of compost.

I ripped open the pouch and let the stuff fall into my left hand. It felt like rotten leaves and burned my skin lightly. I touched a bit of it to my tongue. It tasted like acid. I shouted a Chinese imprecation I'd learned as a student and hurled the mess out the front door. The hairs on the back of my neck were prickling. I was going to starve to death, and soon. I was already four days into it.

It was no way to go, and I knew it. I went over to my Eames chair, trying not to think about my stomach and the way it was beginning to come back to life, and seated myself slowly. I put my naked and dirty feet up on the ottoman. There was a distant humming in my ears. I clasped my sweaty hands behind my neck the way I had learned to in the Great Orbach's office and played his sturdy old Viennese voice in my head: "Relax, Ben. The first thing is to relax." I concentrated on my scalp and forehead, relaxing them. It didn't work. I was tense as hell, as though I were made of stiff, vibrating wires. I looked across the room toward the drug synthesizer and saw a small white mound of fresh morphine powder sitting in its hopper. I quickly averted my eyes. There was not enough yet for an overdose anyway. I knew that I could, if push came to shove, make hydrocyanic acid—or for that matter nicotinic—and erase myself in a half minute. The modern world makes death one of the easiest things in life. If only it worked as well for sex, love and work.

I tried again to relax, concentrating on my calves and

thighs. They felt in need of nourishment. There were flaky spots—my grim vegetable ashes in miniature—before my eyes. There was acid in my stomach. The humming in my ears grew louder. I remembered my near-suicide in Mexico, fifteen years before.

I was in my mid-thirties and so empty inside, so disappointed with life and with all the money I was making, that I began over a long number of sterile weeks to focus my attention on euthanasia. I'd read about it in *Scientific American* and saw a segment on it on a TV show. The new pills had been invented in Germany. Naturally. They were illegal everywhere but Mexico and Bolivia. The Life-Arrest pill put you on hold for up to a thousand years, as long as your body was encased in a box or tube. No refrigeration needed. They had places in Mexico to store you, tagged and ready for revival in the century of your choice. You popped one and you were rigid in three minutes, with no pain, no consciousness. The antidote was a brief flash of high temperature and a massive electrical shock in the chest, like the Frankenstein monster. If you didn't trust Mexican engineering—and who did?—you could be shipped back home in the suspended state without legal problems, as long as you had a birth certificate and some other I.D.—like VISA. There was a place in Brooklyn that would store you underground, safe from nuclear attack and the IRS, and bring you out of it at the appointed time. Nobody explained what course your resurrected self was to take if there had been an H- or R-Bomb attack during your sleep. Maybe there would be another pill and a glass of water on your bedside table.

The other pill was called Permanent Arrest, and differed from the pharmacopoeia of the Borgias only in its speed and lack of pain; it switched you off like a light bulb. Then they dropped you into the crematorium, or recycled you in a Mexican garden. It was the latter I had in mind when I took the train to San Miguel Allende. I had no interest in trying to resume my life in the twenty-eighth or thirtieth century; I would be happy to have my private collection of dancing molecules dance again as poinsettias.

When I got there a Oaxacan Indian in a blue jumpsuit showed me the storage chambers in an old pink church, with row after row of coffin-sized plastic cartons. "These are our Survivors," he explained, in oleaginous English. There was a name stenciled in dark green on each box, a good many of them were Japanese. *Hara-kiri?*

"What about the dead ones? I mean permanently dead?"

"You mean our Terminates," he said. He led me to a stone undercroft lined with bookshelves. These were about half filled with what looked like coffee cans, a name stenciled on each. I shuddered slightly. What a small space to contain a person! What *compression* of a body that it takes so long to grow and age and get comfortable in!

"What about the others," I said, "the ones you plant?"

He took me up some stairs and out into a garden filled with flowers and trees, but my spirit did not rise at the sight. They were shabby trees and unkempt flowers, with a lot of insect damage and sunburn on their leaves. What a misuse of human resources! I decided immediately that I did not want to join that sad aggregation of cloistered plants. At least not yet. I would sweat it out for a few more years in human form and see what happened.

On the train back to Atlanta, where I was living at the time, I thought of how close I'd come to dying, and I felt relieved and clear in the head. I thought of how many people must kill themselves in midlife, by blade or chemical or leap, rather than give up their jobs or divorce their spouses or take up a wicked habit. It struck me that the thing to do was quit the job or slug the boss or whatever. If it didn't work out, if you really fucked it up, *then* you could commit suicide. I went back to work in real estate and took up cigars and love affairs. The real estate did well for me and I doubled my fortune in eight months; the other two were less productive, but they did fill in some empty niches in my being and I forgot about suicide. Until now, on Belson, faced with starvation. What an outcome for a man who loves eating as much as I do!

I lay back in my chair and tried to relax, but my body was stiff with fear and anger and would not let go. A part of me wanted to die and another part was terrified of dying. I tried to generate Orbach's voice in my mind, but nothing happened; there was nothing in my head but the fear of death.

And then I looked across the room and blinked. My mother

was sitting near the far wall, on our old Ohio sofa. Her pink chenille gown was open at the top and her breasts were visible—waxy, shining with sweat. On each side of her, candles burned in Belson air. On her face was emptiness and despair. She looked up at me as I stared and her face broke into a weak smile.

Shockingly, I found myself drawn toward that couch, toward that ruined face and those breasts. Flesh of my flesh; that loosely tied chenille covered the belly where I had once dwelt. There was my first hotel, where I had begun as a coiled marvel of gestation. I sat and stared at her, feeling drawn toward her empty and lonely death, by alcohol and cigarette and self-hatred, wanting to throw my arms around her waist and lean my cheek against her breast. I reached a shaky hand toward her and then I heard myself shouting, "*Goddamn you, Mother!*" and I was out of my chair and running.

Where I ran to was the field of Belson grass half a mile from the shack. I stopped at the edge of it, out of breath and sweating in the noonday sun. I took off my shirt and pants, then my shorts. I was stark naked and covered with four days and nights of morphine perspiration. My muscles felt shriveled and my scalp itched powerfully with all the sweat in my hair.

The humming in my ears was loud now and it was no longer a humming in my ears. It was the grass. It was singing softly. To me. Who else? It was singing to me.

"Forgive me, Love," I said, and walked gently on it. I looked down at my feet. The grass wasn't bleeding. I walked farther, out into the middle of the field, surrounded by song. Tears were streaming down my face and my feet seemed to be damp with cool oil as they pressed the delicate flesh of the grass beneath them.

Without difficulty I found the place that was right for me, the center of the song and the heart of the field. I sat carefully at first, feeling the soft grass like a living carpet on my bare body; then I lay down on it, looking up at the hot blue spirit of Fomalhaut. The grass moved gently beneath my body, pressing my shoulders and back, my buttocks, calves and heels with a delicate massage. I felt a sensation of rocking and closed my eyes. Fomalhaut blazed on my body. The grass held and rocked me. I passed out.

• • •

When I awoke it was night and both moons were up. It took a few moments to realize that I was not hungry. Nor was I hung over, or sore, or frightened.

It was totally silent around me; the grass had stopped singing. At least it had stopped singing aloud; I felt that it might be singing in my veins—my healed veins. I felt awake, at peace, nourished, clean.

Eventually I raised my left arm to look at my watch, and as I did so I felt a series of tiny resistances against my skin and looked over at it by the moonlight: blades of grass had fastened their tips to the length of my arm, and as I raised it they fell away. I was like Gulliver with those Lilliputian ropes, except the grass did not really restrain me. When the arm was free I looked at it closely. There were little pink marks. I knew I had been fed that way, and cleaned out that way; my beloved grass had drawn the used morphine and all its attendant poisons from my bloodstream and replaced that detritus with nutrients of its own devising. I was clean. An interplanetary molecular wedding had taken place while I slept and the chemical soup that filled my veins had been filtered, strained, purified and replenished. It must have read my DNA like a helical braille with the fingertips of its filaments. This planet was a sentient being and it loved me.

Yet if Belson loved me, just who had wiped out my food supply in the first place? For a moment a shudder passed through me and I felt like the awakened Adam, not yet aware that both God and Satan watched his moves and laid their plans for him.

Fomalhaut had begun to rise and pale lavender spread itself across the sky above me. *What the hell*, I thought. *I'm not going to die after all*.

The feeding I'd received that night lasted me throughout the following day. I wanted to stay away from morphine but couldn't. Or wouldn't. I wound up shooting a half-dozen small fixes into myself during the day. I thought of taking my hammer and smashing the drug synthesizer, but I didn't do that. I kept the machine turned on and myself too.

I did nothing to clean up the mess my hydroponic garden had become. I spent the day mostly sitting on my porch reading *The Wings of the Dove*, getting fuzzier in the head as the day wore on. I speak of a Belson day, which is a bit more than nineteen hours. Beneath the fuzziness was a kind of panic at my need for morphine. The way to quell that panic, of course, was to shoot more morphine.

When I became tired I took my clothes off, washed my face and hands, and walked out toward the field of grass. Suddenly I became frightened. What if that rain should fall again, while my naked body was stretched out to the night sky? I stopped, then turned and headed back to the cabin. I could get a bed-sheet to throw over myself. I stopped again. What good would a bedsheet do to protect me against something that had eaten through the heavy plastic food bags? That had even gotten the food in the cabin somehow while I slept? It could have dis-solved me then, in my morphine trance, had it been out to get me. I turned and headed back toward the field.

I slept on my back spread out naked. As I drifted off I felt the soft tips of grass blades caressing my body, sensed their penetration into my skin. They were finding my capillaries and veins, wedding my body's life to their own. The intimacy of this connection hushed my unquiet soul.

That night I dreamed of my father's study again, with the forget-me-nots on the wall and the silent ache in my youthful heart. I sat there in my dream for hours, waiting for my father to speak to me. He did not even look up from what he was do-ing.

Then, in my dream, I did something that felt monstrous and frightening. I willed it to end. I stood up and turned my back to my father and walked out of the room. I shut the door behind me. I was terribly, terribly frightened. I stood outside the room a few steps from the closed door and felt as though I were completely alone, fatherless and motherless, and I knew nothing. Nothing at all.

I awoke on Belson, with no moons up and the sky black except for stars, Sol among them. I was cold and I was crying.

I lay there and cried for hours. It seemed as though the grass were providing the fluid for my tears, that I was merely a channel for liquids that entered the skin of my back and my arms and legs and passed through my bloodstream to my eyes and then flowed out and across my face, hot and merciful. I was limp all over, as limp in my body as I have ever been, and the relief was like a muted continuous orgasm. It was a letting out of pressure that I had felt so long it seemed to be merely the human condition. I exhausted my tears. When I stopped crying there was no tension anywhere in me.

And then a remarkable thing happened. Belson's rings came out, glowing across the entire sky in vast bands of lavender and blue and red, a colossal rainbow to my tears and a sign from heaven. I stared at the sky's refulgence, the illumination this planet was providing me, and my heart leaped up with joy for a long moment. Then the rings and I both eased off into quiet darkness and I slept again.

I must have slept through the next Belson day, because it was twilight when I finally awoke. I sat up carefully, feeling the grass pull away from my body. Then I leaned forward on my face with my arms outspread and embraced the quiet grass. I held that position for several minutes in silence, and then pushed myself up and stood.

I walked to my cabin and smashed my drug synthesizer with a hammer, hitting it a dozen times with all my strength. I lifted the morphine from the hopper and carried it outside to a deep fissure in the obsidian that I used as a toilet. I threw it in. Then I made coffee, thanking Belson that my bags of coffee had remained untouched by the plague that had destroyed my food.

For weeks I kept busy. I cleaned up the mess of my garden and my ruined supplies of food. I cleaned the ash out of the hydroponic equipment, sorted through my remaining seeds—undamaged by the rain—and planted them. They sprouted and I tended them. I finished James's novels and began to read Mark Twain, starting with *Life on the Mississippi*. What a remarkable book! It populated my empty world for me. I read it twice, then set it down and read *Roughing It* and *A Tramp Abroad*. The lettuce and potatoes grew fast. My spirit remained preternaturally calm, except for the occasional fits of morphine lust that would creep up on me. Gradually I reduced my cigars to a half dozen a day. I began to work out again on the Nautilus machines and my body, lean from the lack of food in my diet, toughened up. I spent most of my time naked—since the air on Belson was always a bit above seventy degrees. I read in the nude and slept on the grass in the nude. I became tanned and my hair bleached itself to a very light blond. Veins bulged on my arms and legs. I felt that I was all lean meat, as tough as jerked beef and as seasoned. There was a spring in my step. I thought little and felt little.

When my lettuce matured I began to eat salads, even though I was not hungry. I kept them small and perfect, mixing Bibb and leaf lettuce equally and tossing them in the sunflower oil I got from my big coarse row of those enormous flowers. When preparing the oil I would recite Blake's poem:

> Ah, sunflower, weary of time,
> Who countest the steps of the sun,
> Seeking after that sweet golden clime
> Where the traveller's journey is done.
>
> Where the youth pined away with desire
> And the pale virgin shrouded in snow
> Arise from their graves, and aspire
> Where my sunflower wishes to go.

After a few days my peas matured and I would steam them a few minutes and add them to my lettuce. The salads grew to include onions and Kentucky Wonder Beans. I welcomed these additions, but Belson was still my primary nourishment. No words passed between us, but my planet fed me like the infant I was.

One morning I awoke from a night on the grass with bright cobwebs of sexual dreams in my head and discovered with a kind of awe that my penis was pointing skyward there in the Belson dawn, as firm and erect as it had ever been in my life. I lay there with my brain half asleep and felt strength radiating throughout myself from that red, erect, sky-pointing marvel: my loving member, my true self, risen at last. Great, tingling physical pleasure suffused me. The pleasure grew and I let it grow and grew with it. And then, almost in a swoon, I *willed* for myself an orgasm. Immediately I felt it begin to happen with that lovely sense of inevitability at the crossing of the physical threshold, and I lay there and watched myself come, jetting upward in heartrending delight into the pure air of Belson's dawn.

What glory, to relearn it. I relaxed and my whole body softened. I fell back to sleep.

When I awoke to a distant roar Fomalhaut was high in the sky and I saw descending, riding a bright silver flame, the *Isabel*. A moment later I felt the ground of my planet receiving her, with a profound subcutaneous shudder.

ᛊ Chapter 8

Clearly the *Isabel* had landed several miles away in order not to cook me with her retros. It would be an hour before anyone showed up at my cabin. I felt resentful, knowing it was time to reenter the ordinary world—resentful even against Belson itself, whose timing was remorselessly accurate. I did not want to leave this placental grass and the stillness of my present life. I did not disturb my physical attachment to the grass, and fell back to sleep.

I awoke to shouting from the edge of the field. The voice shounded hollow and the words were indistinct, but I shuddered myself awake to the world of men. What a pain that is! What endless complications! I wished intensely for a moment that the grass could somehow absorb me into itself and fracture my body into a million blades so that I could lie there forever under the sun of Fomalhaut and when the time came, sing.

The voices kept up. Clearly the crew members did not want to walk out to me. Finally I pulled myself upright, breaking off the connections on my arms and back with little pops, feeling all those filaments severing themselves from my body.

"Okay!" I croaked skyward, "I'm coming." My unused voice rasped in my throat. I sat silent for a full minute until my unease subsided.

Then I stood, slowly, and looked over toward them. Charlie the doctor, and Mimi, and three others stood by a green nuclear jeep.

I walked toward them cautiously. As I got near I saw a flicker of self-consciousness on several faces and remembered that I was nude. Wearing my birthday clothes, as they say.

"You okay, Captain?" Charlie said, with a kind of quaver.

"Did you find Isabel?" I said, hoarsely.

They just looked at me.

"Did you find her?"

"No, Captain. No we didn't." It was Charlie speaking again and his voice was soft. "Are you all right?"

I said nothing and walked past them toward my cabin. I could hear them following me, their gym shoes padding on the obsidian. They stopped at the cabin porch while I stepped up on it and walked in.

I crossed the room to my full-length mirror, taken from the *Isabel's* gym. I looked at myself for the first time in months. I saw John the Baptist. My hair was wild and sweaty, and my beard was a bramble. I was all bone and sinew and deep tan— angular and as tough-looking as leather. The most startling thing was my eyes, which were piercing and prophetic—the eyes of a mad seer. My prick and balls were heavy, and the hair on my abdomen and my legs was curled like wires; my eyes were the eyes of some mad old Jew come straight from the desert with his brains permanently addled by the force of the sun and of Jehovah.

I liked the way I looked and I did not want to put on clothes. I had come into the cabin with the thought of dressing myself, but now I did not want to. I wasn't ready to don civilization with blue jeans and Adidas. I might never be ready.

I walked outside and ignored the crew members who stood there silently waiting for me. I walked between Mimi and Charlie, looking at neither of them, and across the bare surface toward my field of grass. I kept walking, crossing the

field and coming back onto obsidian and then walking to
another field. I turned back. I could see them standing, looking in my direction. For a moment I was furious and waved at
them to go away. But of course they didn't. In agitation I lay
on the grass and held myself rigid, waiting for its tendrils to
take hold, waiting for the rocking motion. But nothing happened. There was no movement beneath my body. After a
frustrating twenty minutes, I stood and began walking back,
crossing my first grass field again. I stopped in its middle and
lay down again, but there was no hope in me. I got nothing
from the grass.

I got up and continued walking, a bit less angry and a bit
reconciled, until I came back to the crew of the *Isabel*, still
standing by the cabin porch. They looked at me strangely but
no one spoke. I nodded roughly and went past them and back
into the cabin. I got my jeans and put them on. I slipped my
Adidas over my bare feet and then put on a gray tee-shirt.
Then I went to my pitcher of water, poured some into the bowl
and washed my face and the back of my sun-wrinkled neck.
The skin was shockingly rough to the touch.

I ran my fingers through my hair several times, wincing as I
pulled out tangles. Then I looked in the mirror again and lit a
cigar. I was now John the Baptist, Chairman of the Board. I
took scissors and hacked off some of the bushiness at the sides
of the beard, letting bunches of hair fall on the moonwood
floor, watching myself in the mirror as I did so until what
I saw was less a prophet than Ben Belson himself. Then I
stopped, before all prophecy and mysticism had left my face. I
did not want to forget how my bloodstream had been fed for
two months, nor how my sexual self had spurted a seminal
fountain that very dawn.

I stepped out onto the porch. They were standing around
silently. When they saw me come out looking near-civilized
and dressed again, I could see the relief on their faces. Mimi's
thin features lit up and Charlie smiled gently at me, clearly
glad to find me more recognizable.

Mimi was carrying what looked like a gym bag. She set it
on the edge of the porch, unzipped it, and brought out two
bottles of Mumm's and some champagne glasses. We all
watched while she undid the wires around the corks and then

blasted them out of the bottles like miniature *Isabel*s. She poured mine first and handed it to me. I held it and watched the way Fomalhaut's blue light sparkled on its fizz. When the others all had glasses I held mine aloft for a toast. "To the United States," I said. "Hear, hear," Charlie said, and we drank them off. The taste was strange to my subdued tongue, acquainted of late mostly with salads. The fizz in my throat brought back New York, the opera, and women with white shoulders.

"Well," I said, "how did they like our uranium?"

At first nobody answered. Finally Charlie spoke up, a little grimly. "They didn't, Captain."

"Call me Ben," I said. "What do you mean they didn't like it?"

"It's still on board."

I stared at him.

"That's right," Charlie said. "They wouldn't let us take it off."

I permitted myself a quiet explosion. "Son of a bitch," I said.

"The uranium was classified as a dangerous import," Mimi said. "We were lucky to stay out of jail."

I could see it. The energy lobbies, and Baynes in the Senate. I tossed off the rest of my champagne and held my glass out to Mimi. As she filled it I looked over her shoulder toward the field of Belson grass and gritted my teeth. Biting the umbilical cord. It had to be.

I drank off the second glass of champagne and then I said to Charlie, "Do you have a fresh cigar?"

"I sure do, Ben," he said, and gave me a Sacre Fidel.

I nodded thanks to him and saw relief on his face and the faces of the others. It can be a cause of tension to find a naked madman greeting you right after planetfall. "Still on board," I said. "Son of a bitch."

"You'll be arrested when you go back, Ben," Charlie said. "The only reason we're not in jail is we had to come get you. They couldn't leave you out here to die."

"Who's they?"

"The U.S. District Court," Mimi said. "In Miami. The hearing took a week."

"Someone was on board the ship, with some experts," Charlie said, "while we were in court. There was talk of unloading the *Isabel* into a government warehouse, but the Sons of Denver started picketing. We were in custody awhile."

"What about my lawyers?" I said. "What about Mel and Met Luk . . . ?"

"We couldn't even see them," Mimi said. "They were under an injunction." She shook her head angrily and finished her champagne. "I got in touch with Howard's lawyer and he told me there was nothing he could do. He said you were clearly in violation of the law. Then I got Whan and Summers on the phone . . ."

"What did they say?"

"They couldn't touch it."

"Yeah," I said, thinking, *Baynes got to them*. He would have plugged the holes. I lit my cigar. Things were serious. I was warming to the fight.

"What about my other people?" I said. "I told you to call Earth the minute you got into the warp."

"We did," Charlie said. "We sent your message to Dolum and Flynn and this is what we got." He pulled a folded sheet of paper from his pocket and handed it to me:

PUBLIC LAW 229BR764 of MARCH, 2064, FORBIDS BENJAMIN BELSON THE USE OF COUNSEL. FOREMENTIONED IS NO LONGER A CITIZEN OF THE UNITED STATES. HE HAS BEEN DECLARED A DANGEROUS ALIEN UNDER THE INTERNATIONAL LAWS OF PIRACY . . .

"*Piracy!*" I said. I have to admit it was kind of a thrill. I had grown a beard just in time.

But my citizenship! What in hell had happened to all my friends?

. . . AND THE FIRM OF DOLUM AND FLYNN IS UNDER INJUNCTION TO SEVER ALL TIES WITH THE STATELESS PIRATE, BENJAMIN BELSON. THIS MESSAGE CONSTITUTES A NOTICE OF THE SEVERANCE OF THIS FIRM'S TIES WITH ALL CORPORATE HOLDINGS AND ENTERPRISES ON BEHALF OF THE AFOREMENTIONED BELSON.

"Son of a bitch," I said.

"I didn't believe it at first," Charlie said.

"Let's go inside," I said. "I've got to pack." *I* believed it. I had just underestimated Baynes and whoever was on his side.

"You know, Captain," Charlie said, "driving over here from the ship was . . . wonderful. Bad as our news is, it's great to be here again. Back on Earth I would think about the sky here, and the quiet . . ."

"Are you trying to tell me something?" I said.

"You could stay," he said. "On Earth they'll put you in prison. Belson is a whole lot better than that."

"We could drop you off at Juno," Mimi said. "That place is an Eden . . ."

"Crew," I said, "I'm getting back to New York." I chomped down on Charlie's cigar and inhaled deeply. I was making plans. I felt totally human again. I puffed the cigar and stroked my beard. "Let's get my stuff back on board. Let's do it fast."

Getting those Nautilus machines onto the jeep and back to the ship was a nuisance, but I wasn't going to leave them behind. I wanted to be in top shape when we landed at Islamorada. For a moment I pictured myself wearing a tee-shirt in Washington when I started knocking on doors. I wanted them to see my muscles, those whey-faced charlatans. Make the bastards walk the plank.

We got the machines bolted back in place in the ship's gym and I had Annie take charge of harvesting what she could of my corn and beans and the other stuff. It was sad to see a strange face as pilot, but Ruth was gone, along with her brother, Howard. The new pilot was a quiet little Japanese named Betty. She looked competent enough, but I missed Ruth.

After the ship was ready for takeoff, I told everyone else to stay on board and I went out of the ship one last time. I walked slowly over to my field of grass and stood by its edge. Then I squatted down and held the palms of both hands against the tips of the blades. I felt them touch me back.

"Thank you," I said. "Thank you for feeding me."

The grass was silent.

"I have to leave you now, Love," I said. "I may never come back."

I got up and walked to the ship.

We were strapped down and lifting off in ten minutes. I had my endolin concentrate in the little gym bag that Mimi had brought the champagne in. My red computer was back on my stateroom desk, ready to continue with this memoir. My head was clear. I felt ready to move.

ꙮ Chapter 9

We orbited a couple of times and then I gave the order to slip into warp. I began formulating messages to Earth in my head as the universe outside the portholes began to wrinkle.

Warp travel is a weird business, and although the physics of it doesn't defy comprehension it does transfix it. Trying to picture it can glaze your eyes as speedily as three martinis on an empty stomach. It's a matter of pressuring your vehicle into a place where the effects of movement are grossly exaggerated. Seven-league boots. It's called "analogy travel" by some. When you're doing it there's a side effect that makes message-sending fast and easy; there's no speed-of-light limit because messages don't *travel* from or into spacewarp; they are, in a sense, already *there*.

From Belson there were the regular Einstein limits to contend with. I didn't even have a radio. It would take twenty-three years for an FM "I love you, Isabel" to have gotten to New York, and another twenty-three for a geriatric "Too late, Ben" to come back. Like impotence, only worse.

When we were settled into the warp and the sense of no-time

and loose space began to come down on us like the lull at the end of a party, Charlie asked me if I wanted to log the trip in chemical sleep.

"No, Charlie," I said. "Let's make this flight on coffee."

My first message was to Isabel's old address:

HONEY, I'VE BEEN A SON OF A BITCH. I'M SORRY. I LOVE YOU. WILL YOU MARRY ME?

                                                                    BEN

That felt good even though it had little hope of reaching her. Then I sent one to a friend in Chicago and told him to telephone Arnie my lawyer at his home:

TELL MEL DOLUM I WANT MY CITIZENSHIP BACK. I WANT HIM TO REPRESENT ME AND IF HE CAN'T I WANT HIM TO GET ME A LAWYER WHO CAN. TELL HIM TO CALL BELSON ENTER-PRISES IN PEKING AND HAVE THEM SEND INFORMATION ABOUT THE LAWS OF PIRACY AND HOW I CAN GET TO BE A CITIZEN AGAIN.

The messages were sent scrambled. I had left decoders with the friend in Chicago, with Isabel, and with my brokers, to keep messages private in case I wanted to transmit buy-and-sell orders or do business in general.

I sent a few more messages on the lines of the one to Arnie, trying to find out about my bank accounts and how long it would take to get the uranium unloading problem solved. After about twenty hours my first reply came:

MISS CRAWFORD NO LONGER AT THIS ADDRESS.

Well. What had I expected? I sent a message to Aaron, my accountant, telling him to try finding her for me.

Then I got a reply from Mel:

SORRY, BEN. I CAN'T HELP. THEY'LL DISBAR ME IF I ADVISE YOU.

I smashed my Spode coffee cup on the deck when I read that one.

And right away this came in:

THE ISABEL IS FORBIDDEN TO LAND AT THE ISLAMORADA SPACEPORT BECAUSE OF HAZARDOUS CONDITIONS. REPEAT: DO NOT LAND AT ISLAMORADA.

The sons of bitches. I added forty pounds to the spring tension of the Nautilus double shoulder machine, strapped myself in and heaved against a hundred-sixty-pound drag thirty times. Goddamn, I'm strong when I'm pissed. My muscles bulged beautifully. I felt ready for violence.

By the time we came out of the warp and could see Sol the size of a dollar in the ports from the bridge, I had received a greater accumulation of negative messages than Moses had on Sinai. All of my bank accounts were under court seizure. My apartment was sealed off and barricaded. There was a contingent of mounted police on round-the-clock vigil at Islamorada to arrest me if I landed there. Anna was suing for more alimony. My house in Georgia had been burned to the red clay under it by outraged conservationists. The U.S. Public Health Service and the Narcotics Bureau had warrants out for me as a dangerous drug addict. Isabel had gone to London in *Hamlet* in the company of the young actor who played Laertes. (I thought of trying to negotiate a Mafia hit on him when we got in orbit. It would have been a first.) *Hamlet* had closed in London; Isabel had left no address. My safe-deposit boxes, stock and bond certificates, and Aunt Myra's set of Haviland china were all under government seals. As far as my legal status was concerned, any thug could probably knife me on the streets and not be prosecuted. Belson Enterprises in Peking, Belson Ltd. in Montreal, and Belson and Co. in New York were all shut down and their directors strapped by court orders. My wood lots stood idle. My car had been sold. The Pierre couldn't take me.

"Let's go into an orbit," I said to Betty. "East to west." She bobbed her head down over the console and began punching figures in. "I want to make a few passes over New

York and Los Angeles while I decide where to set down.''

Don't ever trim your beard in free fall. While we were getting into orbit I grabbed a pair of scissors and tried it. It was like leveling a table by sawing the legs: I wound up with a lopsided effect, but stopped in time.

We circled at a hundred twenty miles up; it was nighttime in North America, and although there was little cloud cover it was shocking how few lights there were to see, compared with the photographs taken fifty years ago from the weapons carriers and spacelabs that used to coast around up there. You could barely make out New York, Chicago and Los Angeles; they looked like small towns. Well, they were on their way to *being* small towns.

I sat at one of the tables on the bridge puffing a cigar and watching a dark North America go by, saw the penumbra of dawn over the Pacific and then morning and then noon over Australia and South China. What a lovely blue ball that Earth is! You can't beat it for a place to live. Even with all those bastards down there trying to do me in.

After our fourth orbit I made my decision. ''Betty,'' I said, ''can you find Washington and bring us down there?''

She didn't look up from the console. ''Washington, D.C.?''

''Yes.''

''Certainly, Captain. On the White House lawn?''

''We don't want that kind of attention. How bad a hole would the *Isabel* make in a football field?''

''Pretty bad. More crater than hole.''

I thought about that for a minute. ''If there's anybody there—a night football game or something—can you change your mind and pull back up into orbit?''

She turned her rice-paper face up to me and said, ''Are you out of your *mind*, Captain?''

''I was afraid of that.'' I looked at my watch. August 23, a little past midnight. Well, there wouldn't be any ball games. ''Get out your Washington map and bring us down in Aynsley Field. How long will it take?''

''One hour twenty-three minutes after we leave orbit.''

She was very sharp. ''How many G's?''

''Twelve at maximum, for thirty seconds.''

"Okay," I said. "Let's do it after one more time around. I've got some things to pack."

"Yes sir, Captain."

Bill put Washington into the course console and brought a map of the city onto the screen. He turned lacquered knobs. The two coordinate lines appeared and jiggled a bit and then settled on a black rectangle not far from the Congressional Shelter Complex. Then he pushed a lever in slowly and the map expanded until the rectangles filled the screen and the outlines of Aynsley Field were recognizable. You could see the grid lines of the football field, and the end zones. He gripped a handle and a clear black dot appeared on the screen; he twisted the handle, pushed it forward and the dot found the center of the field. Then he threw the "Lock" switch and the dot locked itself in place. "All set, Betty," he said.

Betty threw a couple of switches and said, "We have our trajectory, Captain, and our atmosphere entry point."

I really loved all this. Like Ruth, I'd watched spaceship shows on TV as a kid. Even though the actual doing of it—determining a point to drop out of orbit and a trajectory to ride down on—was no more difficult than getting a manicure, there was *panache* to it. Especially with our bright-red Chinese equipment.

I flipped on the intercom. "This is the Captain. We'll drop out of orbit next time around, in about two hours. Tie everything down for twelve G's." Then I drew a breath. "I'll be the first person off the ship, and I'm going to run for it. You people are all still citizens and they won't give you too hard a time. I'm the one they want. I'll get you your salaries and bonuses as soon as I'm able. For God's sake don't tell anyone we've been to Aminidab. The important thing is to get the uranium out of here. We'll all be rich. I'll be in touch."

The endolin packets were still in Mimi's gym bag in my stateroom. The gym had a first-aid cabinet; I got a handful of big stretch-Synlon bandages out and, winding them around myself, managed to tape about eight pounds of concentrated endolin to my chest and two or three pounds to each arm. Enough for all the hangovers in Los Angeles. I left my legs free, for running.

Surprise was clearly the thing. They would be expecting me,

but they'd be expecting a middle-aged, potbellied billionaire like one of those Texas fatties. Hell, *past* middle age; I turned fifty-three the day before we landed.

They'd know I was there and they'd have a half hour to be ready. Their radar would have picked up the *Isabel* even before we entered our orbit, but they had no way of knowing where I'd try to set down. Once we left orbit, it would take about three minutes for them to get a fix on our trajectory and conclude I was coming down over Washington; that was the scary part for me, since Washington sure had the wherewithal to blow the *Isabel* out of the sky as if she were an ICBM hot from Aberdeen. That was unlikely, though, since they weren't dumb enough to think I'd attack the United States. What they would do, in the half hour they had after they'd figured we'd come down at Aynsley Field, would be to surround the ship with military police, wait for the landing area to cool, and arrest me. Then into the Chateau d'If with me, while Baynes and his cronies figured out what to do with my uranium.

Thinking all this out calmed my spirit immensely. With a few minutes left before touchdown, the G forces had leveled off. I got out of my landing seat, grabbed the scissors and finished trimming my beard, steady as a rock this time. By then the touchdown counter had started and a red light was blinking over the mirror in the head where I'd been doing this barbering. I set the scissors down, got back into my chair and belted myself in with about three seconds to spare before the *Isabel* burned herself into Aynsley's midfield. I could see nothing through the porthole; rippling heat from our retros crimped the outside air. Suddenly the shudder of the landing began to massage my spine like a demon chiropractor, yet the effect was soothing. I literally *felt* the *Isabel* burn her way twenty feet into topsoil and bedrock like a white-hot coin dropped onto butter. She trembled, gave a sigh, settled in, and came to rest back on the planet where she was made—where we were all made.

I undid my belt and lit a cigar. I looked out the stateroom window and son of a bitch if I didn't see a goalpost! Judging by the distance, Betty must have brought us down right on the fifty-yard line. What an encouraging thing for a first sight on Earth in nine months! What an emblem for my plans! Ben

Belson, broken-field runner. I bent over and retied my shoes. Outside, the ground was smoking; there were spotlights bearing down on us and smoke rose foggily into the beams.

The *Isabel* has two exit hatches. On Belson and Juno, where low gravity and a hard surface had made for less devastating setdowns, we could merely walk out the bottom one, and down a short stairway to the terrain. But for landings like this there was a hatchway thirty feet up, just off the mess hall. And the *Isabel*, being Chinese, had a special gimmick; I was counting on it to add to the surprise. I'd studied spaceships before buying this one and knew that a U.S. or Russian craft might have to wait eight hours for the ground to cool after Betty's hot-pilot landing, before anybody tried getting out and walking. But the *Isabel* had a foldout, magnesium-alloy footbridge that could arch its way over the hot circle of earth the engines had made; it could be sent out thirty feet away from the upper hatch. The only thing was I'd never tested it. On the blueprints it looked flimsy. And I'm no compact Chinese astronaut.

There was no time to sit agonizing about that one. I checked the tapes that held the endolin to my body, made sure I had my billfold, which held exactly forty dollars, some credit cards and a photograph. I patted the pocket of my plaid lumberjack shirt, my basic space-travel shirt; there were three cigars and a lighter. I checked my wristwatch; it was 2:43 A.M., Wednesday, August 23, 2064. I left my cabin, chugging with adrenalin, and scrambled up the ladder to the messroom. The hatchway was just past the dining table.

There was a porthole in the door about a foot across; I had to stoop to look out. There wasn't much to be seen: white vapor rising from the ground, and searchlights. Near the door-release handle was a switch that controlled the footbridge. I flipped its safety off, took a breath, and pulled it. A servo motor began whirring. I looked out the porthole again but could see nothing. The glass had steamed over. I waited, chomping my cigar and feeling my heart beat like a rubber mallet, until the whirring stopped. I grabbed the lug wheel in both hands and spun it. The hatchway lugs pulled in and there was a hiss as the Belson pressure inside the ship equalized with the 14.7 Earth pressure; I could feel warm Earth air rushing in to mingle. I heaved the hatchway open into the breeze; some papers on the table behind me rippled and swooshed to the deck. I looked out. Searchlights. Warm night air. *Earth!* I looked down. There was my narrow, shiny bridge, looking as if made of aluminum foil, as if the weight of a teddy bear would collapse it. Up ahead were lights, steam, the shadows of some kind of equipment. I stuck my head out and looked straight down, to one side of the bridge. Heat from molten ground hit my face. A siren was going somewhere in the distance. Right at the base of the ship was the rim of a serious crater; it actually glowed with a muted crimson. Black, acrid smoke was rising from it. It looked like Dante's hell and smelled like it too. I pulled my head back in the doorway, took a deep breath, and hit the bridge running. It swayed and bobbed sickeningly under my feet. I could hear it creak; a vision of myself being dropped into liquid stone pierced my mind like a spear. I ran on, trying to soften the pounding of my Adidas. Halfway across I looked up ahead. I could see the end of the bridge, swaying from side to side. The fucker had never lowered itself on the turf! It was about fifteen feet above the ground! For a moment I almost turned to go back aboard the *Isabel*, to wait till everything cooled. But if I did there would be at least four men with adamant-steel handcuffs to hold me till the warrants arrived. To hell with that. I did not want to continue my spiritual growth in a federal prison. I kept on going. At a distance I heard someone shouting, but I could see no one. Past the midmark on that Japanese Garden bridgeway my weight started pushing it down. It fell about three feet and stuck, jarring the teeth in my jaws and vibrating like a drumhead. I could feel heat from the walking surface penetrating the soles of my shoes; if I stood there long my feet would start cooking. Life gets that way at times. *The wise man profits from the hot foot.* I was thinking like a fortune cookie, but I'll stick by it still. I ran on to the end of the bridge, stopped, and began to jump up and down, shouting, "Goddamn you, you Chinese puzzle, you fucking aluminum chopstick! Get your ass *down.*" *Thump, thump!* It was like Anna taking off her girdle. That goddamned thing! And hot as blazes by now too. The sirens got louder. The bridge dropped another couple of feet and stuck again. I saw two men in uniform suddenly emerge from the shadows below me, looking up puzzled. A searchlight fanned across my chest and face. What the hell. I jumped.

I landed on what must have been Astroturf, fell forward, and rolled. No pain. The surface felt springy, a little like Belson grass. I sat for a moment and shook my addled brains clear. In front of me was a goalpost! I had landed in the end zone! Six points. From my right two men were approaching me. They were about ten feet away. Cops. But no guns—or none in sight. They seemed a bit dumbfounded. I stood up, looked quickly around. Lots of bleachers. To one side were a couple of trucks, one of which had headlights pointing toward me. Clearly the Army, since only the Army had trucks. Some women with rifles stood by them. Near them were men in business suits. No one was moving in my direction. They were all just watching the show.

The cops walked up, a little more composed by now. One of them came very close to me and put his face in mine. I suddenly realized I was still smoking my cigar, had held it in my teeth through the whole jump, tumble and roll act. "Are you Mr. Belson?" he said, just a shade impolitely.

I'd never hit anyone before in my life. What I did was just extend my right arm the way you do in the Nautilus pectoral machine; in the back of my head was the memory that I'd increased the drag in that machine to a hundred eighty pounds the Thursday before. I caught him in the neck with my forearm and he fell like a stone. Jesus Christ, I'd no idea it was so easy!

The other cop seemed undissuaded by this display of muscle, or he was too confused by it all to react properly. Maybe he had lost heart when he looked up to see me jumping up and down, with my lumberjack shirtsleeves rolled up and a cigar in my mouth, on the end of that flimsy Chinese cantilever. Strong men could quail at such a sight. Anyway, he was not forewarned by his partner's sudden drop and I punched him out with a right cross to the jaw. Then I took off running. I doubled back past the *Isabel*'s crater, looked around and saw an open place in the grandstand facing the fifty-yard line. There were no people or vehicles that I could see in that direction. I poured it on and ran that way, through a gate that, *mirabile dictu*, was open, and out onto a sidewalk. I looked up and down an avenue; it was deserted. Down the street was the Washington Monument, big and clean in the moonlight. I ran that way. Back at the stadium I heard trucks moving up, and people shouting. I ran on, took a left at the bottom of the street and a right at the end of the next one, to confuse the trail. I really stretched my legs. I ran like a night wind down those dark Washington streets, past the shells of old slum houses and then down the Mall, where I ran even more gaily on grass. If you could sing while running, with your chest at the bursting, I would have sung a hallelujah chorus of my own devising. Goddamn, it was good to be home!

⚜ Chapter 10

There was a chance Baynes was back at the stadium, but I didn't think it likely. If I was right he'd be at home and in touch with them by phone. It was his house I was headed for.

I stopped running at the far end of New Mall, across the street from the Mendoza Monument, and sat on the grass for a while to get my breath. It was a warm night; the ground was faintly damp and had that good Earth-grass smell. This grass was not going to say it loved me or feed me, but right now silence was all I wanted. The monument was lit and I lay on my elbow in the quiet for a while panting heavily and contemplated the heroic bronze of Guadelupe Mendoza, the first woman Chief Justice and one of my favorite people in history. When I was a kid I saved bubble-gum cards with her picture; I had always liked her motherly ways and her liberal decisions.

Baynes's house was three blocks from Lupe, a fairly modest mansion—considering its owner's wealth and power—at the eastern edge of the Congressional Compound. I was wary of guards, but there was no need to be; none were around. The place was lit up with the kind of candlepower only a senator could command; even the pair of metal deer on the front lawn had a spotlight.

I considered climbing through a bedroom window but rejected the idea. I hadn't been reborn on Belson to get shot as a burglar. So I walked up the brickwork path and climbed the stairs to the broad porch. I knocked loudly on the door and then checked my watch. It was two-thirty. I knocked again.

The door opened and a young man was standing there blinking at me. I recognized him from a visit I'd paid Baynes a few years before. I gave him my steely, no-nonsense look. "Good evening," I said. "I'm Ben Belson and I'm here to see the Senator." I paused a second and then pushed past him into the enormous living room. On the floor at one end of the room a couple of small black boys wearing pajamas were playing with a modern rarity, an electric train. At the other end, half lying on a Chesterfield sofa, was a thin, elderly black man. He was smiling warmly at me. "Son of a bitch!" he said with a grin. He rose sleepily to his feet, jammed his hands into his bathrobe pockets, and looked at me as friendly as you please. "If it isn't Benjamin Belson!" he said.

"Hello, L'Ouverture," I said, not smiling. I have to admit that he's a charming bastard. And nobody is going to outpoise him.

"They called me a few hours ago, Ben, when they found your ship on the radar." He gestured toward the children and yawned. "Woke up my grandchildren too."

There was a blue viddiphone on the table by the sofa. Just then it began to hum. "L'Ouverture," I said. "Turn the video off and don't tell them I'm here. It'll be in your interest."

He nodded, flicked off the camera switch and answered the phone. After a moment he said, explosively, "Ran away? How is it that thirty MPs can't catch a running billionaire?" He smiled at me, and listened for a bit. Finally he said, "Well, he won't get far. I'm going to bed. And for heaven's sake don't shoot him." He hung up the phone.

"Thanks," I said.

He smiled. "Nothing to thank me for, Ben. I'm curious to know why you came here."

"Sure," I said. "How about some coffee first?"

"Get us some coffee, Morton," he said, "and something light to eat. Melba toast."

Morton left for the kitchen and I looked around me for a moment. It was a homey place, sort of shabby-genteel, with beige corduroy-covered sofas and unmatching overstuffed armchairs. There were a couple of acrylic landscapes on the walls. Baynes was as rich as Croesus, but he lived like a college president. People said he had more opulent digs tucked away in the sun, that he didn't want to put on a show in Washington. Maybe that was it. But I've known other rich people who won't spend serious money on themselves, and I distrust them.

I seated myself in one of the overstuffed chairs and leaned back. I hadn't realized until then how tired I was. Baynes remained standing, stretching now as if trying to wake up. He'd probably spent the evening berating his captive Energy Committee, gone to bed late and then was wakened by being told I was on my way to Washington. Would he have had cops sent to his home? I didn't think so; he had no way of knowing I was coming.

"L'Ouverture," I said, "what in heaven's name made you do me that way? Taking away my *citizenship*. Why do a thing like that?"

"Nobody's trying to hurt you, Ben," he said. "And you're a rich man. You have friends."

I just stared at him. Such a cool son of a bitch. L'Ouverture is very good-looking. He is cheap about his household furnishings and I can't remember his ever picking up a check in a restaurant, but he dresses gorgeously. He looked like an expensive whiskey advertisement in that bathrobe with the monogram over the pocket. The kids in the corner kept buzzing their little green train around its track; through silvery draperies I could see the ghosts of L'Ouverture's lawn deer in frozen grazing; two miles away the *Isabel* was sitting, packed with uranium, waiting for the ground to cool. And here I was in this dumpy living room talking to this elegant man like an angry son just back from college. Somewhere in that sky out there, down south in Pisces Austrinus, shone Fomalhaut, no bigger than a bright pinhead. And Belson? Obsidian Belson, my heart's quiet home? Too small to see from here. Too small and far away. I looked back to L'Ouverture.

Baynes was born in the twentieth century and is a fine grandfatherly figure of a man. Tall, purplish-black and shiny. In his seventies. He must be six feet six—nearly as tall as his celebrated father, one of the finest basketball players who ever lived.

I'm tall enough to be unused to looking *up* at the person I'm talking to. Napoleon claimed that being short was an advantage; it made others feel awkward to bend down to him. But I didn't feel that way with Baynes. A part of me was like a kid with him and I didn't like it. "Being a pirate has style," I said. "It goes with my beard. But I resent the rest of it. And think of the money the government will lose on taxes alone if I don't get my uranium to work."

Baynes seated himself on the sofa and leaned forward, elbows on knees and chin on those big fists of his. It made our heads at the same level. "The Committee discussed that, Benjamin. The loss in revenue will be considerable."

There was a clatter behind me as the toy train derailed. "Motherfucker!" squeaked one of the kids. Neither of them seemed to be more than five years old.

Baynes spoke sharply. "You ought to say 'Goodness!' when a thing like that happens."

"*You* don't," said the kid, matter-of-factly, and set the engine back on its track.

Baynes shrugged and spoke to me. "You went off to wherever it was you went in violation of the law. An act of Congress forbids space travel as wasteful of energy. You attempted to import a dangerous extraterrestrial substance . . ."

"Come on, L'Ouverture," I said. "Why in hell did you throw the book at me? Are you afraid I'll ruin you in the wood business?" I pulled a cigar from my shirt pocket and started getting it ready to light. "Are you still mad at me for bankrupting Exxon?" I'd bought what was left of some energy corporations a few years back, put them into receivership, and made a fortune on the tax losses. Baynes had put his money on the other side and lost.

He laughed pleasantly. "Not at all. Revenge is a waste of time. The Committee just can't let you have a monopoly. There's a delicate balance of energy use in the United States,

Benjamin. We won't have any one person disrupting it . . ."

"Goddamn it!" I said. "That 'delicate balance' means the military gets the oil, the Mafia gets most of the coal, and people like you and me get rich off the leftover coal and wood. It means that what little uranium there is is being saved for bombs. People are *freezing* out there and it may get worse. What if the temperature drops again next winter?" I puffed my cigar furiously for a moment, staring into Baynes's grandfatherly look, into his pose of bemused patience. "You charlatans in Congress have campaigned on the word 'crisis' for so long you think it's only meaningful in TV spots."

"Your concern for the ordinary citizen is touching."

"Oh, come off it!" I said. "That uranium out there is a gift from the heavens. Everybody can profit from it. It'll run the elevators in New York and heat houses in Omaha, enrich the U. S. Treasury and give me a lot of money. What in hell's wrong with that, L'Ouverture?"

"You make it sound idyllic," Baynes said. "A TV spot in its own right. You're ignoring some things, Benjamin, in your polemic. There is currently a forty percent *surplus* of wood in the country. Talk of an ice age is premature. There is enough coal in Wyoming alone to run all the elevators in the world, continuously, until the good Lord sees fit to blink this planet back into chaos. The U.S. has tidal engines, windmills and solar plants. And uranium has a bad reputation. Very bad. Consider what the conservationists did to your country home in Georgia."

"Nonsense!" I said. "The conservationists are being paid by the Mafia; everybody knows that. Uranium's unsafe, but so is coal. Look at the Chinese. They run their whole industrial plant on U235. The U.S. was trying to find safe uranium in space, just like me, back when I was a kid. You can't have elevators and fast cars on solar power, L'Ouverture."

"*Benjamin*," he said, in his gravelly, soothing way. "Benjamin, who needs cars? They had all that in the twentieth century, and all they did was kill and maim one another on the highways."

"In the twenty-first century they stay home and watch TV," I said, "and freeze in winter. There's a price for everything. The Chinese have big bank accounts and their cuisine's deteriorated; you can't buy a Peking duck in Peking. Soyaburgers and fries. They have to come to New York to spend all that money. What kind of civilization is that?"

"The Chinese are known the world over for the quality of their family life."

"Hogwash, L'Ouverture. They watch TV together and send their kids to business colleges. There's more revolutionary zeal in Aberdeen than in all of China." I thought of Isabel, of her sad capitalist love for communism. We should join the Communist Party together and start a revolution somewhere. I'd finance it and she'd write the slogans.

Just then Morton came back in the room with a tray. "Let's have our coffee now," Baynes said. He nodded toward a permoplastic table by the marble fireplace and Morton set the tray there. "Why don't you put the children back to bed, Morton?"

"Shit!" one of the kids said, *sotto voce*.

"Go to *bed*," Baynes said wearily. That seemed to work, and they followed Morton upstairs like lambs. Baynes turned his attention back to me. He was still smiling but clearly tired. It was about four in the morning. "I don't really care about the Chinese," he said. "They're admirable in their way, but East is East . . ."

I leaned forward. It was time to make my pitch. I could feel the intensity in my voice. "L'Ouverture," I said, "there's more safe uranium where that came from." I gestured toward the general direction of Aynsley Field. "A billion tons of it. We can beat those Chinese hustlers at their own game. We can be the richest nation on Earth again, L'Ouverture." I leaned back and chewed my cigar a minute. "And this time we're mellower. We'll do it right. We won't kill ourselves in our cars anymore. No more big horsepower. We won't bully the little countries." I paused a moment, overwhelmed myself by what I was going to say. "We can build a great civilization, L'Ouverture, a great, humane, and beautiful civilization. We can be an electronic Byzantium, a holy city. We can be the Age of Pericles and light up the world. Think of the *talent* in this country! Think of the architecture we can build with cheap power!"

I sat back, moved by my own words. I really believed it.

America is a magnificent, fertile place, and in decline it has lost much of its grossness. What a comeback we could have, with all that power from Juno!

Baynes walked over to the table. "The coffee is ready," he said coolly.

I stared at him, miffed at his ignorning my rhetoric. "Come *on*," I said. "Where's your patriotism, for Christ's sake?"

He began pouring the coffee with a steady hand. "My daddy used to say to me at Fourth of July parades in Louisville, 'Whitey talks pretty, but listen to him closely.' "

I stared at him and almost screamed, *Bullshit*. But I didn't. I remembered the black guys in prison. The U.S. has had two black presidents and a dozen black justices in the Supreme Court; a third of Congress is black—mostly women. But the black prisoners at Leavenworth still had to fight to get shoes that fit, had to pay bigger bribes to get the easy jobs in the prison factory. I shrugged and seated myself at the coffee table.

"Your father made ten times the money my father made," I said.

His face became arctic, just for a second. "What in hell was your father good for?"

There was one final ploy to try, a pretty drastic one, to give myself some operating room. I must at all costs get time and money and stay out of jail. The months on Belson, self-willed though they were, were jail enough. I needed action.

Wouldn't you know the coffee cups were plastic? Here was a man who could afford anything and he used coffee cups like these. I took a deep breath, tried to dismiss things like that from my mind, and said, "L'Ouverture, I'll give you half my share of that uranium outright if you'll get me back my citizenship and my money and drop those charges."

He took a sip of his coffee. "A bribe?"

"What else?" I said. "Draw up papers and I'll sign them around noon, right after I get back my citizenship and the courts cancel that mumbo-jumbo."

He went on sipping his coffee in silence. I leaned back in the little plastic chair by the mantelpiece, feeling at last relaxed. L'Ouverture looked thoughtful and grandfatherly. I felt a part of me yielding to his spell and I didn't mind, now that I'd played my cards. I knew Baynes: he would rather make a quiet deal like this than fool around. I looked at his contemplative, intelligent old face; this was turning out to be a pleasant welcome home. It was as good in its way as finding Isabel would have been. Maybe better, because with Baynes I wouldn't be breaking crockery or screaming at cats. Yet I knew well enough that he could be an authentic blacksnake and a threat to life and limb. *He who sups with the devil must eat with a long spoon.* Oh yes. This man could have me clapped in irons. Still, I let myself love him a bit, dangerously, for his charm. Christ, do I ever want a father! And at my age! What a charming old son of a bitch, with his shiny black head and yellowing teeth and steady hands—so manicured, so well manicured. I wanted to lean across the table and hug him.

He was looking at me. "Have some coffee, Ben," he said.

That reminded me of where I was. I took a sip of the coffee and almost spit it out. Instant coffee. Garbage! What kind of a father was he anyway? Somewhere in his soul was the demon that had dominated my real father: Low Rent. If Western Civilization dies it will drown in instant coffee, processed cheese and TV specials. Men and women in America have been born, lived, and gone to quickly dug graves without ever tasting real coffee, a real hamburger, or a real glass of lemonade. What right did this billionaire, the sharpest man in the Senate, have to drink powdered coffee out of plastic cups? Genghis Khan would have known better.

"L'Ouverture," I said, even though I could go to jail for it, "you should make your coffee with a Chemex. And I need fifty thousand in cash. I mean right away."

"Benjamin," he said, a bit sternly, "I *like* instant coffee. I embrace the modern world and live happily in it. The nineteenth and twentieth centuries do not interest me. Instant coffee is the drink of the times and I drink it with pleasure. I don't keep cash around."

"That's a pity," I said, and tried the coffee again. I needed the caffeine.

L'Ouverture shrugged, still smiling, and spoke in his honeyed old voice, "Snobbery is a waste of energy. The past is dead, Ben. Your father was an historian; mine was a basketball player. Father adapted the crane dance of his ancestors to var-

nished oak floors and sent me to Harvard, where I learned to
prosper even as he had. He hated sports, hated the Olympics,
hated abstractions. Sometimes he slept with a basketball
beside him. I too delight in the real, the contemporary.''

It was seductive, but I knew Baynes too well to believe it.
You're a power jack-off, I wanted to shout, *and the past is
alive! Solipsist!* The son of a bitch probably counted the votes
of his Energy Committee with a hard on. ''Look,'' I said, ''I'd
like to go to a bank in the morning and get some cash. When
can you have my accounts released?''

He smiled benignly. ''Just have an extra croissant for
breakfast, Benjamin, and go to your bank at ten. I'll have
Justice Flaherty call in a reversal. Where did you bring the
uranium from? Fomalhaut?''

Jesus Christ! I thought, *How does he know?* It wasn't
Fomalhaut, thank God; it was Aminidab. Juno. But how did
he know about *Fomalhaut?* From that geologist in Jamaica?
Anyway, I didn't fall for it. ''Come on, L'Ouverture,'' I said.
''That's not the deal.''

He shrugged and set his coffee cup down with an air of
finality. ''If you won't tell me where the uranium comes from,
there is no deal. I'm going to get some sleep.'' He turned his
face toward a doorway and called out, ''All right out there.''

At first I thought he was hailing Morton, but I realized that
was unlikely just as two men in brown suits came in the doorway, each holding a pair of handcuffs. The chair I was sitting
on was low, in a sort of semi-Japanese way, and when I tried
to jump to my feet I knocked over the table. L'Ouverture got
out of the way just in time and I didn't even get the pleasure of
splashing him with hot coffee. They had me by the time I'd
recovered my balance and was, ignominiously, in a semi-
crouch like a small boy with a stubbed toe. The cuffs were of
steel; I had one wrist cuffed to a wrist of each of those
bastards in what seemed to be a single motion. They pulled me
upright from my crouch. Private cops, probably. Cheap ones
too.

One of them began to recite, ''You have the right to remain
silent . . .''

Baynes interrupted him. ''No need,'' he said. ''Mr. Belson
has no rights. He is not a citizen.''

"You son of a bitch," I said.

"Take him to the Reagan Detention Center and book him for illegal entry."

My stomach sank. From rebirth to the Reagan Stir. I checked the two out. Poker-faced. But one of them, the fatter, seemed under his stern patriot look to be troubled by something. "Okay," I said, "let's get out of here." And then to L'Ouverture, who was still smiling amiably, who had almost certainly never stopped smiling, "You are one deceitful son of a bitch."

He went on smiling. "Have a good day," he said.

✦ Chapter 11

The Reagan Stir is way out past Arlington Cemetery, and a long haul. The cops ushered me out the door of Baynes's house and down the block to where they had a little methane-powered Honda with D.C. plates. Twenty miles per hour, maximum. We all squeezed together in the front seat, which forced me to put my knees under my chin. But I didn't feel as uncomfortable as the fat guy looked, sitting on my right with one arm and half his head out the window. We chugged along under the moonlight for about ten minutes, until we were approaching a woodshop, clearly an all-night one, at the corner of Constitution Avenue and D Street.

The fat guy with some effort pulled his head back in the car and I felt his soft belly mash against my side. The thinner one was driving with his left hand, his right being cuffed to my wrist. I really didn't like this kind of physical intimacy one bit and I'd been repeating my mantra for the last two or three minutes. "Billy Bob," the fat one said, "pull over at that store. I gotta use the restroom."

"Can't you *wait?*" Billy Bob said, sounding a whole lot like my mother.

"Hell, no," the fat one said. "I've been waiting back at that house for an hour and a half."

"*Shit*," Billy Bob said. I figured he was going to stop but, like mothers everywhere, was going to exact payment for it. "You might have used the toilet back there."

"Billy Bob," Fatty said, "pull over."

Billy Bob drove up to the woodshop and parked. It took us a minute to get out the same door that we had all gotten in. I felt God had sent me this opportunity. I'd bet a million that whatever cops were at the stadium hadn't told Baynes on the phone that I'd decked two of their number. As far as Fatty and Billy Bob were concerned, I was just an aging tycoon.

There was an old Chinese woman at the cash register inside who looked as if she had seen all there was to see and had built no small part of the Great Wall with her own rough hands. When the three of us came in as a conjoined trio, as it were, she was reading a comic book. She looked up, laid her cigarette on the edge of an overflowing ashtray, and waited.

"I need to use the restroom," Fatty said, clearly ill at ease.

She nodded toward the far wall. A faded print of Mao surrounded by awed children hung there, and under it on a small hook a key.

There was no room for the three of us to walk abreast, but we managed to make it single file with a little shoving around and Fatty got his key. Getting back out the door was a bit confusing, but we made it. The shop was clearly an ancient gas station, with the restroom in back.

"Why don't you piss against a tree, for Christ's sake?" Billy Bob said.

"If I only needed to piss I'd a done it a quarter hour ago." I was surprised at the uncowed quality in Fatty's voice. He had apparently developed a sense of mission over this middle-of-the-night B.M. and he was riding it. Well, I was developing a sense of mission too, although not a cloacal one.

"How in hell you going to stay handcuffed and do that?" Billy Bob said.

"Let's look it over," Fatty said.

In back was a room with MEN on its door. Fatty unlocked it

easily enough and flipped on a little ten-watt light inside. What a grubby-looking place, with wet newspaper on the cracked linoleum floor! And what a smell! The Chinese have one of the most admirable cultural histories in the world. Their cuisine—where it still exists—is right up there with the French. Hell, they make a fine spaceship. But they're in the Middle Ages when it comes to toilets.

As a partner in this venture, so to speak, I could see right away that it was going to be a problem for Fatty. Had I been he, I would have found a dark lawn somewhere, dropped my pants and made the best of it. But either that hadn't occurred to Fatty and Billy Bob, or it was far beyond Fatty's sense of propriety.

The room wasn't big enough for the three of us. The toilet faced the doorway. Fatty tried to cool it. He walked in, dragging me by my wrist halfway into the door, which opened outward. He turned around facing me and began to loosen his belt with his free hand, while getting himself into kind of a crouch. For a moment I panicked; if I had to watch this I would rather do a month in solitary.

But as I had hoped, Fatty suddenly gave up. "Look, Billy Bob," he said, nodding toward the handcuff that joined us, "undo this thing for a minute."

Billy Bob looked doubtful. "What in hell . . .?" he said.

"Come *on!*" Fatty said, in desperation. "He ain't going nowhere with you attached."

"Okay," Billy Bob said. He got the little magnetic key out of his pants pocket, walked in front of me and undid the cuff from Fatty's wrist, letting it dangle from mine. Then he stepped back out the door and I followed him for a step, so that I was now all the way outside.

"Close the door," Fatty said. He was standing in the doorway. I had already seen there was no bolt latch on the inside. Only a knob.

"Sure," I said, casually. I took the knob firmly in my now free right hand, felt the steel heft of the door, and slammed it powerfully right into Fatty's face. The door clicked shut and I could hear a thud. The strength in my pectorals felt like a triphammer. Then I jerked my left arm toward me with everything I had and Billy Bob's head shot past my face and

into the door. I smashed into the back of his head with my
closed fist and felt him go slack. Then I turned the bolt on the
men's room door. It clicked into place beautifully.

Billy Bob was out cold with his face bloody enough that I
could see the mess even by moonlight. I had no pity for him
just then; he had chosen a violent profession for himself and
should have been more alert. I bent down and examined his
left hand for the key. It wasn't there. I'd been afraid of that.
He'd probably dropped it when I'd jerked him. I began looking around the grass as well as I could by moonlight. No luck.
I dragged him over a few feet and looked where he'd been
standing after he'd unlocked Fatty. Still no luck. It was just
too *dark*. From inside the restroom came Fatty's voice now,
shouting, "Get me out of here!" He began banging on the
door.

I was getting worried. I had just about made up my mind to
pick up Billy Bob and carry him back to the car with me when
a small miracle occurred: a light over the men's room came
on. I looked back toward the front of the building and, sure
enough, Chinese Mama stood there, with her cigarette and
comic book in one hand and her other on a light switch. She
must have heard the commotion.

"Thank you, ma'am," I said politely and began searching
the grass with my eyes. And there it was, about a foot the
other side of where Billy Bob had been standing when I'd
decked him. I dragged him a bit farther, stretched out and
got it. I was astonished at how steady my hand was when I unlocked us.

I looked back at Mama. Inscrutable, unperturbed. Billy
Bob and I could have been discussing the weather. And the
louder Fatty shouted and banged the door the calmer she
looked, a genuine flower of heavenly repose all by herself. I
could have kissed her. I checked out Billy Bob and figured
he'd be all right in a few minutes, since his neck wasn't twisted
in any serious way. The poor son of a bitch.

I started walking toward the front of the store, where I'd
seen a cigar-and-candy rack. When I came up to Mama I said,
"What's your name, ma'am?"

She took a puff from her cigarette. "Arabella Kim," she
said. "Are you Captain Belson from outer space?"

I grinned at her. "Oh yes." And then, "I'd like to buy some cigars." I gave her my whole forty dollars for ten cigars—cheap two-dollar ones, but what the hell—and six Mars bars. Mars seemed appropriate for a space pirate. "Keep the change," I told her, "and I'd be obliged if you didn't help these two for a few minutes." I was still out of breath a bit and my voice was husky.

"Many people are on your side, Captain Belson," she said. "People write letters to the Washington *Post* and say we should have your uranium. I think so."

"Why, bless your heart," I said, stuffing the cigars in my shirt pockets and the candy bars in my pants. There was no telephone at the store. I went over to Billy Bob's car, lifted the hood, took out the distributor, and threw it into some bushes.

Then I stood there in the moonlight for a minute and a power realization dawned on me: I was flat broke. Here I was reborn into the world after nine months in the sky, and I had come back to be indeed naked and helpless. I took a deep breath of the night air and felt my heart speed up with it and the small hairs at the back of my neck tingle.

I had to begin somewhere. I turned and walked back into the shop and said, "Arabella, I need some cash."

She just looked at me imperturbably. "How much?"

"I'll sell you my watch for five hundred dollars," I said. It had cost me eight thousand.

"One needs a watch," she said. "I'll see what I can do."

She got up from her chair, went to a closed door at the back of the little shop, and opened it. I peered in. There was a small room filled with tobacco smoke, with Chinese revolutionary posters on the wall, some of them in tatters. At the back of the room was a cot with a wrinkled red coverlet on it and a tiny, wizened Chinese man lying on it reading *Sports Illustrated*. Probably Mr. Kim. She spoke to him in Chinese in a no-nonsense kind of way. He mumbled something that sounded surly but got off the cot meekly enough. She reached under the mattress and pulled out a little red plastic purse, opened it and took out six hundred-dollar coins. She handed them to me, smiled faintly, and said, "Keep your watch and pay me back when you sell the uranium."

I glanced out the window to where the stacks of cordwood

lay piled and said, "That uranium will put you out of business, you know."

"It's a dull business," she said.

I nodded and put the coins in my pocket. "You're a good woman, Arabella," I said. Then I left the shop and took off toward Union Station.

I got about five minutes of exultation out of overcoming my arrest before I remembered that remark L'Ouverture had made about snobbery. The son of a bitch had a way of getting under my skin. In a sense I am a snob about good food, good china and good theater. I like Shakespeare immensely, as a matter of fact, now that I'm not trying to win points with Isabel. Bless her heart, she never knew the competition she entered when she took me on as a lover! But I like the good things of the modern world too. I thought of my running shoes. I'd bought them at a place on Forty-sixth Street a few weeks before the *Isabel* took off. You put your feet in a pretty little device called a Contour Reader, and the son of a bitch makes you a pair of Adidas right there. I mean right on your *feet*. It's weird to watch but it feels good to have the warm polymers and rubber molded to your personal arches and to the ball and the heel and then up over the great toe. Like a Japanese massage. The machine even puts laces in, a sight more interesting to watch than most contemporary movies. And Jesus, do I love those gym shoes! Sky blue and made by electronic wizardry right before my eyes, between Madison and Fifth. Five hundred dollars. Eighty more if monogrammed. Mine have a white "B.B." where the rubber disk used to be on a pair of Converse.

But I was pissed at L'Ouverture. Maybe because he'd pulled racism on me. I pounded along the predawn pavements, through silent suburbs and then along the "Ghost town" where all the poor blacks who did the paperwork for the U.S. Government used to live. Empty high-rise housing glowing dully by moonlight, emptier and spookier than Belson. I felt lucky to have been born in rural Ohio; those places, filled with the smells and sighs of government clerks and their dazed families, back when I was sleeping with Juno, were authentic anger factories. They used to defecate in the elevators in places like that, and do casual rapes on the staircases. No proper life for man at all.

Still, I'd picked up a lot of anger myself in my own loveless home. Anger and hunger—I could hardly tell them apart. *Slap, slap* went my shoes, the products of electronic sorcery and of my unique, large feet. *Whump, whump* went my substantial, furious heart; I could feel my quadriceps bulging against my jeans.

I began to think about railroad schedules. One thing about being a coal and wood tycoon: you learn when the trains run. A half-empty freight would be leaving Washington for New York at 5:15 A.M., and it was usually on time. I looked at my watch. I had twenty minutes.

Sometimes I think God sent me to Belson and Juno. Twenty years of space exploration by three countries had yielded nothing worth having. I, a rank amateur, had found two paradises with hardly any effort. One was a genuine Eden with food and trees and pleasant air; the other its reverse, made for the likes of St. Simeon Stylites, Origen, Cotton Mather and me. Oh, the varieties of religious experience! I had five minutes to find myself a comfortable freight car and get aboard.

The station, being electronic, had nobody around. The train was there when I arrived; it hissed a bit, made those endearing heavy clangs that trains make, and looked energetic. I found a big open car with BELSON MINES clearly stenciled on it—one of my very own. I climbed up the ladder at the side, slipped over, and let myself down. There was some coal dust at the bottom and nothing else. No way to see outside. But what the hell.

I was still panting from the run and had a godawful stitch in my side. My left wrist was painfully swollen from the handcuff when I'd jerked Billy Bob. My feet hurt like hell. Suddenly I remembered that I was a human bomb of endolin! There was no need to feel pain. I got one of the plastic packs from around my left arm, took a pinch, swallowed it with a bite of a Mars bar, and in a few minutes I felt terrific. So much for pain.

After the train got started, with more noise and vibration than the *Isabel* made landing on Belson, I slept for about an hour. When I awoke the sky was beginning to lighten overhead. I climbed up the ladder and was able to perch somewhat uncomfortably on the side of the slow-moving car and watch the sun coming up over misty fields. Now that I had something to compare our Earth with, I enjoyed it even more. Only one sun and one moon and no rings either, but a beautiful planet and one to treasure. Where else would you find a Canyon de Chelly or a Pacific Ocean, a Florida Keys or an India? My heart leaped to see that sweet green of summer grass on Earth, and maple trees in leaf, cattle out in fields, and birds everywhere, determined busybodies in the morning air!

The train had a forty-minute stop in Philadelphia, at a power plant. There were a couple of railroad people there to refuel the engine and oversee the unloading of some coal, but I was able to get out for a break without their noticing me. I left the terminal and did a few simple exercises. My body was stiff and sore and I added a bit of endolin to my Mars bar breakfast. There was a water fountain outside the station—my first Earth water in nine months. The sun was well up, and warm on my face.

I found myself in a shabby part of Philadelphia—one of those "Big House Slums" you read about. Population falls so fast these days that there is ample space for the poor in solar-house suburbs and town houses in the cities. The problem is they can't heat the places in the wintertime and the solars don't work, and the houses were so cheaply made in the first place that they were now, there among the pacified hills of a former suburb, a tatterdemalion aggregate of fallen plastic shingles, ruined lawns, cracked glass roofs and vine-clotted breezeways. It beats sleeping in doorways, but it's a depressing sight.

I found an open drugstore and bought a six-pack of club soda, some beef jerky, a box of cookies and a pack of brown hair dye. Sixty dollars and change. As I was starting to leave the store I saw a pile of *Enquirers*, and sure enough, there I was on the front page. But without the beard, thank God. No one had taken a picture of me with the beard. And in the picture I looked rather well-groomed and serious. The headline read BILLIONAIRE OUTLAW FOILS COPS. I gave the man at the counter his two dollars for the paper. He didn't even look at me. I left, reading.

It was comic in its way. I was called a "berserk eccentric" and a "financial maverick." I especially liked "berserk eccentric," which suited my mood: John the Baptist still slept in me.

Back in my coal car I proceeded to dye my hair, using a couple of the cans of club soda and wishing I had bought a mirror at that drugstore. What I did was pour half the liquid dye into the plastic can of soda, shake it up, and then work it into my hair and beard with my fingertips. I left it there for twenty minutes, while the train chugged its way across the border into New Jersey, and then rinsed it off with another canful. I'd have given a hundred dollars for a pocket mirror. I'd dyed a spot the size of a five-dollar piece on my left forearm, where it was at its hairiest, and I used that for a kind of control; when I rinsed it off after twenty minutes there was a patch of convincing-looking brown on my arm. I hoped that on my head and beard the results were as good.

The day was uneventful and warm. I lay around in the bottom of the car like Huckleberry Finn on his raft, or rode up on the side and watched the countryside go by and ate my beef jerky and Mars bars and drank the four other cans of club soda and had a pretty good time of it. It seemed more of a real journey than traveling halfway across the Milky Way had been.

Close to dusk, the train gave me my first view of the Manhattan skyline. It was breathtaking, as it always is to me. Yet I could have wept to know that the upper floors of all the tall buildings were vacant. It is saddening to see the city at such times and know that it was once a powerhouse and isn't anymore, although those tall old buildings still stand there quiet and aloof from the streets below them. I'm crazy about the *idea* of New York. It's one of the great inventions of the human spirit, like the fugue or the Pythagorean Theorem or the airplane—the apotheosis of the *polis* and still to me the world's greatest city.

We came into Manhattan through the old Pennsylvania

Railroad tunnel and climbed back aboveground at Thirty-fourth and Seventh Avenue, at the Coal Dock. What a dusty, smelly place to see New York from! Almost all the fuel for the entire city came in at that point, and there were heaps of coal the size of small mountains, with the dust from them penetrating the air everywhere; I felt I could get black lung in ten minutes.

There used to be a department store—Macy's, I think—on Thirty-fourth Street; the old building was now used for coal storage. My train stopped there and I was able to climb down from the car unobserved. There were a lot of guards around, but they were there to keep coal thieves out; I merely nodded and walked past them. It was a quarter to eight and there was still some light in the sky. I found Fifth Avenue and headed uptown. A good many people were on the street but nobody paid attention to me. I felt fine—loose and easy in the body and pleasantly tight in the stomach. It was something like my first trip to the city that time I'd come to stay with Aunt Myra; I was an anonymous and rootless tourist, starting a new life, on my own in the world's best place to be on your own.

There was a mirror in the window of a videosphere store at Thirty-ninth Street, and I stopped to see myself at full length. I looked like hell—like a raunchy and fragrant derelict-rapist. The dyed hair and beard were a shock, as was the coal dust smeared on my face. I was something to scare children with. One elbow of my shirt was ripped open; my pants were baggy and filthy with coal and soot; there was a stain from hair dye on my shirt collar; and the dye on my beard and hair was uneven, with dark and light clumps sticking out crazily. I could have slept on park benches for the next twenty years and nobody would have noticed me.

When I was a teenager a fine old skyscraper sat at Forty-second Street between Lexington and Third. It was Aunt Myra's favorite piece of hopeful architecture and she was the first person to name it to me: the Chrysler Building. They tore it down a few years after the elevators were stopped by the legislature in Albany. Elevators have counterweights and the whole thing wasn't really necessary, but Albany wanted to show the world it was energy conscious. Its decree changed

New York in a horrifying way, making the upper floors of all those unconscionably tall buildings inaccessible. Above the eighth it was all emptiness, derelicts and the odd fugitive.

Now where the Chrysler Building had once been there was the Heating Emporium, an open market for coal, wood, and alcohol, together with a few more exotic combustibles; I was glad to see the Belson Fuels corner well stocked and it pleased me to stand there a moment, looking like the raunchiest and most fragrant of bums, and see that each stick of neatly stacked cordwood had the name BELSON stamped on it in purple letters. Next to it was a heap of my coal, and that was not so pleasing. It was all bituminous, and you could tell it would be foul stuff by the color. But the Mafia had all the anthracite, and they weren't about to let go of it in a controlled market.

I walked up Fifth to Fifty-third Street and turned over toward Madison. A couple of cops gave me a hostile eye, and a family of Chinese tourists seemed as boggled by me as a Chinese permits himself to be. A member of the capitalist underclass—one of the dregs. *We do these things better in Hangchow*. Well, in Hangchow I'd be wearing a gray uniform and sweeping the streets with a plastic broom and touching my forelock to the fat Communist bourgeois as they daintily strolled the streets with their chubby families. I liked being a disheveled bum in New York better, with my newfound pirate's soul.

There was no doorman at the building and I walked up to the third floor. The apartment door had three locks. I banged loudly. After a minute the locks began clicking and, finally, the door opened. There was a small Japanese maid standing there, in uniform, staring up at me in shock.

I spoke softly to her, but with authority in my voice. "Tell Miss Belson it's her father," I said.

The maid nodded, shut the door and locked it. I waited. After several minutes it opened again and there was Myra, tall as ever, on crutches, looking at me quizzically for a moment. Finally she said, "Jesus Christ! *Daddy*." She opened the door wider. "Jesus!" she said again.

I came in and hugged her. Gently, because Myra could be hurting almost anywhere. "It's good to see you, honey," I

said. I was crying. I hadn't thought about Myra much in the
past few years—thinking about her could make me feel terrible—but I really loved her.

"Jesus, Daddy," she said, "did you fall in?"

I shook my head. "Something like that."

She laughed in that sort of childish way she has. Myra is
almost thirty. "Let's sit in the living room." I followed her as
she walked with care on her aluminum crutches into the big
living room with windows looking down on Fifty-third Street.
Myra had never met my Aunt Myra but she had somehow arrived, as if by reincarnation, at Aunt Myra's style in interior
decoration. I seated myself on a black velvet sofa, leaned
back, and lit up a cigar. "I'll wash up after a bit," I said. She
nodded and there was an embarrassed silence for a minute.
There usually is, when I see her. "How about some coffee?"
she said, "or whiskey?"

"Coffee."

"Sure," she said, with relief. "Martha, can you fix coffee
for my father, with cream and sugar. I'll have whiskey and
soda."

She turned back toward me and seated herself carefully in
an armchair that faced the sofa I was sitting on. "You were
on the TV news last night." She laughed a bit uneasily. "They
showed some old holos and called you the 'billionaire
fugitive,' but it wasn't clear what the police wanted you for."

"The bastards," I said. "*They* don't know what they want
me for. It's that son of a bitch Baynes, and probably the
Mafia too."

"I thought it was something like that. Is that uranium
dangerous, Daddy?"

"No," I said. "Hell, no. On the contrary. It's the safest
uranium in the universe. I feel like Galileo when those car-
dinals were after his ass. Have they bothered you?"

"No. Do they know you're in New York?"

"I don't think so," I said. "I've been sly about it. How's
your arthritis?"

She shrugged. "Same as always."

"Hurts like hell?"

"Yes, Daddy. It hurts like hell." She smiled at me in a way
that might be described as "bravely" except that I sensed a

hidden edge of blame in it. If only I had been around more during her childhood, had not been off in hotel suites dissolving corporations on paper in the middle of the night or bouncing around in bed with actresses or—let's face it—finding ways of staying away from Anna and her fortitude, her unflinching zeal to be undeceived by the fripperies and fantasies of the world. If I hadn't drunk so much when I *was* at home. If I hadn't fought so much with Myra's mother, bellowing my space pirate's voice down the hallways and across the kitchens of whatever houses and apartments—in California or New York or Atlanta, or wherever my geographical yearnings took us . . .

Well, now I had endolin. "Myra," I said, "I've got something for you."

"Daddy." She frowned. "I don't need any more presents. Not even from outer space."

"Honey," I said, "this is no present." I began unbuttoning my shirt, for a moment embarrassed by the sexual implications of what I was doing, being about to transfer that endolin wrapped to my sweating body to the body of my daughter sitting there in her stiff, arthritic way.

"What the hell . . . ?" Myra said.

"It *is* something from another planet," I said, pulling one of the bags filled with powder out from under the bandage that held it to my chest. I pushed aside a group of ivory netsuke and a Venetian-glass ashtray on Myra's coffee table and set the packet of endolin down. Then I began opening the clear plastic carefully. My fingers trembled a little. "I have great hopes for you and this, Myra," I said. I was shocked to hear my voice: *vibrato*, on the edge of tears. "I think it may be your anodyne . . ." I couldn't finish. I got the bag open and looked at the powder sitting there, like some kind of super fix, a mainline for King Kong, that destructive fellow pirate in New York. *Come on, Kong*, I said to myself, *do something good for someone you love, for a change*.

"I'll need to get a glass of water," I said aloud, holding back tears. I stood up and barged into the kitchen, where Martha was putting ice in Myra's drink of whiskey. I got a glass from a shelf and half-filled it with water. Then I grabbed a silver spoon from the sonic dishwasher and went into the living room again. I put a pinch of endolin into the water and stirred it, shakily.

"What in hell is going *on*, Daddy?" Myra was saying. She really was beginning to look alarmed. "You come in looking like a crazed derelict and then you pull out this Baggie of what looks like dope. They said on TV that you were a drug addict . . ."

I let the glass sit there on the table and leaned back. I began buttoning up my shirt, less shaky now. "Well, there's some truth in what they say, honey. I used morphine quite a bit. Got hooked on it in fact, trying to feed some dumb craving, but this isn't morphine. No high comes with it. It's only a painkiller."

"I'll try it," she said matter-of-factly.

I stared at her. Was it this easy after all?

"Daddy," she said, "I trust you. And I've tried more painkillers than you have any idea of. Believe me, I've swallowed a lot of chemicals in my time." She leaned forward, somewhat stiffly, and picked up the glass. Her hand was far steadier, despite the pain, than mine had been. "What do you call this stuff?"

"Endolin," I said. "Just drink it off. There's no special taste."

She nodded and downed the glassful the way a sailor downs a beer. "Endolin, eh?" she said, with an edge of cynicism in her voice. Well I couldn't blame her for being cynical, considering the number of things she must have tried. It was a testimony to her strength that, having used morphine and probably heavier stuff, she wasn't a junkie herself.

I said nothing. It takes endolin about three minutes to work and there was no point in talking it up. I felt nervous and got up just in time to take my coffee from Martha's tray as she came in the swinging door from the kitchen. I looked at a couple of contemporary holographic etchings on the wall for a moment; but those damned 3-D things always hurt my eyes. I looked out the window down to the street, which was now empty. It was one of those phosphorescent sidewalks that glow green in the dark and it eased my eyes to stare at it for a minute. I was itching in several places. I should take a bath.

Just then Myra said softly, "My God, Daddy!" and I

turned around. She was still seated. Her face was strange and her mouth was half open in astonishment. As I looked at her she shook her head a couple of times.

"Is something wrong?" I said, alarmed.

She shook her head again, more violently, staring at me. I took a step toward her. She was beginning to cry. "Are you all right?" I said.

Her face was very serious and the expression was one I'd never seen before. "How long does it last?" she asked.

"About six hours."

"Will I have a hangover?"

"Nothing, honey," I said. "No hangover."

"Oh my God," she said and burst into tears. I squatted somewhat awkwardly by her chair and put my arms around her and hugged her. I could feel some of that pain that had just gone out of her, feel the shock of it. After a moment she pulled gently away and stood up, not using her crutches. She began walking around the room slowly and taking an occasional little two-step. "I used to take morphine sometimes, or shoot myself full of procaine and dance for an hour or so. But the thing was I couldn't really *feel* my body. And my head would be fuzzy."

"It just takes the pain away," I said.

Myra went over to a bookcase, put a steel ball into a box and Chinese dance music filled the room. She began dancing more confidently, her face open and surprised still. I seated myself and watched. It was overwhelming to see her moving easily like that, still a bit careful in her movements because of her long history of pain.

After a while she stopped, perspiring and smiling now. She turned the box off and came and sat beside me. She let herself cry again for a minute, very openly and easily, holding her hands in front of her and flexing her fingers. We used to play chess with ivory pieces every now and then and sometimes it would make her wince in pain just to pick up a pawn. Now her fingers seemed completely easy and supple. After a moment she stopped crying and said, "How about that, Daddy? I think I always knew you'd come through for me."

"I wish I could have had it twenty years ago . . ."

"Now is good enough," she said. "When the pain is over

it's over.'' She smiled a little wistfully. "Where did it come
from?"

"From the heavens," I said. "From a star." I pointed
downtown. "A star in Pisces Austrinus, called Fomalhaut. It
has a planet with only two living things on it: a kind of
wonderful grass and the little, ugly plant endolin comes
from.''

"What's the planet called? Or does it have a name?"

"It's named Belson, honey."

Myra laughed. "Just like you and me, Daddy."

I looked at her. "And your Great Aunt Myra."

I took a long, hot shower after that. Myra was able to find
some men's clothes that fit well enough, and I picked a denim
work shirt and a pair of jeans that were a little loose in the
waist. It gave me a tinge of pride to find my waist was smaller
than whatever lover of Myra's had left his pants behind. I
brushed off my electronic running shoes and put them on over
a pair of clean white socks. There is nothing quite like a
shower followed by clean white socks. I was becoming a small
fugue of good feelings; what I needed now was Isabel. And a
few million dollars.

After showering and putting on clean clothes I had a quiet
drink with Myra in her living room. She had come down a bit
from her high, but she smiled a lot. She asked me about my
travels in space and I told her about Belson and Juno, although I didn't mention Juno's star. It was fun to talk with
Myra that easily, leaning back into a soft couch with a drink
of good whiskey, seeing her face for once relaxed and her
body at ease. From time to time she would flex the fingers of a
hand or work a shoulder joint just a bit, with a pleasant surprise. She wanted to know everything about endolin, and I
told her everything I knew about it. How we had found it
growing in fissures in Belson's impenetrable obsidian, how I'd
learned to concentrate it and preserve it. It was wonderful to
sit there with the windows open in Myra's big living room with
the barely luminous New York street outside the window
hushed with an August hush, and me with my clean white
socks, my skin clean, my hair still dyed and my beard dyed
and combed and a fresh shirt on my strong chest, letting the

old guilt seep out of my pores and away into the nighttime, off to Fomalhaut and beyond, into the outer reaches.

When I went off to bed a little before midnight, the moon was shining as full as a hundred-dollar silver coin into the bedroom window. On the night before, I had been its fellow orbiter, in a kind of sublunar funk; here I was now, a fugitive, a pirate, dispossessed, but tired and happy going to bed in a New York apartment, ready to sing hymns to the joy of my new life. "For he on honey dew hath fed, and drunk the milk of paradise." Coleridge. Another junkie. What the hell. I slept like a baby for a dozen hours.

Birds were singing when I awoke. Myra was up and had found *Pain Chocolat* and espresso for me and three fresh Havana cigars. Gueveras.

I dressed in jeans and a gray tee-shirt and went barefoot into the kitchen and began making an omelet with a fried banana on the side. There was coffee on the wood stove. Yellow morning sunshine came in the kitchen window as still and humane as in a Vermeer. The cup I drank my coffee from was Spode and had a decoration of two small green frogs, facing each other amiably; my heart glowed warmly to see such frogs, and on such china. Myra was wearing a blue denim smock, and walked as if on air, as if she had never gone to sleep with fire in her joints, as if she had had a childhood of skipping rope and tag and dancing. Her hair was tied loosely in back in a bun, her hazel eyes smiled. "Let me pour you more coffee," she said, and I remembered her as a bright-eyed two-year-old, as lovely and heartwarming a thing as nature ever made. I had forgotten how much I loved my child.

"Honey," I said to Myra, "do you know of an actress named Isabel Crawford? She was in the last *Hamlet*, playing the mother."

Myra pursed her lips a moment and then nodded slowly. "British?"

"Scottish. In her forties. Very good-looking."

"She's a friend of yours then?"

"Sure. Do you know anything about her? I need clues. I can't find her."

"No, Dad, I'm sorry. I haven't any idea at all. You could call her agent."

"I tried that last night on your phone. Called her director too, and her hairdresser. No luck at all. They'd like to know where she is too."

Myra nodded politely while I told her this. When I'd finished she tried to be casual, but I could tell she was picking her words with care. "Dad. Why don't you give Mom a call? She's in New York."

Something went tight in my stomach at that. I tried to sound casual too. It was beginning to feel like acting school. "Oh?" I said. "Where's she staying?"

"At your old place, Dad. The Pierre."

Jesus! I thought, *Anna at the Pierre?* It didn't sound like her at all. "What in hell is your mother doing in New York?" I said. "She always claimed to hate it here."

"She was over for dinner a few nights ago, Dad. She said she was getting bored upstate and came down to do some shopping." She looked at me. "Why don't you ask her for lunch or something?"

For a moment it was a seductive idea. Whatever Anna might possess of a longshoreman's spirit, she was a hell of a person to talk with. I've never really enjoyed *talking* with a woman as much as I did with her. And I'd never had any trouble getting it up with her—maybe because her sexuality was no threat. I thought, standing there with Myra, of how nice sex with Anna would be—a spell of rain after a three-year drought. But then I thought of that damnable popping girdle and that righteous anger and I said, "Myra, it just wouldn't be smart. Not now. I know what you have in mind, bless your heart, and I admit there might be something to it. But I don't need the trauma right now. There's something fragile in my spirit, and seeing Anna might shatter it."

Myra pursed her lips. "Okay, Dad. It's your life."

"Oh yes, honey," I said. "It sure is."

❧ Chapter 12

Isabel was not to be found in New York. I called everyone I dared call and learned nothing but what I had learned from or- bit: Isabel had left for London six months before, in *Hamlet*. *Hamlet* closed four months later and no one had heard from her since, not her agent and not her friends. The agent was try- ing to get her to do the mother in *Mourning Becomes Elektra* —crazy typecasting for childless Isabel, with her teenage figure. She could be in Istanbul or Santa Fe or Aberdeen. I gave up temporarily and concentrated on business.

It's taken over fifty years of living to get my priorities right and to learn that love is more important than money. What fortune-cookie wisdom to spend a lifetime acquiring! But now that I knew it, circumstances forced me to put money first anyway. It was time to peddle endolin.

First I found my friend Millie Shapiro in a little studio apartment on West Fifty-seventh. Millie is a retired makeup artist, once at the top of her profession. I knew her through Isabel; they were both cat fanatics. Millie was grumpy and shaky, but she expertly washed the cheap hair dye out of my hair and redyed it dark brown, with gray at the temples. Her breath was horrible, but when.I looked in her cracked vanity mirror afterward I had to whistle. She also trimmed my hair and beard for me in a kind of movie-star way that was far different from my usual rough-and-ready. She gave me a pair of black-rimmed glasses to wear and suggested I shift from cigars to a pipe and that I wear rings. I dismissed the pipe idea immediately; I have a hearty distrust of pipe smokers and tweedy people in general.

Myra had managed to put together sixty thousand dollars in cash and had bought me a money belt at an Army-Navy store to keep it in. I paid Millie, asked her one more time if she had any notion of where Isabel might be, enjoined her to silence, and left. Good woman, Millie, and I trusted her.

I did as she suggested and bought a couple of classy-looking rings at a costume-jewelry place. At a men's store I finished my metamorphosis: tight Western jeans, army boots and a red silk shirt. In the clothing-store mirror I looked as if I'd been sent from central casting to play an aging gigolo—which was something of a laugh considering my recent troubles. Anyway, most people knew me from the covers of *Time* and *Newsweek*, and on those I'd been beardless and dressed in one of my famous lumberjack shirts. I was known as a ''boyish eccentric'': the beard, red shirt and rings should throw people off as long as I could stand to go on looking that way.

Actually, I figured they weren't searching very hard for me. Baynes had the *Isabel* and the uranium and he knew there was no way I was going to get another spaceship. The next move was mine. The move I had in mind was checkmate. I went to Grand Central and bought a Pullman ticket to Columbus, Ohio.

The train had a parlor car, with armchairs and magazines and little tables to set your scotch and soda on. The furnishings were shabby—frayed green curtains on streaked windows, a peeling mural on one wall—and the upholstery was that woeful green that is one of the perversions of U.S. railroading. But I felt at home instantly in that car. I was the first passenger there and I chose a window seat in the chair with the least-worn upholstery. It was ten-thirty in the morning; I ordered a pot of coffee and toast and settled back, clicking the rings together on my left hand, occasionally stroking my freshly trimmed beard and feeling a pleasant anticipation in my stomach.

After a bit, a couple of priests came into the car and seated themselves prissily at the other end from me. And then a small, sexy woman came in and sat down alone. I began changing plans. Ever since that sight of the thighs of my fantasy sweetie who left my life in New Hope, Penn., I travel with the unconscious expectation of sex. It's an expectation that, up to the point I'm writing about, had never been fulfilled. I'd had opportunities when I was younger and on my way to check out a coal mine or a merger or a commodities possibility —taking a firsthand look at Kansas wheat, say, or North Carolina firewood—but I'd always somehow fumbled or lost out or had gone horribly, maddeningly shy at the sight of a crossed pair of legs under the hem of a skirt. The awful truth is that women turn me on so goddamned much I feel powerless with them. Jesus, do I like asses and breasts and pubic hair and the sweet pungency of vaginal lips! Thighs. The backs of knees.

All this response to a small, pretty woman entering a parlor car! Well. It had been a long time. I'd just got back from outer space and from a stretch as solo gardener on a slippery planet. A stint at impotence before that. It had been three years since I'd genuinely experienced a woman. Seeing her there, about forty, with splendid legs and an intelligent face and light-brown hair and a white blouse draping so nicely over her ample breasts, I immediately lost any notions I'd had of catching up on world news on my trip across country. I no longer cared about what had happened in politics or war or energy or show business or acts of God during my absence; I wanted to share my bed with that woman. She had been in the car about thirty seconds and I was in love with her.

Little wrinkles at the corners of her eyes. How nice! Her back straight and her ass neat and firm under her skirt. Splendid! L&M marijuana cigarettes in the gold pack and a gold lighter to match, set with assurance on the little table by her seat. *Quel délicatesse!* She ordered pernod and water in a soft voice, flitted her eyes quickly around the car, passing over me with just the hint of a pause. Oh my God, how I love all those

things women do! How I love a civilized New York woman
who dresses right and talks warmly and knows how to order a
drink on a train! Monuments should be built to such women.
To hell with generals, admirals, presidents, artists, messiahs; a
civilized, grown-up woman with an education and a firm ass is
worth the whole lot of them.

I was scared too. Fifty-three years old, a pirate, and I was
beginning to panic at the realization that if I wanted something to happen between us I would have to make it happen. I
have lost beautiful women to nobodies because of this fear,
have sat stupidly by because I was afraid, down deep, that I
wasn't wanted and let some dumb, balding insurance salesman
walk off arm in arm with a woman I'd been admiring for an
hour. Oh yes. As easy as I may be with actresses and show-
girls, I can turn prepubescent and unintelligible in a flash, out
in the real world. And damn it, I am a good-looking billionaire and a lamb at lovemaking—a gentle and affectionate
lover when not plagued by psychosomatic wilt.

All this whizzed around in me before my coffee came,
before the train started moving. A minute at most. I knew I'd
better act fast before things got even more complicated.
Before that insurance man came in and plopped down beside
her.

I got up and walked over, fast enough so I wouldn't feel my
lack of poise. "Hello," I said, "I'd like to have my coffee
with you. It's coming in a minute." I tried not to think about
my red shirt, my rings, my dyed beard.

She looked at me with no alarm at all and my heart immediately grew lighter. "Okay," she said.

I sat down with surprising ease and introduced myself as
Ben Jonson, using the name of my favorite Benjamin in the
arts. She was Sue Kranefeld and a professor of history at
Berkeley.

"That's terrific!" I said. "You can tell me about the Punic
Wars and why Alexander the Great didn't live longer."

"I'm in American history," she said, which seemed to end
that. Maybe she thought I was being facetious, but I meant it.
I learned a lot about Scottish communism from Isabel.

Her pernod and my coffee came at the same time, and just
as I was pouring, the train pulled out of Grand Central.

"I really love this," I said. "I love starting a trip. I think I could spend my life doing it."

"Do you travel much?" She poured the water on her pernod and we watched it cloud up.

I wanted to say I had just got back from the stars, zooming through light-years of void, but I replied that I traveled whenever I could and that I was in the coal-and-wood business, as a power-plant designer. Normally I don't like telling lies, but on a train it's part of the ambience.

She brightened. "That's interesting to me," she said. "I've been in New York researching the greenhouse panic of the twenties, and that has a lot to do with coal."

"Yes," I said, glad we had something in common to talk about for a while. She was wearing a perfume that smelled of camellias. That soft voice was really splendid, as relaxed as an oatmeal cookie. Something a bit of the schoolteacher about her, but how pleasant she was! And how turned on I was. What I of course wanted to say was, "I'd sure like to *fuck*, right this minute if you don't mind." I'd have said it too, if I thought it had a prayer of working. Since it didn't, I had to say *something*, and what I chose was, "The coal business would be a lot different if they'd planned it right. There was no need to pump all that black soup into the air." Talk, talk.

"They were greedy," she said. "When they started heating with coal and running elevators with it in the twenty-teens it was on a huge scale. People died. Crops died. They tried scrubbers and precipitators and cattle keeled over in fields. Then the greenhouse effect began."

I was getting nervous with this and was unsure how to stop her. She had adopted the professor mode and was lecturing me. I could see the three-by-five cards in her head flipping over. "Uranium would have been safer," I said somewhat lamely, hoping she didn't know anything about uranium. "Even plutonium."

"Of *course*," she said, as though I were a backward student, "but Denver came at the worst possible time."

"Just before an election," I said.

"Do you work for the Mafia?"

"I work for Belson Mines."

"Oh," she said. "Have you met him?" Her voice, thank

God, left the classroom and came back to our parlor car. Outside, behind her lovely head of brown hair, were more and more trees and fewer crumbling apartment buildings.

"Sure," I said, "a dozen times."

"What do you think of him?"

"I think his heart's in the right place."

She thought about that a minute and finished her drink.

"Want some of my coffee?" I said. I had a big pot of it between us.

She shook her head "No" and flagged down the waiter for a pernod. I poured myself another cup of coffee. "What do you think of Mr. Belson?" I said, as casually as I could.

She lit a joint and looked out the window. "He's an attractive man, but he seems . . . frenetic, from what I've read. And foolish."

"That sounds accurate enough," I said. "I know him to be warmhearted."

She turned and looked at me. "I think he looks a bit like you, judging from the pictures. Are you related?"

"Cousins," I said. "I'd like to take you to lunch at twelve. Okay?"

"Sure." She smiled pleasantly at me.

Beyond the window it was fields now and trees and a blue sky. The train swayed erotically, as did my loins. *What the hell*, I thought, and said what I wanted to say. "You sure are a beautiful woman," I said. *Isabel I'm sorry*.

"Thank you," Sue said.

There were light freckles on her upper arms, and not a wrinkle anywhere. I could have kissed every freckle. I vowed then I would, perhaps while crossing Pennsylvania.

I glanced over at the priests; one had his hand on the other's knee and they were bent toward each other in intimacy. What the hell. What are trains really for anyway?

She had another drink before lunch and I worried that the booze in her might get to be a problem, but she only drank a single glass of wine with her spinach quiche. We had the dining car to ourselves, and over dessert I reached out and took her hand. She leaned toward me and said, "I can't wait until tonight to go to bed with you."

"What a darling you are!" I said. But I was suddenly nervous. How horrible it would be not to get it up after all this. The thought of how a shot of morphine might help came to mind. But with it there was a flash of unaccustomed clarity: the only way to save this was to tell her the truth and tell it right now.

There was no one seated anywhere near us. I leaned forward a bit and said, "Sue, I'm embarrassed to say this, but I have a sexual problem."

She looked at me.

"The last time I went to bed with a woman was over a year ago," I said, "and I was impotent."

She had become a shade distant and she lit up a cigarette now. "Ben," she said, "you're a very attractive man and I like you. But I don't like complications, or embarrassments."

"Sue," I said, "neither do I. But it won't be complicated and it won't be embarrassing." She must have heard the joy-fulness in my voice. Sitting right there in the dining car with a pair of dessert plates between us and watching her light a green marijuana cigarette and click her little lighter shut afterward, watching the freckles on her upper arms and the sweet curve of her neck and smelling her perfume, I felt the unmistakable and joyful response.

I leaned forward and said, "Hallelujah, Sue! I've got an erection!"

She smiled distantly. "It's only a little past noon, Ben. I've brought a book with me I need to read . . ."

"Come on, Sue." I got up carefully—a bit bent over at first. "I'll be back for you in about two minutes."

I found a porter and gave her a fifty-dollar piece and told her to make the bed in my compartment. Then I went back to the diner. Sue was drinking what looked like a double Bour-bon. For a moment the memory of my mother standing at the sink with a martini, with her ruined face, almost withered me in my tracks. But I pulled myself together. My member, though chastened by the necessity of my walking up and down train aisles, was still alive and well and ready to rejoin the rest of me. I walked up to Sue and bent down to where she was sit-ting and kissed her warmly on the cheek. Then on the mouth. She kissed me back, a bit warily. I was right; it was Bourbon. Her mouth was full of the taste and it sent a special electricity into my balls. I was ready for rape, ecstasy, tears. Yes, she got up and walked with me the length of two railroad cars and into my compartment. And yes, the sheet was turned down as white and crisp as you ever saw. There was a little vase with three pink carnations sitting on the washstand; lace curtains softened the light from the windows. We were out of our clothes in no time. I could have shouted with pride for my dear old member; I could have hung our clothes on it.

All I can say is the whole thing was as easy as anything I've ever done in my life, as easy as drinking cold water on a hot day. God what a lovely, relaxed woman. A little drunk, but I thought: *so what, if that's what she needed*. We did everything in bed we could think of doing. Weight fell from my troubled spirit—some of it was weight I hadn't even known was there—and it was like zero-gravity on the bed afterward. Free fall. If only we could live our whole lives in moments like those. I pulled the curtains open, finally, after we had both napped, and we copulated in twilight as the hills of Pennsylvania rolled by under an August moon.

The next morning she was hung over and threw up in the little sink. It seems she'd gone to the parlor car while I was sleeping and had drunk for three or four hours before coming to bed.

"What a crazy thing to do!" I said, exasperated at the way she looked and the way she sounded at the washstand. Her hair was sweaty, and in the morning light I could see a roll of fat at her waist. There were blue veins behind her knees.

"I'm an alcoholic, Ben," she said, washing her face.

"I can't believe that," I said. "You're in too good shape for a boozer."

"I only started about a year ago. After my divorce."

"How do you feel?" I said.

"I've got a terrible headache."

"I can fix that," I said, and got one of the little packets out of my briefcase. "Here. Dissolve this in a glass of water."

She did as I told her. She dried her face and went on talking. "I never had an orgasm with my husband until I started getting drunk."

I just looked at her. After a minute she sat on the bed and sighed. We were both silent. Then she said, "Hey! my headache's gone.'' Her voice was brighter, and with her face freshly scrubbed and her hair combed she was beginning to look good again.

I washed myself up, got dressed and had a silent breakfast while she drank a bloody mary. The morning scenery outside the window began to restore my spirits. Sue's problems were Sue's problems; she had been no problem to me where it counted. I ordered extra toast and coffee and sent a silent prayer of thanks toward Fomalhaut.

At noon she ordered a couple of drinks—martinis this time —and by one we were back in the sack again. I feared failure for one bad moment, thinking that maybe I needed the force of abstinence to impel me. But the fear was dispelled by the salute of my comfortable member. It is a remarkable and wonderful thing to be a man.

During lunch at two-thirty she talked of how coal could supply the world with all its energy, if only it was mined and distributed right. I nodded agreement with her, not going into what I knew about it—considerably more than what any professor knew. That greenhouse effect was only an inconvenience compared to the fights among Mafia families. This was the twenty-first century, for Christ's sake. But the Mafia was run the way General Motors and the Roman Catholic Church had been run in the twentieth. It was an assemblage of bureaucrats whose only loyalty was to the institution.

Well, people like that ran the world in the Middle Ages. The people who run it now are little different. The laws of the Church meant more to the Church than the happiness of mankind. Ditto the Mafia. Ditto General Motors. Ditto Belson Industries? Yes, sometimes. A corporation is more intelligible than life; one can more easily learn its rules and live by them.

I began talking. ''The trouble with coal, Sue, is that it's heavy and dirty. It's hard to get it out of the ground and hard to ship it where you want it. You can gasify it or grind it up and mix it with water and send it through pipes, but the pipes are an invitation to sabotage. They chopped pipes like Christmas ribbons during the gang wars thirty years ago.''

I realized I was talking more heatedly about this than I had planned to. What in hell was I angry with?

She had listened attentively, with an opened book primly in

her lap. I was leaning against the green back of my chair, making gestures with my cigar. I wasn't wearing the rings, since I was already heartily sick of them.

When I finished, Sue leaned forward and spoke quietly. "Ben," she said, "you're Ben Belson, aren't you?"

I stared at her. "What makes you say that?"

"Well, your hair's dyed for one thing. I noticed that last night. And you *talk* like a tycoon."

I thought about that for a moment and almost said I was more pirate than tycoon. But what the hell was the use of being defensive about it? "Okay," I said. "But for Christ's sake don't tell anybody. I'm on the lam."

She laughed. "On the *lam?* That's a quaint way to talk. Didn't the government make you an outlaw or something?"

"A pirate. They took away my citizenship and made me a pirate. Or L'Ouverture Baynes did, the son of a bitch."

"I voted for Baynes when he ran for President," she said.

"He's still a son of a bitch." I drank some coffee angrily.

"I voted for him too. Set a thief to catch a thief."

"Exactly."

"Yeah," I said, looking at the drink in front of her. I had been mulling over an idea ever since breakfast. "Look," I said, "why are you going back to California anyway?"

She closed her book and took a sip from her drink. "To write up my research. I need to publish."

"Do you have to teach?"

"I'm on leave for six months."

"Well, look," I said, "I have two interests in life: spiritual growth and financial resurrection. I'm going to Columbus to make money, so I can take my spaceship away from Baynes. If you'd stay with me I'd be able to continue my spiritual growth."

She raised her eyebrows. "Let me mull it over, Ben."

"Sure," I said.

Well, I needed to mull, myself. One problem was Ruth, my motherly redheaded spaceship pilot. I'd chosen Columbus and Lao-tzu Pharmaceuticals partly because Ruth lived there and I had some idea of staying with her awhile. And Ruth's brother was Howard the biophysicist, whose help I would need before

I saw any of those wily Chinese. Ruth was fond of me, and I was fond of her. I was concerned with how things would work out if I showed up in Columbus with a new sweetie.

Why do I complicate things so much—as Anna would say. As Isabel would say. As Sue would be saying soon enough. Orbach didn't ask that question; he answered it. The reason you complicate things so much, Ben Belson, is that you are trying to get your mother's love and your father's attention. Since they are both dead, it's a complicated thing to do. I had to admit there was truth in that; there are simpler goals in life than jarring the dead loose from their sleep.

Sue suddenly spoke up. "Sure, Ben," she said. "I'd like to stay in Columbus with you."

By mutual consent Sue and I split up for a while. I found a *Newsweek* and read its Energy section. There was another of those pieces about plutonium—that malign transuranite stuff. *Newsweek* did acknowledge that Buenos Aires had been lost to it but claimed plutonium was now safely under lock and key. They talked about the Chinese breeder reactors and about all the cheap energy available in the stockpiles, but they didn't mention what a microgram of plutonium could do to a human lung.

There was another *Newsweek* piece, about coal distribution, full of false hope. I knew far too much about the way coal was moved around to have any faith in it at all. If the United States was going to revive, it was going to be with Juno uranium making steam for the next millennium and beyond. I could feel the straightforward power of it the way I felt my sexual power.

That brought me back to thinking about Sue. I looked at my watch. We were due in Columbus in twenty minutes. I set my magazine down and went back to the parlor car to look for her. I'd been reading in the diner. She wasn't there. The place was empty except for the two priests still in murmured conversation, still with the hand of one on the knee of the other.

I headed briskly toward the sleeping car, pushing my way past a couple of porters, already beginning to feel angry at what I was sure I'd find. And find it I did.

When I opened the door to our bedroom I could smell her. I felt like picking up her fallen-off shoe and beating her in the face with the heel of it. She was sprawled out in the easy chair in a rumpled, red-faced mess, passed out drunk. I might have been able to wake her, but I didn't try.

❧ Chapter 13

I left Sue on the train and felt no guilt in doing it. If that was what she wanted her life to be like, it was her business; I wasn't prepared to dance her loser's dance and get involved in waking her up and feeding her endolin and dragging her into Columbus with me and then hearing the apologies. She knew what *I* wanted with her, and I was beginning to see what *she* wanted. A few years ago I would have become involved, but not now.

In the station I walked directly to a pay phone, got the dollar for a local call and Ruth's telephone number out of my billfold, and stood there for a long moment holding in my hand my worn old billfold and the paper Ruth had given me aboard the *Isabel* with her phone number and address. The little brass dollar was in the other hand. What was I doing, leaving one woman behind me and rushing to another? There in that badly lit train station in Columbus, Ohio, about seventy miles from the little town where I was born, I began to remember my nights on Belson. My shoulders and the backs of my legs tingled with the memory of the grass making its interstellar connection with my physical self. My heels felt sensitive; they remembered the tendrils that had penetrated them. A sigh arose from my soul, and I heard an old woman who stood at the viddiphone next to mine gasp softly, and I saw her turn to stare at me for a moment in alarm. Did I look like John the Baptist again? Had I sighed like a drunken beast, as Isabel claimed that I sighed in my sleep?

Here I was about to embark on another dubious sexual adventure, about to diddle with the life of a person who had shown more concern for me than I had ever shown for her— who might secretly love me, for all I knew—and I was going to do this questionable diddling while involved in whatever steps were necessary to find Isabel, make money, and get the uranium off my spaceship and away from L'Ouverture Baynes. All of this while staying out of prison. *What was I doing?* Where was my Belson calm, my Belson peace? I looked down at my hand. It was trembling. I jammed it, together with the billfold, Ruth's paper and the dollar, back into my pocket. I turned away from the phone, walked out of the station and into an Ohio drizzle.

It was a five-block walk to the John Glenn Hotel. I was soaked by the time I got there and I dripped water onto the blue carpet at the desk while I registered. The clerk stared at me. I ignored him and signed, thinking of Belson nights.

I came for a moment out of this reverie when he asked if I would prefer a heated room, explaining crisply that the John Glenn had a splendid new coal furnace. There was an implication in his voice that I couldn't afford it. Not exactly a stupid inference, considering my bedraggled state and lack of luggage; but bastards like that have no business trying to make their customers feel uncomfortable.

When I didn't reply immediately he said, "Perhaps you would prefer one of our unheated singles, with the heavy blankets?"

I blinked at him. "Come off it," I said. "I want a suite and I want it heated." My voice was hoarse.

He just looked at me.

"What's your best suite?"

"We have the Neil Armstrong Gallery on the third floor . . ."

"What's a gallery?"

"Three rooms and a terrace."

"Is it heated?"

"Every room."

"I'll take it."

It was overpriced, and the gray sofa in the parlor had coffee stains on its arms. But there was space to move around in, and a combination kitchen and dining room of the kind that is dear to my heart. I christened it the Belson Grass Room and decided to use it for meditation.

I had to get out of my wet clothes and I didn't have any dry ones. The suite was warm, so I undressed, wrung out my clothes, hung them on the shower rod in the bathroom and padded around naked. That turned out to be a good thing; it brought me back to my nights on Belson.

There was an oriental carpet under the table in the dining room. I pushed the table over against the wall and lay down naked on my back on the rug. The floor was warm and the carpet thick, with a slightly musty smell. After I had lain there awhile I began again to feel the tingling down my back, neck to heels, that I'd felt in the train station. The confused voices in my head, and the anger that had begun to gather in me while I was registering in the hotel, began to leave me. Eventually I dozed off.

I woke up late in the afternoon and just lay there and contemplated the state of my affairs for a while. What I needed first was money. More cash to supplement what Myra had given me and then some real money. I pushed myself up from the floor, padded into the bathroom to check my clothes. They were still damp. I went to the viddiphone by the living-room sofa and set its lens for a head shot, so my nakedness wouldn't show. I seated myself, touched the switch on the phone, and told it to get me a banker I knew. His home phone. In fact he worked for me, since I owned about 40 percent of his savings and loan. And he owed me a favor.

He didn't recognize me with the dyed hair and the beard. I identified myself, told him to keep quiet about my presence in

Ohio and to have his savings and loan lend me a half million, in large bills. To fit my money belt. "I'll think of something to give you a mortgage on, Gordon," I told him. "Bring papers."

He cleared his throat and looked humble. "Mr. Belson," he said, with some of the soft-mouthed arrogance the hotel clerk had tried on me, "I'm not certain it would be within my authority. As much as I'd like to accommodate you . . ."

"I'll accommodate your ass out of the loan business for the rest of your life," I said. "You dumb son of a bitch. You have those bills here tomorrow morning or you'll be sweeping streets for a living." The pompous little fart. He was one of those Warren G. Harding types, with the silver hair at the temples and the grandfatherly ways. Probably younger than I. Ask him to break a law and he turns Sunday school. "Bring that money personally. If you don't you're a fiscal ruin."

There was silence for a moment. I stared at him and let myself float on my rage.

"I'm sorry, Mr. Belson . . ." His voice was creaky.

"Forget it," I said. "I'll see you tomorrow at ten." I felt righteous, ready to excoriate greedy foolishness and malfeasance in general.

Gordon looked dazed; I felt suddenly a little dazed myself. "See you in the morning," I said and hung up. Then I walked back through the dining room and out onto the terrace. This turned out to be a six-by-eight-foot permoplastic apron with an Astroturf rug on it. So much for Neil Armstrong. So much for his dumb remark about that first step. No feeling in it. No more life than Astroturf. At least I had announced the first human steps on Belson with a yelp and a broken arm.

But where was my peace—my Belson peace? My hands were trembling with anger.

The drizzle had lightened but I didn't stay on the terrace. I had begun thinking of Neil Armstrong and of those bland, tightly smiling descendants of people like him, who were more and more coming to rule the world. The John Glenn Hotel, indeed. John Glenn had been orbited like a fetus a hundred years ago, crouched in the belly of the hurtling whale more for publicity reasons than for engineering ones, and the people of Ohio had allowed him to make laws for all of us because of it.

What folly. What an omen! I'd have voted for him maybe, for his being a sound, middle-aged test pilot before the razzmatazz of NASA, but never for his orbits, those pawn moves in the unholy game my country was playing with Russia at the time. What dangerous idiots we were in those days, with our weapons and our paranoia!

These thoughts about the United States and its long tradition of folly were doing me no good. Why was I so *angry?* My nose was itching. I was catching cold.

My shorts in the bathroom, a sky-blue pair I'd worn halfway across the Milky Way and back, were dry enough to put on, since I'd draped them over a hissing radiator. I took a quick shower, got into the shorts, and with a restored sense of purpose went to the viddiphone in the parlor. For a moment I wanted to call Ruth, but I put that out of my mind. I told the machine to give me her brother's number. I got him on the first try. "Howard," I told him, "I need to see you and for God's sake don't tell anyone I'm in Columbus."

I'd quieted down a bit by the time Gordon got to my room with the money. He tried to be hearty and companionable about it, but I wasn't buying. I signed first-mortgage papers with him for a house I own in Key West and sent him on his way. Then I put what I could of the money into my belt, rolled the rest into a crapshooter's roll and stuffed it in my jeans. When I put the belt on it was like putting a bicycle chain around my waist, but it's the best way I know to carry liquid assets. They'd have to sever me to get at it.

Howard arrived a few minutes after Gordon left and I greeted him with a hug. It was good to see someone from the *Isabel* again.

"Well, Captain," he said, "you look healthy. But I liked you as a blond."

"Me too," I said. "Let me get you a drink."

I poured us both some Chinese wine. The living room had a fake fireplace with a pair of high-backed red armchairs by it; we sat in these facing each other. "Did you marry again, Howard?" I asked.

He shook his head slowly. "After the ship landed in Florida and the court let us go I was excited about finding a new wife.

I felt . . ." He was sitting hunched over his wineglass and holding it in both hands. "I felt like a sailor in port, if you know what I mean." He finished his wine. "But nothing happened."

"You didn't meet any women?"

"It seemed like a lot of trouble for nothing, once I got down to it. I took the bus to Columbus." He smiled shamefacedly. "I suppose I'm getting older."

I stared at him.

"I'm forty-four."

I could have hit him with one of the artificial logs. But I didn't do anything. The man had six divorces behind him. Maybe he knew something.

I got up and went to the bedroom. When I came back to my chair I handed him a packet. "Howard," I said, "I need to have this analyzed by somebody who's really good at it."

"It looks like dope," he said.

"It's endolin. I want to find out if it can be duplicated."

"I know just the man. A professor at Ohio State." He held the packet in his hand as though weighing it. "Endolin didn't look like this on Belson."

"I learned a way to concentrate it." I found myself getting more irritated with this conversation. Also, I was beginning to get a serious cold. I excused myself again and went to the bedroom for a handkerchief and blew my nose violently. My throat was sore and my skin felt prickly. I got out another pack of endolin and took a pinch, chasing it with the rest of my wine.

"Captain," Howard shouted from the other room, "did the grass sing anymore?"

I felt annoyed with the question. "Yes," I said, "once."

He nodded. "Wasn't the grass why you stayed? So you could hear it again?"

"I wanted to consolidate myself."

"You could have done that on Juno."

"I can be very self-defeating in how I live."

He laughed as though I was joking, although I certainly wasn't. "You know," he said. "I wanted to stay myself."

I stood in the doorway and looked at him awhile—at his sad

face and stooped shoulders. He did look old. Then I said, "On Juno or on Belson?"

"Belson," he said.

Oh yes, I thought, furious. *There's a lot of it going around.*

I woke before dawn with my bedsheet wet from sweat and my nose and throat feeling stuffed with steel wool. My head throbbed. I got up shakily, feeling wretched, took some endolin and a glass of warm water and then got back in bed and waited. After a few minutes the throbbing stopped and I felt the fever abate, but the baroque world of predawn sickness was enveloping my spirit.

Eventually I fell asleep again, or something like asleep, with twisting around and fighting with the sheets, which would not seem to get straight and smooth no matter what I did. I remember sitting up in bed sometime that morning after the sun had risen and shouting, "Motherfuckers motherfuckers motherfuckers!" and trying to get the top sheet to cover my toes. "*Motherfuckers!*" Someone below me pounded on the ceiling and, fuming, I became quiet again.

I slept till ten and felt better when I awoke, again, to wet sheets. I called room service and got four soft-boiled eggs and a bloody mary. Then I put on my jeans and my red shirt, went to the living room and called Lao-tzu Pharmaceuticals.

It took about an hour of switching around from office to office before I could get anybody important—which really meant anybody Chinese. She was a junior vice-president in charge of Development and clearly a fan of the National Cultural Revival: Pear Blossom Loo. A young woman of about thirty, with black bangs above a face as inscrutable as a cue ball. Nice teeth, though, as well as I could see. I was sitting with the shades down and in dim light to make sure I wasn't recognized.

"Miss Loo," I said, "my name is Ben Jonson. I'm a professor of biochemistry at Stanford and I've developed an analgesic substance that should be of interest to you."

"I see," she said. "The Research Division of Lao-tzu International is not here. Not in Columbus. Bogotá."

My fever was coming back and for a minute I just wanted to

hang up and go back to bed and drink bloody marys. Damn these uptight Chinese women! Damn doing business anyway! But I pulled myself together as well as I could and tried to sound charming. "Of course," I said, "but the research is done. What you need to do is test it out. That's not really research."

"I'm sorry, Mr. Jonson," she said, "we do not have the personnel or the equipment in Columbus to do what you say."

"Look," I said, "you have a Shartz Analyzer, don't you?"

"We have several."

"That's all you need for now." I sneezed suddenly. "We've run tests for a year at the University. It kills pain as well as morphine and it's not a narcotic."

"I'm not certain, Mr. Jonson, that Lao-tzu . . ."

"Come *on*, Miss Loo!" I said. "You look like a smart woman to me. This will take a half hour of your time and it can give you the most profitable pill since Glandol, or time-release Valium. Since Fergusson, for Christ's sake. Do I sound like a lunatic?"

"Yes you do, Mr. Jonson," Pear Blossom said crisply. I found myself staring at a blank viddiphone screen. She had hung up on me. "Son of a bitch!" I said and began sneezing. Then the sneeze turned into a cough. I got up and went to the bathroom and coughed and sneezed and spat voluminously into the toilet, occasionally stopping long enough to shout, "Motherfucker!" Whoever was below me pounded the ceiling again. I could picture some chubby, balding druggist hitting upward with a broom handle. I went on coughing, bent over and holding my belly. My nose was running.

Eventually the coughing stopped. I called room service for two bloody marys and then reached out for the Repeat button on the phone to get Pear Blossom back, but interrupted myself with another fit of coughing. *What the hell*, I thought, and called Ruth.

She came on looking sweet and chubby and a little disheveled. *Good old Ruth!* I thought, and my heart warmed at the sight of her there in front of me.

She was staring at me, apparently not sure who it was. "Ben?" she said.

"That's right, Ruth," I said warmly, with the cold now in

my voice, since my nose was plugged up. "I'm in Columbus."

She kept staring. Then suddenly she looked almost awed. "Oh *Ben*," she said, "I thought I'd never see you . . ."

"I'm at the John Glenn, Ruth." Just then a knock came on the door. "Wait a minute," I said. I left the phone and walked over, opened the door and took the tray with the drinks from the waiter. I pulled a fifty from my jeans pocket, handed it to him and went back to the phone. "Ruth," I said, "you don't know how much good it does just to see your face." I guzzled one of the bloody marys and snorted.

Ruth looked worried. "Are you drunk, Ben?"

"I'm sick, Ruth honey. I've got a cold. It feels . . . interstellar."

She looked relieved. "Do you want me to bring you some hot soup? I go to work in twenty minutes, and I could drop by . . ."

"Ruth," I said, interrupting, "I want more than soup. I'd like to move in with you for a week or two, while I get over this thing. I need to get a World Viddiphone Line and I need a set of barbells . . ." I sneezed again. "How about it?"

She hesitated, started to say something. Then she said, "Are you all right, Ben? Weren't the police . . . ?"

"I eluded them, Ruth, as the papers said."

"Oh," she said. "Ben, you look *strange*. Did you kick it? Morphine?"

I was starting to feel angry again. "Yes. I changed a lot, on Belson. Can I come and stay for a week?"

She looked at me silently for a moment. Then she shook her head. "Ben, it's too late for that. I have a man living with me. I can bring you some food, and a doctor if you need one . . ."

It was a setback for my vanity, but I managed to hide it well enough. "I'll be all right, Ruth."

She smiled sadly. "Sorry, Ben."

After talking with Ruth I sipped another bloody mary and permitted myself the old childhood gloom, then shook it off. What the hell, it was time to be grown-up about it. I'd tried the alternative enough in my life. There was business to take care of, and Isabel to locate. I pressed the Repeat button on the phone twice and got Lao-tzu again.

"Pear Blossom Loo, please," I said.

The head on the screen disappeared and was replaced by that of Pear Blossom's secretary. He put me through to Pear Blossom with some reluctance.

When she saw me she looked ready to hang up again. "The Research Division of Lao-tzu is in Bogotá, Colombia, Mr. Jonson."

I kept my composure, although I felt like throwing an ashtray at her disembodied head. "Miss Loo," I said, "I'll be in your office tomorrow afternoon. Do you really want me going to Parke-Davis first?"

"I will be in conference all day tomorrow." Her face was a study in blank dislike.

"I'll be there anyway," I said, and hung up. Her head and shoulders disappeared from the screen.

I fumed around the room for a while after that, cursing China in general and Chinese bureaucrats in particular. What Lao-tzu Pharmaceuticals needed was somebody like Arabella Kim to run it, with her good wrinkled face and tobacco-stained teeth. It was about noon, and there were things I wanted to do in Columbus—like getting a set of barbells—before going out to Lao-tzu in the morning, but I was beginning to feel as if I wouldn't be able to do any of it. This cold, or whatever it was I had, was *bad*. I was sticky from sweat and my nose and throat were stinging. I took endolin and it kept down the pain, but it didn't do anything for the cold itself. I knew what I needed was a transfusion from Belson grass, but that was out of the question. I climbed into bed, jabbed out my cigar in an ashtray, put a pillow over my head, and passed out. Falling asleep, I wondered briefly about Sue—about where the train would have been when she came to and found me gone.

I awoke late in the afternoon feeling feverish, dazed and unworldly. I knew I was sick, but I also knew it was only a cold. Something deeper was troubling me, some old loneliness. I'd had a Private World Line installed in the room and could talk through scrambled microwaves with considerable security to any phone in the world. I could do therapy this way. I sat up in bed, adjusted the sheets, relit my cigar, and called Orbach.

Orbach came on with his usual somberness. "Hello, Benjamin," he said. "Welcome back into the world."

"Orbach," I said, "can you spare me an hour? Things are happening."

He shook his head. "I'm sorry. I have a patient arriving. I can connect you with my surrogate . . ."

"Orbach!" I said, desperate. "I don't want to talk to a computer. Give me twenty minutes."

Orbach looked at me sadly. "I'm truly sorry, Benjamin," he said. "I can give you the noon hour on Thursday."

"I don't want Thursday," I said. "Give me your computer."

"It's good to see you back safely, Benjamin," the Great Orbach said. There was a slight click and the screen went milky white. Then Orbach's synthesized voice came from the speaker. "Hello, Benjamin," it said. "We can talk if you'd like."

"Hell yes, I'd like," I said.

"You sound angry," the voice said.

"I'd like to talk to my mother," I said grimly. What the hell.

"Your mother is dead, Benjamin."

"I've heard that you machines can fake it."

"I don't know the voice," the machine said. "I know parts of the personality, from your remarks in the office. Perhaps you can help me."

I nodded. I'd been offered the chance to do this before but refused it as being too contrived. "First, she was a woman. Of sorts."

"Yes," said Orbach's voice, now female.

"I want you to be her at about thirty-five, when I was a teenager. There was a nervous quaver in her voice. She was born in Columbus, Ohio, in 1987 and she spoke with an Ohio accent. She was a narcissistic drunk and she tried to be casual in her speech, but the self-regard and worry were always there."

There was a pause and then the machine said, in a genteel, quavering female voice, "Do I sound like your mother now, Benjamin?"

"That's pretty good," I said grimly.

"If you have a picture I'll put it on the screen and animate it."

"I'm not sure . . ." I said. But I was sure. I was faking it for the benefit of the machine. I did have my mother's picture in my billfold; I'd carried it for over thirty years and never told a soul. I reached over to the table beside the bed, took my billfold, opened it, slipped out a polychrome holo card and squeezed it on. And there sat Mother with a glass in one hand and a cigarette in the other, looking at the camera in a patronizing way. Her brow was furrowed half in irony and half anxiety. Her hair needed combing. I stared at her for a long time, unsure what I was feeling.

"Hold it toward the viewing lens, please." It was the machine speaking but I almost jumped; it had come to seem very like Mother's voice.

I held the picture toward the tiny lens at the bottom of the set, and a moment later the face reappeared on the screen. I leaned back in bed, my head propped slightly against the wall, and puffed my cigar. My palms were sweating and my mouth was dry. "Hello, Mother," I said.

The face moved, quite naturally, talking. "Hello, Benny," it said. It was uncanny. I felt frightened.

"Are you drunk, Mother?" I said.

"Hardly," she said. "It's ten in the morning."

"Oh," I said. Somehow the wind had all gone out of my sails. "What year is it?"

She looked down toward her watch. Mother always wore a watch, which may be why I'd never worn one until recently. Until leaving Isabel. "It's June 8, 2024," she said. "And I feel like hell."

"I hate to see you drinking and smoking like that, Mother," I said. "It makes me nervous."

She looked at me and then puffed her cigarette. "You're just a child, Benny," she said. "You have no idea how badly I feel. And your father's no help . . ."

Some of my anger was coming back. "Have you ever asked him for help?" I said.

"What good would that do? You have no conception of what it's like to deal with that man . . ."

"Damn it, Mother!" I shouted. "You've never noticed,

have you? You've never seen me trying to get him to talk to *me* . . ." And I broke off, startled to hear the quaver in my voice like that in the voice of the woman in front of me.

"He used to hold you on his lap when you were a baby. It was only after you got loud and had dirty fingernails all the time . . ."

"Mother," I said, "you're trying to blame me. Damn your soul."

She laughed, a cruel little self-regarding laugh. "You were hyperactive, Benny. And loud. A real pain in the neck . . ."

I stared at her, telling myself, *It's only a machine, a computer in an analyst's office on Third Avenue in New York. It isn't even her voice. It doesn't really sound like her.* Yet I saw myself as a small boy, dirty-nailed and loud and squirming and I felt hatred toward the child I saw, toward what that mechanical voice had sketched for me so blithely. "Mother!" I said. "Stop it!"

She looked at me and then took a knowing sip from the glass in her hand.

"Mother." I could hear the pain in my voice as though it were someone else's. "I was only a little kid."

She seemed not to hear me. "I never should have had a child."

"I didn't ask you to," I said.

She laughed a little more easily this time and finished her drink. "You were a trial to me even before you were born, Benny. You almost tore out my liver with your feet." She looked meditative. "That's all you were when I was pregnant with you: elbows and feet."

"Goddamn it!" I said, sitting upright in bed. The sheet fell away from me. I was naked there in front of her, exposed. "Goddamn it, you were supposed to be my *mother*."

Somehow she had gotten another glass of what must have been gin and she took a long swallow from it. "To tell the truth, Benny, you were a mistake," she said. "I had too much to drink at the wedding, and took the wrong Fergusson."

"*Orbach!*" I shouted at the machine, "how can you know that? You're not *her*."

Mother's picture remained on the screen, motionless now, and Orbach's voice came on, mechanically synthesized. "It is inferable," the voice said gravely, "from your memories and dreams. You are not being toyed with in therapy. You hear from your mother what you yourself believe to be true."

I lay back in bed again and started to pull the sheet over my body, but did not. I puffed my cigar deeply for a moment, nursing myself as always, and said, "Bring her back and let her talk."

"Benny," she said, more brightly now, "you were sweet enough in your way, but you never knew what *I* was going through. You would slobber kisses on me when I was hung over, and try to crawl in bed with me in the mornings, and when you were two you kept hugging your father's leg until I had to pull you away. You weren't like other children, with good manners and an ability to entertain themselves. You wanted attention all the time, and I was having problems myself. Your father ignored me. The other faculty wives made me a pariah. Life was very difficult for me."

I watched her with appalled fascination, remembering every phrase of it from one time or another. As she went on drinking and talking her face became more relaxed and pleasant. She looked younger and I saw, suddenly, that her breasts were still high under her pale-blue housedress and not the sagging old woman's breasts of the night she had sat with the candles going. "I know I have drunk a bit too much to be the best of mothers," she was saying, "but other mothers get some help from their husbands."

Now you're blaming him, I thought. *You'll blame anybody. Like me with Isabel.* I writhed with this for a moment, lost in a confusion of myself and my chattering mother there on the screen. It wasn't really Mother anyway, only a simulacrum. *And neither am I,* I thought. *I am not my mother either, but only a likeness when it comes to love.*

"I had the whole work of rearing you," she said. "He did not lift one finger. Not one."

"*Mother,*" I shouted from the bed. "You goddamned fraud. You could have loved me anyway. You could have let me love you . . ."

"Benjamin," she said sternly, "you are getting an erection. Cover yourself."

I looked down. It was true. I stared at myself for a long moment, bedazzled. I was shameless; I kept getting harder.

"Well," she said in some kind of crazy voice that was half coy and half reproachful, "I'm glad to see that you're normal. It's more than I can say for your father in there."

I stared at her on the screen. "Shut up!" I said. "Won't you please just shut up?"

Her eyes began to glaze. "Benny," she said, "you'll never know what it's been like for me all these years. God knows I've tried. I've tried to be a good wife and mother and nobody cares anything for me."

"Mother," I said, "I cared. I tried to love you and you pushed me away, just like Daddy. The two of you were a fucking *team* . . ."

"You don't have to use that language," she snapped. "You've forgotten how I nursed you, and fed you . . ."

"That's not how it was, Mother," I said. "You used to feed me Franco-American spaghetti out of a can. Half the time you didn't trouble yourself to heat it." I stared at her. "You were too drunk, Mother."

She looked down at her lap a moment and then took another drink. Her voice had become low and her eyes seemed to look inward as they had that night on the couch, with the candles. "You can abuse me all you like, Benjamin, with your gutter language. But the truth is I'm your mother and I did my best for you."

I sat up in bed, feeling something about to burst in my head. "It wasn't your best and it wasn't enough," I said.

For a long moment we were both silent, staring at one another. I realized, with a shock, that she was much younger than I. Prettiness and weakness met in her face, already showing incipient ruin. My hatred for that face was insatiable; I wanted to crush it like a rotten grapefruit between my hands.

During all this my prick had remained erect. Mother looked at me awhile in a kind of crazy, muted comtemplation. Then she said, "I used to wash your thing for you, Benny, when you were little, and cute. You always enjoyed it."

"Mother," I said, *"I was not a toy.* God did not give you something to fool around with when you had me."

She smiled a faint, smug smile. "Why is your penis so hard, Benny?"

"Why do you think?" I found myself shouting. "And you aren't worth it. You're nothing."

I was sitting straight up in bed. I reached forward abruptly and slammed the telephone's "off" switch with the heel of my hand. Her face, with its smug, flirtatious smile, vanished into the electronic limbo it had been generated from.

I finished my cigar slowly and got Orbach's machine on the phone again. This time the screen was blank. "I hope you are better, Benjamin," the machine said in Orbach's normal voice.

"I don't know. I'm not as angry."

"And things are clearer?"

"Things are," I said. "I had an erection while I was looking at her."

"Congratulations!" the machine said. "Would you like to talk with your father?"

I reached for another cigar and held it for a while in my hand. Then I shook my head. "My father's dead," I said.

"Yes," the machine said, "he is dead."

"Then I've done enough," I said.

In an hour the fever was down and my head was clear. It was getting dark outside, and the rain had stopped. I looked at my watch. Eight o'clock. I would be going out to Lao-tzu in the morning and I needed to do some research first. And I was hungry.

I phoned room service for a hamburger and a glass of ginger ale. Then I called the one local taxi and reserved him for eight in the morning. I hung up, pushed the "Library" button on the viddiphone and began tracking down what was available on Lao-tzu. There was a good deal, much of it in the Shanghai People's Library.

I found two histories of the company, going back to its origins on a Nanking back street in the nineteenth century, and books about the founder. There were annual reports and stock prospectuses in English and Chinese, and a lot of miscellaneous works on the drug business in China. I put it all on "Hold."

On a hunch I checked U. S. Political Science and struck it rich there too: a holo movie called *L'Ouverture Baynes—Man of the Times,* and a book from the University of Kentucky Press, *Kentucky Political Campaigns in the 2050s.* I had texts of these printed out.

My hamburger arrived on a pewter plate with grapes and cheese cubes and Roquefort dressing and piles of evil-looking lettuce: clearly a Renaissance Pope Sandwich. I signed the bill and turned on the TV, switching it to play the material I had on "Hold" on the viddiphone. I threw away the lettuce and began eating, as an introduction to the Chinese ethical drug business came on. There was a panoramic shot of Chang An in Peking and crowds of healthy, prosperous Chinese. "Welcome to China!" a saccharine voice proclaimed. I sighed, had a drink of ginger ale, and called room service again for a pot of coffee. It was going to take a lot of caffeine to get through all this.

About the time my pitcher of coffee arrived, Howard called to say he'd gotten the report on endolin. There was no way to analyze it completely and no way whatever to synthesize it. I was delighted. I thanked him for his help and told him I had to get busy. Then I instructed the viddiphone to select out for me all the information on analgesics and to read it aloud, in English. I poured a cup of coffee and settled back in my chair.

At Lao-tzu in the morning Pear Blossom's secretary told me icily that she was in conference. I told him I'd wait, plumped myself into an armchair and opened my Kentucky Politics printout, brought along for just this purpose. I lit a cigar. It must have been thirty years since anybody had made me wait in an outer office, cooling my heels like a porno-videosphere salesman, but I managed it all right. Pear Blossom came in a little over an hour later dressed in a gorgeous lavender shift and high heels. She saw me sitting there and looked away coolly, about to hurry into her office. Nice legs.

I played my ace in the hole immediately: I spoke to her in Chinese, using the Tradition-Revival forms. "Gracious flower of the arching pear tree," I said, freezing her in her tracks. "I address you unworthily and my outlander's tongue is lame with its mockery of yours." In fact, I was speaking Chinese beautifully and Pear Blossom, judging from her face, knew it. ". . . yet even my poor discourse might add treasure to the bursting storehouse of the exalted Lao-tzu.''

"I'll give you ten minutes," Pear Blossom said.

I followed her into her office, a packet of endolin in my hand.

It took them four days to make the first offer. It was absurdly low, as I explained to Pear Blossom and her boss. By that time they had figured out who I was and had come to take me seriously. They also knew, of course, what endolin could do. They wanted it. Oh yes. It tingled my capitalist balls to sense that.

They doubled the offer the next day, and I told them again what I wanted. Three hundred million for the fifty pounds I had and for a 40 percent option on imports.

They walked out on that, as I thought they might.

The following day we met in a bigger room, with gray silk wall hangings. There was a new person among them, a very old woman in a blue robe, just arrived by plane from Peking. Pear Blossom introduced her to me as Mourning Dove Soong and I knew immediately who she was.

I spoke to her in Chinese. "I am filled with pride to address the distinguished chairperson of the world's most formidable drug company."

She nodded without smiling. "You ask too much for your endolin. A headache is a headache. Aspirin is a fine drug."

This was just what I wanted. My heart felt light. It is exhilarating to see research pay off.

"I agree heartily," I said. "I often buy aspirin from Bayer—a fine company—or Norwich, though that firm tediously outsells Lao-tzu throughout Europe, Scandinavia, and the Gold Coast. Upjohn also purveys a fine U.S.P. aspirin, to be found in twice as many American stores as the Lao-tzu product, unquestionably worthy though the latter is. One might weep at the thought."

Mourning Dove was looking at me thoughtfully, holding a glass of plum wine. Pear Blossom and her boss were on the sofa. I sat in an armchair.

"One must also regard," I said, "those merciful aids to the arthritic which are made with an analgesic as a component. Tao, the illustrious nine-way arthritis remedy, has sadly lost millions of dollars to Anacin alone over the past seven quarters. The new plant in Rio de Janeiro for the manufacturing of Tao will be forced to close, at embarrassing cost, if this tendency is not reversed. Worker riots are spoken of publicly. One wonders what the addition of endolin, in trace amounts, might do to this unhappy competition with Anacin. Then we must consider light anesthesia for minor surgery, and the hospital market . . ."

Mourning Dove was lighting a cigarette, much as Humphrey Bogart might have. "We'll buy it," she said.

I could have hugged her. "Splendid!" I said, in English. "Let's sign the papers here tomorrow."

Mourning Dove nodded, and sipped her wine. "I understand you have no present citizenship, Mr. Belson," she said.

"All too true," I said in English, still feeling some of the Chinese way of speaking in my head. "I have no nationality whatever at present." I hesitated. "Perhaps you and I are sharing a thought." My research had told me Mourning Dove was not only Chairperson of Lao-tzu International; she also sat on the Committee for the Enlargement of the People. The Immigration Bureau.

"Perhaps. Would you like to be Chinese?"

"Mourning Dove, you are marvelous!" I said. "You and I understand each other very well."

"Yes," she said, unsmiling, in her soft, gravelly voice. "I'm certain it will help with your plans, to be free of legal encumbrances. Our embassies protect the People, Mr. Belson."

"Oh, don't I know it," I said, exuberant. I had planned to go for this but hadn't been sure it would work. As a Chinese I could have lawyers; I could use the whole string of multinational and world courts to go after the *Isabel*.

"Yes," Mourning Dove said. "It will make our contract safe from red tape. And from publicity."

"I'm right with you, Mourning Dove," I said. "Do I need to pass any tests? I've read Confucius and the sayings of Chairman Mao. I have a pair of Qin horses by my croquet court in Atlanta, and my sweetheart, Isabel Crawford, is a Maoist." I was high and feeling a bit silly. And I was really liking Mourning Dove, in whose eyes I had begun to detect amusement.

"None of that will be necessary," Pear Blossom said coolly. "It's a matter of form with the Committee for Enlargement, in Peking. The People's Republic does not require performances from prospective citizens."

Mourning Dove ignored her and smiled faintly at me. "Many of the Qin horses are exquisite," she said. "I am pleased with your judgment."

"Thank you," I said. "Thank you for coming all the way from China."

The forms were sent to Columbus by Transpacific Xerox, and by the next afternoon I was Chinese. I signed three papers in the presence of witnesses, made a ceremonial bow, and promised to be orderly in the arrangement of my household. Why not? I could have signed my name in script, but my professor of Chinese had shown me the calligraphic way and I did it like that, using a brush:

本
鏢
修

I became a compatriot of Confucius and Mao with a few strokes. A small world, if you know the right people. Chinese Belson.

I remained undeceived, however, aware that my being Chinese made the endolin contract safer for them. The papers were ready right after the naturalization papers. I signed them briskly. I was now not only a Chinese, but a rich Chinese.

• • •

After I left Lao-tzu with a plastic card that identified me as a Chinese national, my taxi took me to The People's Bank of Shanghai, Columbus Branch, where I set up some accounts. I'd taken a check for ten million from Lao-tzu, for good faith and to tide me over until the transfer of funds was finished. The only possible snag was in Lao-tzu's getting the endolin from the *Isabel*. I wouldn't have any more cash from them until that was brought off. Since the People's Republic maintained a big staff in Washington, and since even L'Ouverture couldn't buck the State Department where Chinese relations were concerned, I hoped they'd have it within a week. I'd told Pear Blossom how to find it in the *Isabel*'s cabin. Pear Blossom was clearly the sort of person who got hold of what was rightfully hers.

Back at the hotel I called London; first a retired actor I knew and then a theatrical agency. No luck from either. There was a subsidiary of Belson Tile and Marble in Fleet Street. I called its director and told him to find out what he could about an actress named Isabel Crawford. I'd call him back next week. His eyes bulged out to see his actual boss talking to him. "Certainly, Mr. Belson," he said. "We shall put our shoulders to the wheel."

When I'd done what I could about finding Isabel, I called the Lieutenant Governor of Kentucky, George Kavanaugh. I'd known him when he was a coal broker. We talked about Baynes, who was up for election in November. "Is he unbeatable?" I asked, after we'd finished the amenities.

"Maybe," George said. "He won strongly last time."

"Who's running against him?"

"Mattie Hinkle. Liberal democrat."

"What chance?"

"A Chinaman's."

"Watch your language, George," I said. "I'm no person to talk to about Orientals that way."

"Some of my best friends are Chinese," George said.

"I believe it. What's Hinkle's program? What's she promising?"

George scratched his head. "Shit, Ben, I don't know. Re-

form, I suppose. She should try to get him from the Left."
Suddenly he looked at me hard. "Didn't you escape from the
Marines or something, Ben? In Florida?"

"It was two private cops, George, and it was Washington.
You said from the Left?"

"Unemployment might work." He paused and grinned.
"God, Ben, you always were a live one. Betty says you ought
to be in movies."

"I don't have the time, George. How can I get in touch with
this Mattie Hinkle?"

"Try Miyagawa and Sumo in Louisville."

"Okay, George," I said. "Thanks for the information. And
don't tell anyone I called you."

"Mum's the word, Benny. Where are you calling from
anyway?"

"I'm staying at a hotel," I said. "In Los Angeles."

Miyagawa and Sumo was an ad agency. I told them I was
Aaron Fine, borrowing the name of my friend and accountant. I said I represented an organization backing liberal
causes. The man on the phone was a clerk in the agency and
clearly bored by all this. "We have impressive sums at our disposal, for key candidates," I said levelly.

"Oh?" He looked more interested. "May I ask the name of
your organization?"

"Something in the order of fifty million dollars," I said.

He stared at me and set down his coffee cup. "That figure is
hard to believe."

"Do I look crazy?"

"No, sir . . ."

"Look," I said, "I'd like to talk to either Miyagawa or
Sumo."

"They're both in conference," he said, for the second time.
This time he seemed less sure.

"Well," I said, "I'm going to hang up and have my bank
send a million for the campaign to show good faith. Then I'll
call back and I want to speak to *both* of them." I hung up.

I called the People's Bank and told them to phone a million
to Louisville. A certified check would pop out of a slot in the

agency's phone in a half minute. I called back and, sure enough, I was talking to two polite Japanese. By that time I'd invented an organization. "I represent the Friends of the Poor. We have been taking an interest in the campaign of Mattie Hinkle."

They both nodded sagely and the smaller of them spoke. "Ms. Hinkle thanks you for sharing."

"That's fine," I said. "What Friends of the Poor is concerned with right now is Ms. Hinkle's stand on safe uranium."

"Safe uranium?" the smaller one said. I took him to be Sumo.

"The uranium aboard the spaceship in Washington. The uranium Senator Baynes won't release for use in power plants."

"You say it's *safe* uranium?"

"I can explain later. The main issue now, for Friends of the Poor, is Ms. Hinkle's stand on that uranium."

They hemmed and hawed for a bit and then admitted Ms. Hinkle had no opinion on the *Isabel*'s uranium. They would be glad for me to enlighten them both on the issue.

"I'll call you back," I said, and hung up.

The next morning Pear Blossom called to say the endolin was off the *Isabel* and in the Chinese Embassy in Washington. I asked about Baynes.

"He did not involve himself," Pear Blossom told me coolly. She was a shade more civil, now that I was Chinese myself, but she still could project a lot of dislike.

"Baynes didn't try to interfere?"

"He was out of town. My colleagues went through the Department of State."

"Pear Blossom," I said, "can I come out this afternoon for my three hundred million?"

"Two hundred ninety million dollars," she said.

"Okay," I said. "Can I get it today?"

Pear Blossom looked petulant about it. I could see how it hurt her actuarial soul to part with that kind of money. She'd been boggled when Mourning Dove agreed to my terms, even though she must understand the drug market well enough to appreciate the impact endolin would make. "Mr. Belson," she said, "Lao-tzu is paying you over sixty thousand dollars an ounce for endolin. I feel we should attempt to market before . . ."

"Come on, Pear Blossom," I said. "You know I get the money when your embassy gets the endolin. *Our* embassy. There are forty-five thousand milligrams in a pound. You'll recover half your investment in six months. You have an exclusive on imports. You've got a bargain."

She shrugged wearily. It was the first human gesture I'd seen her make and my heart warmed to her. "Come on, Pear Blossom, honey. It's going to double the business for you. You'll be a company hero. Don't weaken."

And suddenly I was astonished to see her, there on my big viddiscreen, smiling at me. "Okay, Mr. Belson. I'll have your check ready." What nice teeth she had!

Pear Blossom had thawed enough to be downright agreeable. She congratulated me in Chinese and gave a demure bow as I took the little plastic check. The weather was getting cool and she wore a tight lavender sweater and Synlon jeans. "Pear Blossom," I said, "how'd you like to join me for breakfast?" We were sitting in her big antiseptic office. Behind her desk was a huge photograph of the Chinese Olympic Soccer Team.

"That would be pleasant," she said, almost bowling me over. I really hadn't expected it. "There's a cafeteria on the second floor."

It was about ten-thirty in the morning and we had the room to ourselves. I had figs and a pot of green tea; Pear Blossom had coffee and a danish. After we'd finished I looked for a few moments at the array of photos of bright pill bottles on the walls and then smiled at her. "You really look good in that sweater," I said.

Insensitive as Pear Blossom might seem, she appeared to be alert to the vibrations in my words. "Oh?" she said, coolly.

What the hell? I thought. "You're really a very dandy looking young lady," I said. "It's a nice fall day outside. Why don't you let me take you for a spin in my taxi?" Pear Blossom was probably in her late twenties; it occurred to me I hadn't touched the firm skin of a really young woman in a coon's age. Her jet-black Chinese hair shone in the fluorescent lights and her skin was flawlessly white.

Unfortunately, at my question her eyes had turned to something resembling Belson obsidian. "Mr. Belson," she said, in the voice you use for lunatics, "what do you have in mind?"

I almost backed off, but I felt I'd be damned if I would. "Sex," I said.

She put her little white hands firmly on the table and leaned toward me, speaking very distinctly. *"You old man,"* she said in the crispest English I'd ever heard. "You crazy, arrogant old man. I don't want your body touching mine."

"I'm sorry to hear that," I said, grabbing what composure I could from what was flying out every window in the big room. I could see myself in her eyes: a clumsy old Caucasian wanting to soil her body with lecherous hands.

"I'm going back to my office, Mr. Belson," she said, as distant as Fomalhaut. She got up and walked off, paying my check as she left the cafeteria.

I guess humility is good for you, if it can be kept to short bursts. It took me about three minutes to recover and remember how I really wasn't a dirty old man and that my body was in terrific shape. Besides, I was rich, and gentle, and good with children. I was helpful to the downtrodden. I made excellent fettuccine. Ruth liked me. Anna probably loved me. Isabel ditto, if she still remembered me. I'd cured Myra.

I took the check out of my shirt pocket and read the figures again. I began to feel better.

I hadn't bought Chinese securities for years, had never held a seat on the Peking exchange, and knew next to nothing about how to beat Chinese income taxes. But I didn't want to put my money in anything American, for fear of Baynes's tying it up. I'd have to get a Chinese lawyer, a Chinese broker and a Chinese accountant, for openers, and I didn't want to spend the time right then doing research. I'd done a thorough study of gold about five years before, and there is nothing more comfortably international. What I did was take a quick look at current prices, sigh a little, and buy two hundred fifty million worth of Chinese gold. That meant a new number would be placed on a list in Zurich. The simplicity of gold always scares me. Thirteen thousand four hundred a troy ounce. All it's really good for is filling teeth.

The other forty-eight million went into three bank accounts: one Chinese, one Japanese, and one—for sentiment—Scottish. Using the Chinese account and my Chinese name, I bought a five hundred thousand, paid-up American Express card, for traveling.

Back at the hotel that afternoon my passport card was already in the phone slot, with a scowling hologram of my face on one side and the crimson symbols for the People's Republic on the other, together with the usual date and place-of-birth information and warnings against travel in Russia, Cuba or Brazil. I slipped the card into my billfold, called Miyagawa and Sumo, and told them I wanted to speak to Mattie.

They put her on immediately. She came on the screen as a stocky, no-nonsense type in her mid-fifties, with glasses and closely cut hair. There was a matronly toughness to her, but her voice was soft. "My agency finds no record of a Friends of the Poor," she said, straight-out. "How do you account for that, Mr. Fine?"

I'd figured that might happen, since Miyagawa and Sumo had time to check it out.

"Look, Ms. Hinkle," I said, "I'll be straight with you. I'm not Aaron Fine, I'm Ben Belson. I want you to beat L'Ouverture Baynes so I can get my spaceship back."

She peered at me through her glasses for a moment, impassively, and then said, "That's pretty blatant, Mr. Belson."

"You're absolutely right," I said. "Illegal in every way."

"I understand you're not even an American citizen."

"That's right, too," I said. "They took it away from me." I decided the best defense was no defense at all. She'd have to make up her own mind, if she wanted me to buy her the election.

She pursed her lips and thought about it a moment. "Mr. Miyagawa said you spoke of several millions."

"Fifty. I can let you have it in gold. Five million at a time. I'll give you a number of an account in Zurich; you have it transferred where you want it."

"People get long prison terms for less," she said.

"That's the truth," I said.

"How can I know you aren't setting me up for just that? How can I know this phone call isn't being recorded?"

I was lighting a cigar as she said these things. I took a big puff and then set it in a hotel ashtray. "Well," I said, "you can never be sure. Anyway, I don't think *my* phone is tapped. To answer your first question, why would I want to set you up for anything? So Baynes could beat you? You know as well as I do he's already got you beat."

She pursed her lips again, in a schoolteacherly way. "I have other enemies," she said.

"I don't doubt it. You'll just have to assess the risks. You know who your enemies are; you'll have to figure out why I would be working for them."

She nodded. "May I call you back?"

"No," I said. "Sorry. I'm keeping my whereabouts a secret. I'll call back at noon tomorrow. Shall I go ahead and set up that Swiss account?"

"Don't do that," she said. "Just call. I'm addressing a D.A.C. meeting at noon, so make it at eleven."

"What's D.A.C.?" I said.

"The Daughters of the American Confederacy," Mattie Hinkle said.

I sat there and fidgeted for a minute. Then I decided to go ahead with it despite Mattie. I punched my Bank Dispatch code into the phone and had Shanghai send a twenty-million credit to Geneva under the rubric FRIENDS OF THE POOR FOR MATTIE HINKLE and a notification to Miyagawa and Sumo.

If I didn't hear anything for a week I'd send the rest of it.

I slept well that night and dreamed beatifically of money. Not of graphs on production charts or shorts in corn futures or even of bank accounts, but of crisp green beautifully engraved bills and brightly minted coins. For a while during the night I was a baby wrapped in new thousand-dollar bills, as though in swaddling clothes. I gurgled with the joy of contact with all that sweet money while older folk moved slowly by me, their steps taken as if in a sea of molasses, themselves dressed soberly in gray and brown suits, disdaining my infantile garment of cash. I smiled at them all.

✦ Chapter 14

Some part of me must have been expecting it all along. When I saw the four Marines the next morning standing in the lobby at the foot of the stairs, it had some of the quality of *dèjá vu*. Big sons of bitches. I stared at them and froze. When one of them took me by the right arm I came out of it and tried to pull away from him. It didn't work. I suppose I'd been imagining myself as one of the strongest men in America; this was a rude brush with reality. This youth with the perfect shave was bigger than I in every way. His fingers on my forearm felt like rocks. The other three looked about the same.

When they took me past the desk to the door the clerk looked away, busying himself with some records. Outside the hotel was a gasoline-powered military jeep. I sat in back with a Marine on each side of me and we drove off down Broad Street while people on the sidewalk stared.

I got back a bit of my composure in the jeep. "Men," I said, "where are you taking me?"

"Air base" was all I could get, from the only one who seemed to know how to talk. He had sergeant stripes. "You're not supposed to do this," I said, "I'm a Chinese national." I might as well have been speaking to the wind.

They took me about twenty miles to Kissinger Air Force Base, put me on an F-611 jet fighter, and flew me to Washington at four times the speed of sound. Those military sons of bitches; they burn jet fuel as if it were seawater.

It's quite an experience to fly like that, let me tell you. The *Isabel* could zip through her warp at two hundred times the speed of light, and light goes fast enough to circle the earth seven times in a second; but even so, that little white jet felt a hundred times faster. *Zoom,* Pennsylvania! *Zoom, zoom,* New Jersey! *Zoom,* Maryland! *Zip,* Washington! Good afternoon, Senator.

I wore one of those white spacesuits for altitude and was handcuffed to my seat, feeling like a nailed-down snowman skimming the stratosphere in this military frisbee. When we slowed for a landing the G forces pressed my body like the hand of death. I sat strapped in a tiny cockpit, feeling like hell, feeling like a childish fool, and unable to say a thing to anybody. I couldn't even hear my own voice over the roar of those fuel-wasting jets. Damn the military. They could have sent me back on a Pullman and saved everybody a lot of grief. But I grudgingly had to admit what they were doing made Baynes look good, the son of a bitch. There was class to this operation.

Four MPs at the Washington Air Base got me out of the white suit and into another jeep. They drove me straight to the Reagan Detention Center, where Baynes was waiting, dressed elegantly in gray tweeds. I checked my watch; less than two hours since they'd picked me up. If only they could handle mail like that. "Hello, L'Ouverture," I said, rubbing my wrists where a cop had just taken off the cuffs. We were in a steel-walled room without windows, sitting on wooden benches facing one another through plastic; our voices came through speakers. There was no humanity to this; I'd have felt closer talking to him by viddiphone.

"Ben!" L'Ouverture said, shaking his head in mock dismay. "What a nuisance! What a waste of taxpayers' money!"

"That's exactly what I've been thinking," I said. "How did you find me?"

Baynes shook his head again. "Ben," he said, "it was simplicity itself. You left clues everywhere. People recognized you in Philadelphia and called the FBI. The Chinese Embassy filed a report." He looked at me in a kind of bemusement. "Ben," he said, "I don't see how a man so careless could be so rich."

I felt myself blushing. Caught in my fool's paradise again, playing games. Tom Sawyer Wins An Election.

"Quit rubbing it in," I said. "What is it you want from me?"

"I want to know where that uranium came from, Ben."

"I figured as much," I said, "and I'm not going to tell you."

L'Ouverture leaned toward me, with his elbows on his knees. He was wearing a pale-blue oxford-cloth shirt and I could see silver cufflinks. He folded his long black fingers together. "That's no way to talk, Ben," he said. He smiled amiably. "If you don't tell me, you'll spend the rest of your days in this building."

"The Chinese Government . . ."

"The Chinese Government doesn't know where you are, Benjamin, and I don't think they care. Mourning Dove Soong is a busy woman. She has more to do than keep up with your whereabouts." He smiled again.

"What are the charges against me?"

He threw back his head and laughed, stretching out his long arms from his body. Then he shot his cuffs and set his bony elbows on his knees again. "Oh my my!" he said. "Resisting arrest, twice. Assaulting a police officer, four times. Illicitly importing dangerous drugs. Using same. Telephone fraud. Crossing state lines as an unregistered alien." He laughed again. "There are friends of mine on the bench who would give you ten years at hard labor just for burning up Aynsley Field."

I just looked at him. What was there to say? I knew he was at least partly wrong about Mourning Dove, if only because Lao-tzu needed me for future supplies of endolin; but I wasn't going to tell Baynes that. I wasn't going to tell Baynes *anything* this time.

"Well, L'Ouverture," I said, "you seem to have all the cards."

He nodded and smiled grimly. "You dealt them to me, Ben."

"L'Ouverture," I said, "I don't need this. I'll give you sixty percent of my uranium . . ."

He looked at me very coolly. "I don't want it."

"You don't *want* it? My God, it's worth a king's ransom."

He shook his head. "I'm a king already, Benjamin."

I looked at him. He was certainly *dressed* like a king. "It'll triple your wealth, L'Ouverture. It'll put America back on top of the heap."

He looked at me calmly. "Who are you to talk that way?" he said. "You're Chinese."

"Come off it," I said. "That's an expedient, not a political choice. We can be partners. Belson and Baynes."

He sat there awhile, looking very collected, very urbane. Finally he spoke. "I like things the way they are. I enjoy my work, Benjamin. The United States is doing very well under its energy laws, and I helped frame them."

"And you profit from them."

"They are good laws, for the resources we have."

I just looked at him, feeling nothing. There was no way to get through to this man, and I knew it. He did not want to be partners with anyone, and the only way I could bargain with him now would be to tell him about Juno and how to get there. But then, thinking about that, I realized something I had missed before: if he really wanted to know where my uranium came from he would have found out from the crew. He could have locked them up as conspirators, or pirates, and pressured them until someone told him. And he hadn't done that. "You don't really want to know where I got that uranium," I said.

He looked at me and smiled tiredly. "How perceptive you are, Benjamin."

"You just want to keep things the way they are."

"In a nutshell."

I sat there awhile. Finally I said, wearily, "Can you get me some cigars?"

He smiled. "I'll have a dozen boxes sent." He stood up to his full height on the other side of the plastic. What a hugely tall man he was, and how light on his feet and flexible for his age! The goddamned devious son of a bitch.

"Sacre Fidels," I said. And then, "Do you ever use Nautilus machines, L'Ouverture?"

He smiled down at me. "Daily." He straightened his jacket and patted the pockets with his huge hands, smoothing them. "I have to go now," he said.

I stood up. "What will you do with the *Isabel?*"

"It can stay where it is. Its hatch has been welded shut. And the portholes are covered. It is under perpetual guard."

"Like the Tomb of the Unknown Soldier?"

"Exactly."

"And it'll just stay at Aynsley?"

"I have no interest in football." He turned to leave.

"L'Ouverture," I said, "when am I going to get out of this place?"

He turned back to me and shook his head sympathetically. "Benjamin," he said, "I'd tell you if I knew."

I nodded. It all seemed eerily natural, this conversation with the thick transparent plastic between us. "I know I was spotted in Philadelphia," I said. "But how did you find out I was in Columbus?"

He stood silent for a minute before speaking. Then he said, "Sue Kranefeld. She called my office."

The Reagan Stir is a wretched place—a kind of flophouse of prisons. I was given a cell with a tiny TV and a cold-water shower. There was a library and, thank God, a gym. I worked out with weights and an LAT machine twice a day and sometimes did pushups in my cell. They had me in Diplomatic Isolation, which meant no visitors and no newspapers and no news shows on my TV. I was in Washington, but I didn't know if the public at large knew where I was. After a week I quit caring.

I hate to admit this, but a part of me warmed up to prison. I shifted into the psychic gear I had been in on Belson and all I really missed was my vegetables. I got the complete short stories of Henry James out of the prison library and spent my days between working out, reading and playing chess. At level eight. There was a UV booth in the gym; I added to my Belson suntan, which had faded a good deal. I wasn't allowed to talk to other prisoners—although I always nodded at a woeful Arab who worked out on the LAT machine next to me—and that suited me fine. Ever since Father's forget-me-nots I had known the game of spiritual Robinson Crusoe; I found sweet sadness in playing it yet again.

Sometimes at night I would watch TV, after getting weary with Henry James's games of ethical chess and of people who responded to moral crises by not finishing sentences. The Chinese TV channel was doing a thirty-part dramatization of European history, shot in Peking, and I got hooked on it. It wasn't the European history I had been taught and it was amusing to see it from a Chinese perspective. One Sunday night after a supper of frankfurters and beans I sat on my bunk drinking coffee from a plastic cup and idly watching a segment of the sixteenth century in England, when something about Queen Elizabeth caught my attention. Her walk seemed eerily familiar. I stared. It looked like Isabel in a red wig. I sat upright and turned up the volume. It *was* Isabel, in lace, pearls and heavy silk, looking like an authentic queen, even though it was ludicrous to hear her voice dubbed in high-pitched Chinese.

The Chinese view of Elizabeth was as a kind of virginal nymphomaniac. She was shown turning on Essex, and Cecil and Raleigh. Drake was trying to get into her pants. All of this was very disturbing, and when a scene came on where she was lying in bed with Essex, both of them naked, and she fending him off with chatter, I nearly choked. I wanted to kick the idiot who was playing Essex, grab Isabel by her lovely waist and demonstrate the folly of coyness. I could have pounded my head against the wall for the waste of my five months' impotence with her. There I sat in my cell, staring at her electronic image with an erection—the only erection the sight of her body had ever given me and as useless, now, as an airplane on the moon.

I'd been happy enough with Henry James, chess and weightlifting before that, but it changed everything. I wanted to get out of prison and back to life again. It was toward the end of October; I'd been in stir six weeks, with no trial scheduled and no word from anybody. I stepped out of my Robinson Crusoe daze like stepping out of a pair of dirty socks and found myself in reality. It was awful. I was in prison, horny, angry, and ready to go, but I couldn't get out. Four walls. Bars on the windows. Guards. Frankfurters, beans and instant coffee.

This kept up for two weeks and would have been the death of me if they hadn't, suddenly and without notice, let me out. The eighth of November. Two guards came into my cell after breakfast and told me to pack. That took three minutes, including brushing my teeth. They took me to a desk where I signed papers, got back my billfold, was admonished to "watch my step" and taken to a coal-gas black Maria. I didn't know what in hell was going on, but suspected it had something to do with the election. My prison had been well heated if nothing else; it was icy and gray outside. Glad as I was to get out, a part of me was sorry to leave the warmth of jail. We drove past the Washington Monument, looking bleak in the winter air, and then a few blocks later I looked down a side street and saw sticking up proudly into the sky above tall buildings, covered with snow, the *Isabel!* That cheered me up. I blew her a kiss as we went by.

They pulled up at the Chinese Embassy and the guards ushered me into a back door, where four Chinese soldiers took me into a room with painted screens and modern furniture. Two Chinese ladies fingerprinted me, in red. A tall, thirtyish one who seemed in charge handed me rice paper forms to sign.

"What's all this about?" I asked, in English.

She pulled a cigarette from her robe, lit it and blew smoke toward me. "I am taking you home, Mr. Kwoo."

"Kwoo?" I almost jumped out of my skin. "What the hell is this *Kwoo?*" I still hadn't signed the papers. "Let me have one of your cigarettes if you don't mind, and then explain to me what going home means and about this Mr. Kwoo."

She gave me a cigarette and lit it with a little red electronic. "Mr. Kwoo is your Chinese name," she said.

"That's not what's on my passport," I said.

"We have a new passport. It seemed expedient to change your identity." Her face was hard-looking but the voice pleasant enough. Except for the hardness she was a beautiful woman. "The United States does not want you to leave its shores. Senator Baynes would like to keep you under lock and key until . . . how do you say it in America?"

"The cows come home. Hell freezes over." I began to pace around the room, hands in my jeans pockets. "I wasn't planning to leave any shores, anyway." But it had already dawned on me; they were going to take me to China. What the hell; it beat prison. And Isabel might be there. "Is 'home' China?" I said.

She nodded.

"Okay," I said, "okay. I'll need some clothes." The prison jeans and dungaree shirt I was wearing were all I had. "Does this have to do with endolin?"

"Our interest in you, Mr. Kwoo, is not pharmacological. It is your other cargo that occupies our attention. It has caused us to go to some lengths to take you from prison."

Shit. They wanted the Juno uranium fields. For a moment I chilled with the image of a Chinese dungeon somewhere. What if they had revived the water torture? Meltdowns were a scandal to the People's Republic and the old ladies who ran it; there were radioactive villages and ruined rice paddies sprinkled all over that ancient geography. My well-being, in that context, would mean very little.

"Is Mourning Dove Soong behind this?" I said.

"Madame Soong is Deputy Chairman for the Honshu District. I do not know her position with respect to your case."

"Okay," I said. "I'll go to China. How do we get there?"

She took another cigarette and lit it from the butt of the first. "We'll go by ship, Mr. Kwoo."

"All right," I said. I stubbed my cigarette out in a little jade dish. "But tell me. What does 'Kwoo' mean?"

The shorter woman spoke up, in a quiet voice. "It's an old Mandarin word. It denotes an ancient coin. You could translate it as 'cash.' "

I looked down at her and fingered my beard. "Well," I said, "you people do know how to name the newborn. I accept Kwoo." *Ben Kwoo.*

It was a Chinese jet that took us to the Embarcadero in San Francisco. This time my stratosphere suit was crimson. There was a valve in the mask, so I could sip oolong through a straw during the two-hour flight. My cigarette-smoking friend was

seated behind me, but had little to say on our intercom. I tried
to get her to talk about her family, but she wasn't interested. I
sipped my tea and brooded a bit. Then I did some knee bends
just as we were zooming over the Rockies and started figuring
out ways of getting back into the search for Isabel from
wherever we were going in China.

A gray Mercedes was waiting for us; we drove in silence
from the airfield to a dock. The car pulled up at the gangway
to a coal-burner with rusty sides. On the forepeak lettered in
red was PRS KEIR HARDIE. It was a Scottish ship! "What the
hell?" I said to my chain-smoking companion. She was climbing the gangway alongside me with her short black hair blowing in the offshore wind. "Why aren't we sailing Chinese?"

"This was available," she said, stepping briskly aboard.

My stateroom was ready and she ushered me right to it. My
heart lifted when I walked in. The parlor had a screen painted
with blue morning glories; there were walnut tables and blue
silk poufs. Along one bulkhead was a galley with a refrigerator, a molecular cooker and a freezer. "How long will the
trip take?" I looked at her. "And what's your name?"

"My name is White Heron. Many call me Jane. It will take
us two weeks to cross the Pacific."

There was a bar with relief carvings of birds on its front and
two crystal decanters and glasses. I crossed over to it and
sniffed one of the decanters. Scotch, sure enough. I started to
pour. "Would you like a drink, White Heron?"

"Jane," she said. "I'm on duty."

"Suit yourself," I said and made mine larger. I went to the
refrigerator, filled my glass with ice and clinked it around. I
was still wearing my red stratosphere suit. I took a drink and a
ship's whistle blew, loud, clear and thrilling. Nothing in this
world sounds better than a ship's whistle. "Are we leaving?"

Jane nodded and the deck beneath our feet began to vibrate.
I drank another musty slug of scotch, spreading out my big
feet into a seaman's stance. "Jane," I said, "who assigned me
to these quarters? It wasn't you, was it?"

She looked at me coldly. She'd have had me in the bilges if
she'd been in charge. Then she shrugged. "It was Mourning
Dove Soong," she said. "Your partner at Lao-tzu Pharmaceuticals."

"Yes," I said, and drank off my scotch. "Bless her heart."
I thought of Arabella Kim and her woodlot in Washington.
Old Chinese mothers, the two of them, as good as gold.
Maybe there was something in matriarchy after all.

I played a lot of solo chess during the next few days and then
began to suntan myself on deck when we got far enough into
the South Pacific. I read a few twenty-first-century Chinese
novels, but their vigor wore me out. Everybody was productive and brave in those books, and nobody made love except
after a Confucianist wedding, and then they did it solemnly
and in the dark. Puritanism is like the wheel; if it ever got lost
it would be reinvented fast.

I was allowed no access to the ship's communications equipment, which was probably just as well. I wasn't ready to do
business just yet. I managed to borrow some recent Scottish
magazines from one of the mates and entertained myself with
stories of love among the fens, or brawls on collective farms in
the lowlands. Still dull stuff, but better than the Chinese.
More balls.

The ship plowed across the blue Pacific as if in a dream,
leaving a wake like a glory in that awe-inspiring surface. At
night the stars were magnificent—nearly as bright as from my
toilet seat on the *Isabel*. When we got to our southernmost
point I could see Fomalhaut, near the horizon.

Nobody talked to me much and I didn't try to make friends.
They were probably under orders anyway. There were some
other passengers, all well-to-do Chinese families. It seemed the
Keir Hardie was used by the higher ranks of the Party. As
much as they officially excoriated one another, the Chinese
and the Scots could work things out when it came to luxury.
There's nothing new in that.

I took my meals alone and ate with chopsticks. The officers'
mess supplied what I ordered, and once offered a haggis if I
wanted to try one. I declined politely. I had no television and
no newspapers and didn't care. It was shipboard lull and fine
with me. But I worked out in the ship's gym daily and did
pushups in between, coiling up for whatever lay ahead.

I would see families sometimes standing in a row along the

gunwale, wrapped in their heavy overcoats, staring out to sea.
The children were touching—so solemn and oriental, with
their bangs and quiet black eyes. Sometimes a beautiful child
would peek toward me as I stood nearby, in one of my crazy
capitalist outfits, but there was never any conversation. I'd
like to have adopted about six of those kids. I'd have loved to
cook pot roast for a bunch of them and taught them how to
play chess.

Well. Children are hostages to fortune, as Bacon said. But
what else is there to do with your time?

I can see myself dying by coronary in a parlor suite, clutch-
ing my throbbing shoulder and mumbling, "Hey! I need time
to think about this!" I would be ninety and still in good shape
but without a home or family, without a profession. Tycoon is
no profession. All I do is make money and chase women. And
travel. *"I haven't done anything with my life!"* I would say in
that hotel suite, thrashing about in the kitchen in terminal
anguish, falling dead over the *truite fumée*.

One evening at the beginning of my second week there was a
knock on my door. I was at the table, playing king's gambit
against Myra's board. I got up and opened the door. It was
Jane, wearing a pink silk dress. She was lighting a cigarette.

"Hello," I said.

"Hello. I've come for that drink."

"Sure," I said. "Come in."

It was one of those tight traditional dresses with a slit down
the side. The amount of leg she displayed coming in the door
was alarming; a voice in me immediately said, *Watch it*.

"I'm in the middle of a game," I said.

She nodded and seated herself on my lavender pouf. Her
black hair shone and she wore scarlet lipstick; her face was
dead white and Chinese-round with perfect Mongolian eye-
folds. She looked like a poster ad for a twentieth-century
movie. The Dragon Lady. She watched me silently. I returned
to the sofa and lit a cigar. I was in my prison dungarees—comfortably faded now since I washed them at nights and hung
them on deck to dry. If they got rained on I wore my red silk
stratosphere pants and went barechested, like an Italian
trapeze artist. She was looking me over the way Fu Manchu

might look over a captive American spy. *We have ways of making you talk, Mr. Belson.* "I like big men," she said.

"You're a tall person yourself," I said. "What will happen when we dock in China? To me, I mean."

"You'll be interrogated and given living quarters. Much depends on your cooperation." She lit another cigarette from the butt of the first, and then ground the old one out in one of my jade ashtrays. There was silence for a while, except for the rumble of the ship's engines. I turned back to my game.

I was going for a back-rank checkmate with my queen's rook, but I couldn't get the proper file cleared of pawns. I leaned forward and tried to concentrate. Just as I found the move I wanted, she spoke. "I've never had an American lover," she said.

I brought a knight to bishop five and looked over the board at her. "I'm not American anymore."

"Nonsense. You're the most American person I've ever seen. Like Abraham Lincoln."

"That's good company," I said, "and I thank you for putting me in it. Lincoln was a genius and a man of heart."

She looked at me as though appraising a minor artwork. "A big American man with a big sad soul." She crossed her legs with the sound tight silk makes. "Just like you."

"I feel more affinity with Billy the Kid," I said, nervously. "But thanks anyway. If that actor hadn't plugged Lincoln at the play it would be a different world. What if Chairman Mao had been gunned down in the fifties?"

"Chairman Mao made many errors."

"Maybe," I said. "But Mao was what China needed. You were lucky to have him all those years."

"If one didn't spend one's time being rehabilitated."

"Okay," I said. "Okay. Where is this ship going to dock?"

"At the Port of Celestial Winds, District Four."

"I never heard of it."

"Newly built by the People." She looked me over silently again. I turned back to Myra's board and tried to concentrate. Abruptly she said, "I'd like sex."

"Jane, honey," I looked up again, "I've got other things to think about. My heart wouldn't be in it."

She ignored that and stood up languidly. Then she arched

her arms behind her back and unfastened the neck of her dress. I have a great weakness for the upper arms of beautiful women and I could hardly not see how fine hers were. Firm and perfectly white. While I watched in reluctant fascination, she let the dress drop to her ankles and stepped out of it. She kicked off her sandals. She was wearing scarlet panties and a thin gold necklace. Her body was as white as snow and without a flaw. Tiny white breasts and tiny white feet. I was getting hard. "Come on, Jane," I said. "I'm not in the mood for this kind of thing. I'm fifty-three years old and well past my prime and I'm in love with a Scottish actress."

She walked over to the sofa and sat beside me. "Take off your pants."

"Come *on*, Jane," I said, panicking. The tops of her shoulders were the best I'd ever seen. I blinked with unease.

"There's nothing to be afraid of," she said. And then, "Is your pubic hair blond too?"

"It's got a lot of gray," I said.

"You can lie back on the couch and I'll undress you."

"I tell you, Jane, you're a splendid-looking woman. Enough to drive a man right out of his skull. But I wasn't cut out for this . . . this gigolo thing. I have to pick my own times."

She laughed at the word "gigolo." "There's nothing wrong with your servicing me. Chinese men enjoy the opportunity. Many of them are trained for it, in schools."

At the word "servicing" I stiffened. I could run out onto the deck, or lock myself in the bathroom. Except that my perverse member was now so rigid there was no way I could stand up in those tight prison jeans.

"Mr. Kwoo," Jane said, coolly, "you'll need a good report from me when we arrive in China. If I say your thinking is confused it could cause you hardship."

Jesus Christ! I thought. Am I going to have to do this like a whore? Can a man really do that and satisfy the lady in a state of panic? My member was answering this silent inquiry in the affirmative; it was undaunted. The eager son of a bitch. I felt betrayed by the same partner who had betrayed me the other way with Isabel.

I looked her over. She sure had a fine body, even though it

looked as cold as ice. And I loved the red panties. *What the hell*, I thought. *I used to sleep with a horse*. "Okay, Jane," I said. "But let's go into the bedroom and do it right."

"Here is adequate," she said. She began to unzip my pants.

"Look," I said, pushing her hands away, "I'll do this myself." I unzipped with care and freed myself. I slipped the pants off, and then my shorts. I was already barefoot. I started to get up.

She had already stood. Now she pushed on my chest, with alarming strength from a smallish person, and I sat back. "Just lie back, Mr. Kwoo," she said. "I think your pubic hair is charming, with all those curls."

"Jesus Christ, Jane, I'm no *courtesan*. I can't just . . ."

"Yes you can. Clearly. Just lie back and relax."

I think I was blushing. She was aroused to where she looked dangerous. Her nipples stood out like little Marines. "Okay," I said, defeated. "Okay." I lay back awkwardly, bending my knees to fit my frame to the couch.

She had peeled off her panties by the time I got there, and then she mounted me in a gung-ho way, as though she were a sailor and I a B-girl. I didn't like it at all, but my sexuality was in another world, doing its business in the dark like an Old Testament fanatic. I wriggled despite myself and ground up into her with a twist. "That's it!" she whispered and began pumping in earnest. I pumped back. She began kissing me open-mouthed, smelling of booze. Her nipples pushed into my chest. I began to feel smothered. She pulled back just in time and I could see her face twisted in some kind of unearthly concentration, her eyes upward and sweat on her porcelain forehead, with the bangs now sticking to it. I froze at the sight.

"Don't stop now," she said.

I started pumping again. From the waist down I was a satyr. But my better part was watching in alarmed detachment.

"Yes!" Jane hissed—not to me but to the ceiling. She grabbed my shoulders and I winced when her nails dug in. Then she went slack and fell across my chest.

I don't know why that orgasm of hers didn't provoke one on my part, but it didn't. Suddenly I felt a physical need that was as potent as the need for air when you find it cut off. I started pumping against her limp body.

Abruptly she grew rigid, and then pushed off of me. "What the hell . . . ?" I said, throbbing.

"I'm finished," she said.

"Well, I'm not," I said and reached out to grab her. She stepped back nimbly. I sat up, furious. My groin was beginning to ache. "I can rape you," I said.

"I'd kick you first. You'd never forget it."

She stood there sweating like an Olympic gymnast and I believed her. I leaned back on the sofa. I'd had a lot of practice at sexual frustration—at Isabel's and at the Pierre afterward—and for a moment I gave up. "Suit yourself, White Heron," I said.

"I have suited myself," she said. She bent elegantly to the table by the pouf and took a cigarette. Her back was to me.

I was off the couch and had her around the waist before she could straighten up. I was careful not to hurt her or break a bone; but I had her on the floor in ten seconds. I looked down at her face. It was flushed but composed.

"If you rape me," she said, "I'll put you in prison."

"Mourning Dove Soong likes me," I said, breathing hard. "If you try that, she'll have you in front of the Central Committee." That was mostly bluffing, but it seemed to work. Her face for the first time lost some of its composure. "Then enjoy yourself, Mr. Kwoo."

"I'm Ben Belson," I said, "and I'm not going to rape you." And I wasn't. My member had finally bowed out of the fray.

Jane stayed out of my cabin for the rest of the trip. I didn't see her again until a cold morning when I passed her on deck after coffee and then looked through mists over the port bow to see the coast of China. Right over there. Despite apprehensions and uncertainties, the thrill was exquisite; to sail the Pacific and then see China distant in the mist is an experience that goes right to the marrow of your bones and tingles the back of your skull like a morphine rush. I stared for a moment and then started doing side-straddle hops by the gunwale, wearing my red spaceman's pantaloons, barefoot on the slippery metal deck. Jumping jacks, some people call them. I slapped my hands together over my head and hopped my legs out and in, saying hello to China. The ship's whistle blew. I stopped and held my breath. We were turning starboard and I felt a heart-rending throb as the screws adjusted to a new course. We steamed straight toward the China Coast.

The *Keir Hardie* docked at a long gray pier late that afternoon. The rain had changed to sleet and it was freezing cold. I had no coat. The dock city looked like Cleveland in the nineteenth century—dark satanic mills and grit in the air. Coolie longshoremen lounged on barrels at dockside, in Ghengis Khan hats and overcoats, smoking what might have been opium. The ship was docked by computer, and when it was done a huge red display suddenly lit up on the side of a plastic warehouse, spelling out in neon-like letters: WELCOME TO THE PEOPLE'S REPUBLIC OF CHINA. My teeth chattered. I had thrown a blanket over my shoulders and was wearing my electronic running shoes, but I had no socks, having lost them sometime before in the Reagan Stir, and my toes were freezing.

One of the female crew members found me like this, swigging from my decanter. She approached me warily, as one might examine a sick grizzly.

"If you don't watch out," she said, pronouncing the word "oot," "you'll have pneumonia in the lungs."

"Honey," I said, "I have no coat or socks. This is it."

"I'll bring you something against it," she said. "Hold on now."

She jogged back to a stairway and down. A minute later she came back with a jacket, two pairs of socks, a pair of mittens and a tam. "The mate had these put by," she said, handing them to me. The coat looked pretty small, but I thanked her from the bottom of my heart, went into my cabin again, and managed to get it all on—although my wrists stuck out of the sleeves of the mackinaw and it wouldn't button over my chest. But the mittens were stretchy enough and the tam fit. It had a damn-fool red pom-pom on the top, which I managed to bite off and stuff in my pocket. I looked at myself in a closet mirror before going back out again. It was terrible, with the red silk pants and the rest of it. But what the hell; I stepped back out on deck, head high.

Jane was waiting for me, wearing an army uniform this time with the long gray overcoat and epaulets. A major's insignia and a gray garrison cap. She looked like the Empress of Austria, or a Chinese Greta Garbo in *Ninotchka*.

"Well," I said, holding my composure pretty well, considering my outfit and hers. "So you're a soldier. I had no idea."

"You look a fool," she said, not without some pleasure.

"White Heron," I said, "use your sadism on the troops. I'm not afraid of you."

She lit a cigarette and said nothing. A moment later the gangway went down and the First Officer left the ship. There were four male noncoms with rifles standing at dockside. They must have marched up while I was changing clothes. One signed a paper the officer handed them, returned it, shouted something to the others and then led them up the gangway to where we stood. The leader saluted Jane, who returned it casually, her cigarette between the fingers of the saluting hand.

We marched down the gangway and onto the ancient soil of China. I didn't exactly march, but stumped along because of the two pairs of wool socks stuffed into my running shoes. I was arriving in China even more clownishly than I'd arrived at Aynsley Field by spaceship. Well. Dignity was never my object in life.

They had a staff limousine—an actual nineteen-nineties black Cadillac with power windows and a glass partition; as far as I knew, the only one like it in America was under glass at the Smithsonian. Two flags of the People's Army flew from fenders. A sergeant opened the door and I got in. It was a billionaire's car if there ever was one; I felt immediately at home.

Two soldiers got in back with Jane and me, and sat on the jump seats. We drove in silence away from dockside. The coolie loafers puffed their long pipes and stared at us through the sleet. I relaxed against glove-leather upholstery and lit a cigar. Willynilly, I had my dignity back.

We drove about five miles past industrial buildings before hitting open country. The sleet had lessened; it was getting late in the day. There were houses surrounded by perfectly groomed fields. Pink tile roofs glistened wetly. I saw children playing in front of a barn; they stopped to wave as we drove by. I waved back. Old men drove gray steam tractors or red nuclear jeeps; there were vehicles everywhere. We passed a house with a table in its front yard where four old women sat at tea, their heads together in gossip. Pigs rooted at the edge of the house. An old man sat on the porch in an overcoat, reading a newspaper. *Everybody was Chinese. A whole country full of Chinese!*

A few miles later we drove by a four-story factory building painted bright blue. The sun was setting behind it. There were hundreds of electric cars in a lot near the gate, a sight America hadn't seen for sixty years.

"What do they make there?" I asked Jane.

"Toy airplanes," she said. "For export." *My God*, I thought, *Myra has one of those. I bought it at F.A.O. Schwartz.*

Our destination turned out to be another airport. In a grim, institutional waiting room I changed into a fresh stratosphere suit—yellow this time—and was taken without ceremony to a Confucius 433 jet. Jane was my fellow passenger again. She stubbed out her cigarette while the pilot zipped down the runway; she covered her bangs with her helmet as we shot up for altitude like an arrow of Apollo, leaving behind us a plain that stretched twenty miles from the sea and ended in a vast range of blue mountains, now glowing in the setting sun.

"Where to?" I said into the intercom.

"Peking," Jane said. "The Imperial City."

We landed in darkness a few hours later. I was drowsy now and in need of food and rest. My seat on the plane was designed for a smaller race of person than I, and my ass was sore from it. I hadn't had anything to eat since that breakfast coffee. When we started coming down I asked Jane if I could get a sandwich at the airport.

"No time for that, Mr. Kwoo," she said as we banked into a landing curve.

Two girl soldiers marched us from the plane to a black electric Mercedes. My stomach growled. I lit a cigar. We drove down a dimly lit airport road and then through suburbs of row houses with an occasional corner grocery lighted brightly, where old people shopped. Where were the young? We crossed Chang An Avenue and came into a downtown district with a few bright lights but not many people. It was only nine-thirty, and this appeared to be Peace Blooms Square right in the heart of downtown. A few blocks from Tien An Men. Everybody must be at home watching television. I was gratified to see what appeared to be a drunk, asleep on a bench near a closed bookstore. An American tourist? We drove on. A few blocks from the square we stopped in front of what appeared to be a hotel.

"Where are we?" I said.

Jane answered in Chinese. "You will be a guest in the House of Comradely Love."

I was marched past a grim lobby with four male clerks at a desk. We went into a gritty freight elevator and stared straight ahead as we went up eighteen floors and creaked to a stop. The door opened. The hallway had a gray linoleum floor, with cigarette butts. A dead geranium sat in a cracked pot near a barred window to my right; we turned left, past metal doorways to the end of the hall. There were four locks on the door. The girl who had brought us here produced four electronic keys and unlocked them one by one without getting any of the locks wrong. She stepped aside. Jane pushed open the door into a single room. A bare twenty-watt bulb hung from the ceiling, illuminating the ugliest hotel room I had ever seen. A cockroach scurried along a broken baseboard; the air smelled of cabbage.

"What the hell are you trying to do to me, White Heron?" I said.

She looked at me a moment and then spoke in English. "You should have been more cooperative. Aboard the ship."

"Wait till Mourning Dove hears about this."

"Mourning Dove Soong," White Heron said, "is enjoying a long vacation in Tibet, at a monastery without viddiphone. She will be there meditating, indefinitely. I have been given charge of your case."

I stared at her.

"Welcome to China," Jane said, and clanged the door behind me. I stood transfixed in that cold, cabbagey room. In dim light I saw an oak dresser, a straight-backed chair and a sagging bed. A toilet without a seat was in one corner, and a dirty washstand with one tap at the other. There was no telephone, no TV, no bathtub or shower. There was no food. The one window had bars an inch thick.

I managed to sleep anyway, with my clothes on. There was a cake of rough yellow soap and I got fairly clean with it in the morning and then used the wet towel to wash some of the grit off the window. I looked down between bars eighteen stories to a park. It looked like Gramercy Park, in fact. I was stiff as a board and frightened. My joints ached and I was trembling with cold. I did situps and knee bends for ten minutes, trying not to think about breakfast. Trying not to think at all. They would hardly bring me to China just to starve me.

When I'd finished and was wiping off the sweat with my one other towel the door started unlocking. This time two men were waiting for me, in noncom uniforms. They escorted me silently to the elevator and punched the up button. We arrived at a kind of penthouse on the twenty-sixth floor, which turned out to be the cafeteria. A few old people were sitting at tables, drinking tea.

The guards continued to flank me while I went to the serving counter. The food was piled in steel trays and lit by flickering light bulbs. I got six hard-boiled eggs, a cup of soggy rice and a mug of black tea. There was no cream or sugar.

I took a seat by the balcony with a view of Gramercy Park, and cracked my eggs while the guards watched. The eggs were awfully dry in my mouth, and when I tried to wash them down with tea I spilled some on my beard because my hand was shaking. *Don't weaken, Belson*, I told myself. But there was a gnawing going on at the roots of my soul. I knew what it was I had begun to want the minute I saw that room, that scurrying roach, that awful bed. Morphine.

When I finished, the men marched me back to the elevator. In the lobby two other soldiers met us, both with rifles, and the four of them escorted me out the door and across the street to a building with a big sign that read PEOPLE'S CLOTHING AND AIDS TO HEALTH.

Inside, a chubby middle-aged man looked me over. "Mr. Kwoo?" he said.

"That's right."

"Well, we can certainly make you more fashionable than *that*." He frowned at my yellow spacesuit.

"You're going to make me an outfit?" I said.

"Absolutely!" he said in English. "The very best. We know about you from the newspapers, Mr. Kwoo, and we know your importance."

Thanks a lot, I thought, remembering my hotel room.

The five of them took me to a back room where a big metal box stood, like an upright coffin.

"Just step inside," the man said. "It works like a dream. An absolute dream."

I stepped in. He threw a switch and I heard a hum. An invisible beam must be scanning my body, doing a contour map. "All right now," he said and turned it off.

"How long does it take?" I said.

"About ten minutes. Do you like midnight blue? For the trousers, I mean?"

"How about blue jeans?" I said.

"Sorry," he said. "This isn't Los Angeles. I was planning flannels. We'll cut four or five shirts in different pastels, and then, to cap it all, a simple down jacket in gray silk."

"Don't make it look Italian. And I'll need shoes."

"I'm sorry, Mr. Kwoo," he said, "but our shoemaking equipment isn't working. We can give you fresh hose for those . . ." He looked at my feet with distaste.

"Adidas," I said.

"I'm sure they're *marvelous* for speed." He turned and walked over to a wall where bolts of fabric hung above one another, reached his short arms up, and with some dexterity pulled down a heavy bolt of gray cloth. He smiled benignly toward me and then lugged the fabric over to a large gray machine, slid it into a hopper at one end and delicately pressed a green button on the side. There was a low whirr for about fifteen seconds, a click, and then another louder whirr. A folded pair of pants slid out onto a red enameled tray. He walked over and picked them up. "Perfect," he said. "It's really a superb piece of equipment. Japanese." He handed them to me.

I slipped out of my spacepants right there and pulled on the flannels. They were of good fabric, but they fit over my narrow ass like a glove. "Jesus!" I said, "they're *tight*."

He looked me over, pursing his lips. "Well," he said, "this machine does make them snug. That's the truth of it."

"Isn't it working right?" I said. "I haven't seen anybody on the streets wearing anything like this. The men outside are wearing good Communist baggy pants."

He blushed a little. "To be frank," he said, "I'm under orders from the Army. From Major Feng."

I stared at him. "White Heron?"

He looked up at me helplessly. "Yes, Mr. Kwoo. White Heron Feng. You are to be dressed as a . . . as a courtesan."

"Jesus Christ!" I said. Inwardly I had a sense of my life—my tired and crazy life—coming full circle, with a kind of preordained click. *Okay,* I thought, *I can follow this out to the end*.

They made me a down-filled gray jacket and one of those Ghengis Khan caps, with the earflaps. It all fit well and looked good. They were far better clothes than you could buy in New York. The truth of it is there's nothing first-class made in America except television and French fries. Television *equipment*, that is; the shows are for cretins.

Outside, it was bitter cold and I tucked my head down and started toward the hotel. One of the guards grabbed me by the arm and stopped me. "We go elsewhere," he said in English.

"That's a good thing," I said.

They walked me four blocks through streets crowded with Chinese. Men, women and children, and they all stared at me politely. Most of them looked well-dressed and well-fed. Some carried gold-headed walking canes. There were occasional groups of Japanese among them, in business suits and double-breasted Chicago overcoats, with lapel cameras. I got snapped a half-dozen times, standing out because of my height and my clothes and my rifle-carrying escort. The street we walked along was full of black passenger cars and red taxis. Vendors sold *dim sum* and tea at street corners. There were bookstores and newsstands on every block. Some people walked along reading. The bustle enlivened me, brought back my love of cities. I strode with bounce in my feet and made my escorts scurry to keep up with me in their heavy overcoats and rifles and short legs. The sun was out fully now and the streets were clean, lined with trees, and busy. I began to whistle. *Così fan tutte*. We passed a park with grandmothers and children and swings. Trees everywhere—so unlike New York. Bright theater posters adorned a fence. A big one for *Macbeth* caught my eye, but I didn't stop to read it. The architecture was dreary Old Stalinist, but the feel of Peking was lively—far more so than I'd remembered it. There were soldiers and sailors of both sexes, pretty girls, old Arabella Kim types with shopping bags full of celery and tomatoes, lovers. From time to time electric limousines passed in the street with red flags, carrying Party members. We walked by a *shu mai* vendor with a stack of books on his little wheeled stand. Looking closely I saw *The Complete Works of Leo Tolstoy* and *The Novels of James M. Cain* next to the dumplings. I still had a few American dollars in my billfold; I bought a copy of *Mildred Pierce* in Chinese and stuck it in my shopping bag.

After that, we turned a corner by a construction site and came upon an enormous white marble building, set back in a park where a dozen armed soldiers were patrolling. The building was about thirty stories high, with an entrance like a Turkish mausoleum. Over the doorway hung a huge silk banner with black ideograms: THE DEFENSE OF THE PEOPLE IS THE DUTY OF THE PARTY. Ten-foot-high statues of Mao and a dozen of his successors stood on the grass, surrounding an ICBM of the kind that carries a dozen R-bombs. *My God*, I thought, *this is the Chinese Pentagon*. The headquarters of the most powerful military force in history.

The fence was of wrought iron and twenty feet tall. We stopped at a guard box where four dour matrons in army uniform checked out the papers of my guards and then, steely-eyed, let us pass. They looked at me as though I had been found in a slag heap somewhere. I took a cigar from my pocket and started to light it. One of the women snatched it from my hand. "No smoking," she said, in a bullfrog voice, in Chinese.

"Let me have that back," I said. "I won't light it." My

voice sounded hostile as hell; I'd have slugged her if I hadn't
been surrounded by rifle butts.

"When you leave," she bullfrogged back, and put the cigar
on a metal table in the guard box.

Shit, I thought. I had only one more left, and the Chinese
didn't trade with Cuban deviationists.

We crunched our way down a gravel path bordered in
peonies, blooming crazily here in winter. I bent down and felt
the ground. Warm. *My God, they must use electric wires to
heat it.* I'd never seen such profligate use of power in my life.
The path was about five hundred yards long, and not a candy
wrapper in sight. Bright-green grass all around in the compound too, and no pigeons on the statues. They gleamed in the
sun.

Two workmen were polishing the brass on the doorway
when we came up. They stood aside, nodding deferentially to
my guards, and we went into an enormous Romanesque anteroom with groined arches. This led into a still larger room, a
foyer with a ceiling eight stories high, and narrow windows
that let light slant in and glow on pink marble columns that
seemed to be everywhere, like a forest. It was as vulgar as hell,
but impressive. A kind of junk cathedral with pink marble
floors and crystal chandeliers and the echoing sounds of officers striding around in military boots. A crew of men was
polishing the floor over at one side, while men and women officers, natty in uniform, strode from hallway to hallway like
Prussian officers under Frederick Wilhelm. About six cor-
ridors fed into this grand room and the traffic was heavy.

We took a left and entered a long hall, only three stories
high this time but still lit by crystal chandeliers. We walked
down it, past posters celebrating victories: the Urals Campaign of 2007, where the Chinese had routed half the Russian
Army in a week; the Japanese Peace Mission of 2037, where
the Great Fleet of the People had sailed into Tokyo Bay to
explain to the Diet that Japan must stop rearming. At the end
of this hall was something that stopped me in my tracks. A
simple old realistic painting of young Mao, almost slim, squat-
ting by a hut with a pitifully small bowl of rice in his hand and
his eyes dark with fatigue. Near him sat Lin Piao. The caption

read "The Long March." I could have cried. What men—
what men they were!

My guards took me by the arms and led me to an elevator.
"You sons of bitches," I said, "don't you have any respect?"
But I said it in English and nobody tried to answer me.

The elevator was an express; it shot us right to the top of the
building; we stepped out onto a red-carpeted hallway where
two female guards checked us out again before taking me
from my male ones. The men who brought me were awed by
their surroundings. They were told to go back and return to
their base. I would be watched over from here. The two new
guards took me down the red carpet to a simple teakwood
doorway and knocked. A male orderly let me in.

I looked around. I was in some kind of outer office, something like a doctor's waiting room, with Scandinavian-style
chairs and magazines on coffee tables. The orderly took me
across the room to a teakwood door and knocked softly. We
waited a minute until it opened. A middle-aged woman, with a
general's star on her collar, stared at me. "My God," she said,
in English, "it's Belson."

Thus began one of the strangest episodes of my bewildered
life: my five weeks as a Chinese whore. There was a certain
fascination to it. They weren't monsters; they were hard-
working and competent army officers—the Underchiefs of
Staff of the Army of the People's Republic. Several were very
attractive. There was a bedroom down the hall from one of
their conference rooms; it was decorated in a Chinese idea of
Western Macho. There was a giant fieldstone fireplace at one
end with a moose head over it and crossed dummy rifles by the
hearth. A huge brass bed sat in the middle of the room. The
place was ludicrous, but a lot more pleasant than the House of
Comradely Love, and the steaks sent up from the senior officers' mess were splendid. As long as I behaved myself with
these ladies I could stay there and be left alone at night.
Nobody asked me about uranium, the *Isabel*, or endolin. We
had little conversation; all they told me was that White Heron
had recommended me to their attention.

So I tried to accommodate myself to it as best I could. They

must have had erection pills ground up in my food and drink;
I had a hard on whether I liked it or not at almost all times.
My physical health was excellent and I found myself on my
back for hours a day, my mind often totally divorced from the
movement of my hips and the sensations of my bruised penis
—pleasuring one general or the other, with my eyes squeezed
shut and lines of Shakespeare in my head:

> For God's sake, let us sit upon the ground
> And tell sad stories of the death of kings . . .

Sometimes my thoughts would be jarred by the orgasm of my
partner. I had become a thinking dildo, a mournful captive of
my adolescent dreams.

Sometimes when alone in the room I would stand back from
the bar, a drink in my hand, and look at myself in the big mirror. My work had narrowed my waist and firmed my abdomen
more than the Nautilus machines could, and I was still
tanned. The smell of jasmine and of just-departed flesh might
be in my nostrils. A line from Yeats would sometimes come
into my head:

> In dreams begin responsibilities . . .

and then I would wonder how long it would go on. In a
fashion time-honored in the trade of prostitution, I found
myself going to sleep drunk every night and so hung over in
the mornings that my first two or three tricks might have been
a continuation of the night's unpleasant dreams. My God—
tricks! I had no endolin and no morphine. I ate, drank, slept
and copulated. I had quit exercising, since my work was
vigorous enough. No. I had quit exercising because I didn't
feel like a man anymore. My underwear was always returned
to me perfumed, and sometimes flowers were sent to the room
by one of my lovers. When we drank together the woman
would pour the drinks. The oldest of them—a wiry brigadier
in her fifties—liked to feed me my desserts with a spoon. I ate
them greedily.

It ended as quickly as it had begun. One Thursday morning,
in the week before Christmas, my first visitors were a pair of

policemen in gray uniforms and red armbands. They were polite and clearly intelligent. I had no idea where they were going
to take me and didn't particularly care; my main feeling was
relief that I didn't have an erection when they woke me. I
dressed and left without breakfast.

The day was horribly raw, a Chicago-in-January day in
Peking, with ice everywhere in the streets. Everybody but me
was wearing puffy overcoats and boots and enormous caps.
Fortunately, the limousine was parked near the building and I
made it inside without frostbite. It felt like thirty below. In the
car I was glad to be in the company of men again; I felt I could
live without women forever. I leaned back in the middle of my
seat.

It was a long trip. It took an hour to get out of Peking, and
we followed a winding road through bare, ice-covered trees
for another hour before turning down a narrow path and
beginning to climb a series of hills. At first there were scrubby
bushes flanking the narrow road, then snow. The gray pave-
ment had been plowed flawlessly, although there was no sign
of habitation. After an hour the snow was high on each side of
us and we were humming at a smooth thirty miles an hour
through what felt like a cloud tunnel. I was shockingly hungry. Little spots whirred in front of my eyes against the dead
white of the world outside. It was spooky and peaceful, like a
shared dream, and no one spoke for over an hour. The driver
was a wiry old Chinese with a chauffeur's cap; he kept both
hands on the wheel and both eyes on the road. Once I cried out
when a jackrabbit shot across in front of us like an apparition.
The car was very warm; after a while I fell asleep.

I was awakened by a stop. Outside the driver's window two
guards, so muffled around the faces I couldn't tell whether
they were men or women, were standing like huge chessmen.
The driver opened the back door with a switch; icy air stung
my face; one of the guards bent down toward me, staring over
a high collar and muffler and from under an enormous furry
cap. Sunlight glinted on a bayonet. I stared back into sharp,
ambiguous eyes; the guard nodded, said something to the
driver and closed the door. We drove on.

We were on top of the hills now, rumbling through plowed
snow along a flat plain. There were no features, no sign of life.

It was like a snow-covered Belson. I stretched and rubbed my eyes. Somehow my hunger had gone. The sun was out; we drove through streamers of mist that were now lambent, along a perfectly straight road across the plain. After ten minutes I could see in the distance a red pagoda roof.

As we came closer and slowed, I made out a house or temple about the size of my parents' home in Ohio, with a few wooden steps and a simple door in front. Snow had been cleared away from all around for a radius of about fifty feet. The roof was bright in the sun. On it sat a large bird or the image of a bird, head tucked under its wing. A dove.

Our car pulled up to the front steps. A tall, muffled guard was waiting, with no rifle this time. He held an enormous greatcoat open for me. I stepped from the warm car into it, pulling its huge collar around my ears. The guard took me firmly by the elbow and led me up the steps. The door opened. I walked inside, the weight of the coat giving gravity to my movement. I felt astonishingly calm, and the wearing of that coat for only a minute conferred dignity on my spirit as well as heft, as though it had been the robe of a Manchu emperor or Prospero's magic cloak.

I was in a small room with no furniture. The bare floor was teak; ink brush drawings of birds hung on the walls.

There was a wide, green-lacquered door at the far side of the room. I walked toward it and as it swung open I saw daylight and green foliage. I heard the sound of falling water. Standing in the doorway I looked up at a skylight, with a willow tree brushing its top against it. Through ferns, light sparkled on water. I took a step forward and saw the surface of a pool. A gravelly, womanly voice said, "Come in, Mr. Belson."

"Mourning Dove!" I said. "I hoped it would be you."

I stepped forward onto gravel, turned at the feathery stand of ferns, walked around the pond and its small waterfall. A couple of abrupt *chunks* startled me; frogs had jumped into the water at my approach and were now peering at me from wet bubble eyes, the rest of their dark bodies floating below the surface in subaqueous murk.

At the other side of the pond on a raised wooden dais between willow trees sat Mourning Dove Soong in a white wicker chair. Her hair was white and she wore a plain black robe. She looked much older and terribly frail. Her face was chalky and, as I came closer, massively wrinkled around the intelligent black eyes. She was looking at me steadily. On her lap slept a gray cat. I walked to the chair across from her and took it.

She looked at me for several moments. Then she said, in English, "You are calm now, Mr. Belson."

"Yes. A lot has happened since we first met. Some of the experiences have been calming." I wondered if she knew what I had been doing in that room back in Peking. "I hope your life has been a pleasure for you."

"It has not been," she said.

"I'm sorry," I said, truly feeling sorry. "Is it the endolin?"

"I am not concerned with endolin," she said. "Would you like tea?"

"Yes. And food too, if I may?"

"You were not fed in Peking?"

"Not since last night."

She nodded. "That would be Major Feng. I told her to treat you well, but she believes I do not care anymore. I will remind her eventually." She pressed a button on the arm of her chair, and I heard a soft buzz in another room. A boy of about twelve came in, dressed in a black robe like Mourning Dove's. He stood before her and bowed slightly.

"Bring us food from the kitchen, Deng," she said gently, in Chinese. Then to me, in English, "There will be no meat, Mr. Belson, since I do not eat it. But what we have is good."

I said nothing and watched Deng as he walked across the gravel and left. When he was gone I said, "Mourning Dove, I am very seldom calm. All my life I have been in a hurry and I'm not even sure what for."

"You make the simple difficult," she said. "Perhaps because the difficult is simple for you."

A voice in me was saying *Fortune-cookie wisdom*. Yet if anyone on Earth was wise, it was this woman. I could feel wisdom around her presence like a magnetic field. "I've been bored with making money," I said. "But when I stop I just seem to crash around and hurt other people, like Isabel."

"Miss Crawford is a strong person and can profit from the experience."

"You know Isabel!"

"I had your history examined when I learned of your cargo."

"The uranium?"

"Yes."

"And you know where Isabel is now?"

Mourning Dove nodded, stroking her cat. The cat stretched itself and yawned.

"Mourning Dove," I said in agitation, "I'd be relieved if you'd tell me where she is."

"Mr. Belson," she said, "I do not wish to play cat and mouse with you and I wish you well in life. But I am not ready to tell you that. Maybe later."

I stared at her. "Mourning Dove, I love her. I need to know where she is."

She looked at me calmly. "Mr. Belson," she said, "China needs safe uranium. Our sources of power have caused far more pain than you feel for your Isabel."

The way she said it gave me pause. "Has something happened?" I said.

She took her hand from the back of the cat and laid her thin arms on the arms of the chair. "While you were crossing the Pacific there was an accident in the North, near the village of Wu. Thousands of cubic feet of radioactive gas were emitted and many died. Wu is my home village and it was I who ordered the reactor built forty years ago, to show good faith in my policy."

"Your policy?"

"I am one of the sponsors of the use of nuclear fission in China, Mr. Belson. I agreed that the price in lives would be worth the profit—in the contribution to China's future."

I could feel her pain, even though her face didn't show it. "And you had family members in Wu?"

"Yes. My daughter and three sons. Seven grandchildren. They are dead now, or in hospitals dying."

"That's unbearable," I said. I wanted to hold her and try to comfort her. "Do you blame yourself?"

She looked at me. "Who else is to blame?" she said. "I championed nuclear fission. I had the plant built near Wu."

I just looked at her. What could I say? "What are you going to do?" I said, eventually.

"I am going to have lunch," she said.

Deng had come back from the kitchen carrying a flat basket and a low table. He set the table between us and put the basket on it. It was full of fruit and vegetables. Another boy, who might have been Deng's brother, followed with a ceramic teapot and two cups. He set the cups down and poured.

"I don't see how you stand it," I said, watching the boy pour the steaming tea and thinking of those corpses and of a provincial hospital somewhere, with the ruined faces of the dying.

"The big things are simpler than the small. One doesn't complicate them. I went to a monastery in Tibet and fasted. Necessities arrive unbidden, like dreams. It was necessary to grieve properly and I have grieved." She handed me a cup of tea. "I planned to greet you in Peking, Mr. Belson, to buy your uranium. I am sorry to have caused you a long wait."

"That's unimportant. I too underwent a kind of . . . purgation. I hope your pain will relent. I wish I could help."

"I see that you do," she said calmly and sipped her tea. "The broccoli is nourishing. It has been steamed in ginseng."

I took a bite. It was delicious and my appetite returned in a flash. "Did you visit Wu afterward?"

"Yes," she said, drinking tea. "I took endolin to the survivors. They are not in pain."

"I'm glad it helped," I said. I finished a floret of broccoli and then took a big peach and ate in silence, looking at the water of the pond and at the green ferns that surrounded it. I thought of Juno, of all that safe uranium there, enough to power our world forever. "Mourning Dove," I said, "I still love America, even though it has treated me badly. And I'm crazy about New York. I don't want my country to be an outpost of a Chinese empire."

"Your country is China now."

"By adoption. And I think I could be a Confucianist. But right now I would like to settle in New York, with Isabel if she'll have me, and devote the rest of my life to making it into a great city again."

She was silent for a moment. Then she said, "Crashing around?"

"Maybe I can do it calmly." I said this with surprising passion. "I've learned a lot in the last year, Mourning Dove. I may be ready to enjoy the rest of my life." My head was feeling very clear, and there were no more spots in front of my eyes. This was one of the loveliest rooms I had ever been in and I felt I was with the oldest and best of friends.

She nodded. " 'The road of excess leads to the palace of wisdom.' "

"That's William Blake!" I said. "I hope it's true."

"It is true. I was excessive when young, as you are, Mr. Belson, and I have become wise. I believe that in my case one brought about the other." She returned her attention to the cat. "I read Blake in college, in London. I desired to know everything when I was young, and to be infinitely rich and to become a member of the Central Committee of the Party. I have had four husbands and alienated them all. They are all dead now and I have forgotten them. But I got what I desired." She looked at me. "I have not forgotten my mother and my father. My mother would beat me for nothing . . ." Suddenly her old face tightened alarmingly. "*For nothing,* Mr. Belson. She has been dead fifty years and I hate her still. I hate my father for letting her do it, and he too is long dead."

"Jesus!" I said. "It sounds familiar."

"It is not uncommon. The thing is to rule it and not to let it rule." She paused. "One cannot attract the attention of the dead, though many try."

"Oh yes," I said, blinking, "many try." My voice sounded strange.

"You are crying," Mourning Dove said. "As much as I hate my mother I also love her. With a mother it is hard to do otherwise. Perhaps you love yours still."

Orbach had tried to tell me that, but I wouldn't listen—not in my stomach or heart or wherever it is. I looked at Mourning Dove through tears. They were pouring out, some of them slopping down on my big hairy right hand that held a half-eaten peach. I could see my mother's face, lost in self-regard. Grief suffused my body, starting in my stomach and spreading to my chest and shoulders and heaving the muscles of my abdomen and my face.

Gradually it subsided. I heard the pond waterfall again. I leaned back and stretched. I could feel the strength of my limbs, the soundness of my heart. My beard was wet. I took a bite from the peach, letting the juice mix with tears.

"You are a remarkable man, Mr. Belson," Mourning Dove said.

I nodded and swallowed. "Would you call me Benjamin?"

"Benjamin," she said, "I want your uranium."

I nodded. "You can have half of it."

Her voice was quiet. "No. All. China needs it."

I looked at her. Her face was unshakable. "I can't do that. There will be enough to go around. I can send the *Isabel* back."

She just looked at me. "You can be made to tell us where it is from. Chemicals . . ."

"I know. But they aren't reliable."

"Torture," she said, as if mentioning a stock option.

I shuddered. "Oh, I know. You could do that and it would work. But it wouldn't give you what's on the *Isabel*. That's in Washington, and L'Ouverture Baynes is no fool."

She had finished her tea but was still holding the cup. She leaned over now and set it on the table beside the basket. "L'Ouverture Baynes will be out of office next week. He was defeated in November, Benjamin."

I stared at her and said, "Mattie . . . ?"

"Miss Hinkle campaigned with tales of the *Isabel*'s uranium, claiming the needs of employment in Kentucky. She will be sworn in in January. You will be able to recover the *Isabel*. I want it brought to Honshu."

"Mourning Dove," I said. "I can't do that. I can let you have half of it. That's thirty tons. You can replace all the U235 in China with thirty tons and it will keep you till I get more." My heart had begun beating wildly again, thinking of how L'Ouverture had been defeated and that I could get hold of my spaceship again.

"Why would I want the United States to be powerful?"

I stared at her. "Oh Jesus, Mourning Dove," I said. "Don't do to us what the British did to you, with the opium and all that bullying. The world doesn't have to be run that way."

"There is danger in a house without a master."

"Oh, come off it," I said, exasperated with her. "That's fortune-cookie wisdom and it sounds fascist."

"It's Confucius."

"I'm sorry, but it's still no good. Remember your mother? She was a master, wasn't she? Who needs that?"

That seemed to touch her. She pursed her lips silently for a moment. I waited. "America will waste the fuel," she said, "as it wasted the oil of Texas and of the Persian Gulf. America built tall buildings with sealed windows and burned oil to cool them in summer."

"You sound like L'Ouverture. It doesn't have to be that way anymore. America has changed. We're more civilized, less crazy about dumb toys. Cheap power can permit a beautiful life as easily as a crass one."

Her face had softened a bit, but now it hardened. "Benjamin," she said, "the person who supported me as a child and comforted me after Mother's beatings was my great-uncle, Too Moy. The boys who served us are his great-great-grandsons and my nephews. They are all the family I have left."

"I'm glad you had someone to comfort you," I said. "With me it was a horse named Juno."

"One takes what one can find. Too Moy was very old and crippled. He had seen Mao himself. He was a peasant. In Wu our water power came from the power of human legs. A man or a woman sat astride a device like a wooden bicycle, across a stream, and pedaled the water into rice paddies. Sometimes for ten or twelve hours a day. There is slight fulfillment in such work and a great deal of pain. My great-uncle walked little and took much aspirin for the cramps in his legs. I was able to get medication for him, and it helped, but at times he would lie on his pallet in the room behind my mother's house and groan. Paddling was all he ever did, and he did it for over fifty years. Yet he was an intelligent man, with a loving heart. I might have been a cruel person without his love."

"It's awful to spend a life like that," I said.

Her face was rigid. "Yes," she said. "All the labor that Too Moy did in his lifetime could have been done better by one of the motors Americans were cutting their lawns with when he was young."

I nodded. I had nothing to say.

"You Americans did not create that oil you used for your

cars, your air conditioners, your lawn mowers, or for the plastic films you wrapped toys and pens and vegetables in. The oil was made by the world itself, when great ferns covered Texas and the Persian Gulf. It took millions of years to make it. You and the Arabs threw it away in a century, on foolishness. With that oil, my great-uncle could have had a happier life. There were many like him all over China. When my great-uncle was young, people like you in America called such people the 'yellow peril' or 'faceless millions.' " She leaned over toward me in quiet fury. "My Great-Uncle Too Moy was not a peril, was not faceless. He did not mope in impotence. He was a better man than you, Mr. Belson."

I sat there stunned for a long while. I stared at the water, trying to spot the frogs. But they were out of sight now. Minutes passed in silence. I thought of counterarguments, thought of mentioning the cars and jets the Chinese had transported me in, the luxurious life that Party members like Mourning Dove herself lived, the red flag limousines and the graft in the military. But I could not get that great-uncle out of my mind. My vision had somehow become very clear; on an impulse I took off my glasses and slid them into my shirt pocket. I could see everything with a preternatural sharpness, every wrinkle in Mourning Dove's impassive face, every leaf of the willow. Back at the other end of the pond were the eyes of a frog, just on the still surface of the gray water, looking toward me.

"Mourning Dove," I said, "I would like to be your son."

She did not look at me. "I have no son now."

"I know. I would like you to adopt me."

She raised her eyes slowly. "Why?"

"I need a mother."

She kept looking at me for a long while. "Perhaps you are only trying to win an argument."

"God, *no!*" I said passionately. "I have let that go for now. I truly love you and want you to be my parent, the way Too Moy was yours and saved your soul for you." I paused and looked at her, not crying now but feeling as though the slightest breath of air could bring tears. "I want my soul to be like yours. I want you in my memory to drive away the drunken fool who lives in there." I kept looking at her.

She remained impassive for a long time. Then she reached out a fragile white hand and placed it on the back of mine, on the arm of the wicker chair. "Benjamin," she said. "Benjamin. You may keep half of the uranium."

I felt as I had felt when, naked to Fomalhaut, I had slept on the grass that fed me and awakened to the magnificent yet distant rings of Belson.

✦ Chapter 15

The theater occupied the bottom floors of a hideous new office building—one of dozens along Chang An Avenue a mile east of Tien An Men Square. We drove up to it in a chauffeured limousine. It was I who arranged the demolition of Mitsubishi Tower in New York twenty years before; this Chinese abomination resembled that Japanese one, except for the statues. Flanking the doorway were massive bronzes of a peasant and a soldier, shirtsleeves rolled, staring tight-lipped toward the future. What in hell is so holy about the future? Anyone who feels that way about it should be forced to read history at gunpoint. The crowd was mostly young; they wore blue jeans or quilted Synlon pants, and bright foul-weather jackets. They were probably students from the Institute of Life Enrichment and Managerial Skills, a few blocks away. Some stared as the theater manager led us past the ticket queue and into the lobby. Conspicuous as I was with my height and blond beard, it was Mourning Dove who attracted the stares; she responded with a thoughtful frown.

A flunky had rushed ahead of us, and when we were

ushered into our box he was hanging a painting of Chairwoman Chu, arms folded in her turn-of-the-century black jacket. He left the picture crooked for a moment, held Mourning Dove's chair for her obsequiously, murmuring praises as she seated herself, then quickly straightened Madame Chu and left.

When we were alone I said, "Some of those looks downstairs were mean."

She lit a Lucky Strike with a stainless-steel Zippo and held the closed lighter in her frail hand for a moment. I saw with surprise that the hand was trembling. She put the lighter in the pocket of her gown and said, "The accident near Wu has affected my standing with the people."

I remembered my agitation at being hanged in effigy on Madison Avenue. "Are you in any danger, Mourning Dove?"

"I have enemies."

"I bet you have." I thought of White Heron.

The play had been running for two months; it would close in a week. We had been driven into Peking that afternoon, had gone to the People's Hall of Records for a brief ceremony and then, at Mourning Dove's instructions, were driven here.

While we waited for the curtain, people kept looking up at us from time to time. Some seemed only curious to see a Party official and her blond escort, but some showed open hostility. I settled back into my Victorian opera chair, rested my elbow on one of its little antimacassars, and lit a cigar. It was like a box in a movie Western: the chairs were upholstered in dark-purple velvet; the oil painting of China's first Party Chairwoman hung over velvet draperies behind us; there was a brass railing in front of us with yet more purple velvet hanging from the rail to the floor. But it was comfortable and spacious. And I knew that what you pay for in China is privacy and space. China may be down to half a billion souls, but it still teems. I chewed nervously on my cigar and left Mourning Dove to her thoughts, almost bursting with impatience for the curtain to rise. By the time it went up I had cleaned my glasses twice and my cigar was a mess. I ground it out in the ashtray and leaned forward toward the stage below.

The witches were adequate but no thrill. They were got up as Japanese Shinto priests and their English was more comical than scary. But their old faces did look like something to be reckoned with, and the blasted heath they stood on made me think of those vast acres of obsidian I had lived on so long:

> Fair is foul, and foul is fair;
> Hover through the fog and filthy air.

Macbeth was a big Australian named Wellfleet Close, with an Aussie's red face and a bellowing voice; he looked as if he had the required gift for murder. Duncan and Banquo were Southeast Asians. I know the play pretty well, having a certain spiritual familiarity with that dangerous couple; I knew when to expect her first appearance. But when the scene abruptly cut to Lady Macbeth with a big letter in her hands, I was startled. There she was, and yet not really. She wore a long russet gown and no wig; the bright lights made her gray hair shine and her eyes seem large and commanding. I knew it was Isabel, yet it was Lady Macbeth too.

She began reading the letter aloud,

They met me in the day of success and I have learned . . .

Even while pouring tea Isabel could dazzle with her voice. Here in Peking, after all the uncertain accents that preceded her entrance, the sound of her own Scottish speech, the real English language, was electrifying. Even these Chinese became hushed at the authentic ring of it. The play went on through its blood and dreams, and Isabel took every scene she was in, dominating the stage. She was a first-rate actress. I'd had no idea. When it ended with Macbeth's head on the pole, I glanced over at Mourning Dove. She seemed lost in thought. Applause filled the theater.

During the curtain calls I stood and shouted, "Isabel!" and she looked up to stare at me a moment. I could have climbed down to the stage, but something in her look made me keep my distance. Maybe Lady Macbeth was still in there, and I didn't want any part of that.

When she looked away from me I sat and leaned back in my seat, trying to calm myself. Mourning Dove was lighting a cigarette. The sound of the applause became fragmentary.

Voices began calling out. Men and women in the front rows were standing, not facing the stage now but facing our box, staring up in anger, shouting, "Comrade Soong. Comrade Soong."

Mourning Dove rose, stepped to the front of the box and held the rail with both hands. She looked very old and frail, but her voice was steady. She spoke in Chinese. "I am Mourning Dove Soong. What is wanted of me?"

"An accounting," someone shouted, "an accounting of the Death Tax for Electricity. An explanation of Wu." More shouts repeated this. I came over beside her for moral support, but she seemed not to need any. I was in more need of help than she, with emotions flying around in my stomach like leaves in a monsoon.

"I will come to the stage," Mourning Dove said. I stared at her, shocked. She put her hand on my arm and said, "One is accountable to the People."

"Let me go down there with you, Mourning Dove," I said.

"If you wish." We left the box, went down a staircase and through a small door that led backstage. I looked around for Isabel. She was not in sight.

Then suddenly I was onstage with the curtain up, blinking out across bright lights at a bunch of angry Chinese, most of them standing. Beside me stood Mourning Dove, only as high as the middle of my chest, with a cigarette in her hand and her eyes straight ahead.

"Nine hundred seventy died at Wu," Mourning Dove said. "Another thousand will die before this winter is a memory. It was I who ordered the reactor built."

They were silent for a moment. Then someone shouted out, "Murderess." And someone else shouted, "Lady Macbeth! Bloody hands!" I began to be afraid for her.

"This theater is well-lighted and warm," Mourning Dove said. "China has power everywhere because of uranium. You do not labor on foot in rice paddies, nor do your mothers or fathers. You study at universities and attend the theater. Your homes are warm. A price is paid for this."

"Too high," someone shouted—a young woman with traditional bangs and an army jacket. "It is too high a price."

"Have you considered the alternative?" Mourning Dove said.

There was silence for a moment, and then a lean young man in the third row shouted, "China has coal, and wind, and tides."

Mourning Dove was lighting another cigarette. When she closed her Zippo she looked at the man who had spoken and said, "Coal blackens the skies and the lungs. It is dangerous to mine. The wind and tides are a perpetual delight, but they will not power the factories of Hangchow nor warm the hearths of Shanghai. That is a dream."

The young man only looked more furious. "Coal may be burned with precision and the skies made safe from its breath. One must take pains."

Before Mourning Dove could speak I said, in English, "Coal has its own tax of death, its own blight. I am a merchant of coal and speak from experience."

A heavy man with a Charlie Chan mustache sat in the second row, wearing a business suit. "Who speaks?" he said loudly. "Who is this pale devil with the voice of a bear?"

"I'm Benjamin Belson," I said. "I do not endorse Mourning Dove's decision to build reactors. I cannot speak for the dead. But the decision was not a foolish one and Madame Soong has taken responsibility for it."

Several voices cried out, "Foreign devil!" And then Charlie Chan stood and said, "Your English tongue is that of the killer Macbeth. Take your English and go home."

I remembered those student rioters who had burned my effigy and told me to go home. I am proud of my Chinese; it was a thrill to use it. "*I am home*," I said in Chinese. "I am a citizen of the People's Republic, and Mourning Dove Soong is my foster mother. I bring a new uranium, star-born, that will not destroy life."

At my first words in their own language, many of them were clearly shocked. Several seated themselves, as if mulling it over. But the older man was relentless. "I cannot accept your professed gift to China. China has been promised gifts from white devils before. Opium was such a gift."

"I am not British," I said angrily. "I love China. I am dis-

mayed to see its ancient culture discarded and its men become
soft. But China's greatness is everywhere manifest, as was that
of America in the time of my grandfathers. I too mourn the
accident at Wu and know the cost of China's wealth is in-
calculable. In this case the dead speak."

The old man was adamant. "Only the devil calculates with
lives."

Mourning Dove was watching his face. She spoke directly to
him. "Someone must," she said.

They stared at each other for a long moment. Finally he
said, between his teeth, "Murderess," and sat down. Another
voice, from the back, picked up the cry of "Murderess" and
then another. I heard a man shout, "Capitalist!"

And then a voice rang out from behind me and I turned to
see Isabel standing by me with her hands on her hips, facing
the audience. The part in the curtain was still moving from
where she had just stepped through. She was in Lady
Macbeth's russet gown, but the stage makeup was gone from
her face and it looked pale under the lights.

"What kind of Communists are you?" she said.

"English," someone hissed.

Isabel's voice could have waked the dead. "I am *not*
English," she said, spacing the words out. "And you are
hypocrites. You make me ashamed for the great Mao and for
his discipline." She pointed at the old man. "Your jacket is
from Saks. Solar power cannot make such jackets."

Several of the more thoughtful ones had become quietly at-
tentive. Finally a young woman who had been silent spoke up
from about twenty rows back. "Yes, we live well. Must others
die for that?"

Mourning Dove answered. "Yes."

And immediately I said, "Not anymore."

The anger was still in the air, but less powerfully. For a long
minute everyone was silent, wondering if it would start up
again. Then a couple in the back row got up and left the
theater. More followed, and after a while the three of us were
alone onstage with the footlights still blazing on us.

"Mother," I said, "I'd like you to meet Isabel."

•

In the gutters of Chang An Avenue lay occasional clumps of leftover red confetti, from some parade or other that afternoon. It was bitterly cold and halos of frozen mist surrounded the streetlamps. An occasional official car droned by under electric power, its red fender flags flapping. Party officials were on their way to meet sweethearts or were coming back from gambling clubs. A sleek electric bus hummed past us, with most of its seats empty.

"Did you mean that, Ben? That China was wise to use nuclear power?" Isabel said.

"I did at the time," I said. "But I was defending Mourning Dove. God knows how many have died of leukemia alone."

"I've thought of that."

"Isabel," I said, "I'm not impotent anymore."

"That should ease your temper."

"Yes." There was a lighted skyscraper between us and Tien An Men Square and we were heading toward it. It looked a bit like the Empire State Building. "They've lost a quarter million people," I said. "Maybe twice that. If they'd burned it right, coal would have been more humane. But they were in a hurry, and they had all that uranium at Sinkiang and Kiangsi . . ." I felt a sudden wave of sadness.

"Mourning Dove didn't need your help," Isabel said.

Two Mercedes limousines hummed past us, down the middle of the broad old avenue. From one of them came the muffled sound of Broadway music, a new musical called *Oriental Blues*. What strange transactions the modern world conducted!

"Anyway, it's over. I'll have my ship back in three weeks, and they'll start changing cores."

Isabel was wearing an enormous down-filled coat and a black watchcap pulled over her ears. I had my hands jammed in my pockets against the cold. Expert opinion said it was not an ice age, but here we were in another horror of a winter. "You were magnificent in the play," I said, for the second time. "I've never seen a Lady Macbeth like you."

"Ben," she said, "it's a fine play, but sometimes it felt like Fifty-first Street, with you."

That annoyed me. "I'm no murderer."

"That's not what I mean. You can be awfully bombastic."

"I've changed," I said.

"I hope you have," she said, a bit grimly. We walked in silence for a while. Abruptly she stopped and turned to me. "Ben," she said, "I don't want to be a supporting actress in your melodrama."

That hit home, and I said nothing. We were coming up to the skyscraper. There were ideographs incised on an arch over its entrance. We stopped and looked at them.

"I can't read Chinese," Isabel said.

"It says INSTITUTE FOR THE ADVANCEMENT OF HAPPINESS BETWEEN MEN AND WOMEN."

She hesitated. "You weren't the only cause of those fights," she said. "When I let you move in, my life felt empty and I expected you to fill it."

"And did I?"

"With a vengeance."

"Look," I said, "that's all past. You've got a career that's clearly taking off. Fieler wants you to do Ibsen in New York. I have to buy into Con Ed or start up my own company. I've got to mount another voyage for endolin and uranium. We won't be focusing on each other all the time. Besides, I can get it up now. Sometimes I can't get it down."

She looked at me closely. Under the lights by the building I could see the redness of her cheeks and the red tip of her nose. "I gave up my apartment in New York," she said, "and my sister has Amagansett and William." She hesitated. "You won't be going after the uranium yourself?"

I shook my head. "There's a new captain." She hesitated and I said, "I'll be moving back into my mansion and I want you with me. I want the cats too. I'd like you to marry me."

"Things have gone very well since you left," she said. "The *Times* ran my picture during *Hamlet* and I did television here in Peking before *Macbeth* . . ." She stopped. "Ben, you require more attention than I want to give."

"Honey," I said, "don't forget the good times. We used to take walks and eat in restaurants and go to concerts. We really enjoyed each other."

"Sometimes."

I shrugged. "I'll take you home," I said. "Where are you staying?"

"I have an apartment near Tien An Men. We can walk."

I started walking and suddenly I felt Isabel's arm interlink itself with mine. I remembered how we used to hold each other on those cold nights in her apartment, sleeping wrapped up with one another.

She must have been thinking of the same thing because she said, "You can spend the night with me, if you'd like."

The apartment was quiet and warm. There were no cats. We made love easily, in silence, and then lay on Isabel's blue Chinese bed holding each other as tightly as yang and yin. Gradually we separated enough that we could lie on our backs with our feet touching.

I lit a cigar. "How long does the play run?" I said, breathing easily and as relaxed in the body as on Belson grass.

"Eight more performances." She rolled over and kissed my neck. "Oh my, Ben," she said. "It was about time."

"We could get married in Peking," I said.

She rolled over, stretched her arms out and yawned. "New York, Ben. We ought to get married in New York."

ᕔ Chapter 16

The elevator had been double-checked. Workmen had taken it up and down a dozen times. But there was a lot of embarrassed tension among us. Then there were rumblings beneath our feet, a sturdy whine overhead, and we began moving upward.

"Well, for one thing," the Deputy Mayor said, trying to break the tension, "the Maintenance Workers' Union is solidly Democratic."

The rest of us said nothing, but as we approached the top floors the ride began to smooth out and I started feeling an exhilaration like blasting off for Fomalhaut two years before. I stood with the four of them silent in the middle of that freshly painted car with its polished brass handrails and its gray floor, and the old rush of fast travel expanded my soul for a moment. As we slowed near the top I felt Isabel's hand take mine and squeeze it. The car stopped, the door hummed open and we stepped out onto a red carpet laid on a floor still covered with scuffmarks from the last group of tourists to leave, thirty years before. Someone had opened a few windows, but the air was still musty. There were graffiti on the walls—one could have been an imprecation from a hidden tomb. DEATH TO INTERLOPERS it read, in spray-paint orange under a veil of dust. There was a crew of a half-dozen workmen cleaning up. I hoped they would get that one off soon. Heavy blinds covered the windows we faced; it was west that way, and the late-afternoon sun in June would be blinding. I started to head back around to where I could look out to the east, but Isabel put her hand on my arm and said, "Take it easy, Ben. Let's wait a few minutes."

"Okay," I said, remembering my breakneck rush onto Belson. "Let's get a drink." A bar was being set up under the shaded windows and several bottles and some glasses were already out.

Isabel was looking around her, at the long-closed souvenir stand, the grimy coffee urns, the high-ceilinged room with metal girders overhead, and the yellowing photograph of Manhattan on the wall above the elevator—Manhattan as it was around 2025, with all the Japanese skyscrapers. Above this was written in faded letters: OBSERVATION DECK.

We went to the bar and she handed me a canape. As I gave her a drink I noticed the light on the window blinds wasn't so bright anymore; the sun must be hidden by another tall building. I walked a few steps over and pulled the cord. There had been a lot of talking in the room, with the laborers and two foremen and the Deptuy Mayor and his secretary and a holovision crew that was just getting their equipment out of the elevator. But when the blind began to go up a hush spread itself around me. Before I looked out myself I glanced around the room. Everyone was staring toward the window.

I turned and there it was: the New York skyline. The sun glowed from behind the cylinder of the Bank of Hangchow, and its light made quasi-silhouettes of the giant old buildings of the West Side—all of them empty but still astounding to see from this solid old masterpiece of a skyscraper: those solemn black shapes, pushed skyward in turn-of-the-century confidence, almost all of them taller than the one we stood on.

"My God," Isabel said finally. "It's New York City!"

Somebody laughed softly and the silence was swallowed again in chatter. More people kept coming from the elevator.

Ice tinkled all over now. A five-piece band was setting up in a room behind us; above the other hubbub came the occasional spurt of a trumpet, the nervous clang of a cymbal. I walked around the tower several times, looking out toward the Hudson and the East River and the southern tip of the island. A few weak lights down near street level came on—the twenty-watt fluorescents we had all lived with for a third of a century, but all the upper stories remained dark. At the northern end of the deck, facing uptown, was a table draped with red, white and blue bunting and faced by rows of chairs. On it sat the black switchbox and a microwave transmitter dish like a tea saucer aimed toward New Jersey. The switch had been locked into the "off" position with a key. I looked at my watch; fifty more minutes. Booming male laughter was coming from the anteroom. I turned and walked in. Sticking up over the crowd was L'Ouverture's shiny black head, his big toothy smile. He was stretching his long arms out and laughing while several other people looked up admiringly. He did look beautiful, in a pale-blue seersucker suit with a crisp white shirt and red tie.

Just then he saw me coming. *"Benjamin!"* he shouted. "Benjamin Belson, Intergalactic Pirate."

People pulled away to let me pass. I walked up to him. "Piracy is as piracy does, L'Ouverture," I said. I heard my voice. It sounded dangerous.

"Ben," he said, his arms still out above heads, "I'm not even a senator anymore. You've got your spaceship and I'm in commerce. Let me congratulate you."

I was right up to him now, looking up at his flawlessly shaved face, the bright silk of his necktie, smelling his cologne and hearing the rustle of his suit as he now brought his grotesquely long arms down from the gesture my arrival had attracted. "L'Ouverture," I said, "I accept your congratulations." Then I thought, *What the hell.* I handed my drink to someone and put my arms around Baynes. His arms came around me. We hugged hard for a long time and I could feel the warmth of his enormous hands across my shoulders. "Ben," he whispered in my ear, lowering his head to say it, "you are a child of mine after all."

I pulled back and looked up at him. "If I am," I said, "I've left home for good."

He smiled benignly. "What could be more in tune with the order of things?"

"I'll get you a drink," I said. The Mayor arrived and the holo filming began. During a lull in that he handed me a pair of Xerograms and I pressed them on. One was a formal thank you from President Weinberg with a White House logo glowing in gold on its projection; the other was in strong calligraphy: "I am pleased with my son," it said. "Your journey has relighted the world." The Mayor tapped my arm, ready to begin his speech. I followed him to the dais and stood at the bunting-draped table. Someone had unlocked the power switch. Isabel sat in the front row in her blue dress; she looked smart and strong.

The Mayor went on longer than I had expected and I began to get impatient. He talked about the simultaneous ceremonies in Boston, Dallas and Chicago, about the new electric heating that would soon be flowing into Montreal and Vancouver, about Juno uranium plants scheduled for Zimbabwe and Rio and Paris, about the new reciprocity in U.S. relations with China, while I stood with impatience, wanting to get on with it and occasionally slipping a look at my watch. For a moment I became appalled at myself. Did the road of excesses lead only back to this? Had I lost my impotence and quieted my rages only to become another impatient rich man with a distended ego? I looked down at myself. There was my Ralph Lauren cotton jacket of midnight blue, my Bert Pulitzer shirt, my blue silk Marley tie, my gray trousers gently resting their cuffs on English shoes. Under all this a body still firm and a set of genitals no longer in spiritual orbit. I looked up and there was Isabel with a light smile on her lips, looking not at me but at the dull man at my side. Had it all only come to this, then: the speech of a politician, expensive clothes, and boredom?

In a seat behind Isabel a relaxed-looking man whom I didn't recognize shifted his weight in his chair. He glanced down toward his watch. I looked around the room, from well-dressed person to well-dressed person: others were restless too. L'Ouverture, the biggest man there, sat in the back row looking bored out of his skull.

My discomfort subsided and I became easy again with my clothes and my life. I thought of how well Isabel's career was going, how she worked at her acting and at getting our home in order. I thought of the *Isabel*, now in the limbo of analogy travel from Belson with a load of endolin aboard and a crew ready to fill the empty holds on Juno. Ruth was captain this time, sleeping in my old suite with the porthole in the bathroom, but the Nautilus machines were at our home on Madison Avenue in the room with the pool table. Mourning Dove was presiding over installing new cores in the reactors of the Middle Kingdom. The world was not ready to wind down yet, and New York was not ready to become a memory like Samarkand or Constantinople.

While this verbal fugue was playing in my head, a part of my attention was picking up Mayor Wharton's speech. He was praising the work of the *Isabel* and the abundance it had brought. Then he paused, turned to me and said, "With us now to close the circuit is the captain of the *Isabel*." I took a step forward and spoke. "I am an impatient man and I want to throw this switch, but I want my wife with me when I do it." I looked at Isabel. She stood up, walked around the table and took my arm. We gripped the heavy handle, hesitated a moment and pulled it together, looking toward the window behind the rows of chairs. The switch clicked into place and the microwave blipped its signal off to the power plants across the river. No more than a dozen windows lighted up outside. Isabel looked up at me. "Is that all?" she said. "Is something wrong?" People were standing and looking out and a few were murmuring; the ceremoniousness had evaporated.

"As we know," Mayor Wharton was saying, "there will be a delay while the elevators are going up and people are entering the high floors." I could picture those old offices and apartments. People with flashlights, people who were part of this big Manhattan party just now beginning, would be wandering about on dusty floors, putting bulbs into sockets and finding long-disused switches and trying to get them to work. The elevators had been checked out over the past months, but there had not been enough professionals to climb all the stairs and get all the rooms open. Now it would be mostly volunteers: clerks, actors, bankers and sanitation workers and their lovers. Children too. People with martinis or beer bumping around in musty old rooms and hallways, in executive washrooms with rusted plumbing and office suites with peeling walls and dust-covered light fixtures and musty carpets. Elevator shafts would be groaning and rumbling again with their cables, so long slack, now going suddenly taut. I thought of the remnants of final office parties, the empty champagne bottles and the uneaten cheese and canapes sitting on empty desks, there since the last office workers had left in 2031, when the legislators in Albany had stopped the use of elevators. In some rooms there would be napkins strewn about, unemptied wastebaskets, an occasional umbrella or a forgotten purse.

Isabel brought me out of this reverie. "Ben," she whispered, "follow me."

People had broken up into groups and were chattering, glancing from time to time toward the windows. A few more lights had come on in the lower stories, but the city was still dark. Isabel had me by the hand. She led me away from the crowd and out into the anteroom with the elevator. Behind us the band had started playing. To the right of the elevator was a door with a small table in front to keep it from being opened. Isabel pulled the table aside. "I checked this out a while back," she said. She turned the knob and opened the door. Fresh air hit my face. "Come on!" she said.

We walked down a short hall into a cool breeze. It was dark and I nearly stumbled, but we had left the doorway open and enough light came from the room behind us that I could find my way with Isabel leading. The noise of the band behind us faded. I felt I was in a windy tunnel, now hearing only the purposeful clicking of Isabel's heels. I was just starting to protest when I saw her stop in front of me by a black staircase. I blinked. It was an old escalator, not working. I looked up and saw a rectangle of black, with stars. "Come on up," Isabel said, leading the way. I followed her and the starry rectangle above grew larger and the air windier.

We stepped out onto a dark metallic surface. I looked up; the mooring mast of the building, that useless tower intended as a home for dirigibles, loomed up over us. I looked outward. The panorama of a dark Manhattan was in front of us. We walked a few steps toward the edge of the platform, our steps clanging, and just as we arrived at the steel railings, with wind now blowing strongly in our faces, just as Isabel took my

hand, a horizontal row of lights came on in a building in front
of us. I caught my breath. More lights came on, to our left.
Then to our right. We stood silently in the night air, staring.

Landing on Belson the first time, Ruth had slid the *Isabel*
into a single orbit under the rings and I, standing on the bridge
in gym shorts in my newly strong body, had felt my heart stop
at the sight that wheeled before us: those magnificent rings in
airless rainbow above a circle of void. Below them hung the
gray curve of Belson itself. The *Isabel* moved from the sunless
side of the rings to their illuminated side, and light suddenly
filled the windows of the bridge and bathed our faces in
a refulgence beyond all knowing. A small pale moon hung
poised between the rings and the planets, shimmering as the
Isabel must be shimmering in that splendor, poised in New-
tonian certainty of hurl and granitic heft, floodlit by magic as
we ourselves were. There is beauty in our galaxy that the
human mind can only reach out for and brush against before
recoiling. There is a sweep and color that our history upward
from warm amoebic seas has hardly prepared eyes and nerves
for. I had to look away.

Here in New York, as the lights of its own metropolitan
scale came winking on randomly at left, at center, at right and
up and down and middle in scrambled array, with the pale,
limited incandescence of tungsten and of phosphors, filling in
the pieces of the great architectural jigsaw, I did not this time
turn away. I am not able to forget the Belson rings, nor do I
ever want to. I am not one to forget either that this human
world of ours has beauty that can stun the mind—the rain
forests, the canyons, coasts, the gray skin of deep ocean, the
grim antarctic mists. New York was built by pressure and
noise, yet its beauty—far beyond the human noise that made
it—penetrates to the marrow. I felt Isabel's warm body beside
me and heard her breath catch in her throat as we watched
Manhattan create itself before us. I would have given my
whole lovely fortune for Aunt Myra to be there with us and to
have heard her own breath catch as she saw New York
reawaken. I hugged Isabel to my side. It was good to be home.

BESTSELLING
Science Fiction
and
Fantasy